D1279954

BLASPHEMY

DOUGLAS PRESTON

CENTER POINT PUBLISHING
THORNDIKE, MAINE

This Center Point Large Print edition
is published in the year 2008 by arrangement with
St. Martin's Press.

The text of this Large Print edition is unabridged. In other
aspects, this book may vary from the original edition.
Printed in the United States of America.
Set in 16-point Times New Roman type.

ISBN: 978-1-60285-136-8

Library of Congress Cataloging-in-Publication Data

Preston, Douglas J.
   Blasphemy / Douglas Preston.--Center Point large print ed.
      p. cm.
   ISBN 978-1-60285-136-8 (lib. bdg. : alk. paper)
     1. Scientists--Fiction. 2. Arizona--Fiction. 3. Religious fiction. 4. Large type books.
   I. Title.

PS3566.R3982B57 2008b
813'.54--dc22

2007040947

For Priscilla,
Penny, Ellen, Jim, and Tim

I

JULY

KEN DOLBY STOOD BEFORE HIS WORKSTATION, his smooth, polished fingers caressing the controls of Isabella. He waited, savoring the moment, and then he unlocked a cage on the panel and pulled down a small red bar.

There was no hum, no sound, nothing to indicate that the most expensive scientific instrument on earth had been turned on. Except that, two hundred miles away, the lights of Las Vegas dimmed ever so slightly.

As Isabella warmed up, Dolby began to feel the fine vibration of her through the floor. He thought of the machine as a woman, and in his more imaginative moments he had even imagined what she looked like—tall and slender, with a muscular back, black as the desert night, beaded with sweat. Isabella. He had shared these feelings with no one—no point in attracting ridicule. To the rest of the scientists on the project, Isabella was an "it," a dead machine built for a specific purpose. But Dolby had always felt a deep affection for the machines he created—from when he was ten years old and constructed his first radio from a kit. Fred. That was the radio's name. And when he thought of Fred, he saw a fat carroty-haired white man. The first computer he had built was Betty—who

7

looked in his head like a brisk and efficient secretary. He couldn't explain why his machines took on the personalities they did—it just happened.

And now this, the world's most powerful particle accelerator . . . Isabella.

"How's it look?" asked Hazelius, the team leader, coming over and placing an affectionate hand on his shoulder.

"Purring like a cat," said Dolby.

"Good." Hazelius straightened up and spoke to the team. "Gather round, I have an announcement to make."

Silence fell as the team members straightened up from their workstations and waited. Hazelius strode across the small room and positioned himself in front of the biggest of the plasma screens. Small, slight, as sleek and restless as a caged mink, he paced in front of the screen for a moment before turning to them with a brilliant smile. It never ceased to amaze Dolby what a charismatic presence the man had.

"My dear friends," he began, scanning the group with turquoise eyes. "It's 1492. We're at the bow of the *Santa Maria,* gazing at the sea horizon, moments before the coastline of the New World comes into view. Today is the day we sail over that unknown horizon and land upon the shores of our very own New World."

He reached down into the Chapman bag he always carried and pulled out a bottle of Veuve Clicquot. He held it up like a trophy, his eyes sparkling, and thumped it down on the table. "This is for later tonight, when we set foot on the beach. Because tonight, we bring Isabella to one hundred percent full power."

Silence greeted the announcement. Finally Kate Mercer, the assistant director of the project, spoke. "What happened to the plan to do three runs at ninety-five percent?"

Hazelius returned her look with a smile. "I'm impatient. Aren't you?"

Mercer brushed back her glossy black hair. "What if we hit an unknown resonance or generate a miniature black hole?"

"Your own calculations show a one in quadrillion chance of that particular downside."

"My calculations might be wrong."

"Your calculations are never wrong." Hazelius smiled and turned to Dolby. "What do you think? Is she ready?"

"You're damn right she's ready."

Hazelius spread his hands. "Well?"

Everyone looked at each other. Should they risk it? Volkonsky, the Russian programmer, suddenly broke the ice. "Yes, we go for it!" He high-fived a startled Hazelius, and then everyone began slapping each other on the back, shaking hands, and hugging, like a basketball team before a game.

FIVE HOURS AND AS MANY BAD coffees later, Dolby stood before the huge flat-panel screen. It was still

9

dark—the matter–antimatter proton beams had not been brought into contact. It took forever to power up the machine and cool down Isabella's superconducting magnets to carry the very large currents necessary. Then it was a matter of increasing beam luminosity by increments of 5 percent, focusing and collimating the beams, checking the superconducting magnets, running various test programs, before going up to the next 5 percent.

"Power at ninety percent," Dolby intoned.

"Christ damn," said Volkonsky somewhere behind him, giving the Sunbeam coffeemaker a blow that made it rattle like the Tin Man. "Empty already!"

Dolby repressed a smile. During the two weeks they'd been up on the mesa, Volkonsky had revealed himself as a wiseass, a slouching, mangy specimen of Eurotrash with long greasy hair, ripped T-shirts, and a pubic clump of beard clinging to his chin. He looked more like a drug addict than a brilliant software engineer. But then, a lot of them were like that.

Another measured ticking of the clock.

"Beams aligned and focused," said Rae Chen. "Luminosity fourteen TeV."

"Isabella work fine," said Volkonsky.

"My systems are all green," said Cecchini, the particle physicist.

"Security, Mr. Wardlaw?"

The senior intelligence officer, Wardlaw, spoke from his security station. "Just cactus and coyotes, sir."

"All right," said Hazelius. "It's time." He paused dramatically. "Ken? Bring the beams into collision."

Dolby felt a quickening of his heart. He touched the dials with his spiderlike fingers, adjusting them with a pianist's lightness of touch. He followed with a series of commands rapped into the keyboard.

"Contact."

The huge flat-panel screens all around suddenly woke up. A sudden singing noise seemed to float in the air, coming from everywhere and nowhere at once.

"What's that?" Mercer asked, alarmed.

"A trillion particles blowing through the detectors," said Dolby. "Sets up a high vibration."

"Jesus, it sounds like the monolith in *2001*."

Volkonsky hooted like an ape. Everyone ignored him.

An image appeared on the central panel, the Visualizer. Dolby stared at it, entranced. It was like an enormous flower—flickering jets of color radiating from a single point, twisting and writhing as if trying to tear free of the screen. He stood in awe at the intense beauty of it.

"Contact successful," said Rae Chen. "Beams are focused and collimated. God, it's a perfect alignment!"

Cheers and some ragged clapping.

"Ladies and gentlemen," said Hazelius, "welcome to the shores of the New World." He gestured to the Visualizer. "You're looking at an energy density not seen in the universe since the Big Bang." He turned to Dolby. "Ken, please increase power in increments of tenths to ninety-nine."

The ethereal sound increased slightly as Dolby worked on the keyboard. "Ninety-six," he said.

"Luminosity seventeen point four TeV," said Chen.

"Ninety-seven . . . Ninety-eight."

The team fell into tense silence, the only sound now the humming that filled the underground control room, as if the mountain around them were singing.

"Beams still focused," said Chen. "Luminosity twenty-two point five TeV."

"Ninety-nine."

The sound from Isabella had become still higher, purer.

"Just a moment," said Volkonsky, hunching over the supercomputer workstation. "Isabella is . . . slow."

Dolby turned sharply. "Nothing wrong with the hardware. It must be another software glitch."

"Software *not* problem," said Volkonsky.

"Maybe we should hold it here," said Mercer. "Any evidence of miniature black hole creation?"

"No," said Chen. "Not a trace of Hawking radiation."

"Ninety-nine point five," said Dolby.

"I'm getting a charged jet at twenty-two point seven TeV," said Chen.

"What kind?" asked Hazelius.

"An unknown resonance. Take a look."

Two flickering red lobes had developed on either side of the flower on the central screen, like a clown's ears gone wild.

"Hard-scattering," said Hazelius. "Gluons maybe. Might be evidence of a Kaluza-Klein graviton."

"No way," said Chen. "Not at this luminosity."

"Ninety-nine point six."

"Gregory, I think we should hold the power steady here," said Mercer. "A lot of stuff is happening all at once."

"Naturally we're seeing unknown resonances," Hazelius said, his voice no louder than the rest, but somehow distinct from them all. "We're in unknown territory."

"Ninety-nine point seven," Dolby intoned. He had complete confidence in his machine. He could take her to one hundred percent and beyond, if necessary. It gave him a thrill to know they were now sucking up almost a quarter of the juice from Hoover Dam. That was why they had to do their runs in the middle of the night—when power usage was lowest.

"Ninety-nine point eight."

"We've got some kind of really big unknown interaction here," said Mercer.

"What is problem, bitch?" Volkonsky shouted at the computer.

"I'm telling you, we're poking our finger into a Kaluza-Klein space," said Chen. "It's incredible."

Snow began to appear on the big flat panel with the flower.

"Isabella is behave strange," said Volkonsky.

"How so?" Hazelius said, from his position at the center of the Bridge.

"Glacky."

Dolby rolled his eyes. Volkonsky was such a pain. "All systems go on my board."

Volkonsky typed furiously on the keyboard; then he swore in Russian and whacked the monitor with the flat of his hand.

"Gregory, don't you think we should power down?" asked Mercer.

"Give it a minute more," said Hazelius.

"Ninety-nine point nine," said Dolby. In the past five minutes, the room had gone from sleepy to bug-eyed awake, tense as hell. Only Dolby felt relaxed.

"I agree with Kate," said Volkonsky. "I not like the way Isabella behave. We start power-down sequence."

"I'll take full responsibility," said Hazelius. "Everything is still well within specs. The data stream of ten terabits per second is starting to stick in its craw, that's all."

"Craw? What means 'craw'?"

"Power at one hundred percent," said Dolby, a note of satisfaction in his laid-back voice.

"Beam luminosity at twenty-seven point one eight two eight TeV," said Chen.

Snow spackled the computer screens. The singing noise filled the room like a voice from the beyond. The flower on the Visualizer writhed and expanded.

14

A black dot, like a hole, appeared at the center.

"Whoa!" said Chen. "Losing all data at Coordinate Zero."

The flower flickered. Dark streaks shot through it.

"This is nuts," said Chen. "I'm not kidding, the data's vanishing."

"Not possible," said Volkonsky. "Data is not vanish. Particles is vanish."

"Give me a break. Particles don't vanish."

"No joke, particles is vanish."

"Software problem?" Hazelius asked.

"Not software problem," said Volkonsky loudly. "Hardware problem."

"Screw you," Dolby muttered.

"Gregory, Isabella might be tearing the 'brane," said Mercer. "I really think we should power down now."

The black dot grew, expanded, began swallowing the image on the screen. At its margins, it jittered manically with intense color.

"These numbers are wild," said Chen. "I'm getting extreme space-time curvature right at CZero. It looks like some kind of singularity. We might be creating a black hole."

"Impossible," said Alan Edelstein, the team's mathematician, looking up from the workstation he had been quietly hunched over in the corner. "There's no evidence of Hawking radiation."

"I swear to God," said Chen loudly, "we're ripping a hole in space-time!"

On the screen that ran the program code in real time, the symbols and numbers were flying by like an express train. On the big screen above their heads, the writhing flower had disappeared, leaving a black void. Then there was movement in the void—ghostly, batlike. Dolby stared at it, surprised.

"Damn it, Gregory, power down!" Mercer called.

"Isabella not accept input!" Volkonsky yelled. "I lose core routines!"

"Hold steady for a moment until we can figure out what's going on," said Hazelius.

"Gone! Isabella gone!" said the Russian, throwing up his hands and sitting back with a look of disgust on his bony face.

"I'm still green across the board," said Dolby. "Obviously what you've got here is a massive software crash." He turned his attention back to the Visualizer. An image was appearing in the void, an image so strange, so beautiful, that at first he couldn't wrap his mind around it. He glanced around, but nobody else was looking: they were all focused on their various consoles.

"Hey, excuse me—anybody know what's going on up there on the screen?" Dolby asked.

Nobody answered him. Nobody looked up. Everyone was furiously busy. The machine sang strangely.

"I'm just the engineer," said Dolby, "but any of you theoretical geniuses got an idea of what that is? Alan, is that . . . normal?"

Alan Edelstein glanced up from his workstation distractedly. "It's just random data," he said.

"What do you mean, random? It's got a shape!"

"The computer's crashed. It can't be anything but random data."

"That sure doesn't look random to me." Dolby stared at it. "It's moving. There's something there, I swear—it almost looks alive, like it's trying to get out. Gregory, are you seeing this?"

Hazelius glanced up at the Visualizer and paused, surprise blossoming on his face. He turned. "Rae? What's going on with the Visualizer?"

"No idea. I'm getting a steady blast of coherent data from the detectors. Doesn't look like Isabella's crashed from here."

"How would you interpret that thing on the screen?"

Chen look up and her eyes widened. "Jeez. I've no idea."

"It's moving," said Dolby. "It's, like, emerging."

The detectors sang, the room humming with their high-pitched whine.

"Rae, it's garbage data," Edelstein said. "The computer's crashed—how can it be real?"

"I'm not so sure it is garbage," said Hazelius, staring. "Michael, what do you think?"

The particle physicist stared at the image, mesmerized. "It doesn't make any sense. None of the colors and shapes correspond to particle energies, charges, and classes. It isn't even radially centered on

CZero—it's like a weird, magnetically bound plasma cloud of some kind."

"I'm telling you," said Dolby, "it's moving, it's coming out. It's like a . . . Jesus, what the hell is it?" He closed his eyes hard, trying to chase away the ache of exhaustion. Maybe he was seeing things. He opened them. It was still there—and expanding.

"Shut it down! Shut Isabella down now!" Mercer cried.

Suddenly the panel filled with snow and went dead black.

"What the hell?" Chen cried, her fingers pounding the keyboard. "I've lost all input!"

A word slowly materialized in the center of the panel. The group fell into silence, staring. Even Volkonsky's voice, which had been raised in high excitement, lapsed as if cut off. Nobody moved.

Then Volkonsky began to laugh, a tense, high-pitched laugh, hysterical, desperate.

Dolby felt a sudden rage. "You son of a bitch, you did this."

Volkonsky shook his head, flapping his greasy locks.

"You think that's funny?" Dolby asked, getting up from the workstation with clenched fists. "You hack a forty-billion-dollar experiment and you think it's *funny?*"

"I not hack anything," said Volkonsky, wiping his mouth. "You shut hell up."

Dolby turned and faced the group. "Who did this?

Who messed with Isabella?" He turned back to the Visualizer and read out loud the word hanging there, spat it out in his fury. GREETINGS.

He turned back. "I'll kill the bastard who did this."

2

SEPTEMBER

WYMAN FORD GAZED AROUND THE 17TH Street office of Dr. Stanton Lockwood III, science adviser to the president of the United States. From long experience in Washington, Ford knew that while an office was designed to show the outer man, the public man, it always betrayed somewhere the secret of the inner man. Ford cast his eyes about, looking for the secret.

The office was done up in that style Ford called IWPB—Important Washington Power Broker. The antiques were all authentic and of the finest quality—from the Second Empire desk, as big and ugly as a Hummer, to the gilded French portico clock and the hushed Sultanabad rug on the floor. Nothing that hadn't cost a bloody fortune. And of course, there was the obligatory "power wall" of framed diplomas, awards, and photographs of the office's occupant with presidents, ambassadors, and cabinet members.

Stanton Lockwood wanted the world to see him as a man of importance and wealth, powerful and discreet. But what came through to Ford was the grimness of the effort. Here was a man determined to be something he wasn't.

Lockwood waited until his guest was seated before he eased himself into the armchair flanking the other side of a coffee table. He crossed his legs and smoothed a long white hand down the crease in his garbardine pants. "Let's dispense with the usual Washington formalities," he said. "I'm Stan."

"Wyman." He settled back and observed Lockwood: handsome, late fifties, with a hundred-dollar haircut, his fitness-club physique beautifully draped in a charcoal suit. Probably a squash player. Even the photo on the desk of three perfect towheaded children with their attractive mother had all the individuality of a financial-services advertisement.

"Well," said Lockwood, in a meeting-now-underway tone, "I've heard excellent things about you, Wyman, from your former colleagues at Langley. They're sorry you left."

Ford nodded.

"So awful what happened to your wife. I'm so terribly sorry."

Ford willed his body not to stiffen. He never had been able to figure out a way to respond when people mentioned his dead wife.

"They tell me you spent a few years in a monastery."

Ford waited.

"The monastic life not to your liking?"

"It takes a special kind of person to be a monk."

"So you left the monastery and hung up your shingle."

"A man's got to make a living."

"Any interesting cases?"

"No cases at all. I've just opened the office. You're my first client—if that's what this is about."

"It is. I have a special assignment for you, to start immediately. It will last for ten days, maybe two weeks."

Ford nodded.

"There's a little catch I need to mention up front. Once I've described the assignment, rejecting it is not an option. It's in the United States, it doesn't involve risk, and it won't be difficult—at least in my opinion. Succeed or fail, you can never talk about it, so I'm afraid you can't use it to buff up your résumé."

"And the remuneration?"

"One hundred thousand dollars cash under the table, plus an aboveboard G-11 salary commensurate with your cover position." He raised his eyebrows. "Ready to hear more?"

No hesitation. "Go ahead."

"Excellent." Lockwood slid out another folder. "I see you have a B.A. in anthropology from Harvard. We need an anthropologist."

"Then I'm afraid I'm not your man. That was just my B.A. I went on to MIT and took a doctorate in cybernetics. My work for the CIA was mostly in cryptology and computers. I left anthropology far behind."

Lockwood waved his hand dismissively, his Princeton ring flashing in the light. "Not important. Are you familiar with, ah, the Isabella project?"

"Hard to avoid hearing about it."

"Forgive me if I repeat what you already know then. Isabella was completed over two months ago—at a cost of forty billion dollars. It's a second-generation superconducting supercollider particle accelerator. Its purpose is to probe the energy levels of the Big Bang and explore some exotic ideas for generating power. This is the president's pet project—the Europeans just completed the Large Hadron Collider at CERN and he wanted to maintain America's lead in particle physics."

"Naturally."

"Getting Isabella funded was no cakewalk. The left carped that the money should have been spent on the halt and the lame. The right whined that it was just another big-government spending program. The president steered a course between Scylla and Charybdis, rammed Isabella through Congress, and saw it to completion. He sees it as his legacy and he's anxious to have it running smoothly."

"No doubt."

"Isabella is essentially a circular tunnel, three hundred feet underground and forty-seven miles in circumference, in which protons and antiprotons are circulated in opposite directions at almost the speed of light. When the particles are brought into collision, they duplicate energy levels not seen since the universe was a millionth of a second old."

"Impressive."

"We found a perfect site for it—Red Mesa, a five-hundred-square-mile tableland on the Navajo Indian Reservation, protected by two-thousand-foot cliffs and riddled with abandoned coal mines, which we converted to underground bunkers and tunnels. The U.S. government pays six million a year in leasing fees to the Navajo tribal government in Window Rock, Arizona, an arrangement which was most satisfactory to all parties involved.

"Red Mesa is uninhabited, and there's just one road to the top. There are a few Navajo towns near the base of the mesa. These are traditional people—most of them still speak Navajo and live by herding sheep, weaving rugs, and making jewelry. That's the background."

Ford nodded. "And the problem?"

"In the past few weeks, a self-proclaimed medicine man has been stirring up people against Isabella, spreading rumors and misinformation. He's gaining traction. Your assignment is to deal with the problem."

"What's the Navajo government doing about it?"

"Nothing. The Navajo tribal government is feeble. The former tribal chairman was indicted for embezzlement, and the new chairman's just taken office. You're on your own with this medicine man."

"Tell me about him."

"His name is Begay, Nelson Begay. Not clear how old he is—we haven't been able to turn up a birth cer-

23

tificate. Claims the Isabella project is desecrating an ancient burial ground, that they were still using Red Mesa for grazing sheep, and so on. He's organizing a horseback ride in protest." Lockwood pulled a soiled flyer from a folder. "Here's one of his notices."

The blurry photocopy showed a man on horseback holding a protest sign.

RIDE TO RED MESA!
STOP ISABELLA!

SEPTEMBER 14 & 15

Protect the Diné Bikéyah, the Land of the People! Red Mesa, Dzilth Chíí, is indwelled by the sacred Pollen Being who brings forth flowers and seeds. ISABELLA is a mortal wound in her side, spilling radiation and poisoning Mother Earth.

Join the ride to Red Mesa. Meet at the Blue Gap Chapter House, Sept. 14 at 9:00 A.M., for the ride up the Dugway to the old Nakai Rock Trading Post. Camp at Nakai Rock with Sweat Lodge and one-night Blessing Way. Take back the land with prayer.

"Your assignment is to join the scientific team as the anthropologist and establish yourself as a liaison with the local community," said Lockwood. "Address their concerns. Make friends, calm everyone down."

"If that doesn't work?"

"Neutralize Begay's influence."

"How?"

"Dig some dirt out of his past, get him drunk, photograph him in bed with a mule—I don't care."

"I'm going to consider that a feeble attempt at humor."

"Yes, yes, of course. You're the anthropologist; you're supposed to know how to handle these people." Lockwood's smile was bland, generic.

Silence gathered. Ford finally asked, "So what's the real assignment?"

Lockwood clasped his hands and leaned forward. The smile widened. "Find out what the hell's really going on out there."

Ford waited.

"The anthropology bit is your cover. Your real assignment must remain absolutely secret."

"Understood."

"Isabella was supposed to be calibrated and online eight weeks ago, but they're still messing around with it. They say they can't get it to work. They have every excuse under the sun—bugs in the software, bad magnetic coils, leaky roof, broken cable, computer problems. You name it. At first I bought the excuses, but now I'm convinced I'm not getting the real story. There's something wrong—I just think they're lying about what it is."

"Tell me about the people."

Lockwood leaned back, inhaled. "As you certainly

25

know, Isabella was the brainchild of the physicist Gregory North Hazelius, and he leads a handpicked team. The best and the brightest America has to offer. The FBI vetted them thoroughly, so there's no question of their loyalty. In addition, there's a senior intelligence officer assigned by the Department of Energy, and a psychologist."

"DOE? What's their involvement?"

"One of the major research goals of the Isabella project is to look for exotic new forms of energy— fusion, mini black holes, matter–antimatter. DOE's nominally in charge, although—if I may be frank— I'm running the show at this stage."

"And the psychologist? What's his role?"

"It's like the Manhattan Project out there—isolated, high security, long hours, no families permitted. A high-stress environment. We wanted to make sure nobody went nuts."

"I see."

"The team went out there ten weeks ago to get Isabella up and running. It was supposed to take two weeks maximum, but they're still at it."

Ford nodded.

"Meanwhile, they're burning a hell of a lot of electricity—at peak power, Isabella eats up the megawattage of a medium-sized city. They run the damn machine at a hundred percent power again and again, all the while claiming it isn't working. When I press Hazelius for details, he has answers for everything. He charms you and cajoles you until he convinces you black is white. But something's wrong and they're covering it up. It could be an equipment problem, a software problem—or, God knows, a human problem. But this comes at a terrible time. It's September already. The presidential election's in two months. This would be a hell of a time for a scandal."

"Why the name Isabella?"

"The chief engineer, Dolby, the guy who headed the design team, nicknamed it that. It sort of stuck—sounded a lot better than SSCII, the official name. Maybe Isabella's his girlfriend or something."

"You mentioned a senior intelligence officer. What's his background?"

"Tony Wardlaw's the name. Former Special Forces, distinguished himself in Afghanistan before joining the DOE's Office of Intelligence. First-rate."

Ford thought for a moment, and then spoke. "I'm still not sure, Stan, what makes you think they're not telling the truth. Maybe they really are having the problems you mentioned."

"Wyman, I've got the best bullshit meter in town, and that's not Chanel Number Five I'm smelling out in Arizona." He leaned forward. "Members of Congress on both sides of the aisle are sharpening their long knives. They lost the first time around. Now they smell a second feeding."

"Sounds just like Washington: build a machine for forty billion dollars and then kill the funding to run it."

"You got that right, Wyman. The only constant in

this town is its yearning for imbecility. Your assignment is to find out what's really going on and report back to me personally. That's it. Don't take any action on your own. We'll handle it from here."

He went to his desk, pulled a stack of dossiers from a drawer, and smacked them down beside the phone. "There's one here for each scientist. Medical records, psychological evaluations, religious beliefs—even extramarital affairs." He smiled mirthlessly. "These came from the NSA, and you know how *thorough* they are."

Ford looked at the top dossier, opened it. Stapled to the front was a picture of Gregory North Hazelius, an enigmatic look of amusement dancing about in his brilliant blue eyes.

"Hazelius—you know him personally?"

"Yes." Lockwood dropped his voice. "And I want to . . . *caution* you about him."

"How so?"

"He has a way of focusing on a person, dazzling him, making him feel special. His mind burns with such incredible intensity that it seems to throw a spell over people. Even his most offhand comment seems charged with hidden importance. I've seen him point out something as common as a lichen-covered rock and speak about it in a way that makes you feel that it's extraordinary and filled with wonder. He showers you with attention, treats you as if you're the most important person in the world. The effect is irresistible—something a dossier can't capture. This may sound odd, but it's . . . it's almost like falling in love, the way the man draws you in and lifts you out of the humdrum world. You have to experience it to understand. Forewarned is forearmed. Keep your distance."

He paused, looking at Ford. The muffled sounds of tires, car horns, and voices from the street seeped into the silence. Ford clasped his hands behind his head and looked across at Lockwood. "The FBI or the intelligence arm of the DOE would normally conduct an investigation of this kind. Why me?"

"Isn't it obvious? There's a presidential election in two months. The president wants this thing fixed fast, on the quiet, with no paper trail. He needs speed and deniability. If you screw up, we don't know you. Even if you succeed, we don't know you."

"Yes, but why me *specifically?* I've got a B.A. in anthropology and that's it."

"You've got the background—anthropology, computers, ex-CIA." He pulled a dossier out of the pile. "And you have another asset."

Ford didn't like the sudden shift in tone. "Meaning?"

Lockwood pushed the folder across the table to Ford, who opened it and stared at the photograph stapled to the inside cover—a smiling woman with glossy black hair and mahogany eyes.

He slapped it shut, pushed it back at Lockwood, and rose to go. "You call me in here on a Sunday morning and pull a trick like this? Sorry, I don't mix work with my personal life."

"It's too late to withdraw."

A cold smile. "You going to stop me from walking out?"

"You were CIA, Wyman. You *know* what we can do."

Ford took a step forward, towering over Lockwood. "I'm trembling in my boots."

The science adviser looked up, hands clasped, smiling mildly. "Wyman, I'm sorry. That was a stupid thing for me to say. But you of all people should know the importance of the Isabella project. It'll open the doors on our understanding of the universe. Of the very moment of creation. It could lead us to an unlimited source of carbon-free power. It would be a huge tragedy for American science if we flushed that investment down the toilet. *Please* do this—if not for the president or for me, then for your country. Isabella, quite frankly, is the best thing this administration has done. It's our legacy. When all the political sound and fury has passed, this is the one thing that will make a difference." He passed the folder back to Ford. "She's the assistant director of Isabella. Thirty-five now, Ph.D. from Stanford, a top string theorist. What happened between you and her was a long time ago. I met her. Brilliant, of course, professional, still single, but then I don't suppose that'll be an issue. She's an entrée, a friend, someone to talk to—that's all."

"Someone to pump for information, you mean."

"The most important scientific experiment in

human history is at stake." He tapped the dossier, then raised his eyes to Ford. "Well?"

When Ford returned the gaze, he noticed that Lockwood's left hand was nervously caressing a pebble that had been sitting on the desk.

Lockwood followed his eyes and smiled sheepishly, as if having been caught. "This?"

Ford could see a sudden guarded look in Lockwood's eyes. "What is it?" he asked.

"My lucky stone."

"May I see it?"

Lockwood reluctantly passed the stone to Ford. He turned it over to see a small fossil trilobite embedded in one side.

"Interesting. Any special meaning?"

Lockwood seemed to hesitate. "My twin brother found this the summer we turned nine, gave it to me. That fossil is what started me on the road to science. He . . . drowned a few weeks later."

Ford fingered the stone, polished by years of handling. He had found the inner man—and, unexpectedly, he liked him.

"I really need you to take this assignment, Wyman."

And I need it, too. He laid the rock gently on the desk. "All right. I'll do it. But I work in my own way."

"Fair enough. But don't forget—no action on your own."

Lockwood rose and pulled a briefcase from his desk, shoved in the dossiers, shut and locked it. "In there you'll find a satellite phone, laptop, orientation packet, wallet, money, and your official cover assignment. A helicopter's waiting. The guard outside my office will escort you. Your clothing and sundries will be sent separately." He locked the briefcase and gave the dial a twirl. "The combination is the seventh to tenth digits of the number pi." He smiled at his cleverness.

"What if we don't agree on the meaning of 'no action on my own'?"

Lockwood shoved the briefcase across the desk. "Remember," he said, "we never knew you."

3

BOOKER CRAWLEY LEANED BACK IN HIS Grundlich CEO chair and studied the five men seating themselves around the bubinga-wood conference table. In his long and fruitful lobbying career, Crawley had learned that you can indeed judge a book by its cover, at least most of the time. He looked at the man opposite him with the preposterous name of Delbert Yazzie, taking in his watery eyes and sad face, the off-the-rack suit, the belt buckle sporting a half pound of silver and turquoise, the cowboy boots that appeared to have been resoled several times. Yazzie, in short, looked manageable. He was a rube, a hayseed Indian playing cowboy who had somehow found himself the newly elected chairman of the so-called Navajo Nation. Previous employment: school janitor.

Crawley would have to explain to Yazzie that in Washington, people made appointments. They didn't just show up—especially on a Sunday morning.

The men seated to Yazzie's left and right formed the so-called Tribal Council. One looked like a real live Injun, with a beaded headband, long hair tied up in a bun, velvet Indian shirt with silver buttons, and turquoise necklace. Two wore JCPenney suits. The fifth man, suspiciously white, sported a tailored Armani suit. That would be the guy to watch out for.

"Well!" said Crawley. "I'm delighted to meet the new leader of the Navajo Nation. I didn't know you were in town! Congratulations on your election—and to all of you, members of the Tribal Council. Welcome!"

"We're pleased to be here, Mr. Crawley," said Yazzie, his voice low and neutral.

"Call me Booker, please!"

Yazzie inclined his head, but did not offer to be called by his own first name. *Well, no wonder,* thought Crawley, *with a name like Delbert.*

"Can I offer anyone a drink? Coffee? Tea? Pellegrino?"

Everyone wanted coffee. Crawley pressed a buzzer, gave the order, and a few minutes later his man came in pushing a cart loaded with a silver coffeepot, creamer, sugar bowl, mugs. Crawley watched with a shudder while teaspoon after teaspoon of sugar crystals slid into the blackness of Yazzie's coffee, five in all.

"It's been such a pleasure for me personally to work with the Navajo Nation," Crawley continued. "With Isabella almost up and running, this is truly a moment of celebration for all of us. We value our relationship with the Navajo people and look forward to working with you for a long time to come."

He leaned back with a friendly smile and waited.

"The Navajo Nation thanks you, Mr. Crawley."

Nods and murmurs of approval went around the table.

"We're grateful for all you've done," Yazzie continued. "The Navajo Nation feels a great satisfaction in being able to make such an important contribution to American science."

He spoke in a slow, deliberate way, as if he had rehearsed the words, and Crawley felt a small, cold place harden in his gut. They might want to chisel his fees. Well, they were welcome to try—they had no idea who they were dealing with. What a bunch of sand monkeys.

"You've done an excellent job getting Isabella sited on our land and negotiating fair terms with the government," continued Yazzie, his sleepy eyes raised toward Crawley, but somehow not quite on him. "You did what you said you would do. This is something new in our experience in dealing with Washington. You kept your promises."

Was that all this visit was about? "Thank you, Mr. Chairman, that's most kind. I'm delighted to hear it. We certainly do keep our promises. I have to tell you

34

quite frankly that the project involved a lot of hard work. If I may be forgiven a little self-congratulation, this was one of the most challenging lobbying projects I have ever been involved in. But we pulled it off, didn't we?" Crawley beamed.

"Yes. We hope the compensation you received was a sufficient return for your work."

"As a matter of fact, the project was far more expensive at our end than we anticipated. My accountant has been in a foul mood these past weeks! But it's not every day we can help American science while bringing jobs and opportunity to the Navajo Nation."

"Which brings me to the subject of our visit."

Crawley sipped from his mug. "Fine. Love to hear it."

"With the work completed and Isabella running, we no longer see the need to continue with your services. When our contract with Crawley and Stratham expires at the end of October, we will not be renewing."

Yazzie spoke so bluntly, with so little finesse, that it took Crawley a moment to absorb the blow, but he kept his smile steady.

"Well, now," he said, "I'm very sorry to hear that. Is it anything we did—or failed to do?"

"No, it's just as I said: the project's completed. What's left to lobby?"

Crawley took a deep breath and set down the mug. "I don't blame you for thinking that—after all,

Window Rock is a long way from Washington." He leaned forward, his voice dropping to a whisper. "Let me tell you something, Mr. Chairman. In this town, nothing is ever *completed.* Isabella isn't actually online yet, and there's an old K Street saying that goes, 'There's many a slip twixt the cup and the lip.' Our enemies—*your* enemies—have never given up. Many in Congress are still itching to kill the project. That's the way it is in Washington—never forgive, never forget. Tomorrow they could introduce a bill that would cut funding for Isabella. They might try to renegotiate the lease payments. You need a friend in Washington, Mr. Yazzie. And I'm that friend. I'm the man who kept his promises. If you wait until bad news reaches Window Rock—it'll be too late."

He watched their faces, but could read no reaction. "I would strongly recommend that you renew the contract for at least six months—as a form of insurance."

This man Yazzie was as inscrutable as a damned Chinaman. Crawley wished he were still working with the previous chairman, a man who liked his steaks rare, his martinis dry, and his women well-lipsticked. If only he hadn't been caught with his hand in the tribal cookie jar.

Yazzie finally spoke. "We have many pressing needs, Mr. Crawley—schools, jobs, health clinics, recreational facilities for our youth. Only six percent of our roads are paved."

Crawley held his smile as if for a camera. The

ungrateful sons of bitches. They were going to collect their six million a year from now until doomsday, and he would get none of it. But he hadn't been lying—this lobbying assignment had been a bitch-ride from start to finish.

"If this 'slip twixt the cup and lip' should occur," Yazzie continued, in his slow, sleepy fashion, "we would call on your services again."

"Mr. Yazzie, we're a boutique lobbying firm. There's just me and my partner. We take only a few clients, and we have a long waiting list. If you drop out, your slot will be filled immediately. Then, if something happens and you need our services again, well—?"

"We'll take the risk," said Yazzie, with a dryness that goaded Crawley.

"I might suggest—indeed I *strongly recommend*—continuing the contract for another six months. We could even discuss renewing it at a half-retainer. That would at least keep your seat at the table."

The tribal leader looked at him steadily. "You were well compensated. Fifteen million dollars is a lot of money. In looking over your billable hours and expenses, some questions come to mind. But that is not of concern to us at the present time—you succeeded and we're grateful. We'll leave it at that."

Yazzie rose, then the others.

"Surely you'll stay for lunch, Mr. Yazzie! My treat, of course. There's a fabulous new French restaurant just off K Street, Le Zinc, run by an old frat buddy.

They do a mean dry martini and steak au poivre combo." He had never known an Indian to turn down a free drink.

"Thank you, but we have much to do here in Washington and can't spare the time." Yazzie extended his hand.

Crawley could hardly believe it. They were leaving—just like that.

He rose to see them out with limp handshakes all around. After they left, he leaned his bulk against the great rosewood door of his office. Rage burned in his gut. No warning, no letter, no telephone call, not even an appointment. They'd simply walked in, fired him, walked out—a real screw-you. And they'd implied he'd cheated them! After four years and fifteen million dollars' worth of lobbying, he had gotten them the goose that laid the golden egg, and what had they done? Scalped him and left him for the buzzards. This wasn't how things were done on K Street. No, sir. You took care of your friends.

He straightened up. Booker Hamlin Crawley never went down with the first punch. He was going to fight back—and an idea of how was starting to form in his mind already. He entered his inner office, locked the door, and removed a telephone from the bottom drawer of his desk. It was a landline phone registered in the name of a batty old lady in the nursing home around the corner, paid for by a credit card she didn't even know she owned. He rarely used it.

He pressed the first digit, then stopped, tugged by

the hint of a memory, the briefest flash of how and why he had come to Washington as a young man, bursting with ideas and hope. A sick feeling settled in his belly. But immediately the anger resurfaced. He would not give in to the one mortal sin in Washington: weakness.

He punched in the rest of the number. "May I please speak with the Reverend Don T. Spates?"

The phone call was short and sweet and the timing had been perfect. He hit the OFF button, feeling a surge of triumph at his brilliance. Within a month, he'd have those bareback-riding savages back in his office, begging to hire him—at *twice* the retainer.

His moist rubbery lips twitched with pleasure and anticipation.

4

WYMAN FORD LOOKED OUT THE WINDOW of the Cessna Citation as it banked over the Lukachukai Mountains and aimed for Red Mesa. It was a striking landform, an island in the sky walled all around by cliffs, seamed in layers of yellow, red, and chocolate sandstone. As he watched, sunlight spilled through an opening in the clouds and hit the mesa, lighting it on fire. It was like a lost world.

As they neared, details began to resolve themselves. Ford could make out landing strips that crossed like two black Band-Aids, with a set of hangars and a helipad. Three massive sets of high-tension power lines, strung on thirty-story trusses, came from the north and west and converged at the edge of the mesa, where there was a secure area, protected by a double fence. A mile away, a cluster of houses were nestled in a valley of cottonwoods, alongside green fields and a log building—the old Nakai Rock Trading Post. A brand-new asphalt road cut across the mesa, from west to east.

Ford's eye traveled down the cliffs. About three hundred feet down, a massive square opening had been quarried into the side of the mesa, with a recessed metal door. As the plane continued to bank, he could see the only road up the mesa, twisting up the face of the cliff like a snake clinging to a tree trunk. The Dugway.

The Cessna nosed into a cone of descent. The surface of Red Mesa revealed itself to be riven and split by dry washes, valleys, and boulder fields. A thin scattering of juniper trees alternated with the gray skeletons of piñons, patches of grassland and sagebrush, and areas of slickrock pocked by dunefields.

The Cessna touched down on the runway and taxied up to a Quonset hut terminal. Several hangars stood behind, gleaming in the light. The pilot threw open the door. Ford, carrying only Lockwood's briefcase, stepped onto the warm tarmac. There was no one there to greet him.

With a parting wave, the pilot remounted, and in a moment the small plane was back in the air, a glint of aluminum shrinking in the turquoise sky.

Ford watched the plane disappear, and then he ambled over to the terminal.

A wooden signboard hung on the door, hand-painted in Wild West–style letters.

KEEP OUT

TRESPASSERS WILL BE SHOT
THAT MEANS YOU, PARDNER!

G. HAZELIUS, MARSHAL

He gave it a push with his finger, listening to it creak back and forth. Beside it, on metal posts sunk into concrete, a bright blue government sign spelled out, in dry bureaucratic language, pretty much the same thing. Wind gusted across the runway, coiling dust a long the asphalt.

He tried the terminal door. Locked.

Ford stepped back and looked around, feeling like he's dropped into the opening sequence of *The Good, the Bad and the Ugly.*

The rasping of the sign and the moaning of the wind brought on a flash of memory—that moment, every day, when he would arrive home after school, lift the key from around his neck, unlock the door to the family home in Washington, and stand alone inside that vast echoing mansion. His mother was always off at some reception or fund-raiser, his father away on government business.

The roar of an approaching vehicle pulled him back to the present. A Jeep Wrangler topped a rise, disappeared behind the terminal, and reappeared tearing across the tarmac. With a squeal the car leaned into a turn, then stopped hard in front of him. A man jumped out, wide smile on his face, hand extended in greeting. Gregory North Hazelius. He looked just like the dossier photograph, wired with energy.

"Yá'át'ééh shi éí, Gregory!" said Hazelius, clasping Ford's hand.

"Yá'át'ééh," Ford answered. "Don't tell me you speak Navajo."

"Just a few words I learned from a former student of mine. Welcome."

Ford's brief review of Hazelius's file indicated the man allegedly spoke twelve languages, including Farsi, two dialects of Chinese, and Swahili. No mention had been made of Navajo.

At six feet four, Ford routinely had to look down to meet other men's eyes. This time he had to peer down more than usual. Hazelius was five feet five, a casually elegant figure in neatly pressed khakis, a cream-colored silk shirt—and a pair of Indian moccasins. His eyes were so blue, they looked like chips of backlit stained glass. An aquiline nose joined a high, smooth forehead, topped by wavy brown hair, neatly combed. A small package carrying an outsized energy.

"I wasn't expecting the great man himself."

Hazelius laughed. "We all do double duty. I'm the resident chauffeur. Please, get in."

Ford folded his frame into the passenger seat, while

42

Hazelius slipped into the driver's seat with birdlike grace. "While we got Isabella up and running, I didn't want a lot of support staff hanging around. Besides"—Hazelius turned on him with a brilliant smile—"I wanted to meet you personally. You're our Jonah."

"Jonah?"

"We were twelve. Now we're thirteen. Because of you, we might have to send someone out to walk the plank." He chuckled.

"You're a superstitious lot."

He laughed. "If only you knew! I never go anywhere without my rabbit's foot." He pulled an ancient, vile, and almost hairless amputated appendage out of his pocket. "My father gave it to me when I was six."

"Lovely."

Hazelius jammed his foot on the accelerator and the Jeep shot forward, pressing Ford back into the seat. The Wrangler flew across the tarmac and squealed onto a freshly laid asphalt road that wound among junipers. "It's like summer camp, Wyman. We do all our own work—cooking, cleaning, driving. You name it. We've got a string theorist who grills a mean tenderloin, a psychologist who helped us lay in an excellent wine cellar, and various other multitalented folk."

Ford gripped the handle as the Jeep slewed around a corner with a whine of rubber.

"Nervous?"

"Wake me up when we arrive."

Hazelius laughed. "Can't resist these empty roads—no cops and sightlines that go for miles. What about you, Wyman? What are your special talents?"

"I'm a killer dishwasher."

"Excellent!"

"I can split wood."

"Marvelous!"

Hazelius drove like mad, picking a line and taking it at maximum speed while totally disregarding the center stripe. "Sorry I wasn't there to meet your plane. We're just finishing up a run on Isabella. Can I give you a quick tour?"

"Great."

The Jeep topped a rise at high speed. Fleetingly, Ford's body felt weightless.

"Nakai Rock," Hazelius said, pointing to the stone spire Ford had seen from the plane. "The old trading post took its name from that rock. We call our village Nakai Rock, too. Nakai—what does it mean? I've always wanted to know."

"It's the Navajo word for 'Mexican.' "

"Thank you. I'm awfully glad you could come at such short notice. We've managed to get on the wrong side of the locals, unfortunately. Lockwood speaks highly of you."

The road looped down into a sheltered valley, thick with cottonwoods and surrounded by red sandstone bluffs. Along the outside of the loop stood a dozen or more fake-adobe houses placed artfully among the cottonwoods, with postage-stamp lawns and picket fences. An emerald playing field in the center of the loop formed a vibrant contrast against the bluffs. At the far end of the valley, like a presiding judge, stood the tall hobgoblin rock.

"Eventually we'll build quarters for up to two hundred families. This'll be quite a little town of visiting scientists, their families, and support staff."

The Jeep swept past the houses, making a broad turn. "Tennis court." Hazelius gestured to the left. "Barn with three horses."

They reached a picturesque structure made of logs chinked with adobe and shaded by massive cottonwoods. "The old trading post, converted to dining hall, kitchen, and rec room. Pool table, ping-pong, foosball, movies, library, canteen."

"What's a trading post doing way up here?"

"Before the coal company moved them off, the Navajo ran sheep on Red Mesa. The post traded food and supplies for the rugs they wove from the wool. Nakai Rock rugs are less well known than Two Grey Hills, but just as fine—finer, even." He turned to Ford. "Where did you do your field research?"

"Ramah, New Mexico." Ford didn't add, *It was just for the summer and I was only an undergrad.*

"Ramah. Wasn't that where the anthropologist Clyde Kluckhohn did research for his famous book, *Navaho Witchcraft?*"

Hazelius's depth of knowledge surprised Ford. "That's right."

"Do you speak fluent Navajo?" Hazelius asked.

"Just enough to get myself into trouble. Navajo is possibly the most difficult language on earth."

"As such it always interested me—helped us win World War Two."

The Jeep shrieked to a stop in front of a casita, small and neat, with a fenced yard enclosing a patch of artificially green lawn, along with a patio, picnic table, and barbecue.

"The Ford residence," Hazelius said.

"Charming." In fact, it was anything but. It looked crushingly suburban, this tacky little subdivision done up in imitation Pueblo-revival style. But the setting was magnificent.

"Government housing is the same everywhere," Hazelius said. "But you'll find it comfortable."

"Where is everybody?"

"Down in the Bunker. That's what we call the underground complex that houses Isabella. By the way, where are your bags?"

"They're coming tomorrow."

"They must have been anxious to get you out here."

"Didn't even give me time to collect my toothbrush."

Hazelius gunned the Jeep and took the final curve of the loop at rubber-stripping speed. Then he stopped, shifted into four-wheel drive, and coaxed the vehicle off the pavement onto two uneven ruts through the brush.

"Where are we going?"

"You'll see."

They spun their wheels in gullies and bounced around boulders as the Jeep climbed up through the strange, twisted forest of junipers and dead piñons. They bounced along for a few miles. A long steep slope of red slickrock sandstone loomed ahead.

The Jeep stopped, and Hazelius hopped out. "It's just up here."

His curiosity growing, Ford followed him up the slope to the summit of the peculiar sandstone bluff. The top was a huge surprise: he found himself unexpectedly at the edge of Red Mesa, the cliffs dropping away almost two thousand feet. There was no sense that the mesa edge had been coming up, no warning that a cliff lay ahead.

"Nice, eh?" Hazelius asked.

"Scary. You could drive over the edge before you knew it."

"In fact, there's a legend about a Navajo cowboy, chasing a maverick on horseback, who rode off here. They say his *chindii,* his ghost, still rides off the edge on certain dark, stormy nights."

The view was breathtaking. An ancient land spread out below them, humps and pillars of rock the color of blood, windblasted and sculpted into strange shapes. Beyond lay mesas layered on mountains beyond mountains. It could have been the edge of Creation itself, where God had finally given up, in despair of bringing order to an unruly land.

"That great island mesa in the distance," said

Hazelius, "is No Man's Mesa, nine miles long and a mile broad. They say there's a secret trail to the top that no white man has ever found. To the left is Piute Mesa. Shonto Mesa is the one in front. Farther back are the Goosenecks of the San Juan River, Cedar Mesa, the Bears Ears, and the Manti-La Sal mountains."

A pair of ravens rode an air current up, then dipped and glided back into gloomy depths. Their cries echoed among the canyons.

"Red Mesa is accessible at only two points—the Dugway, back behind us, and a trail that starts a couple of miles over there. Navajos call it the Midnight Trail. It ends in Blackhorse, that little settlement down there."

As they turned to go, Ford noticed a series of marks on the face of a huge boulder that had split down the bedding plane.

Hazelius following his gaze. "See something?"

Ford walked over and laid his hand on the uneven surface. "Fossil raindrops. And . . . the fossilized track of an insect."

"Well, well," the scientist said in a low voice. "Everyone's been up here to look at the view. But you're the first person to have noticed that—beyond myself, of course. Fossil raindrops from a shower that fell in the age of dinosaurs. And then, after the rain, a beetle walked across the wet sand. Somehow, against all odds, this little moment in history got fossilized." Hazelius touched it reverently. "Nothing we humans have done on this earth, none of our great works—not the *Mona Lisa* or Chartres Cathedral or even the pyramids of Egypt—will last as long as that beetle's track in wet sand."

Ford was strangely moved by the thought.

Hazelius traced his own finger along the insect's wandering path, and then straightened up. "Well!" he said, grasping Ford's shoulder and giving it an affectionate shake. "I can see you and I are going to be friends."

Ford remembered Lockwood's warning.

Hazelius turned southward, gesturing back across the mesa top. "In the Paleozoic, all this was an immense swamp. It gave us some of the thickest coal seams in America. They were mined out in the fifties. Those old tunnels were perfect for retrofitting Isabella."

The sun lit Hazelius's nearly unlined face as he turned to smile at Ford. "We couldn't have found a better place, Wyman—isolated, undisturbed, uninhabited. But to me the most important thing was the beauty of this landscape, because beauty and mystery have a central place in physics. As Einstein said, 'The most beautiful thing we can experience is the mysterious. It is the source of all true science.'"

Ford watched the sun slowly die in the deep canyons to the west, like gold melting into copper.

Hazelius said, "Ready to go underground?"

5

THE JEEP JOSTLED BACK TO THE road. Ford gripped the roof handhold, trying to look relaxed as Hazelius accelerated hard past the airstrip, hitting eighty on the straight road.

"See any cops?" Hazelius asked with a grin.

A mile beyond, the road was blocked by two gates in a double set of chain-link fences topped with concertina wire, walling off an area along the edge of the mesa. He braked at the last minute, the wheels squealing.

"All that's inside is the Security Zone," said Hazelius. He punched a code into a keypad on a post. A horn squawked and the gate rolled open. Hazelius drove in and parked the Jeep next to a row of other cars. "The Elevator," he said, nodding toward a tall tower perched on the edge of the cliffs, festooned with antennae and satellite dishes. They walked up to it, and Hazelius swiped a card through a slot beside the metal door, then placed his hand on a palm reader. After a moment a husky female voice said, "Afternoon, sugar. Who's the cat with you?"

"This is Wyman Ford."

"Gimme some skin, Wyman."

Hazelius smiled. "What she means is, lay your palm on the reader."

Ford placed his hand on the warm glass. A bar of light moved down it.

"Hold on while I check with the *man.*"

Hazelius chuckled. "You like our little security interface?"

"Different."

"That's Isabella. Most computer voices are of the HAL variety, too white-bread for my taste." He mimicked a stage-trained white voice: " *'Please listen carefully, as our menu items have changed.'* Isabella, on the other hand, has a *real* voice. Our engineer, Ken Dolby, programmed it. I believe he got some rap singer to lend him her voice."

"Who is the real Isabella?"

"I don't know. Ken's rather mysterious on that point."

The voice rolled out like honey. "The man says cool. You in the system now, so don't get yo ass in no trouble."

The metal doors swished open, revealing an elevator cage that ran down the side of the mountain. A small porthole window showed the view as they descended. When the elevator halted, Isabella warned them to watch their step.

They stood on a spacious outdoor platform cut into the side of the cliff in front of the huge titanium door Ford had seen from the air. It appeared to be twenty feet wide and at least forty feet high.

"This is the staging area. Another nice view, eh?"

"You should build condos."

"This was the opening to the great Wepo coal seam. They took fifty million short tons of coal from this seam alone, and left huge caverns behind. A perfect setup for us. It was critical to get Isabella deep underground, to protect people from radiation when Isabella is running at high power."

Hazelius approached the titanium portal set back into the cliff. "We call this fortress the Bunker."

"I need yo number, sugar," Isabella said.

Hazelius punched in a series of numbers on a small keypad.

A moment later the voice said, "Come on in, boys." The door began to rise.

"Why such high security?" Ford asked.

"We have a forty-billion-dollar investment to protect. And much of our hardware and software is classified."

The door opened on a vast echoing cavern carved out of stone. It smelled of dust and smoke, with a hint of mustiness that reminded Ford of his grandmother's cellar. It was cool and pleasant after the heat of the desert. The door rumbled down, and Ford blinked to adjust to the sodium lighting. The cavern was huge, perhaps six hundred feet deep and fifty feet high. Straight ahead, at the far end of the cavern, Ford could see an oval door, which opened into the side of a tunnel filled with stainless steel pipes, tubes, and bundles of cable. A fog of condensates poured out of the door, flowing over the ground in little rivers that vanished. To the left a cinder block wall had been built across another opening in the rock, with a steel door in it. The door was marked THE BRIDGE. Along the other side of the cavern there were stacks of steel caissons, I-beams, and other leftover construction materials, along with heavy equipment and half a dozen golf carts.

Hazelius took his arm. "Straight ahead is the oval opening to Isabella itself. That fog is condensation from the superconducting magnets. They have to be cooled with liquid helium at close to absolute zero to maintain superconductivity. That tunnel runs back into the mesa, forming a torus fifteen miles in diameter, where we circulate the two particle beams. The fleet of electric golf carts over there is transportation. Now let's go meet the gang."

As they strolled across the cavern, their footfalls echoing in the cathedral-like space, Ford asked casually, "How are things going?"

"Problems," said Hazelius. "One damn thing after another."

"Like what?"

"Software, this time."

They approached the door marked THE BRIDGE. Hazelius opened it for Ford, exposing a cinder block corridor painted slime green and illuminated with fluorescent strips in the ceiling.

"Second door on the right. Here, let me get it for you."

Ford stepped through into a circular room, brightly lit. Huge flat-panel computer screens lined the walls, giving the room the appearance of the bridge of a spaceship, with windows looking into deep space.

The screens were not operating, and a starship screen saver running simultaneously on them completed the illusion of a spaceship passing through a starfield. Below the screens were massive banks of control panels, consoles, and workstations. The room had a sunken center, with a retro-futuristic swivel chair in the middle.

Most of the scientists had paused in their work to look at Ford curiously. He was struck by their haggard appearance, their pale, cave-creature faces and rumpled clothes. They looked worse than a bunch of grad students at the bitter end of final exams. His eyes instinctually searched for Kate Mercer, and then he immediately upbraided himself for his interest.

"Look familiar?" Hazelius asked, an amused twinkle in his eye.

Ford looked around, surprised. It did look familiar—and he suddenly realized why.

"To go where no man has gone before," he said.

Hazelius laughed delightedly. "Right you are! It's a replica of the bridge of the original starship *Enterprise* from *Star Trek*. It happened to make an excellent design for a particle accelerator control room."

The illusion that this was the bridge of the U.S.S. *Enterprise* was partly spoiled by a trash barrel overflowing with soda cans and frozen pizza boxes. Papers and candy wrappers lay scattered about the floor, and an unopened bottle of Veuve Clicquot lay on its side against the curving wall.

"Sorry about the mess—we're wrapping up a run.

Only about half the team is here—you can meet the rest at dinner." He turned to the group. "Ladies and gentlemen, allow me to introduce to you the newest member of our team, Wyman Ford. He's the anthropologist I requested to act as a liaison with the local communities."

Nods, murmurs of greeting, a fleeting smile or two—he was little more than a distraction. Which was just fine with him.

"I'll just go around the room and introduce everyone quickly. We can get better acquainted at dinner."

The group waited wearily.

"This is Tony Wardlaw, our senior intelligence officer. He's here to keep us out of trouble."

A man as solid as a butcher's block stepped forward. "Nice to meet you, sir." He had a whitewall marine haircut, military posture, no-nonsense expression—and the gray face of exhaustion. As Ford expected, the man's grip tried to crush his hand. He crushed back.

"This is George Innes, our team psychologist. He leads weekly chat sessions and helps keep us sane. I don't know where we'd be without his steadying presence."

A few exchanged glances and rolled eyes told Ford where the others felt they'd be without Innes. Innes's handshake was cool and professional, just the right pressure and length. He looked outdoorsy, in neatly pressed L.L. Bean khaki pants and a checked shirt.

Fit, well groomed, he looked like the type who thought everyone but himself had problems.

"Good to meet you, Wyman," he said, peering over the rim of his tortoiseshell glasses. "I imagine you must feel a bit like a new student entering school in the middle of the semester."

"I do."

"I'm here if you ever feel the need to talk."

"Thank you."

Hazelius swept him forward toward a wreck of a young man, early thirties, thin as a rail, with long greasy blond hair. "This is Peter Volkonsky, our software engineer. Peter hails from Yekaterinburg, Russia."

Reluctantly Volkonsky detached himself from the console he had been hunched over. His restless, manic eyes roved over Ford. He didn't offer his hand, merely nodded distractedly, with a curt "Hi."

"Good to meet you, Peter."

Volkonsky shifted back to his keyboard and resumed typing. His thin shoulder blades stuck out like a child's under his ragged T-shirt.

"And this is Ken Dolby, our chief engineer and the designer of Isabella. Someday there'll be a statue of him in the Smithsonian."

Dolby strode over—big, tall, friendly, African-American, maybe thirty-nine, with the laid-back air of a California surfer. Ford liked him immediately— a no-nonsense kind of guy. He, too, looked frayed, with bloodshot eyes. He extended his palm. "Welcome," he said. "Hope you don't mind we're not at our best. Some of us have been up for thirty-six hours."

They moved on. "And this is Alan Edelstein," Hazelius continued, "our mathematician."

A man Ford had barely noticed, sitting away from the others, raised his eyes from the book he was reading—Joyce's *Finnegans Wake*. He raised a single finger in greeting, his penetrating eyes steady on Ford. His arch look suggested supercilious amusement with the world.

"How's the book?" Ford asked.

"A real page-turner."

"Alan is a man of few words," said Hazelius. "But he speaks the language of mathematics with great eloquence. Not to mention his powers as a snake charmer."

Edelstein acknowledged the compliment with an incline of his head.

"Snake charmer?"

"Alan has a rather controversial hobby."

"He keeps rattlesnakes as pets," said Innes. "He has a way with them, it seems." He said it facetiously, but Ford thought he detected an edge in his voice.

Without looking up from his book, Edelstein said, "Snakes are interesting and useful. They eat rats. Which we have quite a few of around here." He shot a pointed glance at Innes.

"Alan does us a double service," said Hazelius. "Those Havahart traps you'll see in the Bunker and

scattered about the facility keep us rodent—and hantavirus—free. He feeds them to his snakes."

"How do you catch a rattlesnake?" Ford asked.

"Carefully," Innes answered for Edelstein, with a
tense laugh, pushing his glasses back up his nose.

Once more Edelstein's dark eyes met Ford's. "If
you see one, let me know and I'll show you."

"I can't wait."

"Excellent," said Hazelius hastily. "Now let me
introduce you to Rae Chen, our computer engineer."

An Asian woman who looked young enough to be
carded jumped off her seat and stuck out her hand,
her waist-length black hair swinging. She was
dressed like a typical Berkeley student, in a grubby T-
shirt with a peace sign on the front and jeans patched
with pieces of a British flag.

"Hey, nice to meet you, Wyman." An unusual intelligence lurked in her black eyes, and something that
resembled wariness. Or maybe it was just that she,
like the others, looked exhausted.

"My pleasure."

"Well, back to work," she said with artificial bright-
ness, nodding at her computer.

"That mostly does it," said Hazelius. "But where's
Kate? I thought she was running those Hawking radiation calculations."

"She took off early," said Innes. "Said she wanted
to get dinner started."

Hazelius circled back to his chair, gave it an affectionate slap. "When Isabella is running, we're peering

into the very moment of creation." He chuckled. "I get a kick out of sitting in my Captain Kirk chair, watching us go where no man has gone before."

Ford watched him settle in his chair, kicking his feet up with a smile, and he thought—he's the only one in this room who doesn't look worried sick.

6

SUNDAY EVENING, THE REVEREND DON T. SPATES fitted his bulk into the makeup chair so as not to crease his pants and handmade Italian cotton shirt. Once in, he adjusted his large bottom, moving it from side to side with a flurry of creaks and squeaks in the leather. He carefully leaned his head back against the headrest. Wanda stood to one side, holding the barbershop robe.

"Do me good, Wanda," he said, closing his eyes. "This is a big Sunday. A *real* big Sunday."

"You're going to look just great, Reverend," said Wanda, snapping the robe over him and tucking it in around his neck. Then, with a soothing clinking of bottles, combs, and brushes, she set to work, paying special attention to the reverend's liver spots and the spiderlike clusters of varicose veins on his cheeks and nose. She was good at what she did and she knew it. Regardless of what the others might say, she thought the reverend a fine, handsome man.

Her long white hands worked with expert economy, swift and precise, but the reverend's ears were always a challenge. They stood out from the head a trifle too much, and were lighter and redder than his adjacent skin. Sometimes, as he strode about the stage, the backlight would catch his ears, turning them into pink stained glass. To bring them to their proper tonal value, she covered them with a heavy base makeup three shades darker than his face, and finished with a face powder that made them virtually opaque.

As she smoothed, stroked, brushed, and dabbed, she checked her work in a color-balanced video monitor that displayed a feed from a camera trained on the reverend. It was essential to see her handiwork as it would appear onscreen—something that looked perfect to the eye could show up as a ghastly two-tone on the monitor. She worked on him this way twice a week: for his televised sermon on Sunday, and for his Friday talk show on the Christian Cable Service.

Yes, the reverend was a fine man.

REVEREND DON T. SPATES FELT COMFORTED AND cosseted by her professional bustle. It had been a bad year. His enemies were out to get him, twisting his every word, attacking him mercilessly. Every sermon seemed to generate vilification from the atheist left. It was a sad time when a man of God was attacked for speaking the simple truth. Of course, there'd been that unfortunate incident in the motel with the two prostitutes. The ungodly liars had had a field day with that. But the flesh is weak—as the Bible repeatedly confirms. In Jesus' eyes, we are all hopeless, backsliding sinners. Spates had asked for and received God's forgiveness. But the hypocritical, evil world forgave slowly, if at all.

"Time for your teeth, Reverend."

Spates opened his mouth and felt her expert hands applying the ivory dentine fluid. In the bright lights of the camera, it would make his teeth flash as pearly white as the gates of heaven.

After that she worked on his hair, carefully grooming the wiry, orangish helmet until it was just right. She gave it an indirect spritz of hair spray and puffed on a bit of powder to tone the color down to a more respectable ginger.

"Your hands, Reverend?"

Spates extracted his freckled hands from under the cover and laid them on a manicure tray. She bustled over them, applying a makeup base designed to minimize wrinkles and color variations. His hands had to match his face. In fact, Spates was particularly insistent that his hands be perfect. They were an extension of his voice. Botched makeup there could ruin the impact of his message, as camera close-ups of laying on of hands revealed flaws unnoticed by the eye.

The hands took her fifteen minutes. She gouged dirt from under the nails, applied clear fingernail polish, repaired nicks, sanded the nails, cleaned and cut off excess skin, and, finally, covered them with an appropriate shade of makeup base.

A final check in the TV monitor, a few touch-ups, and Wanda stepped back.

"All ready, Reverend." She turned the monitor toward him.

Spates examined himself in the monitor—face, eyes, ears, lips, teeth, hands.

"That spot on my neck, Wanda? You missed that spot—again."

A quick swipe of the sponge, a touch-up with the brush, and it vanished. Spates grunted his satisfaction.

Wanda flicked off the coverings and stood back. From out of the wings, Spates's aide, Charles, rushed in with the reverend's suit jacket. Spates rose from the chair and held out his arms, while Charles slipped on the jacket, tugged and smoothed down the cloth, gave it a quick brushing, plumped up the shoulders, smoothed and tucked the collar, and adjusted the tie.

"How are the shoes, Charles?"

Charles gave the shoes a few swipes with a shine cloth.

"Time?"

"Six minutes to eight, Reverend."

Years ago, Spates had had the idea to schedule his Sunday sermon for prime time in the evening, to avoid the televangelist morning crush. He called it *God's Prime Time.* Everyone predicted he'd fail, going up against some of the strongest programming of the week. Instead, it had proved a stroke of genius.

Spates strode from the room toward the wings of the stage, Charles following. As he came close, he could hear the rustle and murmur of the faithful—thousands of them—taking their seats in the Silver Cathedral from where he broadcast *God's Prime Time* for two hours every Sunday.

"Three minutes," murmured Charles in his ear.

Spates inhaled the air in the shadows of the wings. The crowd quieted as the audience prompts scrolled across the screens and the appointed time neared.

He felt the glory of God energize his body with the Holy Spirit. He loved this moment just before the sermon; it was like nothing else in this world, a surge of rising fire, triumph, and anticipatory exultation.

"How's the audience?" he whispered to Charles.

"About sixty percent."

A cold knife stabbed into the heart of his joy. Sixty percent—last week it had been seventy. Just six months ago people had been lining up for tickets, Sunday after Sunday, and had to be turned away. But since the motel incident, on-air donations were down by half and the ratings for the broadcast had fallen forty percent. The bastards at the Christian Cable Service were about to cancel his *Roundtable America* talk show. God's Prime Time Ministry was heading into the darkest night since he had founded it in a vacant JCPenney thirty years before. If he didn't get an infusion of cash soon, he'd be forced to default on the "Own a Piece of Jesus" bonds he had sold over the air to hundreds of thousands of parishioners to finance the building of the Silver Cathedral.

His thoughts turned back to the meeting with the

lobbyist Booker Crawley earlier that day. What a sign of God's grace that Crawley's proposal had come his way. If handled right, this might be just the issue he'd been looking for to rejuvenate the ministry and galvanize financial support. The evolution versus creationism debate was old hat, and it was getting hard to gain traction on that one—especially with so much competition from other televangelists. Crawley's issue, on the other hand, was fresh, it was new, and it was ripe for the plucking.

Damned if he wasn't going to pluck that fruit—now.

"It's time, Reverend," came Charles's low voice from behind.

The lights went up and a roar came from the crowd as the Reverend Spates strode onstage, his head bowed, his hands raised and clasped together, shaking rhythmically.

"God's Prime Time!" he rolled out in his richly timbred bass voice, full of vibrato. *"God's Prime Time! The Prime Time of God's Glory Is Nigh!"* At stage center, he stopped sharply, raised his head, and stretched his arms outward to the audience, as if beseeching them. His fingertips trembled. His words rolled over the audience.

"Greetings to all of you in the precious Name of our Lord and Savior, Jesus Christ!"

Another roar rose from the giant Silver Cathedral. He lifted his hands high, palms up, and the roar went on—sustained with the help of the prompters. He lowered his arms, and silence fell once again, like the aftermath of thunder.

He bowed his head in prayer, then said, in a soft, humble voice, "Where two or three are gathered together in My Name, there am I."

He raised his head slowly, keeping his profile to the audience, and spoke in his richest tone, raising one arm, inch by inch, drawing out each word to its fullest.

"In the beginning," he throbbed, "God created the heavens and the earth. And the earth was without form, and void; and *darkness* was upon the face of the deep."

He paused, inhaling dramatically. "And the Spirit of *God* moved upon the face of the waters."

His voice suddenly boomed through the Silver Cathedral like the notes of an organ. "And God said, *Let there be light!*"

A dramatic beat, and he continued, in the barest whisper. "And there was light."

He strode to the edge of the stage and beamed a folksy smile on the worshippers. "We all know those opening words of Genesis. Some of the most powerful words ever written. No ambiguity there. Those are the very words of God, my friends. God is telling us in His own words how He created the universe."

He strolled casually along the edge of the stage. "My friends, will it surprise you if I tell you the government is spending your hard-earned taxpayer dollars in an effort to prove God wrong?"

He turned, eyeing the silent audience.

"You don't believe me?"

A murmur rose from the sea of faces.

He pulled a piece of paper from his suit-coat pocket and snapped it in the air, his voice suddenly full of thunder. "It's right here. I downloaded it off the Internet less than an hour ago."

Another murmur.

"And what did I learn? That our government has spent forty billion dollars to prove Genesis wrong— forty billion dollars of *your* money to attack the holiest Scripture in the Old Testament. Yes, my friends, it's all part of the government-sponsored, secular humanist war on Christianity, and it's *ugly*."

He paced the stage. He shook the paper in his fist, crackling it.

"Right here it says they've built a machine in the Arizona desert called Isabella. Many of you have heard of it."

A big murmur of agreement.

"I had, too. I just thought it was another government boondoggle. Only recently was I made aware of its *pur-pose*."

A sudden halt in his pacing, and a slow turn to face the audience.

"Its *pur-pose,* my friends, is to investigate the so-called Big Bang theory. That's right, you heard it, there's that word 'theory' again!"

His voice was laced with scorn.

"The Big Bang *theory* goes like this: thirteen billion

years ago a teeny-weeny point in space blew up and created the entire universe—without the helping hand of God. You heard me: Creation without God. *Ay-thee-istic Creation.*"

He waited while a disbelieving silence grew. He shook the paper again. "That's what it says, folks! A whole Web site, hundreds of pages devoted to explaining the Creation of the Universe, and not one mention of God!"

Another glare around the hall.

"This Big Bang theory is no different from the *theory* that says our great-granddaddies were monkeys. Or the *theory* that says life's complexity was created by an accidental rearrangement of molecules in a puddle of mud. This Big Bang theory is just another secular humanistic, anti-Christian, antifaith theory *no different from evolution,* except that this one's worse. *Much, much worse!*"

Spin, turn, pace.

"Because *this* theory attacks the very notion that God created the universe. Make no mistake about it: *Isabella is a direct attack on Christian faith.* The Big Bang theory says this *beautiful,* this *exquisite,* this *God-given* universe of ours happened all by itself, by sheer accident, thirteen billion years ago. And as if that Christian-hating theory wasn't enough, now they want to spend forty billion dollars of *our* money to prove it!"

He raked the audience with a fierce eye.

"How about if we asked the savants in Washington

for equal time? What if we asked them for forty billion dollars *to prove the Truth of Genesis?* What about that! The professional Jesus-hating liberals in Washington would gnash their teeth and foam at the mouth! They'd trot out that old saw about separation of church and state! These are the folks who've banned Jesus from the classrooms, yanked the Ten Commandments from our courtrooms, outlawed Christmas trees and crèches, mocked and spat on our beliefs—and then these same secular humanists think nothing of spending *our* money to prove the Bible wrong, to *make a lie out of our Christian faith!"*

The hubbub swelled. A few people stood up, then more, then the entire congregation. They surged upward like a tsunami, their voices merging into a single roar of disapproval.

The prompters remained dark, unneeded now.

"This is a *war* on Christianity, my friends! It's a war to the finish, and they're taxing you and me to wage it! *Are we going to let them spit on Christ and charge us for the privilege?"*

The Reverend Don T. Spates stopped dead at stage center, breathing heavily, gazing out over the seething audience in the Virginia Beach cathedral, flabbergasted at the effect of his words. He could hear it, he could see it, he could *feel* it—the frenzied swell, the upwelling of righteous anger, the very air crackling with the electricity of outrage. He could hardly believe it. He'd been throwing rocks all his life, and suddenly he'd lobbed a grenade. This was the issue he'd been praying for, hoping for, searching for.

"God and Jesus be praised!" he cried out, throwing his arms toward heaven and raising his eyes to the glittering ceiling. He sank to his knees in loud, quavering prayer. "Lord Jesus, with Your help, we will stop this insult to Your Father. We will destroy that infernal machine out there in the howling desert. We will put an end to this blasphemy against You called Isabella!"

7

AT QUARTER TO EIGHT, WYMAN FORD stepped out of the two-bedroom casita and stood at the end of the driveway, inhaling the fragrant night air. The windows of the dining hall were rectangles of yellow floating in darkness. Above the swish of the sprinklers on the playing field, he could hear the faint sounds of a boogie-woogie piano tune and the murmur of voices. He couldn't imagine Kate as any different from the irreverent, pot-smoking, argumentative graduate student he had known. But she must have changed—a lot—to become assistant director of the most important scientific experiment in the history of physics.

His mind seemed to slide naturally into memories of her and their time together, thoughts that had the unfortunate tendency to become X-rated. He hastily shoved them back into the id corner of his mind from which they had sprung. This was not, he thought, a responsible way to begin the investigation.

He skirted the sprinklers, reached the front door of the old log trading post, and entered. Light and music spilled from a recreation room to his right. He walked in. People were playing cards or chess, reading, working on laptop computers. Away from the Bridge, they appeared almost relaxed.

Hazelius himself sat at the piano. His tiny fingers jumped around the keys for several more bars and then he rose. "Wyman, welcome! Dinner is just ready." He met Ford halfway across the room, took his arm, and led him toward the dining hall. The rest began to rise and follow.

A heavy pine table set with candles, silver, and fresh wildflowers dominated the dining room. A fire blazed in a stone fireplace. Navajo rugs hung on the walls; Nakai Rock style, Ford guessed from the geometric designs. Several bottles of wine stood open, and the smell of grilled steak wafted in from the kitchen.

Hazelius acted the genial host, seating people, laughing, joking. He ushered Ford to a seat in the middle, next to a willowy blonde.

"Melissa? This is Wyman Ford, our new anthropologist. Melissa Corcoran, our cosmologist."

They shook hands. A mass of heavy blond hair tumbled down around her shoulders, and her pale green eyes, the color of sea glass, turned on him with curiosity. A smattering of freckles dusted an upturned

70

nose; a beaded Indian vest, both stylish and simple, set off her pants and shirt. But Corcoran's eyes, too, were faintly bloodshot and rimmed in red.

The seat on his other side was empty.

"Before you start on Wyman," Hazelius said to Corcoran, "I'd like to finish introducing him to those who didn't meet him earlier."

"Go ahead."

"This is Julie Thibodeaux, our quantum electrodynamicist."

A woman opposite Ford gave him a curt hello before returning to a querulous monologue aimed at the white-haired, leprechaun-like man next to her. Thibodeaux resembled the stereotype of the female scientist: dowdy, overweight, dressed in a dingy lab coat, her short hair stringy from lack of washing. A set of pens in a plastic pocket protector completed the caricature. Her file said she suffered from something called "borderline personality disorder." Ford was curious to see just how that manifested itself.

"The gentleman talking to Julie is Harlan St. Vincent, our electrical engineer. When Isabella is running at full power, Harlan manages the nine hundred megawatts of electricity pouring in here like Niagara Falls."

St. Vincent stood and extended his hand across the table. "Pleased to meet you, Wyman." When he sat back down, Thibodeaux went on with her disquisition, which seemed to involve something called a Bose-Einstein condensate.

"Michael Cecchini, our Standard Model particle physicist, is the gentleman at the far end."

A short, dark man rose, extended his hand. Ford took it, struck by his curiously flat, opaque gray eyes. The man looked dead inside—and the handshake was the same: clammy and lifeless. And yet, as if in defiance of the nihilism at the center of his existence, Cecchini had taken fastidious care with his dress; his shirt was a white so brilliant it hurt the eyes, there was a knife-edge crease in his slacks, and his hair was parted with military precision and groomed to perfection. Even his hands were immaculate, as soft and clean as patted dough, the nails emery-boarded and polished to a high gloss. Ford caught a faint scent of an expensive aftershave. But nothing could completely cover up the whiff of existential despair clinging to him.

Hazelius finished the introductions and disappeared into the kitchen, and the noise level grew.

Ford still hadn't met Kate. He wondered if that was a coincidence.

"I don't believe I've ever met an anthropologist before," Melissa Corcoran spoke to him.

He turned. "And I've never met a cosmologist."

"You'd be amazed at how many people think I do hair and nails." Her smile seemed an invitation. "What exactly will you be doing here?"

"Getting to know the locals. Explaining to them what's going on."

"Ah, but do *you* understand what's going on?" Her voice had taken on a teasing tone.

"Maybe you'll help me out."

Smiling, she reached across the table and grasped a bottle. "Wine?"

"Thank you."

She examined the label. "Villa di Capezzana, Carmignano, 2000. I have no idea what it is, but it's good. George Innes is our wine connoisseur. George? Tell us about the wine."

Innes broke off a conversation at the other end of the table, a smile of pleasure lighting his face. He tucked his glasses up. "I was lucky to snag that case—I wanted to serve something special tonight. Capezzana is one of my favorites, from an old estate in the hills west of Florence. It was the first DOC to permit cabernet sauvignon in the blend. It exhibits good color, red and black currant aromas mingling with cherries, and good depth of fruit."

Corcoran turned back to Ford with a smirk. "George is a frightful wine snob," she said, pouring a generous portion into his glass, then refilling her own. She raised it. "Welcome to Red Mesa. A horrible place."

"Why is that?"

"I brought my cat—I couldn't bear to be parted from her. Two days after we arrived, I heard a howl and saw a coyote running off with her."

"How terrible."

"You see them all over, the mangy, slinking brutes. Then there are the tarantulas, scorpions, bears, bobcats, porcupines, skunks, rattlesnakes, and black widow spiders." Reciting the words seemed to please her. "I hate this place," she said with relish.

Ford smiled with what he hoped looked like embarrassment and asked the dumbest question he could think of. No point in people thinking he was smart. "So, what's Isabella supposed to do? I'm just an anthropologist."

"In theory, it's quite simple. Isabella smashes subatomic particles together at almost the speed of light, to re-create the energy conditions of the Big Bang. It's like a demolition derby. Two separate beams of particles accelerate in opposite directions in a huge circular pipe, forty-seven miles in circumference. The particles go faster and faster, round and round inside the ring, until they're moving at 99.99 percent the speed of light in opposite directions. The fun begins when we bring them together in a head-on collision. In that way we re-create the violence of the Big Bang itself."

"What kinds of particles do you smash together?"

"Matter and antimatter—protons and antiprotons. When they come together—pow! E equals mc squared. The sudden blast of energy creates a spray of all kinds of different particles. That spray gets caught in the detectors and we can figure out what each particle is and how it was created."

"Where do you get antimatter?"

"We mail-order it from Washington."

Ford smiled. "And I thought they only had black holes."

"Seriously, we create our own antimatter on-site by blasting a gold plate with alpha particles. We collect the antiprotons in a secondary ring, then feed them into the main ring as needed."

"So where does the cosmology part come in?" Ford asked.

"I'm here to study dark things!" She rolled her eyes dramatically. "Dark matter and dark energy." Another sip of wine.

"Sounds scary."

She laughed. He watched her green eyes traveling across him, appraisingly, frankly, and wondered how old she might be. Thirty-three? Four?

"About thirty years ago, astronomers began to realize that most of the matter in the universe wasn't the usual stuff you could see and touch. They called it dark matter. It seems that dark matter is all around us, invisible, passing through us undetected, like a shadow universe. Galaxies sit in the middle of huge pools of dark matter. We don't know what it is, why it exists, or where it came from. Since dark matter must have been created along with regular matter during the Big Bang, I hope to use Isabella to make some of it."

"And dark energy?"

"Lovely, creepy stuff. Back in 1999, cosmologists found that some unknown energy field was causing the universe to expand, faster and faster, blowing it up like a giant balloon. They christened it dark energy. Nobody has the *slightest* idea what it is or where it comes from. It appears to be malevolent."

Across the table Volkonsky snorted, his voice shrill. "Malevolent? Universe is indifferent. It not give a shit about us."

"The fact is," said Corcoran, "dark energy will eventually wreck the universe—in the Big Rip."

"The Big Rip?" Until now, Ford had been feigning ignorance, but the Big Rip was new to him.

"It's the latest theory of the fate of the universe. Pretty soon the expansion of the universe will become so fast that galaxies will be ripped apart, then the stars, the planets, you and me—down to the very atoms themselves. Everything gone, poof! Existence will come to an end. I wrote the article about it on Wikipedia. Check it out."

She took another sip, and Ford noticed she wasn't the only one enjoying the wine. The conversations around them had swelled in volume, and half a dozen bottles already stood empty.

"Did you say 'pretty soon'?"

"No more than twenty, twenty-five billion years from now."

"*Soon* depends on perspective," said Volkonsky with a harsh laugh.

Corcoran said, "We cosmologists take the long view."

"And we computer scientists take short view. Like millisecond short."

"Milliseconds?" said Thibodeaux scornfully. "My work in quantum electrodynamics deals in femto-seconds."

Hazelius came out of the kitchen carrying a platter heaped with medallions of grilled tenderloin. He set it down to a chorus of approval from the table.

Kate Mercer appeared behind him, carrying a bowl of steak frites. Without looking Ford's way, she set it down and vanished back into the kitchen.

Nothing Ford imagined had prepared him for this first glimpse of her since they broke up. At thirty-five, she was even more beautiful than she had been at twenty-three—except that her long, unruly cascade of black hair was now short and stylish; the unkempt graduate student in jeans and oversized men's shirts had grown up. Twelve years had passed since he last saw her—but it felt like only a few days.

He felt a nudge in his ribs and turned to see Corcoran holding out the platter. "I hope you're not a vegetarian, Wyman."

"Not at all." He selected a slab oozing blood and passed the dish on, trying to appear relaxed. Kate's appearance had unnerved him.

"Don't think we eat like this every night," she said. "Your arrival makes it special."

A spoon tinkled against glass, and Hazelius rose, holding up his wine. Conversation stopped.

"I prepared a little toast of welcome—" He looked around. "*Now* where's our assistant director?"

The door to the kitchen opened and Kate bustled out, quickly seating herself next to Ford with her eyes fixed ahead on the table.

"I was just saying, I wanted to offer a toast of welcome to the newest member of our team: Wyman Ford."

Ford kept his eyes on Hazelius as he took in Kate's slender presence beside him, the warmth of her body, her scent.

"As most of you know, Wyman is an anthropologist and his field of study is human nature—a far more complex subject than anything we're working on." He raised his glass. "I'm looking forward to getting to know you, Wyman. A very, *very* warm welcome from us all."

A round of applause.

"And now, before I sit down, I wanted to say a few words about our disappointment last night. . . ." He paused. "We're engaged in a struggle that has been going on since a human being first gazed up at the stars and wondered what they were. The search for truth is the greatest of all human endeavors. From the discovery of fire to the discovery of the quark, this is the very *essence* of what it means to be human. We—the thirteen of us here—are the true heirs of Prometheus, who stole fire from the gods and gave it to mankind."

He paused dramatically.

"You know what happened to Prometheus. In retribution, the gods chained him to a rock for eternity. Every day, an eagle flies down, tears opens his side, and devours his liver. But because he's immortal, he cannot die, and must endure the torture forever."

The room was so quiet, Ford could hear the crackle of the fire in the grate.

"The search for truth is a hard, *hard* thing, as we are finding out." Hazelius raised his glass. "To the heirs of Prometheus."

People drank solemnly to the toast.

"Our next run will begin Wednesday at noon. From now until then, I want each of you to concentrate every fiber of your being on the task at hand."

He sat down. People picked up their knives and forks, and the conversation gradually resumed.

When the voices had grown loud enough, Ford said quietly, "Hello, Kate."

"Hello, Wyman." Her eyes were guarded. "This is a surprise, to say the least."

"You look well."

"Thank you."

"Assistant director—that's quite an achievement." He had felt like a voyeur, reading her dossier. But he couldn't stop himself—it had intrigued him. She had had a rocky life since they parted.

"And you—what happened to your CIA career?"

"I gave it up."

"And now you're an anthropologist?"

"Yes."

Neither said more. The sound of her voice, the musical lilt of it with just the hint of a lisp, hit him even harder than her appearance. He quickly stepped down on the flood of memories. The reaction was absurd—they had broken up long ago. Since then he had half a dozen relationships and a marriage. It hadn't been a pretty breakup either—no "let's just be friends" about it. They had said unforgivable things to each other.

Kate had turned and was speaking to someone else. He took a sip from his wine, lost in thought. His mind went back to when he had first seen her at MIT. Early one afternoon he'd been searching for a quiet reading corner at the back of the Barker Engineering Library when he noticed a woman sleeping under a table—a not-unusual sight. Her right cheek rested on her hand; the other arm lay across her shirt. Her long glossy hair fanned across the carpet. She was slender and cool, with the fine, delicate features often seen in people with dual Asian-Caucasian ancestry. She looked like a sleeping gazelle. The pale hollow at the base of her curved neck, next to her clavicle, struck him as the most erotic thing he had ever seen. His eyes lingered on her, shamelessly drinking in every erotic detail of her sleeping body. He couldn't seem to move on. He just stared.

A fly grazed her cheek. Her head jerked, and her mahogany eyes flew open, fixing on him. He felt busted.

She blushed and scrambled awkwardly out from under the table. "What's your problem?"

He mumbled something about having wanted to make sure she was okay.

She softened, embarrassed. "I must've looked kind of weird, lying on the floor. Usually there's no one around at this time of day. I can sleep for ten minutes and wake up refreshed."

His only interest in her, he assured her again, had been concern for her health. She made a throwaway comment about needing a double shot of espresso before hitting the books. He said he could use one, too—and that was their first date.

They were so different. That was part of the appeal. She was small-town working class, he big-city elite. She liked Blondie; he liked Bach. She sometimes smoked pot, which he found faintly scandalous. He was Catholic; she was a strident atheist. He was in control; she was unpredictable, spontaneous, even wild. On their second date, it was she who made the moves on him. On top of that, she was academically brilliant—perhaps even a genius. She was so smart, it scared him and turned him on at the same time. Even outside of physics, she had a fanatical drive to understand human nature. She was fiercely partisan, outraged at the unfairness of the world, a petition-signer, marcher, and letter-to-the-editor writer. He remembered their arguments on politics and religion that went on to the wee hours, and how surprised he was at her insight into human psychology, despite the raw emotionalism of her views.

His decision to join the CIA had ended their relationship. For her, either you were one of the good guys or you weren't. The CIA was definitely in the "weren't" category. She called it the Catastrophe-

Inducing Agency—and that was when she was being polite.

"So, Wyman," Kate said, "why'd you give it up?"

"What?" Ford came back to the present.

"Your CIA career. What happened?"

Ford wished he could just make himself say it: *Because my wife got car-bombed while we were working undercover.*

"It didn't work out," he said lamely.

"I see. Is it . . . is it too much to hope you changed your views?"

Is it too much to hope you changed yours? Ford thought, but let it pass. It was so like her: to get right to the heart of the matter, damn the cost. He'd loved that part of her, and he'd hated it.

"The dinner looks great," he said, trying to keep things bland. "Last I remember, you were empress of the microwave."

"Fast food was making me fat."

Again, silence.

Ford felt a nudge in his ribs from the other direction. Melissa Corcoran was holding out a bottle, offering to refill his glass. She looked flushed.

"Steak's perfect," she said. "Nice work, Kate."

"Thanks."

"Rare—just the way I like it. But hey," she said, gesturing at Ford's plate. "You haven't touched yours!"

Ford took a bite, but he had lost his appetite.

"I bet Kate's been telling you all about string

theory. It's pretty cool stuff—even if it's sheer speculation."

"Not at all like dark energy," said Kate, an edge to her voice.

Ford immediately sensed a history between these two women.

"Dark energy," said Corcoran coolly, "was discovered experimentally. By *observation*. The problem with string theory is just the opposite—it only exists as a bunch of equations with no testable predictions. It's not really science."

Volkonsky leaned over the table, and Ford caught a whiff of stale cigarette smoke. "Dark energy, strings, phffft! Who cares? I want to know what anthropologist does."

Ford was relieved by the distraction. "We go and live with a remote tribe and ask a lot of stupid questions."

"Ha-ha!" Volkonsky said. "Maybe you heard, the redskins are coming to Red Mesa. I hope it isn't scalping party!" He gave an Indian whoop and looked around for approval.

"That's not funny," said Corcoran acidly.

"Lighten yourself up, Melissa," Volkonsky shot back, tilting up his chin, the tuft of hair on it quivering with sudden anger. "Don't PC me."

Corcoran turned to Ford. "He can't help it. His doctorate was in horse's-assery."

More history, thought Ford. He would have to be careful to avoid getting hit in the crossfire until he figured out just where everyone stood in relation to one another.

Volkonsky said, "I think Melissa has drink the wine a little too well this evening. As usual."

"Ja, of courrrse," she drawled, in a devastating imitation of Volkonsky's accent. "Better I shoot vodkas like you, late in ze night!" She raised her glass, "Za vas!" and downed the heel of wine.

"Now, if I may interrupt for a moment," Innes began, his voice rotund with professionalism. "While it's good to get feelings into the open, I would suggest—"

Hazelius waved him silent and looked steadily at Volkonsky and Corcoran, back and forth, the pressure of his gaze inducing silence. Volkonsky sat back, the corner of his mouth twitching. Corcoran crossed her arms.

Hazelius allowed the awkwardness to build before he said, "We're all a little tired and discouraged." His voice was low and mild. In the silence, the fire crackled. "Right, Peter?"

Volkonsky said nothing.

"Melissa?"

Her face was red. She nodded curtly.

"Just let it go. . . . Easy does it. . . . Forgiveness and mildness . . . For the sake of our work."

His voice was calm, soothing, with a rhythmical, hypnotic quality—like a trainer calming a spooked horse. Unlike Innes's, it held no trace of condescension.

"That's right," said Innes, jumping in, his voice shattering the extraordinary calm Hazelius had created. "Absolutely. This has been a healthy exchange. We can air some of these same issues at the next group meeting. As I said, it's good to get these issues out in the open."

Volkonsky stood up so abruptly, he knocked his chair over. He balled up his napkin and chucked it on the table. "Screw group meeting. I have work to do."

The door slammed as he departed.

No one spoke. The only sound was the rustle of paper as Edelstein, having finished his dinner, turned another page of *Finnegans Wake*.

8

PASTOR RUSS EDDY EXITED THE TRAILER, threw a towel over his skinny shoulders, and paused in the yard. Monday had dawned brilliantly clear at the mission. The rising sun threw a golden light across the sandy valley, gilding the branches of the dead cottonwood next to the little house trailer. Behind, Red Mesa rose up gigantically on the horizon, a pillar of fire in the early morning sun.

He looked up to the sky, placed his palms together, bowed, and said, his voice clear and strong, "Thank You, Lord, for this day."

After a moment of silence, he shuffled over to the Red Jacket pump in his front yard and tossed the towel over an old hitching post. He gave the handle a dozen energetic creaks. A stream of cold water gushed out into a galvanized washtub below. Russ dashed a handful on his face, slipped a cake of soap into the water, sudsed up, shaved, and brushed his teeth. He washed his face and arms, dashed more water over his face and concave chest, plucked the towel off the post, and gave himself a vigorous drying off. Then he inspected himself in the mirror hung on a rusty nail in the fence post. His face was small, thin tufts of hair on his head sticking out. He hated his body; he looked like a wobbly little bird. Long ago, the doctor had told his mother it was a "failure to thrive." The implication that his physical weakness was somehow his fault, a personal failure, still stung.

He combed the hair carefully over the thinning spots, grimaced, inspected the crooked teeth he could never afford to get fixed. Somehow, he was reminded of his son, Luke—he'd be eleven now—and the feeling of anguish deepened. He hadn't seen Luke in six years, all the while being stuck with child support he had no hope of paying. A sudden vision of the boy flashed through his mind—the way he ran all skinny through a sprinkler one hot summer day. . . . The memory was like a knife slitting his throat—the way he had seen a Navajo woman slit the throat of a lamb, which struggled and bleated, still living but already dead.

He trembled, thinking of the injustices of his life, his money problems, his wife's unfaithfulness, the divorce. He had been victimized again and again, through no fault of his own. He had come to the Rez with nothing but his faith and two cartons of books. God was testing his faith with a hardscrabble existence and a constant shortage of money. Eddy hated owing money all over, especially to Indians. But the Lord must know what He was doing, and Eddy was slowly building his congregation, even if they seemed more interested in the free clothing he gave away than in the sermon. None of them ever laid more than a few dollars in the collection basket— some weeks it held only twenty dollars. And a lot of them went on to Mass at the Catholic Mission to load up on free eyeglasses and medicine, or the LDS Church in Rough Rock, for the food bank. That was the trouble with the Navajos: they couldn't tell the voice of Mammon from the voice of God.

He paused for a moment to look around for Lorenzo, but his Navajo helper had not yet made his appearance. At the thought of Lorenzo, he flushed. The collection-plate money had disappeared for the third time, and now he had no doubt it was Lorenzo. It was only fifty-odd dollars, but it was fifty dollars his mission desperately needed—and, worse, it was stealing from the Lord. Lorenzo's soul was in danger for a lousy fifty bucks.

Eddy was fed up. Last week he had decided to fire Lorenzo, but for that he needed proof. And he would soon have it. Yesterday, between the collection and the end of the service, he had marked the bills in the collection plate with a yellow highlighter. He'd asked the trader in Blue Gap to keep an eye out for anyone spending them.

Pulling on his T-shirt, he stretched his skinny arms and glanced over his humble mission with a mixture of affection and disgust. The trailer he lived in was falling apart. Near it stood the ProPanel hay barn he had bought from a rancher in Shiprock, disassembled, transported, and reerected to be his church. A backbreaking labor. Plastic chairs in different sizes, shapes, and colors substituted for pews. The "church" was open along three of the four sides, and during his sermon yesterday the wind kicked up and blew sand through the congregation. The only thing he owned of any value was back in the trailer, an iMac Intel Core Duo with a twenty-inch screen, sent to him by a Christian tourist passing through Navajoland who had been impressed by his mission. The computer was a godsend, his lifeline to the world beyond the Rez. He spent many hours a day on it, visiting Christian newsgroups and chat rooms, sending and receiving e-mail, and organizing donations of clothing.

Eddy walked into the church and began straightening out the chairs, putting them back in neat rows, and sweeping the sand off the seats with a hand brush. As he worked, he thought about Lorenzo and he became angrier, banging the chairs around and shoving them roughly into place. This was something Lorenzo was supposed to do.

When he finished adjusting the chairs, he carried a

push broom to the wooden preaching platform and started sweeping the sand off the far end. As he swept, he saw Lorenzo appear in the yard. Finally. The Navajo always walked the two miles from Blue Gap, and he had a tendency to arrive silently, unexpectedly, like a ghost.

Eddy straightened up and leaned on the broom handle as the young Navajo walked into the shade of the church.

"Hello, Lorenzo," said Eddy, trying to keep his voice even. "May the Lord bless you and guide you today."

Lorenzo flipped his long braids back. "Hi."

Eddy scrutinized his sullen face for signs of drug or liquor intoxication, but the eyes slid away from his as Lorenzo silently took the broom from his hands and began sweeping. Navajos were hard to read, but Lorenzo was harder than most, a loner, silent, keeping his own council. It was hard to tell if anything was going on in that head of his, beyond a craving for drugs and alcohol. Eddy couldn't recall a single instance in which Lorenzo had ever spoken a complete sentence. Incredible to think he'd attended Columbia University, even if he didn't graduate.

Eddy stepped back and watched Lorenzo sweep, his strokes slow and inefficient, leaving streaks of sand. He suppressed the urge to say something to Lorenzo now about the collection money. Eddy himself barely had enough to eat, and he had had to borrow money for gas again, and here was Lorenzo stealing God's money, no doubt to buy drugs or liquor. He felt a growing agitation at the thought of confronting Lorenzo. But he had to wait to hear from the trader first, because he needed proof. If he accused Lorenzo and the boy denied it—which he would, the liar— what could he do without proof?

"When you finish up here, Lorenzo, could you please sort through the clothing that just came?" He pointed to several boxes that had arrived on Friday from a church in Arkansas.

The man grunted to signify he had heard. Eddy watched his fumbled sweeping a few moments longer. Lorenzo was high, there was no question about it—he had stolen the collection to buy drugs. And now Eddy wouldn't be able to get through the week without borrowing money for gas and food.

He trembled with rage—but he said nothing, turned, and walked stiffly back into the trailer to make his meager breakfast.

9

FORD PAUSED AT THE THRESHOLD OF the barn. The Monday morning sun slanted in, lighting up a storm of dust motes. He could hear the sounds of horses shifting in their stalls, munching feed. He ventured inside and walked down the center aisle, stopping to look at the horse in the first stall. A paint horse, working a mouthful of oats, looked back at him.

"What's your name, pardner?"

The horse nickered, then lowered his head to scoop up another mouthful.

A pail rattled toward the other end of the barn. He turned to see a head poke out of the far stall: Kate Mercer.

They stared at each other.

"Morning," said Ford, mustering what he hoped passed for an easy smile.

"Morning."

"Assistant director, string theorist, cook, and . . . stable hand? You're a woman of many talents." He tried to keep his voice light. There were other talents of hers he'd been hard-pressed to keep out of his mind.

"You might say that."

She pressed the back of a gloved hand against her forehead, then walked over, carrying a pail of grain. A wisp of straw was tangled in her glossy hair. She wore tight jeans and a battered denim jacket over a white, crisp man's shirt. It was unbuttoned at the collar, and he glimpsed the soft swell of her breasts.

Ford swallowed, unable to think of anything to say except an inane "You cut your hair."

"Hair does have that tendency to grow, yes."

He wouldn't rise to the bait. "It looks nice," he said blandly.

"It's sort of my version of a traditional Japanese hairstyle called *umano-o.*"

Kate's hair had always been a touchy point. Her Japanese mother did not want her daughter to be

Japanese in any way. She refused to allow Japanese to be spoken in the house, and insisted Kate wear her hair long and loose, like an all-American girl. Kate had given in on the hair, but when her mother began hinting that Ford would make an ideal American husband, it made her look all the harder for flaws.

It occurred to Ford what the new hairstyle must mean.

"Your mother?"

"She passed away four years ago."

"I'm sorry."

A pause. "Going for a ride?" Kate asked.

"I was thinking about it."

"I didn't know you knew how to ride."

"I spent a summer at a dude ranch when I was ten."

"In that case, I wouldn't advise riding Snort." She nodded to the paint. "Where do you plan to go?"

Ford shuffled a USGS map from his pocket and unfolded it. "I wanted to pay a visit to Blackhorse to see the medicine man. By car it looks like twenty miles over bad roads. But it's only six miles by horse, if you take the trail on the back side of the mesa."

Kate took the map and examined it. "That's the Midnight Trail. Not for novice riders."

"It'll save me hours."

"I'd still take the Jeep if I were you."

"I don't want to arrive in a car emblazoned with government logos."

"Hmmm. I see your point."

They lapsed into silence.

"All right," said Kate. "The horse you want is Ballew." She lifted a halter off a hook, entered a stall, and led out a dirt-colored horse with a ewe neck, rat-tail, and a big hay belly.

"He looks like a reject from the dog-food factory."

"Don't judge a horse by his looks. Old Ballew here's bombproof. And he's smart enough to keep his cool going down the Midnight Trail. Grab the saddle and pad off that rack and let's tack up."

They brushed and saddled the horse, bridled it, and led it outside.

"You know how to mount?" she asked.

Ford looked at her. "Foot in the stirrup, step up—right?"

She held the reins to him.

Ford fumbled with the reins, looped one over the horse's neck, held the stirrup, and stuck his foot in.

"Wait, you need to—"

But he was already swinging up. The saddle slipped sideways and Ford stumbled to the ground, landing on his butt in the dirt. Ballew stood there indifferently, saddle hanging sideways on his flank.

"I was going to say, you need to check the cinch." She seemed to be stifling a laugh.

Ford got up, slapping off the dust. "Is that how you break in the dudes out here?"

"I tried to warn you."

"Well, I'd best be off."

She shook her head. "Of all the places in the world you could be, I can't believe you're here."

"You don't sound happy."

"I'm not."

Ford suppressed a retort. He had a job to do. "I got over all that a long time ago. I hope you can, too."

"Oh, don't worry about that—I'm *so* over it. It's just that I don't need this kind of complication right now."

"And what complication is that?" Ford asked.

"Forget it."

Ford fell silent. He wasn't going to get embroiled in anything personal with Kate. *Keep your mind on the mission.* "You heading back into the Bunker today?" he asked lightly, after a moment.

"Afraid so."

"More problems?"

Her eyes slid—warily, he thought. "Maybe."

"What kind?"

She looked up at him, looked away. "Hardware glitches."

"Hazelius told me it was software."

"That, too." Again her eyes looked away.

"Is there anything I can do to help?"

She faced him directly, her mahogany eyes veiled and troubled. "No."

"Is it something . . . serious?"

She hesitated. "Wyman? You do your job and let us do ours—okay?"

She turned abruptly and walked back toward the barn. Ford watched her until she vanished into the shadowed interior.

10

RIDING BALLEW, FORD GRADUALLY RELAXED, TRYING to keep his mind off Kate, where it had been dwelling far too much for his liking. It was one of those glorious late summer days, tinged with melancholy, that reminded him the season would soon be over. Snakeweed bloomed golden among the dry grasses. Prickly pears were turning furzy with spines, and the tips of the Apache plumes had traded their blossoms for the puffs of red-and-white feathers that signaled autumn's approach.

The trail petered out, and Ford continued cross-country, navigating by compass. Ancient corkscrewed junipers and hoodoo rock formations made the mesa top feel prehistoric. He crossed the track of a bear in sand, the paw prints looking almost human. *Shush,* the long-forgotten Navajo word for "bear" popped into his head.

Forty minutes later, he reached the edge of the mesa. The cliff dropped away sheer for a few hundred feet before stepping down through shelves of sandstone toward Blackhorse, two thousand feet below. The settlement looked like a cluster of geometric marks on the desert, about a half mile from the base of the mesa.

Ford got off and searched the edge of the cliffs until he found the slot in the rimrock where the Midnight Trail descended. It was marked on the map as an old uranium prospecting road, but rockfalls, landslides, and washouts had turned it into an intermittent track. It plunged through the rimrock and switchbacked down the face before crossing a rib of mesa and zigzagging down more switchbacks to the bottom. Just tracing the line of the trail, in places barely more than a few feet wide, made him dizzy. Maybe he should have taken the Jeep after all. But he sure as hell wasn't turning around.

He led Ballew to the edge and began walking down, trailing the horse. Unfazed, the horse lowered his head, gave a sniff, and followed Ford down. He felt a twinge of admiration, even affection, for the old gut-bucket.

Half an hour later they emerged at the bottom. Ford mounted and rode the last bit of trail down a shallow tamarisk-shaded canyon to Blackhorse. Cow pens, corrals, a windmill, a water tank, and a dozen shabby trailers completed the town. Behind one trailer stood several eight-sided hogans built of split cedar, with mud roofs. Near the center of town, a half dozen preschool children romped on a dilapidated swing set, their voices shrill in the desert's emptiness. Pickup trucks were parked beside the trailers.

Ford nudged Ballew with his heels. The old horse moved slowly over the flats on the outskirts of town. A steady wind blew. The children stopped playing and stood like miniature statues, watching him. Then, as if on cue, they ran off squealing.

Ford halted Ballew fifty feet from the closest trailer

and waited. He knew, from Ramah, that Navajo personal space began well before the front door. A moment later a door banged, and a rangy man in a cowboy hat with bowlegs came hobbling down from one of the trailers. He raised his hand to Ford. "Tie your horse over there," he called, over the sound of the wind.

Ford dismounted, tied Ballew, and loosened the flank cinch. The man approached, shielding his eyes from the bright sun. "Who are you?"

Ford stuck out his hand. *"Yá'át'ééh shi éí* Wyman Ford *yinishyé."*

"Oh no, not another *Bilagaana* trying to speak Navajo!" the man said cheerfully, then added, "at least your accent is better than most."

"Thanks."

"What can I do for you?"

"I'm looking for Nelson Begay."

"You found him."

"Got a moment?"

Begay squinted, looked at him more closely. "You come down off the mesa?"

"I did."

"Oh."

Silence.

Begay said, "That's a hell of a trail."

"Not if you walk your horse."

"Smart man." Another awkward pause. "You're . . . you're from the government, then?"

"Yes."

97

Begay squinted at him again, gave a snort, then turned and limped back to the trailer. A moment later the door slammed. Silence took over the town of Blackhorse, except for the wind, unfurling skeins of yellow dust around Ford as if weaving a blanket.

Now what? Ford stood in the swirling dust, feeling like an idiot. If he knocked on the door, Begay wouldn't answer, and all he'd do is establish himself as another pushy *Bilagaana*. On the other hand, he had come here to speak to Begay, and speak to Begay he would.

Screw it, the guy can't stay in his trailer forever. Ford sat down.

The minutes dragged on. The wind blew. The dust swirled.

Ten minutes passed. A stink beetle marched purposely through the dust on some mysterious errand, becoming a little black dot as it went off and disappeared. His mind wandered, and he thought about Kate, their relationship, the long journey his life had made since then. Inevitably, his thoughts turned to his wife. Her death had wrecked any sense of security he had felt in life. Before, he hadn't known how arbitrary life could be. Tragedy happened to others. Okay, lesson learned. It could happen to him. Move on.

He saw the faint movement of a curtain in a window, which suggested Begay was watching him.

He wondered how long it would take the guy to get the message that he wasn't moving. He hoped soon—

sand was starting to filter into his pants, work itself into his boots, sift down his socks.

The door slammed, and Begay came stomping out on the wooden stoop, arms crossed, looking mightily annoyed. He squinted at Ford and then shambled down the rickety wooden steps and came over. He extended his hand and helped Ford up.

"You're about the patientest goddamn white man I ever met. I suppose you'll have to come in. Broom yourself off before you ruin my new sofa."

Ford slapped off the dust and followed Begay into the living room, and they sat down.

"Coffee?"

"Thanks."

Begay returned with mugs of liquid as watery as tea. Ford remembered this, too—to save money, Navajos used the same coffee grounds multiple times.

"Milk? Sugar?"

"No, thanks."

Begay heaped sugar into his mug, followed by a good pour of half-and-half from a carton.

Ford took in the room. The brown crushed-velvet sofa he sat on looked anything but new. Begay eased himself into a broken Barcalounger. An expensive giant-screen television set sat in one corner, the only thing of any value in the house as far as he could see. The wall behind it was plastered with family photographs, many showing young men in military uniform.

Ford turned a curious gaze on Begay. The medicine

man wasn't what he had expected—neither a young, fiery activist nor a wise and wrinkled elder. He was lanky, with neatly trimmed hair, and looked to be in his early forties. Instead of the cowboy boots most Navajo men wore in Ramah, Begay wore high-top Keds, battered and faded, their rubber toe-caps peeling off. The only gesture to being Native American was a necklace of chunk turquoise.

"All right, now what is it you want with me?" He spoke in a soft woodwind voice with that peculiar Navajo accent that seemed to give weight to each word.

Ford gestured to the wall with his head. "Your family?"

"Nephews."

"They're in the military?"

"Army. One's stationed in South Korea. The other, Lorenzo, finished a tour in Iraq and now he's . . ." A hesitation. "Back home."

"You must be proud of them."

"I am."

Another silence. "I hear you're leading a protest ride against the Isabella project."

No answer.

"Well, that's why I'm here. To listen to your concerns."

Begay crossed his arms. "Too late for listening."

"Try me."

Begay uncrossed his arms and leaned forward. "Nobody asked people around here if we wanted this Isabella. The whole deal was done down in Window

Rock. They get the money and we get nothing. They told us there'd be jobs—then you people brought in construction workers from outside. They said it would bring economic development—but you people truck in your food and supplies from Flagstaff. Not once have you folks shopped in our local stores in Blue Gap or Rough Rock. You built your housing in an Anasazi valley, desecrating graves, and took away grazing land that we were still using, without compensation. And now we're hearing talk about smashing atoms and radiation."

He placed his big hands on his knees and glared at Ford.

Ford nodded. "I hear you."

"I'm glad you're not deaf. You're so damn ignorant of us, I bet you don't even know what time it is." He arched his eyebrows quizzically. "Go ahead—tell me what time you think it is."

Ford knew he was being set up in some way but played along anyway. "Nine."

"Wrong!" said Begay triumphantly. "It's ten."

"Ten?"

"That's right. Here on the Big Rez, half the year we're in a different time zone from the rest of Arizona, half the year in the same zone. In the summer, when you enter the Rez, we're one hour later than the rest of the state. Hours and minutes are a *Bilagaana* invention anyway, but the point is, you geniuses up there know so little about us that you don't even have your clocks set right."

Ford looked at him evenly. "Mr. Begay, if you're willing to work with me to make some real changes, I promise you I'll do all I can. You've got some legitimate grievances."

"Who are you, a scientist?"

"I'm an anthropologist."

There was a sudden silence. Then Begay eased himself back. A dry laugh shook his frame. "An anthropologist. Like we're some kind of primitive tribe. Oh, that's *funny*." He stopped laughing. "Well, I'm an American, just like you. I got relatives fighting for my country. I don't like you folks coming out here to *my* mesa, building a machine that's scaring the hell out of everyone, making a lot of promises you don't keep, and now they send an *anthropologist* like we're savages with bones through our noses."

"They sent me here only because I spent time over in Ramah. What I'd like to do is invite you up to the Isabella project for a tour, to meet Gregory Hazelius, to see what we're doing, to get acquainted with the team."

Begay shook his head. "The time for tours is over." He paused, then asked, almost reluctantly, "What kind of research *are* you doing over there? I been hearing some weird stories."

"Investigating the Big Bang."

"What's that?"

"That's the theory that the universe came into existence thirteen billion years ago in an explosion and has been expanding outward ever since."

"In other words, you people are shoving your noses into the Creator's business."

"The Creator didn't give us brains for nothing."

"So you all don't believe that a Creator made the universe."

"I'm Catholic, Mr. Begay. In my view, the Big Bang was simply how He did it."

Begay sighed. "Like I said: enough talk. We're riding up the mesa on Friday. That's the message you can take back to your team. Now, if you don't mind, I've got work to do."

FORD RODE BALLEW BACK TO WHERE the trail ascended. He looked up at the boulders and crags and cliffs. Now that he knew Ballew could navigate the switchbacks and rough spots, there was no reason to walk. He would ride the old horse.

When they passed through the rock opening at the top of the mesa an hour later, Ballew burst into a trot, eager to get back to the barn. Ford clung to the saddlehorn in a panic, thankful there was nobody around to see what a fool he must look. At around one o'clock Nakai Rock loomed up, and the low bluffs around the valley came into view. As he rode down into the cottonwoods, he heard a harsh laugh and saw a figure walking furiously along the path from Isabella to the settlement.

It was Volkonsky, the computer programmer, his long greasy hair in disarray. He looked haggard and angry, but at the same time he was grinning like a madman.

Ford hauled Ballew to a stop, dismounted quickly, and used the horse to block the trail.

"Hello."

"Excuse me," said Volkonsky, trying to dodge around.

"Nice day, don't you think?"

Volkonsky halted and stared, his face full of furious mirth. "You ask: Is it nice day? And I answer you: Never been better day!"

"Is that so?" Ford asked.

"And why is that your business, Mr. Anthropologist?" He tilted his head, his brown teeth exposed in a grimace of false hilarity.

Ford stepped so close, he could have touched the Russian. "From the way you look, I'd say you're having anything but a nice day."

Volkonsky laid a hand on Ford's shoulder in an exaggerated, mock-friendly way and leaned forward. A wash of liquor and tobacco-laden breath enveloped Ford. "Before, I worry. Now I am fine!" He tilted his head back and roared with harsh laughter, his unshaven Adam's apple bobbing.

The sound of steps came from behind. Volkonsky straightened abruptly.

"Ah, Peter," said Wardlaw, approaching down the trail. "And Wyman Ford. *Greetings.*" His voice, pleasant and oddly ironic, emphasized the final word.

Volkonsky started at the salutation.

"Coming from the Bunker, Peter?" Wardlaw's words seemed laced with menace.

Volkonsky maintained the manic grin, but Ford now saw uneasiness in his eyes—or was it fear?

"The security log says you were there all night," Wardlaw continued. "I'm worried about you. I hope you're getting enough sleep, Peter."

Silently, Volkonsky stepped past him and walked stiffly down the trail.

Wardlaw turned to Ford as if nothing out of the ordinary had happened. "Nice day for a ride."

"We were just chatting about that," said Ford dryly.

"Where'd you go?"

"I went to Blackhorse to meet the medicine man."

"And?"

"We met."

Wardlaw shook his head. "That Volkonsky . . . he's always worked up about something." He took a step down the trail, then stopped. "He didn't say any thing . . . *odd* to you, did he?"

"Such as?" Ford asked.

Wardlaw shrugged. "Who knows? The man's a little unstable."

Ford watched Wardlaw strolling off, meaty paws thrust in his pockets—a man like the rest of them, close to the breaking point, only far better at hiding it.

11

EDDY STOOD OUTSIDE HIS TRAILER, A glass of cold water in his hand, watching the sun sink toward the distant horizon. Lorenzo was nowhere to be seen—he had disappeared sometime around noon, vanished as silently as he had come, without having finished his chores. A heap of unsorted clothing lay on a table and the sand around the church hadn't yet been raked. Eddy stared at the distant horizon, burning with resentment. He never should have agreed to take in Lorenzo. The young man had been in prison for involuntary manslaughter, plea-bargained down from second-degree murder—knifed someone in a drunken brawl in Gallup. Served only eighteen months. Eddy had agreed to hire him, at the request of a local family, to help him satisfy his conditions of parole.

Big mistake.

Eddy took a sip of the cool water, trying to suppress the hot resentment and anger that boiled inside him. He hadn't heard yet from the trader in Blue Gap, but he had no doubt he would soon. And when that happened, he would have the proof he needed and could get rid of Lorenzo for good—send him back to prison, where he belonged. Eighteen months for murder—no wonder the crime rate on the Rez was sky high.

He took another sip and was surprised to see the faint outline of a man, walking down the road toward the mission, silhouetted against the setting sun. He stared, squinting.

Lorenzo.

Even as he approached he could see, from Lorenzo's uncertain gait, that the man was drunk. Eddy crossed his arms and waited, his heart accelerating at the thought of the coming confrontation. He would not let it pass—not this time.

Lorenzo came to the gate, leaned for a moment on the post, then came in.

"Lorenzo?"

The Navajo slowly turned his head. His eyes were bloodshot, his silly braids half undone, the bandanna around his head askew. He looked terrible, his whole frame stooped, as if the weight of the world were on his shoulders.

"Come here, please. I'd like to have a word with you."

Lorenzo merely looked at him.

"Lorenzo, didn't you hear me?"

The Indian turned and shambled on toward the clothes pile.

Eddy quickly moved and stood in Lorenzo's path, blocking him. The Indian stopped and raised his head, looking at him. The sour smell of bourbon washed over him.

"Lorenzo, you know very well that drinking alcoholic beverages is a violation of your parole."

Lorenzo just stared.

"You also left without finishing your work. I'm

supposed to certify to your parole officer that you're doing an adequate job here, and I won't lie to him. I won't lie. I'm letting you go."

Lorenzo dropped his head. For a moment Eddy thought it was a gesture of contrition, but then he heard a hawking sound, as Lorenzo scoured up a gob of phlegm and slipped it from his lips, depositing it into the sand at Eddy's feet like a raw oyster.

Eddy felt his heart pounding. He was furiously angry. "Don't you spit when I'm talking to you, mister," he said, his voice high.

Lorenzo tried to take a step to the side to go around Eddy, but the pastor quickly stepped in his way again. "Are you listening to me, or are you too drunk?"

The Indian just stood there.

"Where'd you get the money for liquor?"

Lorenzo lifted his hand, let it drop heavily.

"I asked you a question."

"A guy owed me." His voice was hoarse.

"Is that so? Which guy?"

"Don't know his name."

"You don't know his name," repeated Eddy.

Lorenzo made another halfhearted attempt to go around, which Eddy blocked. He felt his hands trembling. "I happen to know where you got that money. You stole it. From the collection plate."

"No way."

"Yes way. You stole it. Over fifty dollars."

"Bullshit."

"Don't swear at me, Lorenzo. I saw you take it."

The lie was out before he even realized he was telling it. But it didn't matter; he might as well have seen him—guilt was written all over his face.

Lorenzo said nothing.

"That was fifty dollars of money that this mission desperately needs. But you didn't just steal from the mission. You didn't just steal from me. *You stole from the Lord.*"

No response.

"How do you think the Lord will react to that? Did you think about that when you took the money, Lorenzo? And if thy right hand offend thee, cut it off, and cast it from thee: for it is profitable for thee that one of thy members should perish, and not that thy whole body should be cast into hell."

Lorenzo turned brusquely and began walking the other way, back toward town. Eddy lunged forward and grabbed his shirt at the shoulder. Lorenzo jerked his shoulder away and kept going. Suddenly he veered and went off toward the trailer.

"Where are you going?" Eddy cried. "Don't go in there!"

Lorenzo disappeared inside. Eddy ran after him, pausing at the door. "Get out of there!" He hesitated to follow him inside, fearful of being jumped. "You're a thief!" he shouted in. "That's what you are. A common thief. Get out of my house now! I'm calling the police!"

A crash came from the kitchen, a silverware drawer flung across the room.

"You'll pay for the damage! Every cent!"

Another crash, more scattered flatware. Eddy desperately wanted to go in, but he was afraid. At least the drunk Indian was in the kitchen and not in the back bedroom where his computer was.

"Get out of there, you drunkard! Human garbage! You're dirt in the eyes of Jesus! I'm reporting this to your parole officer and you'll go back to prison! I guarantee it!"

Suddenly Lorenzo appeared in the entryway, a long bread knife in his hand.

Eddy backed up and off the stoop. "Lorenzo. No."

Lorenzo stood on the stoop, uncertainly, waving the knife and blinking in the setting sunlight. He did not advance.

"Drop the knife, Lorenzo. Drop it."

His hand lowered.

"Drop it, now." Eddy could see his whitened grip on the handle relaxing. "Drop it or Jesus will punish you."

A gargle of rage suddenly came from Lorenzo's throat. "I screw your Jesus up the ass, like this!" He jabbed the knife into the air so violently that it almost threw him off balance.

Eddy staggered back, the words landing on him like a kick to the gut. "How—dare—you—*blaspheme* our Savior? You sick—you *evil* man! You'll burn in hell, Satan! You—!" Eddy's high-pitched voice was choked off by hysteria.

A raucous, phlegmy laugh erupted from Lorenzo's

throat. He waved the knife around, grinning, as if enjoying Eddy's horror. "That's right, *up* the ass."

"You'll burn in hell!" Eddy cried, with a rush of courage. "You'll call on Jesus to moisten your parched lips, but He won't be listening. Because you're *scum*. Human garbage scum!"

Lorenzo spat again. "Right on."

"God will strike you down, mark my words. He will smite you and curse you, blasphemer! You stole from Him, you dirty Indian thief!"

Lorenzo rushed at Eddy. But the preacher was small and quick, and as the knife came at him in a wide, inefficient arc, Eddy skipped aside and seized Lorenzo's forearm in both his hands. The Navajo struggled, trying to turn the knife back on Eddy, but Eddy held on with both hands like a terrier, twisting and wrenching the arm, trying to shake the knife loose.

Lorenzo grunted, strained, but in his drunken state he didn't have the strength. His arm suddenly went limp and Eddy held on.

"Drop the knife."

Lorenzo stood there, uncertainly. Eddy, seeing his chance, threw a shoulder into Lorenzo, spinning him sideways, and grabbed the knife. Losing his footing, Eddy fell backward with Lorenzo falling on top of his chest. Even as Lorenzo fell, however, Eddy had taken the knife by the handle. Lorenzo fell on it, the knife impaling his heart fore and aft. Eddy felt hot blood gush on his hands and with a cry he released the blade and pulled himself out from under the Navajo. The knife was in Lorenzo's chest, right over his heart.

"No!"

Incredibly, Lorenzo rose to his feet, the knife sticking out of his chest. Staggering back, with one final effort he wrapped both his hands hard around the knife handle. He stood there for a moment, hands gripping the handle, straining to pull it out with rapidly ebbing strength, his face blank, his eyes filming over. Toppling forward, he fell heavily into the sand, the force of the fall driving the point of the knife out his back.

Eddy stared, his mouth working. Below the supine body, he saw a pool of blood running into the sand, soaking into the thirsty ground, leaving jellylike clots on the surface.

The first thought Eddy had was, *I will not be a victim again.*

THE SUN HAD LONG SET AND a chill was in the air by the time Eddy finished the hole. The sand was soft and dry and he had dug it deep—very deep.

He paused, drenched in sweat and shivering at the same time. He climbed out of the hole, pulled up the ladder, placed his foot against the body, and rolled it in. It landed with a wet thump.

Working with great care, he shoveled all the bloody sand into the hole, digging down as far as it went, not missing a grain. Then he stripped off his clothes and tossed them in next. Finally, in went the bloody bucket of water he had washed his hands in, bucket and all, followed by the towel he had dried himself with.

He stood shivering at the edge of the dark hole, stark naked. Should he pray? But the blasphemer deserved no prayer—and what good would prayer do for someone already writhing and shrieking in the blast furnaces of hell? Eddy had said God would smite him down, and not fifteen seconds later God had done just that. God had directed the blasphemer's hand against himself. Eddy had actually witnessed it—had seen the miracle.

Still naked, Eddy filled in the hole, shovelful by shovelful, working hard to keep up his body warmth. By midnight he was finished. He raked out the evidence of his work, put away his tools, and went into the trailer.

As Pastor Eddy lay in bed that night, praying as hard as he had ever prayed in his life, he heard the night wind come up, as it so often did. It moaned and rocked and rattled the old trailer, the sand hissing against the windows. By morning, Eddy thought, the yard would be swept clean by the wind, a smooth expanse of virgin sand, all trace of the incident erased.

The Lord is scouring the ground clean for me, just as he forgives me and scours clean the sin from my soul.

Eddy lay in the dark, shaking and triumphant.

113

12

THAT EVENING, BOOKER CRAWLEY FOLLOWED THE maître d' to the back of the dim steak house in McLean, Virginia, and found the Reverend D. T. Spates already parked at a table, perusing the five-pound leather-bound menu.

"Reverend Spates, how good to see you again." He took the man's hand.

"A pleasure, Mr. Crawley."

Crawley took his seat, shook out the elegant twist of linen that was his napkin, and strung it across his lap.

A cocktail waiter glided over. "May I get you gentlemen anything to drink?"

"Seven and seven," said the reverend.

Crawley cringed, glad he had picked a restaurant where no one would recognize him. The reverend smelled of Old Spice, and his sideburns were a centimeter too long. In person he looked twenty years older than on-screen, his face liver-spotted and mottled with that reddish sandpaper texture that marked the drinking man. His orange hair glistened in the indirect light. How could a man with so much media savvy tolerate such a cheap hair job?

"And you, sir?"

"Bombay Sapphire martini, very dry, straight up with a twist."

"Right away, gentlemen."

Crawley mustered a broad smile. "Well, Reverend, I saw your show last night. It was . . . *terrific.*"

Spates nodded, a plump, manicured hand tapping the tablecloth. "The Lord was with me."

"I was wondering if you've received any feedback."

"Sure did. My office has logged over eighty thousand e-mails in the last twenty-four hours."

A silence. "Eighteen thousand?"

"No, sir. *Eighty* thousand."

Crawley was speechless. "From whom?" he asked finally.

"Viewers, of course."

"Am I right in assuming this is an unusual response?"

"That you are. The sermon really touched a nerve. When the government spends taxpayer money to put the lie to the Word of God—well, Christians everywhere rise up."

"Yes, of course." Crawley managed a smile of agreement. *Eighty thousand.* That would scare the piss out of any congressman. He paused as the waiter brought their drinks.

Spates wrapped a plump hand around his frosty glass, took a long drink, set it down.

"Now there's this matter of the pledge you made to God's Prime Time Ministry."

"Naturally." Crawley touched his jacket above the inner pocket. "All in good time."

Spates took another sip. "What's the reaction in Washington?"

Crawley's contacts had learned that a significant number of e-mails had also arrived for various congressmen, along with heavy telephone traffic. But it wouldn't do to inflate Spates's expectations. "An issue like this needs to be pushed awhile before it penetrates the hard shell of Washington."

"That isn't what I heard from my viewers. Lots of those e-mails were copied to Washington."

"No doubt, no doubt," said Crawley hastily.

The waiter came by and took their order.

"Now, if you don't mind," said Spates, "I'd like to collect that donation before the food comes. I wouldn't want to get grease on it."

"No, no, of course not." Crawley slipped the envelope out of his pocket and laid it unobtrusively on the table, then cringed as Spates reached over and held it up ostentatiously. Spates's jacket sleeve slipped back, exposing a meaty wrist well furred in orange hair. So the orange was real. How could the thing that seemed most fake about Spates turn out to be the one real thing? Was there something else, more urgent, that he was missing about this man? Crawley pushed down his irritation.

Spates turned the envelope over and tore it open with a lacquered fingernail. He slid out the check, held it to the light, and examined it closely.

"Ten thousand dollars," he read slowly.

Crawley glanced around, relieved they were alone in the back of the restaurant. The man had no class at all.

Spates continued to study the check. "Ten thousand dollars," he repeated.

"I trust it's in good order?"

The reverend slid the check back into the envelope and stuffed it inside his jacket. "You know how much it costs to run my ministry? Five thousand a *day.* Thirty-five thousand a week, almost two million a year."

"That's quite an operation," said Crawley evenly.

"I devoted an entire hour of my sermon to your problem. I hope to take it up again on *Roundtable America* this Friday. You watch it?"

"Never miss it." Crawley knew the Christian Cable Service aired Spates's weekly talk show, but he'd never seen it.

"I plan to keep on top of this until I've aroused the righteous anger of Christians across this land."

"I'm very grateful, Reverend."

"For this, ten thousand dollars is hardly a drop in the bucket."

Goddamned Holy Joe, thought Crawley. How he hated to deal with people like this. "Reverend, forgive me, but I was under the impression that you would take up the issue in return for a one-time donation."

"And I did: one-time donation, one-time sermon. Now I'm talking about a *relationship.*" Spates tipped the glass up to his wet lips, drained the last of the drink through the column of ice cubes, replaced the glass on the table, and wiped his mouth.

"I handed you an excellent issue. Judging from the reaction, it seems worth pushing, regardless of the, ah, pecuniary aspects."

"My friend, there's a *war* on faith going on out there. We're fighting the secular humanists on multiple fronts. I could shift my battle lines at any moment. If you want me to keep fighting at your salient, well, then—you've got to *contribute*."

The waiter brought their filets mignons. Spates had ordered his well done, and the thirty-nine-dollar cut of meat was now the size, shape, and color of a hockey puck. Spates clasped his hands and bowed over the plate. It took Crawley a moment to realize he was blessing his food, not smelling it.

"Can I get you gentlemen anything else?" the waiter asked.

The reverend raised his head and lifted his glass. "Another." He narrowed his eyes at the waiter's departing form. "I believe that man's a homosexual."

Crawley took a long level breath. "So what kind of a relationship are you suggesting, Reverend?"

"A quid pro quo. You scratch my back; I scratch yours."

Crawley waited.

"Say, five thousand a week, with a guarantee I'll mention the Isabella project in each sermon and take it up on at least one cable show."

So that's how it was going to be. "Ten thousand a *month,*" said Crawley coolly, "with a guaranteed minimum of ten minutes devoted to the topic in each sermon. As for the cable show, I'll expect the first show to be devoted entirely to Isabella, with later shows pushing the subject. My donation will be made at the *end* of the month *after* the airing. Each payment will be duly recorded as a charitable contribution, with a letter to that effect. That is my first, last, and only offer."

The Reverend Don T. Spates gazed pensively at Crawley. Then his face turned into an enormous smile, and a freckled hand extended across the table, once more exposing the orange hairs.

"The Lord will give you value for your money, my friend."

13

EARLY TUESDAY, BEFORE BREAKFAST, FORD SAT at the kitchen table in his casita staring at the stack of dossiers. There was no reason why having a high IQ would somehow protect you from the vicissitudes of life, but this group seemed to have more than their share of problems: difficult childhoods, dysfunctional parents, sexual identity problems, personal crises, even a few bankruptcies. Thibodeaux had been in therapy since she was twenty, diagnosed with the borderline personality disorder he'd read about before. Cecchini had gotten tangled up with a religious cult as a teenager. Edelstein had suffered bouts of depression. St. Vincent had been an alcoholic. Wardlaw had suffered from PTSD after witnessing his squad leader's head blown off in a cave in the Tora Bora mountains. At thirty-four, Corcoran had been married and divorced—twice. Innes had been reprimanded for sleeping with patients.

Only Rae Chen didn't seem to have anything untoward in her own background—just a first-generation Chinese-American whose family owned a restaurant. Dolby, also, seemed relatively normal, except that he'd grown up in one of the worst neighborhoods in Watts, and his brother had been paralyzed by a stray bullet in a gang shootout.

Kate's dossier had been the most revealing of all. He read through it with a kind of sick, guilty fascination. Her father had committed suicide not long after they'd broken up—shot himself after failing in business. Her mother had then gone into a long physical decline, ending up in a nursing home at seventy, unable to recognize her own daughter. After her mother died, there was a two-year gap in the record. Kate had paid two years' rent on her apartment in Texas and disappeared, returning two years later. It impressed the hell out of Ford that neither the FBI nor CIA could find out where she had gone or what she did. She refused to answer their questions—even at the risk of not gaining the security clearance she needed to be assistant director of the Isabella project. But Hazelius had stepped in, and the reason wasn't hard to see—they had been having a relationship. It seemed to have been more a friendship than a passion, and it had ended amicably.

He packed away the files, disgusted at the violation of privacy, the gross intrusion of government into a person's life, represented by the dossiers. He wondered how he could have stomached it all those years in the CIA. The monastery had changed him more than he'd realized.

He pulled out the dossier on Hazelius and opened it up. He had read it over quickly, and now he began going through it with more care. It was arranged chronologically, and Ford read it in order, visualizing the arc of the man's life. Hazelius came from a surprisingly mundane background, an only child in a solid middle-class family of Scandinavian roots from Minnesota, father a storekeeper, mother a homemaker. They were sober, dull, churchgoing people. An unlikely environment to produce a transcendental genius. Hazelius had quickly shown himself to be a true prodigy: summa cum laude from Johns Hopkins at seventeen, doctorate from Caltech at twenty, full professor at Columbia at twenty-six, Nobel Prize at thirty.

Beyond his brilliance, the man was hard to pin down. He was not your typical narrow academic. At Columbia his students had adored him for his dry wit, playful temperament, and surprising mystical streak. He played boogie-woogie and stride piano in a band called the Quarksters at a dive on 110th Street, filling the place with worshipful undergrads. He took students to strip joints. He developed a "strange attractor" theory of the stock market and made millions before selling the system to a hedge fund.

After winning the Nobel Prize for his work on quantum entanglement, Hazelius moved easily into his role as the heir to physics superstar Richard Feynman. He published no fewer than thirty theoretical papers on the incompleteness of quantum theory, shaking the very foundations of the discipline. He won the Fields Medal in mathematics for proving Laplace's third conjecture, the only person to have won both a Nobel and a Fields. He added a Pulitzer to his list of prizes for a book of poetry—strangely beautiful poems that mixed expressive language with mathematical equations and scientific theorems. He had set up a rescue program in India to provide medical help to girls in regions where it was customary to allow sick girls to die; the program also included subtle but intensive educational programs aimed at changing societal values about girls. He had contributed millions to a campaign to eradicate female genital mutilation in Africa. He had patented—and this Ford found comical—a better mousetrap, humane but effective.

He often appeared on Page Six of the *Post*, hobnobbing with the rich and famous, dressed in his trademark suits from the seventies with fat lapels and massive ties. He bragged he bought them at the Salvation Army, never paying more than five dollars. He was a regular guest on Letterman, where he could always be counted on to make outrageous un-PC pronouncements—he called them "unpleasant truths"—and wax eloquent about his utopian schemes.

At the age of thirty-two, he astonished everyone by marrying the supermodel and former *Playboy* bunny Astrid Gund, ten years his junior and legendary for her cheerful vacuity. She went everywhere with him, even on the television talk circuit, where he gazed at her adoringly while she chattered happily about her warm and fuzzy political opinions, once declaring famously, in a discussion of 9/11, "Gee, why can't people just *get along?*"

That was bad enough. But during this period, Hazelius had said something that so outraged the zeitgeist that it became immortal, in the manner of the Beatles' claim that they were more popular than Jesus. A reporter asked the physicist why he had married a woman "so far beneath you intellectually." Hazelius had taken great offense. "Who would you have me marry?" he roared at the journalist. "Everyone's beneath me intellectually! At least Astrid knows how to love, which is more than I can say for the rest of you moronic human beings."

The smartest man in the world had dissed everyone else as morons. The uproar was enormous. The *Post* ran a classic headline:

HAZELIUS TO WORLD:
YOU'RE ALL MORONS

The talk-radio mobocrats and their fellow travelers worked themselves into a self-righteous fury. Hazelius was condemned from every pulpit and soapbox in America, pilloried as anti-American, antireligious, unpatriotic, a misanthrope, and a member of that most despicable of species—a sherry-sipping, ivory-tower Eastern establishment elitist.

Ford laid the papers aside and poured another cup of coffee. So far the dossier didn't fit the Hazelius he was getting to know, who weighed his every word and acted as peacemaker, diplomat, and team leader. He had yet to hear a single political opinion from the man.

Some years ago, Hazelius had experienced a tragedy. Perhaps that had changed him. Ford skipped ahead in the file until he found it.

Ten years ago, when Hazelius was thirty-six, Astrid had dropped dead of a cerebral hemorrhage. The death devastated him. For several years he had retreated from the world into a Howard Hughes–like seclusion. Then, quite suddenly, he emerged with the plan for Isabella. He was indeed a changed man: no more talk shows, offensive statements, utopian schemes, or lost causes. He shed his society connections and dropped the ugly suits. Gregory North Hazelius had grown up.

With extraordinary skill, patience, and tact, Hazelius had pushed the Isabella project forward, enlisting allies in the science community, wooing big foundations, and courting those in power. He never missed an opportunity to remind Americans that the United States had fallen seriously behind the Europeans in nuclear physics research. He maintained that

Isabella might lead to cheap solutions to the world's energy needs—with all the patents and the know-how in American hands. With that, he had accomplished the impossible: cajoling forty billion dollars out of Congress during a time of budget deficits.

He was a consummate master at persuasion, it seemed, working quietly behind the scenes, a cautious visionary, yet willing to take a bold, calculated risk. This was the Hazelius that Ford was getting to know.

Isabella was Hazelius's brainchild, his baby. He had traveled the country and handpicked a team from the elite ranks of physicists, engineers, and programmers. Everything had proceeded smoothly. Until now.

Ford closed the file and ruminated. He still felt he had not yet peeled back the inner layers to reveal the core human being. Genius, showman, musician, utopian dreamer, devoted husband, arrogant elitist, brilliant physicist, patient lobbyist. Which was the real man? Or was there a shadowy figure behind them all, manipulating the masks?

Parts of Hazelius's life weren't so different from his own. They had both lost their wives in horrifying ways. When Ford's wife had died, the world as he knew it had blown up with her, leaving him wandering in the ruins. But Hazelius had reacted in the opposite way: his wife's death seemed to have focused him. Ford had lost the meaning in his life; Hazelius found his.

He wondered how his own dossier would read. He

had no doubt it existed—and that Lockwood had read it, just as he was reading theirs. How would it look? *Child of privilege, Choate, Harvard, MIT, CIA, marriage.* And then: *Bomb.*

After *Bomb,* what then? *Monastery.* And finally, *Advanced Security and Intelligence, Inc.,* the name of his new investigation company. It suddenly seemed pretentious. Who was he kidding? He'd hung out his shingle four months ago and he'd gotten one assignment. Admittedly, it was a plum job, but then there were special reasons why he'd been chosen. And he couldn't put it on his résumé.

He glanced at the clock: he was late for breakfast, and he was wasting time with self-pitying musings.

Shoving the dossier in the briefcase, he locked it and headed out toward the dining hall. The sun had just risen over the red bluffs, and the light was shooting through the leaves of the cottonwoods, setting them aglow like shards of green and yellow glass.

The dining hall was rich with the smell of cinnamon buns and bacon. Hazelius was seated in his accustomed place at the head of the table, deep in conversation with Innes. Kate sat at the other end, near Wardlaw, pouring herself coffee.

At the sight of her, Ford felt a twist in his gut.

He took the last empty seat next to Hazelius and helped himself to scrambled eggs and bacon off the platter.

"Morning," said Hazelius. "Sleep well?"

"Never better."

Everyone was there except Volkonsky.

"Say, where's Peter?" Ford ventured. "I didn't see his car in the driveway."

Conversation trickled into silence.

"Dr. Volkonsky seems to have left us," said Wardlaw.

"Left? Why?"

At first, no one spoke. Then, in an unnaturally loud voice, Innes said, "As the team psychologist, I can perhaps shed light on that question. Without violating any professional confidences, I think I can say without contradiction that Peter was never happy here. He had a hard time adjusting to the isolation and stressful schedule. He missed his wife and child back at Brookhaven. It's no surprise he decided to go."

"You said he *seems* to have left?"

Hazelius answered smoothly. "His car's gone, his suitcase and most of his clothes are missing—that was our assumption."

"He didn't say anything to anyone?"

"You seem alarmed, Wyman," said Hazelius, peering at him rather markedly.

Ford stopped. He was getting ahead of himself, and a man as observant as Hazelius wasn't likely to miss it.

"Not alarmed," said Ford. "Just surprised."

"I could see this coming for some time, I'm afraid," said Hazelius. "Peter wasn't cut out for this kind of life. I'm sure we'll hear from him when he gets home.

Now Wyman, tell us how your visit went with Begay yesterday."

Everyone turned to listen.

"Begay's angry. He has a list of complaints against the Isabella project."

"Such as?"

"Let's just say that a lot of promises were made that weren't kept."

"We made no promises to anybody," said Hazelius.

"It appears the DOE promised all kinds of jobs and economic benefits."

Hazelius shook his head disgustedly. "I don't control the DOE. Did you at least manage to talk him out of this protest ride?"

"No."

Hazelius frowned. "I hope you can do something to head this off."

"It may be better to let it happen."

"Wyman, the slightest whiff of trouble could make national news," said Hazelius. "We can't afford bad publicity."

Ford gazed steadily at Hazelius. "You've been holed up here on the mesa, engaged in a secret government project, avoiding all contact with the locals—naturally there would be rumors and suspicion. What in the world did you expect?" It came out a little sharper than he intended.

Everyone stared at him, as if he had just cursed the priest. But they relaxed as Hazelius slowly relaxed. "All right, I'd say I deserved that rebuke. Fair enough. Perhaps we haven't handled this as well as we could have. So . . . what's the next step?"

"I'm going to pay a friendly visit to the local Navajo chapter president at Blue Gap, see if I can set up a sort of town meeting with the locals. Which you will attend."

"If I can spare the time."

"I'm afraid you'll have to spare the time."

Hazelius waved his hand. "We'll cross that bridge when we come to it."

"I'd like to take a scientist with me today, too."

"Anyone in particular?"

"Kate Mercer."

Hazelius looked around. "Kate? You don't have anything going today, do you?"

Kate's face flushed. "I'm busy."

"If Kate can't, I'll go," said Melissa Corcoran, tossing her hair with a smile. "I'd love to get the hell off this godforsaken mesa for a few hours."

Ford glanced at Kate and back at Corcoran. He felt reluctant to tell them he'd rather not show up at Blue Gap with a six-foot, blue-eyed, blond Anglo bombshell. At least Kate, with her black hair and half-Asian face, looked almost Indian.

"Are you really all that busy, Kate?" Hazelius asked. "You said you'd almost completed the new black hole calculations. This is important—and you are, after all, the assistant director."

Kate glanced at Corcoran with an inscrutable expression. Corcoran returned the glance coldly.

"I suppose I could finish the black hole stuff later," said Kate.

"Great," Ford said. "I'll swing by your place with the Jeep in an hour." He headed for the door, feeling strangely elated.

As he passed Corcoran, she cast him a sideways smirk. "Next time," she said.

BACK IN THE CASITA, FORD LOCKED the door, took the briefcase into the bedroom, drew the curtains, removed the sat phone, and dialed Lockwood.

"Hello, Wyman. Got any news?"

"You know the scientist, Peter Volkonsky, the software engineer?"

"Yes."

"He disappeared last night. His car's gone, and they say he packed up his clothes. Can you find out if he's showed up or contacted anyone?"

"We'll try."

"I need to know ASAP."

"I'll call you right back."

"A couple of other things."

"Shoot."

"Michael Cecchini—his dossier says he joined a religious cult as a teenager. I'd like to know more about that."

"Will do. Anything else?"

"Rae Chen. She seems . . . How can I put it? Too normal."

"That's not much to go on."

"Look into her background, see if there's something odd there."

Ten minutes later the ring light blinked. Ford pushed the RECEIVE button and Lockwood's voice came on, considerably more tense. "Regarding Volkonsky, we called his wife, his colleagues at Brookhaven—nobody's heard from him. You say he left last night? At what time?"

"I'm guessing sometime about nine."

"We're putting out an APB on his car and plate. It's a forty-hour drive back to his home in New York State. If he's headed that way, we'll find him. Did something happen?"

"I ran into him yesterday. He'd spent the entire night at Isabella and he'd been drinking. He was full of forced hilarity. He said to me, 'Before, I worry. Now I am fine.' But he looked the opposite of fine."

"Any idea what he meant by that?"

"None."

"I want you to search his quarters."

A hesitation. "I'll do it tonight."

Ford cradled the receiver and looked at the cotton-wood trees outside the window. Lying, spying, deceiving, and now breaking and entering. A fine way to launch his first year out of the monastery.

14

FORD TOOK IN BLUE GAP, ARIZONA, with a single sweep of his eyes. It lay in a dusty basin surrounded by rimrock and the gray skeletons of dead piñons. The town was little more than a pair of intersecting dirt roads, asphalted a hundred yards from their point of intersection. There was a gas station of adobe-colored cinder block and a convenience store with a cracked window. Plastic grocery bags flapped like banners from the barbed-wire fence behind the gas station. Next to the convenience store stood a small middle school building surrounded by a chain-link fence. To the east and north, two grids of HUD housing had been laid out in rigid symmetry in the red dirt.

In the near distance, the purple silhouette of Red Mesa formed a towering backdrop.

"So," said Kate as the Jeep reached the pavement, "what's your plan?"

"Get gas."

"Gas? The tank's half-full, and we get all the free gas we need back at Isabella."

"Just follow my lead, will you?"

He pulled into the gas station, got out, and filled up. Then he tapped on Kate's window. "Got any money?" he asked.

She looked at him with alarm. "I didn't bring my purse."

"Good."

They went in. A large Navajo woman stood behind the counter. A few other customers—all Navajo—were browsing in the store.

Ford picked out a pack of gum, a Coke, a bag of chips, and the *Navajo Times*. He strolled to the counter, plunked them down. The woman rang them up with the gas.

Ford dipped into his pocket, and his expression changed. He made a show of looking through his pockets.

"Damn. Forgot my wallet." He glanced at Mercer. "You got any money?"

She glared. "You know I don't."

Ford spread his hands and smiled sheepishly at the lady behind the counter. "I forgot my wallet."

She returned the gaze, unmoved. "You have to pay. At least for the gas."

"How much is it?"

"Eighteen fifty."

Again he made a great show of searching his pockets. The other customers had stopped to listen.

"Can you believe it? I don't have a dime on me. I'm really sorry."

A heavy silence followed. "I *got* to collect the money," the woman said.

"I'm sorry. I really am. Listen, I'll go home and get my wallet and come straight back. I promise. Gosh, I feel like such an idiot."

"I can't let you go without collecting the money," said the woman. "It's my job."

A small, skinny, restless-looking man in a dun cowboy hat, motorcycle boots, and shoulder-length jet-black hair strode forward and slid out a battered wallet on a chain from his jean's pocket. "Doris? This'll take care of it." He spoke grandly and handed her a twenty.

Ford turned to the man. "That's damn nice of you. I'll pay you back."

" 'Course you will, don't worry about it. Next time you come, just give Doris the money. Someday you'll return the favor, right?" He cocked his hand, winked, and pointed a finger at Ford.

"You bet." Ford held out his hand. "Wyman Ford."

"Willy Becenti." Willy grasped his hand.

"You're a good man, Willy."

"Damn right about that! Isn't that so, Doris? Best man in Blue Gap."

Doris rolled her eyes.

"This is Kate Mercer," said Ford.

"Hey, Kate, how's it going?" Becenti grasped her hand, bowed, and kissed it like a lord.

"We were looking for the chapter house," said Ford. "We want to see the chapter president. Is he around?"

"You mean 'she.' Maria Atcitty. Hell, yeah. Chapter house is down that road there. Take your last right before it turns to dirt. It's the old wooden building with the tin roof right next to the water tower. Say hi to her for me."

As they drove out of the gas station, Ford said, "That trick never fails on the Rez. Navajos are the most generous people in the world."

"For cynical manipulation you get an A-plus."

"It's for a good cause."

"Well, he did look like a bit of a hustler himself. What do you bet he charges interest?"

They pulled into the parking lot of the chapter house, next to a row of dusty pickups. On the front door someone had taped up one of Begay's notices for the protest ride. Another fluttered from a nearby telephone pole.

They asked for the chapter president. A neat, solid woman in a turquoise blouse and brown dress pants appeared.

They shook hands and introduced themselves.

"Willy Becenti said to say hi."

"You know Willy?" She seemed surprised—and pleased.

"In a way." Ford gave a sheepish laugh. "He loaned me twenty bucks."

Atcitty shook her head. "Good old Willy. He'd give his last twenty to some bum, then stick up a convenience store to reimburse himself. Come on in and have a cup of coffee."

At a coffeepot on the counter they collected mugs of weak Navajo coffee, then followed Atcitty into a small office heaped with paper.

"So, what can I do for you folks?" she said with a big smile.

"Well, I almost hate to admit this, but we're from the Isabella project."

Her smile faded. "I see."

"Kate's the assistant director of the Isabella project, and I've just arrived as the community liaison."

Atcitty said nothing.

"Ms. Atcitty, I know people are wondering what the heck is going on up there."

"You've got that just about right."

"I need your help. If you can get people together here at the chapter house—say, some evening this week—I'll bring Gregory North Hazelius down in person so he can answer questions and explain what we're doing."

A long silence, then, "This week is too soon. Make it next week. Wednesday."

"Excellent. Things are going to change. From now on, we'll be doing some of our shopping down here and over at Rough Rock. We'll gas up our cars down here, buy our groceries and supplies."

"Wyman, I really don't think—," Mercer began, but he stopped her with a gentle hand on her shoulder.

"That would help," said Atcitty.

They rose and shook hands.

As the Jeep left Blue Gap behind in a cloud of dust, Mercer turned to Ford. "Wednesday next week is too late to stop the ride."

"I have no intention of stopping the ride."

"If you think we're going to shop in that store and eat Doritos, mutton, and canned beans for dinner, you're crazy. And the gas down there costs a fortune."

"This isn't New York or Washington," said Ford. "This is rural Arizona, and these people are your neighbors. You need to get out and show them you're not a bunch of mad scientists about to destroy the world. And they could use the business."

She shook her head.

"Kate," Ford said, "what happened to all your progressive notions? Your sympathy for the poor and downtrodden?"

"Don't you lecture me."

"I'm sorry," he said, "but you need lecturing. You've become a member of the big bad establishment and you don't even know it." He concluded with a little laugh, trying to keep it light, but only too late realized he'd scored a direct hit on her feelings.

She stared at him, white-lipped, then looked out the window. They drove up the Dugway in silence and headed down the long blacktop road for the Isabella project.

Halfway across the mesa, Ford slowed the Jeep and squinted through the windshield.

"Now what?"

"That's quite a column of buzzards."

"So?"

He stopped the car and pointed. "Look. Fresh tire tracks going off the road to the west—right toward those vultures."

She wouldn't look.

"I'm going to check it out."

"Swell. I'm already going to be up half the night doing calculations."

He parked in the shade of a juniper and followed the tracks, his feet crunching in the crusty dirt. It was still blazing hot, as the ground gave up the heat it had sucked in all day. In the distance, a coyote slunk away, carrying something in its mouth.

After ten minutes, Ford came to the edge of a deep, narrow arroyo and looked down. A car rested at the bottom, upside down. Buzzards were perched in a dead piñon, waiting. A second coyote had his head stuck through the broken windshield, jerking and pulling at something. When it saw Ford, it let go and ran off, its bloody tongue dangling.

Ford climbed down the sandstone boulders toward the car, holding his shirt over his nose to soften the stench of death, which mingled with a strong smell of gasoline. The buzzards rose in a flapping, awkward mass. He crouched and peered inside the smashed interior.

A body was jammed sideways on the seat. The eyes and lips were gone. One arm, flung out toward the broken window, had been stripped of flesh and was missing its hand. Despite the damage, the body was recognizable.

Volkonsky.

Ford remained very still, his eyes taking in every detail. He backed away, careful not to disturb anything, turned, and scrambled up the side of the arroyo.

When he could, he took several slow, deep breaths of fresh air, then jogged back toward the road. In the distance, silhouetted against a rise, he could see the two coyotes yipping and squabbling over a floppy chunk of meat.

He reached the car and leaned in the open window. Resentment etched Kate's face.

"It's Volkonsky," he said. "I'm sorry, Kate. . . . He's dead."

She blinked, gasped. "Oh my God . . . You're sure?"

He nodded.

Her lip twitched. Then, in a hoarse voice, "Accident?"

"No."

Swallowing a feeling of nausea, Ford slipped his cell phone out of his back pocket and dialed 911.

15

LOCKWOOD ENTERED THE OVAL OFFICE, HIS shoes soundless on the thick carpet. As always, being so close to the still point of power in the turning world gave him a thrill.

The president of the United States came around from behind his desk, hand outstretched, giving him a real politician's welcome.

"Stanton! Good to see you. How's Betsy and the kids?"

"Just great, thank you, Mr. President."

While continuing to clasp his hand, the president

grasped Lockwood's forearm and directed him to the chair closest to the desk. Lockwood sat, placing the file on his knees. Through the east-facing windows, he could see the Rose Garden settling into a mellow late-summer twilight. The president's chief of staff, Roger Morton, entered and occupied another chair, while the president's secretary, Jean, was ensconced in the third, ready to take notes the old-fashioned way, with a steno pad.

A heavy man in a dark blue suit entered and settled himself in the nearest chair without invitation. He was Gordon Galdone, chairman of the president's reelection campaign. Lockwood couldn't abide the man. He was everywhere these days, in every meeting, ubiquitous. Nothing was decided, nothing happened, without his blessing.

The president resumed his own seat behind the desk. "All right, Stan, you begin."

"Yes, Mr. President." Lockwood took out a folder. "Are you familiar with a televangelist by the name of Don T. Spates? He runs an operation out of Virginia Beach called God's Prime Time Ministry."

"You mean the fellow caught cornholing those two prostitutes?"

A gentlemanly chuckle rippled through the room. The president, a former trial lawyer from the South, was well known for his colorful vocabulary.

"Yes sir, that's the one. He brought up the subject of the Isabella project in his Sunday sermon on the Christian Cable Service. He went on a real tear. His

140

line was that the government has spent forty billion taxpayer dollars trying to disprove Genesis."

"The Isabella project has nothing to do with Genesis."

"Of course. The problem is, he seems to have touched a nerve. I understand a number of senators and congressmen are getting e-mails and phone calls. Now our office is, too. It's big enough that it may require some kind of response."

The president turned to his chief of staff. "Is it showing up on your radar, Roger?"

"Almost twenty thousand e-mails logged so far, ninety-six percent opposed."

"Twenty *thousand?*"

"Yes, sir."

Lockwood glanced at Galdone. The man's slab of a face betrayed nothing. Galdone's game was to wait and speak last. Lockwood hated people who did that.

"It's worth pointing out," said Lockwood, "that fifty-two percent of Americans don't believe in evolution—and among self-identified Republicans, it's sixty-eight percent. This attack on Isabella is an extension of that. It could get partisan—and ugly."

"Where'd you get those figures?"

"A Gallup poll."

The president shook his head. "We stay on message. The Isabella project is a crucial part of keeping American science and technology competitive in the world. After years of lagging, we've pulled ahead of the Europeans and Japanese. The Isabella project is good for the economy, good for R and D, good for business. It may solve our energy needs, free us from dependence on Middle Eastern oil. Stan, issue a press release to that effect, organize a press conference, make some noise. Stay on message."

"Yes, Mr. President."

Galdone's turn had come. He heaved his bulk about in the chair. "If good news were flowing from the Isabella project, we wouldn't be so vulnerable." He turned to Lockwood. "Can you tell us, Dr. Lockwood, when the problems out there will be fixed?"

"In a week or less," he said. "We've got a good handle on it."

"A week is a long time," Galdone said, "when you've got a man like Spates beating his tom-toms and oiling his guns."

Lockwood winced at the mixed metaphor. "Mr. Galdone, let me assure you we're doing everything we can."

Galdone's suetlike face moved as he spoke. "One week," he said, his voice heavy with disapproval.

Lockwood heard a voice at the door to the Oval Office, and his heart just about stopped to see his own assistant being ushered in. It would have to be something big to interrupt him in a meeting with the president. She came ducking along with almost comic obsequiousness, handed Lockwood a note, and exited swiftly. With a feeling of dread, he unfolded the note.

He tried to swallow and couldn't. For a moment he contemplated saying nothing, then changed his mind: better now than later. "Mr. President, I've received word that one of the Isabella project scientists has just been found dead in a ravine on Red Mesa. It got called into the FBI about thirty minutes ago. Agents are on their way to the scene."

"*Dead?* How?"

"Shot—in the head."

The president stared at him without speaking. Lockwood had never seen his face flush so deeply, and it frightened him.

16

BY THE TIME THE NAVAJO TRIBAL Police arrived, Ford had watched the sun disappear in a swirl of bourbon-colored clouds. Four squad cars and a van came humming down the shimmering asphalt, lights flashing, and pulled up, each with a perfectly calibrated squeal of rubber.

A barrel-chested Navajo detective got out of the lead car. He was gaunt, about sixty, with a grizzled crew cut, followed by a cadre of Navajo Nation policemen. Wearing a pair of dusty cowboy boots, he walked with bow legs down the tire tracks toward the rim of the arroyo, followed by his people, and they began setting up the perimeter of the crime scene and stringing tape.

Hazelius and Wardlaw arrived in a Jeep, pulling it

off the road and getting out. They watched the police work in silence, and then Wardlaw turned to Ford. "You say he was shot?"

"Point-blank to the left temple."

"How do you know?"

"Significant powder tattooing."

Wardlaw regarded him, his eyes hard and narrow with suspicion. "You watch a lot of *CSI* on television, Mr. Ford? Or you just make a hobby of crime-scene investigation?"

The Navajo detective, having secured the site, creaked toward them, voice recorder in hand. He walked with great deliberation, as if every movement hurt. His badge read BIA, and his rank was lieutenant. He wore mirrored wraparound sunglasses that made him look dopey. Ford sensed that he was anything but dumb.

"Who discovered the victim?" Bia asked.

"I did."

The glasses turned toward him. "Your name?"

"Wyman Ford." He heard suspicion in the man's tone, as if the lies had already begun.

"How'd you find him?"

Ford described the circumstances.

"So you saw the buzzards, saw the tracks, just decided to get out and walk a quarter mile across the desert in the hundred-degree heat to investigate—just like that?"

Ford nodded.

"Hmm." Bia scribbled some notes, his lips pursed.

Then the glasses turned toward Hazelius. "And you are—?"

"Gregory North Hazelius, director of the Isabella project, and this is Senior Intelligence Officer Wardlaw. Will you be in charge of the investigation?"

"Only on the tribal side. The FBI will lead on this one."

"The FBI? When will they be here?"

Bia nodded toward the sky. "Now."

A chopper materialized in the southwest, the *thwap* of its rotors growing steadily louder. A few hundred yards away, it came into a hover in a storm of dust, then settled down on the road. Two men stepped out. Both wore sunglasses, open-necked short-sleeved shirts, and baseball caps with FBI stitched across the front. Despite their differing skin color and heights, they could almost have been twins.

They marched over, and the tall one pulled out his shield. "Special Agent in Charge Dan Greer," he said, "Flagstaff Field Office. Special Agent Franklin Alvarez." He slipped the shield back into his pocket and nodded at Bia. "Lieutenant."

Bia nodded back.

Hazelius stepped forward. "And I'm Gregory North Hazelius, director of the Isabella project." He shook Greer's hand. "The victim was a scientist on my team. I want to know what happened here, and I want to know now."

"And you will. As soon as our investigation is complete." Greer turned to Bia. "Site secure?"

"Yes."

"Good. Now listen up: I'm going to ask everyone from the Isabella project to please return to their base. Dr. Hazelius, I'd like you to gather everyone at some central meeting place at . . ." He looked at the sky, then his watch. "Seven o'clock. I'll be there to take everyone's statement."

"I'm sorry to say that won't be possible," said Hazelius. "We can't spare everyone all at once. You'll have to take our statements in two shifts."

Greer pulled down his glasses and stared hard at Hazelius. "I will expect everyone in the same place at seven o'clock. Understood?" He spoke precisely, enunciating every word.

Hazelius returned the gaze, his face mild, unthreatening. "Mr. Greer, I'm in charge of a forty-billiondollar machine inside this mountain, and we are in the middle of a critical scientific experiment. I'm sure you wouldn't want anything to go wrong, especially if I had to tell DOE investigators that the machine had been left unattended—at your insistence. I have to keep three team members in the mountain tonight. They'll be available for questioning tomorrow morning."

A long pause, then Greer nodded curtly. "Fine."

"We'll be at the trading post by seven," said Hazelius. "It's the old log building—you can't miss it."

Ford headed back to the Jeep and climbed in, Kate following. He turned the key, and they pulled back onto the road.

"I can't believe it," said Kate, her voice shaking, her face pale. She fumbled in her pocket, tugged out a handkerchief, and wiped her eyes. "This is terrible," she said. "I just . . . can't believe it."

As the Jeep hummed down the road, Ford had a final glimpse of the two coyotes, who had finished their meal and were hanging back, skulking out of range, hoping for a second helping.

For all its beauty, he thought, Red Mesa was a hard place.

AT SEVEN O'CLOCK SHARP, LIEUTENANT JOSEPH Bia followed Greer and Alvarez into the former Nakai Rock Trading Post. He remembered the place from his childhood, when old man Weindorfer was the trader. He felt a twinge of nostalgia. In his mind he could still see the old store—the flour bin, the piles of stovepipe for sale, the halters and lassos, the candy jars. In the back had been the stacks of rugs Weindorfer was taking in trade. The drought of 1954–55 killed half the sheep on the mesa, but not before they had peeled the land. That was when Peabody Coal was hauling out twenty thousand short tons a day. The Tribal Council, with money from the coal company, had paid off everyone who lived on the mesa and resettled them in HUD housing in Blue Gap, Piñon, and Rough Rock. His parents had been among those moved down below. It was the first time Bia had been back in fifty years. The place looked completely different, but he could still smell the old scent of woodsmoke, dust, and sheep's wool.

The scientists had gathered, nine of them, tense and waiting. They looked like hell, and Bia had the feeling something else was wrong besides Volkonsky's death. Something that had been wrong for a while. He wished Greer hadn't drawn the case. Greer had been a good agent once, until what happened to all good agents happened to him: he'd been promoted to special agent in charge and then ruined by spending most of his time shifting paper from point A to point B.

"Good evening, folks," said Greer, slipping off his dark glasses, with a warning look to Bia to do the same.

Bia left his on. He didn't like people telling him what to do. He had always been like that—it ran in the family. Even his name, Bia, came about because his grandfather refused to give his last name when he was hauled off to boarding school. So they wrote down "BIA"—for Bureau of Indian Affairs. A lot of other Navajos had done the same, making Bia a common surname on the Rez. He was proud of that name. The Bias, even though they weren't related, all had something in common—they didn't like to be pushed around.

"We'll get through this as quickly as possible," Greer was saying. "One at a time in alphabetical order."

"Have you made any progress?" Hazelius asked.

"Some," said Greer.

"Was Dr. Volkonsky murdered?"

Bia waited for Greer's answer. None came. They'd been dealing with the question from the get-go, but the forensics would have to be analyzed. There'd be a wait for the ME's report. All being handled in Flagstaff. He doubted he'd see more than a summary. He'd been included only because some FBI bureaucrat needed a name to fill a blank space on some form—proof that the Tribal Police had been "liaised with," to use the favored FBI term.

Bia told himself he had no interest in the case anyway. These were not his people.

"Melissa Corcoran?" said Greer.

An athletic blonde rose to her feet, looking more like a tennis pro than a scientist.

Bia followed them into the library, where Alvarez rearranged a table and some chairs and set up a digital recorder. Greer and Alvarez handled the questioning; Bia listened and took notes. The questioning went fast, one after the other. It didn't take long for a consistent line to develop: They'd all been under pressure, things weren't going well, Volkonsky was an excitable type and he'd been taking it especially badly, he'd begun drinking, and there was a suspicion of harder drugs. Corcoran said he'd banged on her door drunk one night, wanting to sleep with her. Innes, the team psychologist, talked about the isolation and said Volkonsky was depressed and in denial. Wardlaw, the SIO, said the Russian had been acting erratic and was careless with security.

All this had already been confirmed by a search of Volkonsky's place: empty vodka bottles, traces of methylated amphetamine powder in a mortar and pestle, ashtrays overflowing with butts, stacks of porn DVDs, all in one trashed little house.

The stories were consistent and believable, with just enough contradictions to be unrehearsed. Working the Rez, Bia had seen a lot of suicides, and this looked pretty straightforward, aside from a few elements. It wasn't easy to shoot yourself and roll your car into a ravine at the same time. On the other hand, if this had been a murder, the killer would have torched the car. Unless he was smart. Most killers weren't.

Bia shook his head. He was thinking instead of listening. It was his worst habit.

By eight thirty, Greer was done. Hazelius saw them to the door, where Bia, who until now had said nothing, stopped. He removed his shades, tapped them on his thumbnail. "A question, Dr. Hazelius?"

"Yes?"

"You said Volkonsky and the rest of you are under a lot of stress. Why exactly is that?"

Hazelius answered calmly. "Because we've built a machine that cost forty billion dollars and we can't get the goddamned thing to work." He smiled. "Does that answer your question, Lieutenant?"

"Thank you. Oh—and another thing, if you don't mind?"

"Lieutenant," said Greer, "don't you think we've covered enough ground here?"

Bia continued as if he hadn't heard. "Will you hire a new person to take over Mr. Volkonsky's responsibilities?"

A beat, and then, "No. Rae Chen and I will handle them."

Bia slipped the shades back on and turned to go. There was something about this case he didn't like, but he was damned if he could put his finger on it.

17

THREE O'CLOCK IN THE MORNING. FORD eased open the back door of his casita and slipped into the shadows, a rucksack on his back. Stars jammed the sky. A chorus of coyote yips rose in the distance, then died. The moon was nearly full, and the high desert air was so clear that light silvered every detail of the landscape. It was a beautiful evening, thought Ford. Too bad he didn't have time to appreciate it.

He scanned the little settlement. The other casitas were dark, except for the last one at the far end of the loop: Hazelius's, where a yellow glow in the back bedroom diffused through the curtains.

Volkonsky's casita lay a quarter mile the other way down the loop.

Ford darted across the moonlit yard and gained the shadows of the cottonwoods. He moved slowly, avoiding the puddles of moonlight, until he reached Volkonsky's house. He scanned the grounds, but neither saw nor heard anything.

Moving behind the house, he flattened himself in the shadow next to the back door. It was sealed with crime-scene tape. Delving into the rucksack, he removed kid gloves and a knife. He tried the door-knob—locked, of course. Briefly he weighed the consequences of breaking the seal, decided it was worth it.

He slit the tape, pulled a hand towel from his pack, wrapped it around a rock, and pressed it steadily against the window until the glass gave with a shiver. After plucking out the loose slivers, he reached inside, unlocked the door, and slipped in.

The smell of Volkonsky's despair hit him: stale smoke from cigarettes and marijuana, bad liquor, boiled onions, rancid cooking oil. He slipped an LED flashlight out of the pack and shined it around low. The kitchen was a mess. Green-and-gray mold grew on a paper plate of cooked cabbage and miniature peppers that must have been sitting out for days. Beer bottles and vodka minis had spilled out of the overflowing recycling bin. Some had shattered on the Saltillo tile floor, the pieces swept into a corner.

He moved into the living/dining area, the rug gritty with dirt, the sofa stained. No decoration of any sort hung on the walls, except for a couple of kid's drawings taped to a door. One showed a spaceship, the other the mushroom cloud of an atomic bomb. Beyond that, there were no photographs of wife or children, no sentimental details.

Why hadn't Volkonsky taken the drawings? Probably he wasn't much of a father. Ford had a hard time imagining him as a father at all.

The door to the bedroom stood open in the hallway, but still the room smelled stale. The bed had the ratty look of one that was never made, the sheets never changed. Dirty laundry dangled out of the hamper. In the closet, half-full of clothes, Ford found a suit. He felt the material—fine wool—and paged through the rack. Volkonsky had brought a lot of clothes to the wilderness, some of them chic in a kind of Eurotrash way. He must not have realized what he was getting into here, at least socially. But why hadn't he taken them when he left?

Ford moved down the hall to the second bedroom, which had been turned into an office. The computer was gone, but the unhooked USB and FireWire cables remained, along with a printer, a specialized high-speed modem, and a wi-fi base station. Computer CDs lay scattered about. It looked as though they had been sorted through in a hurry, the unwanted ones discarded.

He opened the top drawer of the computer desk to more mess: leaking pens, chewed pencils, and stacks of printed-out assembly language program code, the kind of stuff that would take years to analyze. In the next drawer he found an untidy stack of file folders. He sorted through them—more printed fragments of code, notes in Russian, software flowcharts. He pulled the pile up, and there, underneath, was an envelope, sealed and stamped, unaddressed, and torn in half.

Ford lifted the two pieces out, unfolded them, and found not a letter, but a page of hexadecimal computer code. Handwritten. The date at the top was Monday, the day Volkonsky left. Nothing more.

Questions flooded Ford. Why had Volkonksy written this, then torn it in half? Why had he stamped it, but not addressed it? Why had he left it behind? What did the code mean? Above all, why had he handwritten it? Nobody handwrote computer code. It took forever and was ridiculously error prone.

Ford had a thought: in a high-security computing environment like the Isabella project, you couldn't copy, print, transmit, or e-mail any data without the action being logged. But the computer wouldn't know if you copied it by hand. He stuffed the pieces into his pocket. Whatever they were, they mattered.

From the back porch came the crackle of grit under a footfall.

He switched off the LED and froze. Silence. Then the faintest crick of something between the sole of a shoe and the kitchen floor.

He could not exit either door—the kitchen or the front—without being seen.

Another whispery crunch of a footfall, closer. The intruder knew he was there and was coming for him, moving very slowly, no doubt hoping to ambush him.

Silently Ford crossed the carpet to the back window and reached up. He turned the circular latch and grasped the upper divider, giving it a little upward pressure. It stuck.

He was just about out of time.

A hard shove and the window sash gave. A split second later the intruder made his rush. Ford dived headlong through the window, ripping through the plastic screen just as two rapid shots from a silenced small-caliber handgun shattered the window above him. He rolled on the ground, glass showering around him.

In a flash he was up and running, zigzagging through the shadows under the cottonwoods. At the far end of the trees he sprinted across open ground, heading up the valley. The moon was so bright that he could see his shadow running beside him.

The dull whine of low-muzzle-velocity rounds passed his ears. It had to be Wardlaw—nobody else would have a silencer or shoot like that.

Ford sprinted toward the dark shape of Nakai Rock, swung left behind the rock, and ran up the trail toward the top of the low bluffs. The waspy hum of another round passed to his left. He made a quick jog off the trail and scrambled up through tumbled boulders toward the rim, keeping to cover. A few moments later he came out on top, his legs burning from the effort, and paused to look back. Two hundred yards below he glimpsed a dark figure darting up through the rocks after him.

Ford sprinted along a low spine of slickrock. It was devoid of vegetation and offered no cover—but at least it wouldn't record his footprints. Ahead he could make out several small gullies that zigzagged toward the far edge of the mesa. In a moment he had reached the first. He leapt and ran down the dry wash at the bottom until it angled sharply as it approached the mesa edge. He flattened himself behind a fin of rock and looked behind. His pursuer had halted at the rim and was examining the sandy ground with his flashlight.

It was unmistakably Wardlaw.

The SIO rose and played the beam about the arroyo, clambered down, and began moving in his direction, gun at the ready.

Ford scrambled up the hidden side, keeping out of sight. As he topped the ravine, briefly showing himself, two more shots followed in quick succession, one kicking off a spray of chips from a nearby rock.

Ford ran across an open expanse of sand, hoping to reach the far side before the SIO reached the top of the canyon. He sprinted over the sandy flat so hard, it felt as if someone were knifing his lungs. Toward the far end he angled toward a scabland of naked, hollowed-out bedrock. It was absurdly open, but beyond lay a crazy mass of hoodoo rocks that would provide cover and a possible means of escape. He jumped off the last dune and ran into the scabland, momentarily obscured from Wardlaw's view.

He suddenly saw his chance, and changed his idea. Halfway across the scabland was a hollow in the bedrock with a pool of moonshadow just deep enough to hide him. With a quick turn he dropped into it and huddled down. It wasn't much of a hiding place—all Wardlaw had to do was point his flashlight in the right direction. But he wouldn't—because he would assume Ford had headed into the excellent cover of the hoodoo rocks beyond.

A few minutes passed—and then he heard the fall of Wardlaw's running feet on stone, his rasping breath pass by.

He counted to sixty, then cautiously peeked above the shadow. Beyond, in the hoodoo rocks, he could see the play of Wardlaw's Maglite as he searched deeper and deeper into the rock maze.

Ford leapt up and sprinted back toward Nakai Valley.

AFTER TAKING A CONVOLUTED ROUTE HOME, Ford crept up behind his casita. He circled around, satisfying himself that Wardlaw wasn't keeping a lookout, then slipped in the back door. The moon had set and dawn was just lightening the eastern sky. The distant scream of a mountain lion drifted across the mesa.

He went into the bedroom, hoping to grab at least a few moments of sleep before breakfast. He paused, staring at the bed.

An envelope lay on the pillow. He plucked it up and pulled out the note. *Sorry I missed you,* read the generous, looping script. It was signed, *Melissa.*

Ford dropped it back on the pillow and thought wryly that the hazards of the assignment were only now beginning to reveal their true dimensions.

18

AN HOUR LATER, FORD ARRIVED AT breakfast to the reviving smell of coffee, bacon, and flapjacks. He paused in the doorway. It was a reduced group—several team members were down in the Bunker and others were being interviewed by the FBI in the rec room. Hazelius occupied his usual place at the head of the table.

With a deep breath, Ford entered the room. If the scientists seemed haggard before, they looked like zombies now, eating in silence, their red-rimmed eyes staring off into space. Hazelius in particular looked like hell.

Ford poured himself a mug of coffee. When Wardlaw arrived a few minutes later, Ford observed him out of the corner of his eye. In contrast to the others, the man seemed rested, unperturbed, and unusually friendly, nodding as he made his way to his seat.

Kate went back and forth from the kitchen, laying down platters of food. Ford tried to keep his eyes off her. A desultory conversation arose around him, trivialities. Nobody wanted to talk about Volkonsky. Anything but Volkonsky.

Corcoran took a seat beside him. He could feel her eyes on him, and he turned, to see a knowing smile on her face. She leaned over and spoke sotto voce. "Where were you last night?"

"Out for a walk."

"Yeah, right." She smirked and her eyes slid over to Kate.

She thinks I'm sleeping with Kate.

Corcoran turned to the group and said, "We're all over the news this morning. You hear about it?"

Everyone paused in their eating.

"No one?" Corcoran looked around with an air of triumph. "It's not what you think. There was nothing in the news about Peter Volkonsky—at least, not yet."

Again she surveyed the group, enjoying the attention. "This is something different. Weird. You know that televangelist, Spates, who runs a megachurch over in Virginia? There was a story about him and us in the *Times* online this morning."

"Spates?" Innes leaned in from across the table. "The preacher who was busted with those prostitutes? What could he possibly have to do with us?"

Her smile broadened. "His sermon last Sunday was *all* about us."

"I can't imagine why," said Innes.

"Said we were a bunch of godless scientists putting the lie to the book of Genesis. The whole sermon is available as a podcast on his Web site. 'Ah greet yeew in the nayum of our Lorud and Saveeyore Cheesus Chraiyst,'" she intoned in a near-perfect imitation of his southern drawl, once again demonstrating her ability to mimic.

"You've *got* to be kidding," said Innes.

She nudged Ford under the table with her leg. "You hadn't heard this?"

"No."

"Who has time to surf the news?" Thibodeaux said, her voice high and irritated. "I can't get my work done as it is."

"I don't get it," said Dolby. "How are we putting the lie to the book of Genesis?"

"We're researching the Big Bang—that secular humanist theory which claims the universe was created without the guiding hand of God. We're part of the war on faith. We're Christ haters."

Dolby shook his head in disgust.

"According to the *Times*, the sermon's caused an uproar. Several southern congressmen are calling for an investigation, threatening to kill our funding."

Innes turned to Hazelius. "Did you know about this, Gregory?"

Hazelius nodded wearily.

"What are we going to do about it?"

Hazelius laid down his coffee mug, wiped his eyes. "The Stanford-Binet curve demonstrates that seventy percent of human beings fall in the average or below-average range in intelligence. In other words, more than two-thirds of all human beings are average, which is stupid enough, or they're clinical morons."

"I'm not sure I follow your point," said Innes.

"What I'm saying is, this is the way of the world, George. Live with it."

"But surely we need to issue a statement refuting

the accusation," said Innes. "As far as I'm concerned, the Big Bang theory is perfectly consistent with a belief in God. One doesn't exclude the other."

Edelstein's eyes rose from his book, suddenly glittering with amusement. "If that's what you really think, George, then you understand neither God nor the Big Bang."

"Just a second, Alan," said Ken Dolby, interrupting. "You can have an entirely physical theory, like the Big Bang, and still believe God was behind it."

Edelstein's dark eyes turned to him. "If the theory is fully explanative—which a good theory must be—then God would be unnecessary. A mere spectator. What kind of a useless God is that?"

"Alan, why don't you tell us what you really think?" said Dolby sarcastically.

Innes spoke loudly, shifting into his professional voice. "Surely the world is big enough for God and science."

Corcoran rolled her eyes.

"I would object to any statement made in the name of the Isabella project that mentions God," said Edelstein.

"Enough discussion," said Hazelius. "There will be no statements. Let the politicians handle it."

The door to the rec room opened and three scientists came out, followed by Special Agents Greer and Alvarez, and Lieutenant Bia. The room fell silent.

"I wanted to thank you for your cooperation," said Greer stiffly, clipboard in hand, addressing the group.

161

"You have my card. If there's anything you need or if you think of anything useful, please call me."

"When will you know something?" Hazelius asked.

"Two, three days."

There was a silence. Then Hazelius said, "May I ask a question or two?"

Greer waited.

"Was the gun found in the car?"

Greer hesitated, then said, "Yes."

"Where?"

"On the floor on the driver's side."

"As I understand it, Dr. Volkonsky was shot in the right temple at point-blank range, while he was sitting behind the wheel. Correct?"

"Correct."

"Were any of the car's windows open?"

"They were all closed."

"And the AC was on?"

"Yes."

"Doors locked?"

"That is correct."

"Keys in the ignition?"

"Yes."

"Did Dr. Volkonsky's right hand test positive for powder residue?"

A silence. "The results aren't in yet," Greer said.

"Thank you."

Ford recognized the significance of the questions, and it was clear Greer did, too. As the agents filed out of the room, the meal resumed in tense silence. The unvoiced word "suicide" seemed to hang in the air.

As the meal concluded, Hazelius rose. "A few words." His tired eyes traveled around the room. "I know all of you are deeply shaken, as am I."

People shifted positions uncomfortably. Ford glanced at Kate. She looked more than shaken—she was devastated.

"The problems with Isabella fell hardest on Peter—for reasons we all know. He made a superhuman effort to fix the software problems with Isabella. I guess he must have given up. I'd like to share a few lines to his memory, from a poem by Keats about that transcendent moment of discovery."

He recited from memory:

Then felt I like some watcher of the skies
When a new planet swims into his ken;
Or like stout Cortez when with eagle eyes
He star'd at the Pacific—and all his men
Look'd at each other with a wild surmise—
Silent, upon a peak in Darien.

Hazelius paused, then looked up. "I've said it before: no discovery worth a damn in this world comes easy. Any great exploration into the unknown is dangerous—physically and psychologically. Look at Magellan's voyage around the world, or Captain Cook's discovery of Antarctica. Look at the Apollo program or the space shuttle. We lost a man yesterday to the rigors of exploration. Regardless of how the investigation turns out—and I think most of us can guess which way it will go—I'll always consider Peter a hero."

He paused, choking up with emotion. After a moment he cleared his throat. "The next run of Isabella begins at noon tomorrow. You all know what you have to do. Those of us not already in the mountain will gather here, in the rec room, at eleven thirty and head over as a group. The Bunker doors will close and lock at eleven forty-five. This time, ladies and gentlemen, I swear, we will gaze like stout Cortez on the Pacific."

There was a fervor in his voice that struck Ford—the fervor of the true believer.

19

THAT SAME MORNING, THE REVEREND D. T. SPATES eased himself into his office chair, pressing a lever to adjust his lumbar support and fiddling with other levers to get it to his liking. He was feeling good. The Isabella project had proved to be a red-hot subject. He owned it. It was his. The money was pouring in and the phone banks were jammed. The question was how to advance the subject on his Friday night Christian talk show, *Roundtable America*. In a sermon, you could play on emotion, you could roll out the blood and thunder. But *Roundtable America* worked on a more cerebral level. It was a respected show. And for that he needed firm facts—which he had precious few of, beyond what he could glean from the Isabella project Web site. He had already canceled the guests he had booked weeks ago and had found a new one, a physicist who could talk about the Isabella project. But he needed more: he needed a surprise.

His assistant, Charles, entered with the morning folders. "The e-mails you requested, Reverend. Messages. Schedule." He laid them down, side by side, with quiet efficiency.

"Where's my coffee?"

His secretary entered. "Good morning, Reverend!" she said brightly. Her frosted bouffant hair bobbed and glittered in the morning sun. She set a tray in front of him: silver coffeepot, cup, sugar, creamer, a Mrs. Fields macadamia-nut cookie, and a freshly ironed copy of the *Virginia Beach Daily Press*.

"Shut the door when you leave."

In the restful quiet that followed, Spates poured a cup of coffee, leaned back in his chair, raised the cup to his lips, and took that first bitter, delectable sip. He rolled the brew around in his mouth, swallowed, exhaled, and placed the cup down. Then he picked up the e-mail folder. Every day Charles and three helpers culled through the thousands of e-mails that arrived, selecting those from people who had given or seemed prepared to give at the "1,000 Blessings" level, and those from politicians and business leaders who needed cultivation. This was the result, and they required a personal response, usually a thank-you for money or a request for money.

Spates plucked the first e-mail off the pile, scanned it, scribbled a response, laid it aside, picked up the second one, and in this way worked through the pile.

Fifteen minutes into the pile, he hit one Charles had flagged with a Post-it: *Looks intriguing.*

He took a nibble of the cookie and read.

Dear Rev. Spates,

Greetings in Christ. This is Pastor Russ Eddy, writing you from the Gathered in Thy Name Mission, Blue Gap, Arizona. I've been bringing the Good News to Navajoland since 1999, when I founded the mission. We're a small operation—in fact, it's just me.

Your sermon on the Isabella project really hit home, Reverend. I'll tell you why. Isabella is our next-door neighbor—it's right up there on Red Mesa above me, I can see it out my window as I type this. I've been getting quite an earful about it from my flock. There are a lot of ugly rumors. And I mean *ugly.* People are scared; they're frightened about what's going on up there.

I won't take up any more of your time, Reverend—just a word of thanks for fighting the Good Fight and alerting Christians everywhere about this godless machine out here in the desert. You keep it up.

Yours in Christ,
Pastor Russ Eddy
Gathered in Thy Name Mission
Blue Gap, Arizona

Spates read the e-mail, then read it again. He drained his coffee cup, laid it on the tray, mashed his thumb on the last moist cookie crumb and licked it off. He leaned back, thinking. Seven fifteen in Arizona. Country pastors got up early, right?

He picked up the receiver and tapped in a phone number from the end of the e-mail. It rang several times before a high-pitched voice answered.

"This is Pastor Russ."

"Ah, Pastor Russ! This is Reverend Don T. Spates from God's Prime Time Ministry, Virginia Beach. How are you today, Pastor?"

"I'm just fine, thank you." The voice seemed doubtful, even suspicious. "Now who did you say you were?'

"Reverend Don T. Spates! God's Prime Time!"

"Oh! Reverend Spates! This is quite a surprise. You must've gotten my e-mail."

"I certainly did. It was *very* interesting."

"Thank you, Reverend."

"Please call me Don. I can see that your proximity to this machine, your access to this scientific experiment, could be a Gift from God."

"How's that?"

"I need an inside source of information on what's

going on out there, someone on the scene. Maybe God means you to be that source. He didn't move you to write that e-mail for nothing, Russ. Am I right?"

"Yes sir. I mean, no, He didn't. I listen to your sermon every Sunday. We don't get any television reception out here, but I do have a high-speed satellite Internet connection and I listen to the Webcast, without fail."

"I'm glad to hear that, Russ. It's good to know our new Webcast's reaching out. Now, Russ, you mentioned rumors in your e-mail. What kind of rumors you been hearing?"

"All kinds. Radiation experiments, explosions, child abuse. They say they're creating freaks up there, monsters. That the government is testing a new weapon to destroy the world."

A slug of disappointment congealed in Spates's gut. This so-called pastor sounded like a nutcase. No wonder, living out there in the desert with a bunch of Indians.

"Anything a little, ah, more . . . solid?"

"There was a killing up there, yesterday. One of the scientists found with a bullet in his head."

"Is that right?" This was better. Praise the Lord. "How do you know?"

"Well, in a rural area like this, rumors spread fast. The mesa was crawling with FBI agents."

"You saw them?"

"Sure did. The FBI only comes on the Rez when

168

there's been a homicide. The Tribal Police handle almost all other crimes."

Spates's spine tingled.

"One of my flock has a brother in the Tribal Police. The latest rumor is that it was actually a suicide. All hush-hush."

"The dead scientist's name?"

"Don't know."

"You're sure it was one of the scientists, Russ, and not somebody else?"

"Believe me, if it had been a Navajo, I'd know. This is a very tight-knit community."

"Have you run into any of the scientists on the team?"

"No. They pretty much keep to themselves."

"Is there a way you can make contact?"

"Well, sure. I suppose I could drop by, introduce myself as the local pastor. Real friendly-like."

"Russ, that is an *excellent* idea! I'm interested in finding out more about the fellow who runs Isabella, guy named Hazelius. You heard about him?"

"The name's familiar."

"He declared himself the smartest man on earth. Said everyone was beneath him, called us all a race of morons. Remember that?"

"I think I do."

"That's quite a thing to say, isn't it? Especially coming from a man who doesn't believe in God."

"It doesn't surprise me, Reverend. We live in a world that worships evil."

"That we do, son. Now: Can I count on you?"

"Yes, sir, Reverend, you bet you can."

"Here's something important: I need this information in two days, so I can use it on Friday's *Roundtable America*. You ever listen to my show?"

"Since you've Webcast it, I never miss it."

"This Friday, I've got a physicist on the show, someone with a Christian perspective, to talk more about the Isabella project. I've just *got* to have more information—not the usual PR stuff. I'm talking *dirt*. Like this death—what happened? Talk to that Navajo cop you mentioned. You understand, Russ?"

"Absolutely, yes, you got it, Reverend."

Spates replaced the phone in its cradle and gazed pensively out the window. Everything was falling into place. The power of God knew no bounds.

20

ON HIS RETURN FROM BREAKFAST, FORD was about to enter his casita when Wardlaw stepped from the side of the house and blocked his entry.

Ford had been expecting something like this.

"Mind if we chat?" Wardlaw said, his voice sham-friendly. He worked a piece of gum with his jaw, the muscles above his ears bulging rhythmically.

Ford waited. This wasn't the moment for a showdown, but if Wardlaw wanted it, he would get it.

"I don't know what your game is, Ford, or who you really are. I'm assuming you're operating in some kind of semiofficial capacity. I sensed it from the day you arrived."

Ford waited.

Wardlaw stepped so close, Ford could smell his aftershave. "My job is to protect Isabella—even from you. I'm guessing you're here undercover because some bureaucrat back in Washington needs to cover his ass. That doesn't offer you much in the way of protection, does it?"

Ford remained silent. Let the man vent.

"I'm not going to mention your little escapade last night to anyone. Course, you'll report it to your handlers. If it gets brought up, you know what my defense will be. You were an intruder and my rules of engagement are shoot to kill. Oh, and if you think the broken windowpane and screen are going to get Greer in a lather, they've been fixed. None of this goes beyond the two of us."

Ford was impressed. Wardlaw had actually thought things through. He was glad that the SIO was no fool. He had always found it easier to go up against an intelligent adversary. Stupid people were unpredictable. He said, "Are you finished with your little speech?"

The carotid artery pounded in Wardlaw's thick neck. "Watch your back, cop." He stepped aside, just barely, to allow Ford to pass.

Ford took a step forward and then paused. He was so close to Wardlaw, he could have kneed the SIO in the groin. He looked at the man, inches from his face, and said pleasantly, "You know what's funny? I haven't the slightest idea what you're talking about."

The shadow of a doubt flickered across Wardlaw's face as Ford moved on.

He went in the house and slammed the door. So Wardlaw wasn't absolutely certain that Ford had been the man he'd chased. That uncertainty would slow him down, make him cautious. Ford's cover had been compromised, but it wasn't blown.

When he was sure Wardlaw had left, he threw himself on the sofa, annoyed and frustrated. He'd been on the mesa almost four days, but he knew scarcely more than he had back in Lockwood's office.

He wondered why he had ever thought this would be an easy assignment.

The time had come for him to take the next step, the step he had hoped to avoid ever since Lockwood showed him Kate's dossier.

AN HOUR LATER, FORD FOUND KATE in the stables feeding and watering the horses. He stood in the doorway, following her with his eyes as she filled buckets with oats, broke open a bale of alfalfa, and tossed a flake or two into each stall. He watched the way she moved, her body slender and supple, performing the banal tasks with sureness and grace, despite her obvious exhaustion. It felt like twelve years ago, watching her sleep under that table.

Rock music, turned down low, filtered from inside the barn.

She tossed the last flake and then turned, seeing him for the first time. "Going for another ride?" she asked, her voice subdued.

He stepped into the cool shade. "How are you, Kate?"

She put her gloved hands on her hips. "Not so good."

"I'm very sorry about Peter."

"Yeah."

"Can I give you a hand?"

"All done."

The music played on softly in the background. He recognized it now. "Blondie?"

"I often play music while working with the horses. They like it."

"Do you remember—?" he began.

She cut him off. "Yes."

They faced each other silently. At MIT, she used to start the day at the LEES lab, the electronics lab, by blasting "Atomic" out across Killian Court. When he got there, she was usually dancing around the room, earphones on and coffee mug in hand, making a spectacle of herself. She had enjoyed spectacles—like the time she'd poured a pint of gasoline into Murphy Memorial Fountain and lit it on fire. He felt a sudden pang at the memories, the time gone. How full of naïve hopefulness she had been, how sure that life was always going to be a laff-riot. Life eventually clobbered everyone—her especially.

He shook off the memories and focused on the mission. With Kate, the most direct way was always the best. She hated people who beat around the bush. Ford swallowed. Would he ever forgive himself for what he was about to do?

Point-blank he asked the question: "Okay, what are you all hiding?"

She looked at him steadily. No feigned surprise, no protest, no pretense of ignorance.

"None of your business."

"It is my business. I'm part of the team."

"Then ask Gregory."

"I know you'll be straight with me. Hazelius—I don't know what to make of him."

Her face softened. "Trust me, Wyman, you don't want to know."

"I do want to know. I *need* to know. It's my job. This isn't like you, Kate, keeping secrets."

"What makes you think we're keeping secrets?"

"Ever since I arrived, I've had the feeling you're hiding something. Volkonsky alluded to it. So did you. Something's seriously wrong with Isabella, isn't it?"

Kate shook her head. "God, Wyman, you never change—always that damnable curiosity." She looked down at her shirt, plucked a piece of straw from her shoulder, frowned.

Another long silence. Then she focused her intelligent brown eyes on him and he saw she had reached a decision. "Yes. Something's wrong with Isabella. But it's not what you might think. It's uninteresting.

174

Stupid. It has nothing to do with you or your work here. I don't want you to know because . . . well, it could get you into trouble."

Ford said nothing. He waited.

Kate issued a short, bitter laugh. "All right. You asked for it. But don't expect some big revelation."

He felt a hideous flush of guilt. He shoved the emotion down—he would deal with it later.

"You'll understand, when you hear this, why we've been keeping it secret." She looked at him steadily. "Isabella's been sabotaged. A hacker is making fools of us."

"How so?"

"Someone planted malware in the supercomputer. It seems to be a kind of logic bomb that goes off just as Isabella is about to reach one hundred percent power. First it produces a bizarre image on the Visualizer; then it shuts down the supercomputer and posts a stupid message. It's incredibly frustrating—and extremely dangerous. At that high energy level, if the beams kink or get thrown off track, we could all be blown up. Even worse, a sudden energy fluctuation could create dangerous particles or miniature black holes. It's the *Mona Lisa* of hacks, a real masterpiece, the work of an incredibly sophisticated programmer. We can't find it."

"What's the message?"

"You know, GREETINGS or HELLO or ANYBODY THERE?"

"Like the old AI programming saw, HELLO, WORLD."

"Exactly. An inside joke."

"And then what?"

"That's it."

"It doesn't say more?"

"There's no time for it to say more. With the computer crashed, we're forced to initiate an emergency shutdown of the system."

"You haven't engaged it in conversation? Gotten it talking?"

"Are you kidding? With a forty-billion-dollar machine about to blow up? Anyway, it wouldn't help—it would only spew out more crap. And with the supercomputer crashed, running Isabella is like driving at night on a wet road at a hundred miles an hour with the headlights off. We'd be crazy to sit around chatting with it."

"And the image?"

"Very strange. It's hard to describe—really spectacular, all deep and shimmery like a ghost. Whoever did this was an artist in his own way."

"You can't find the malware?"

"No. It's devilishly clever. It appears to be moving itself around the system, erasing its tracks as it goes, evading detection."

"Why not tell Washington and get a specialized team out here to fix it?"

She was silent for a moment. "It's too late for that. If it came out that we were flummoxed by a hacker, there'd be a furious scandal. The Isabella project just barely scraped by the Congress. . . . It would be the end."

"Why didn't you report it right away? Why are you hiding it?"

"We were going to!" She brushed back her hair. "But then we decided it would be better to delete the malware before we reported it, so we could say we'd already taken care of the problem. A day went by, then another and another, and we couldn't find the malware. A week passed, ten days—and then it dawned on us we'd waited too long. If we reported it, we'd be accused of a cover-up."

"That was a blunder."

"I'll say. I don't quite know how it happened. . . . We were just crazy with stress, and it takes a minimum of forty-eight hours to complete a single run cycle. . . ." She shook her head.

"Any idea who's behind it?"

"Gregory thinks it may be a sophisticated group of hackers who planned a deliberate act of criminal sabotage. But there's always the unspoken fear . . . that the hacker might be one of us." She paused, breathing hard. "You see the position we're in, Wyman."

A horse nickered softly in the shadows.

"This must be why Hazelius seems to think Volkonsky's death was a suicide," Ford said.

"Of course it was a suicide. As the software engineer, the humiliation of being the victim of a hacker fell on him like a ton of bricks. Poor Peter. He was so fragile, an emotional twelve-year-old, just a hyperactive, insecure kid in T-shirts that were too big for him." She shook her head. "He couldn't take the pressure. The guy never slept. He was in there with the computer day and night. But he couldn't find the slag code. It tore him to pieces. He started drinking and I wouldn't be surprised if he got into harder stuff."

"What about Innes? Isn't he supposed to be the team psychologist?"

"Innes." Her brow furrowed. "He means well, but he's hopelessly outgunned intellectually. I mean, these once-a-week 'rap' sessions, this let's-talk-it-all-out crap, it might wash with normal people, but not with us. It's so easy to see through his tricks, his leading questions, his little strategies. Peter detested him." She brushed away a tear with the back of her gloved hand. "We were all very fond of Peter."

"All except Wardlaw," said Ford. "And Corcoran."

"Wardlaw . . . Well, he doesn't really like any of us, except Hazelius. But you have to realize, he's under even more pressure. He's the team's intelligence officer, the guy who's supposed to be in charge of security. If this came out, he'd go to prison."

No wonder he's a little high-strung.

"As for Melissa, she's had dustups with quite a few of the team members. It wasn't just Volkonsky. I'd . . . be careful of her."

Ford thought of the note, but said nothing.

She pulled off her gloves and tossed them in a basket hung on the wall. "Satisfied?" she asked, an edge in her voice.

As Ford walked back to his casita, he repeated the question to himself. *Satisfied?*

21

PASTOR RUSS EDDY HAD GOTTEN INTO his old Ford pickup and was staring at the gas gauge, calculating if he had the gas to get up the mesa and back, when he saw the telltale corkscrew of dust on the horizon that indicated an approaching vehicle. He got out of the truck and leaned against it, waiting.

A few moments later a Navajo Tribal Police car eased to a stop in front of the trailer, the plume of dust spiraling away in the wind. The door opened and a dusty cowboy boot appeared. A tall man unfolded himself from the inside and straightened up.

"Morning, Pastor," he said, touching his hat.

"Morning, Lieutenant Bia," said Eddy, trying to keep his voice easy and loose.

"Going somewhere?"

"Oh, no, just checking the gas level in the truck," said Eddy. "Actually, I was thinking of driving up to the mesa, introducing myself to the scientists up there. I'm concerned about what's going on up there."

Bia gazed around, his mirrored sunglasses reflecting the endless horizon in every direction he looked. "Haven't seen Lorenzo around lately, have you?"

"No," said Eddy. "Haven't seen him since Monday morning."

Bia hitched up his pants, his dangling accoutrements clinking like a giant charm bracelet. "Funny thing is, he hitched a ride to Blue Gap around four o'clock Monday, told the folks there he was heading out this way to finish up his work. They saw him walking down the mission road—and then he seems to have disappeared."

Eddy let a beat pass. "Well, I never saw him. I mean, I saw him in the morning, but he left around noon or maybe before and I haven't seen him here since. He was supposed to be working for me, but . . ."

"Hot out here today, eh?" Bia turned and grinned at Eddy, and glanced toward the trailer.

"Can I talk you into a cup of coffee?" Bia asked.

"Of course."

Bia followed Eddy into the kitchen and sat down at the table. Eddy filled the percolator pot with fresh water and turned on the burner. Navajos habitually reused their grounds, and Eddy figured Bia wouldn't mind.

Bia laid his hat on the table. His hair was plastered down in a wet ring. "Well, I'm actually not here about Lorenzo. I personally think he took off again. The folks at Blue Gap said he was pretty drunk when he came through on Monday."

Eddy nodded. "I noticed he'd started hitting the juice."

Bia shook his head. "Too bad. That kid had just about everything going for him. If he don't show up soon, they'll revoke his parole and he'll go back to Alameda."

Eddy nodded again. "A shame."

The coffee began to perk. Eddy took the opportunity to busy himself getting out the mugs, sugar, and Cremora, placing them on the table. He poured out two cups and sat down again.

"Actually," said Bia, "I'm here about something else. I was talking to the trader in Blue Gap yesterday, and he told me about the . . . problem you'd had with the collection money."

"Right." Eddy took a swallow of coffee, burned his mouth.

"He told me how you marked up some money and asked him to keep an eye out for it."

Eddy waited.

"Well, yesterday a bunch of those bills showed up."

"I see." Eddy swallowed. *Yesterday?*

"It's kind of an awkward situation," said Bia, "which is why the trader talked to me about it, instead of calling you. I hope you'll understand what I'm about to tell you. I don't want to make a big deal about it."

"Sure thing."

"You know old lady Benally? Elizabeth Benally?"

"Of course, she attends my church."

"She used to graze her sheep up on the mesa every summer, had an old hogan up there near Piute Spring. It wasn't her land, she didn't have any right to it, but she'd been using it most of her life. When the tribal government took over the mesa for that Isabella project, she lost that grazing land and had to sell her sheep."

"I'm sorry to hear that."

"It wasn't so bad for her. She's in her seventies, and they got her into a nice HUD house down in Blue Gap. Problem is, with a house like that, you suddenly have electric bills, water bills—you know what I mean? She's never had to pay a bill in her life. And now her income's down to just her government stipend because she doesn't have any more sheep."

Eddy said he understood.

"Well, this week her granddaughter's having her tenth birthday and yesterday old lady Benally bought her a Gameboy at the Trading Post as a present, had it gift-wrapped and everything." He paused, looking steadily at Eddy. "She paid for it with your marked bills."

Eddy sat there, staring at Bia.

"I know. Pretty surprising." Bia removed a wallet from his back pocket. His big dusty hand slipped out a fifty and pushed it across the table. "No point in making a big deal over it."

Eddy could not move.

Bia rose, put the wallet away. "If it happens again, just let me know and I'll cover the loss. Like I said, there's no point in the law getting involved. I'm not sure she's all that *compos mentis* anyway." He picked up his hat and fitted it back down over the sweat mark on his salt-and-pepper hair.

"Thanks for your understanding, Pastor."

He turned to go, then paused. "And if you see Lorenzo, give me a holler, okay?"

"Sure will, Lieutenant."

Pastor Russ Eddy watched as Lieutenant Bia walked out the front door and disappeared, then reappeared through the window, striding across his front yard, right over where the body was buried, his cowboy boots kicking up streamers of dust.

His eye fell on the soiled fifty-dollar bill, and he felt sick. And then angry. Very angry.

22

FORD ENTERED HIS LIVING ROOM AND stood at the window, gazing at the crooked form of Nakai Rock rising above the cottonwoods. He had completed his assignment, and now he faced a decision: Should he report it?

He flung himself into a chair and dropped his head into his hands. Kate was right: if the news got out, it would fatally damage the project. It would destroy their careers—Kate's included. In the field of science, the whiff of a cover-up or a lie was a career killer.

Satisfied? he asked himself again.

He got up and angrily paced the room. Lockwood had known all along that he would find the answer by asking Kate. He'd been hired not because he was some brilliant ex–CIA agent turned PI, but because he just happened to have dated a certain woman twelve years ago. He should've walked out on Lockwood when he had the chance. But he'd been intrigued by the assignment. Flattered. And, if the truth be told, way too attracted to the idea of seeing Kate again.

For a moment he longed for his life at the monastery, those thirty months when life seemed so simple, so clean. Living there, he'd almost forgotten the awful grayness of the world and the impossible moral choices it forced on you. But he never would have made a monk. He had gone into the monastery hoping it would give him back his certainty, his faith. But it had done just the opposite.

He bent his head and tried to pray, but it was just words. Words spoken into silence.

Maybe there wasn't any such thing as right or wrong anymore—people did what they did. He made his decision. There was no way he was going to take a step that would damage Kate's career. She had had enough hard knocks in her life. He would give them two days to track down the malware. And he would help them. He strongly suspected that the saboteur was a member of the team. No one else would have the access or the knowledge.

Walking out the front door, Ford took a turn around the house as if taking the air, making sure Wardlaw wasn't hanging around. Then he went into his bedroom, unlocked a filing cabinet, and removed his briefcase. He punched in the code to unlock it and tapped in the number.

Lockwood answered so fast, Ford thought the science adviser must have been waiting by the phone.

"News?" Lockwood asked breathlessly.

"Not much."

A sharp sigh of exasperation from Lockwood. "You've had four days, Wyman."

"They simply can't get Isabella to work. I'm beginning to think you're wrong, Stan. They're not hiding anything. It's just like they say—they just can't get the machine to work properly."

"Damn it, Ford, I don't buy it!"

He could hear Lockwood breathing hard on the other end. This was a career-breaker for him, too. But the fact was, he didn't give a shit about the man. Let him go down. Kate was what mattered. If he could buy them a few more days to find the malware, there was no reason for Lockwood to ever know.

Lockwood went on. "You heard about this preacher, Spates, and his sermon?"

"Yes."

"This shortens the time frame. You have two, maybe three days, max, before we pull the plug. Wyman, you find out what they're hiding—you hear me? Find it!"

"I understand."

"You searched Volkonsky's place?"

"Yes."

"Find anything?"

"Nothing special."

Silence from Lockwood, then, "I just got the preliminary forensic report on Volkonsky. Looking more and more like suicide."

"I see."

Ford heard a rustling of papers over the line.

"I also looked into some of the research you asked me to. As for Cecchini . . . The cult was called Heaven's Gate. You probably remember, back in '97, that cult whose members committed mass suicide, thinking their souls were going to board an alien spaceship that was approaching Earth behind Comet Hale-Bopp? Cecchini joined the cult back in '95, stayed in it less than a year, and left before the mass suicide."

"Any evidence he still believes it? The guy seems a bit like an automaton."

"The cult doesn't exist anymore, and there's no evidence he believes it. He's had a normal life since—if a bit of a loner. Doesn't drink or smoke, no girlfriends to speak of, few if any friends. Focused everything on his career. The man's a brilliant physicist—totally dedicated to his work."

"And Chen?"

"Her dossier says her father was an illiterate laborer who died before she and her mother emigrated from China. Not so. He was a physicist with the Chinese nuclear-weapons-testing facility out at Lop Nor. And he's still alive, back in China."

"How'd the false information get in the dossier?"

"Immigration files—and from the interview with Chen herself."

"So she's lying."

"Maybe not. Her mother took her out of China when she was two. Could be her mother's the liar. But there could be an innocent explanation for the falsehood: the mother wouldn't have gotten a visa to come to America if she'd told the truth. Chen may not even know her father's alive. No evidence she's passing information."

"Hmm."

"We're running out of time, Wyman. You keep pushing. I know they're hiding something big—I just *know* it."

Lockwood rang off.

Ford went back to the window and stared again toward Nakai Rock. Now he was one of them—hiding the secret. But unlike them, he had more than one secret.

23

AT ELEVEN TWENTY, PASTOR RUSS EDDY sped along the brand-new asphalt road that cut across the top of Red Mesa in his battered 1989 F-150 pickup. The wind blowing through his open windows fanned the pages of the King James Bible on the seat beside him, and his blood pounded with a sense of confusion, anger, and anxiety. So it wasn't Lorenzo after all. Still, he'd been drunk, he'd been insolent—and he'd blasphemed the Lord in the most heinous way. Eddy had had nothing to do with his death—he'd killed himself. But in the end, it was all God's plan. And God knew what He was doing.

God moves in mysterious ways.

He said it to himself again and again. All his life he

had awaited the call—the revelation of God's purpose for him. It had been a long, difficult journey. God had tested him as sorely as Job, taken from him his wife and child in divorce, taken his career, his money, his self-respect.

And now this thing with Lorenzo. Lorenzo had blasphemed God and Jesus using the most horrific words of vileness, and before his very eyes God had smote him dead. *Before his very eyes.* But Lorenzo hadn't been the thief: Eddy had accused him unjustly. What did it mean? Where was God's will in all this? What was God's plan for him?

God moves in mysterious ways.

The pickup coughed and rattled along the shining black asphalt, took a broad curve, passed between sandstone bluffs—and there below him lay a collection of adobe houses half-hidden among cottonwoods. To the right, about a mile off, lay the two new runways of the airstrip and a set of hangars. Beyond that, at the edge of the mesa, was the Isabella complex itself, surrounded by a double set of chain-link fences.

Most of Isabella, he knew, was deep below ground. The entrance must be inside the fenced-off area.

Dear Heavenly Father, please guide me, he prayed.

Eddy drove down into the little green valley. There was a log building at the far end, which must be the old Nakai Rock Trading Post. Two men and a woman were walking toward it. Others moved about near the door. God had gathered them together for him.

He took a deep breath, slowed the pickup, and parked in front of the building. A hand-painted sign above the door read, NAKAI ROCK TRADING POST, 1888.

Through the screen door, he counted eight people inside. He knocked on the wooden frame. No answer. He knocked louder. The man at the front of the room turned, and Russ was struck by his eyes. They were so blue, they seemed to jolt you with electricity.

Hazelius. It had to be.

Russ whispered a quick prayer and stepped inside.

"What can I do for you?" the man asked.

"My name's Russ Eddy. I'm the pastor of the Gathered in Thy Name Mission down in Blue Gap." It came out in a rush. He felt foolish and self-conscious.

With a warm smile the man detached himself from the chair he'd been leaning on and strode over. "Gregory North Hazelius," he said with a hearty handshake. "Good to meet you, Russ."

"Thank you, sir."

"What can I do for you?"

Russ felt panic welling up. Where were the words he had rehearsed as the truck climbed the Dugway? Then his tongue found them. "I heard about the Isabella project, and I decided to come and tell you about my mission and offer you all the benefits of my spiritual assistance. We meet every Sunday at ten o'clock, over in Blue Gap, about two miles west of the water tower."

"Thank you very much, Russ," said Hazelius, his voice warm and sincere. "We'll visit you sometime soon—and perhaps you'd also enjoy a tour of Isabella one of these days. Unfortunately, right now we're in a very important meeting. Perhaps you'd care to come back next week?"

Heat crept up Russ's face. "Well, sir, no, I don't think so." He swallowed. "You see, my flock and I, we've been concerned about what's going on up here. I came to get some answers."

"I understand your concern, Russ, I really do." Mr. Hazelius glanced at a man standing close to him—tall, angular, and ugly. "Pastor, let me introduce you to Wyman Ford, our community liaison person."

The man stepped forward, his hand extended. "Glad to meet you, Pastor."

Hazelius was already retreating.

"I came to talk to him, not you," said Eddy, the high-pitched voice he hated cracking with effort.

Hazelius turned. "Excuse me, Pastor. We didn't mean any disrespect. We're a little tied up right now. . . . Could we meet tomorrow, same time?"

"No, sir."

"May I respectfully ask why is it so important to deal with this now?"

"Because I understand there's been a . . . a sudden bereavement, and I think that needs to be addressed."

Hazelius gazed at him. "You're referring to the death of Peter Volkonsky?" His voice had become quiet.

"If that's the man who took his own life, yes, I am, sir."

The man named Ford stepped forward again. "Pastor, I'd be happy to work with you on these issues. The problem is, right now Dr. Hazelius is about to direct another test of Isabella, and he doesn't have the time he'd like to devote to you. But I could."

Eddy wasn't going to let himself be bundled off to some PR lackey. "Like I said, I want to talk to *him*—not you. Isn't he the one who claimed he was the smartest man on earth? The one who said the rest of us were morons? The one who built this machine to challenge the Word of God?"

There was a short silence.

"The Isabella project has nothing to do with religion," said the PR man. "It's strictly a scientific experiment."

Eddy felt his anger swelling—righteous, furious anger at Lorenzo, at his ex-wife, at the divorce court, at all the injustice in the world. This was how Jesus must have felt in the Temple, when he cast out the money changers.

He pointed a trembling finger at Hazelius. "God will punish you anew."

"That's quite enough—," said the PR man, his voice sharp now, but Hazelius interrupted.

"What do you mean by 'anew'?"

"I've been reading up on you. I know about your wife, who pornographically bared her body in *Playboy* magazine, who glorified herself, and lived deliciously, like the whore of Babylon. God punished you by taking her. Still, you did not repent."

The room went deathly silent. The PR man said, after a moment, "Mr. Wardlaw, please escort Mr. Eddy from the premises."

"No," said Hazelius. *"Not yet."* He turned to Eddy with a terrible smile that chilled the preacher's soul. "Tell me, Russ. You're the pastor of a mission near here?"

"That's right."

"To what denomination do you belong?"

"We're unaffiliated. Evangelical."

"But you are—what? Protestant? Catholic? Mormon?"

"None of the above. We're born-again, fundamentalist Christians."

"What does that mean?"

"That we've accepted Jesus Christ into our hearts as our Lord and Savior, and we've been born again through water and the spirit, the only true way to salvation. We believe every word of the Scriptures is the divine, unerring word of God."

"So you think Protestants and Catholics aren't real Christians and God will send them to hell—am I correct?"

Eddy felt uneasy at this detour into fundamentalist dogma. But if that's what the smartest man in the world wanted to talk about—it was fine with Eddy.

"If they haven't been born again—then, yes."

"Jews? Muslims? Buddhists? Hindus? The uncertain, the seekers, the lost? All damned?"

"Yes."

"So most people on this little mud-ball out here in the outer arm of a minor galaxy are going to hell—except for you and a select few like-minded individuals?"

"You have to understand—"

"That's why I'm asking you these questions, Russ—to *understand.* I repeat: Do you believe that God will send most people on earth to hell?"

"Yes, I do."

"Do you know this for a fact?"

"Yes. The Scriptures repeatedly confirm it. *'He that believeth and is baptized shall be saved. He that believeth not shall be damned.'*"

Hazelius turned to the group. "Ladies and gentlemen: I give you an insect—no, a *bacterium*—who presumes to know the mind of God."

Eddy's face flushed. His brain boiled with the effort to come up with a reply.

The ugly man named Ford spoke to Hazelius. "Gregory, please, don't ask for trouble."

"I'm merely asking questions, Wyman."

"What you're doing is creating a problem." The man turned again to the security officer. "Mr. Wardlaw? Once again I will ask you to escort Mr. Eddy from the premises."

The security officer said evenly, "Dr. Hazelius is in charge and I take my orders from him." He turned. "Sir?"

Hazelius did not speak.

Eddy wasn't finished with the speech he had prepared in his head on the drive up. He had mastered his anger, and he spoke with cold, cold certainty, facing those blue eyes squarely. "You think you're the smartest man in the world. But how smart are you, really? You're so smart, you think the world started in some accidental explosion, a Big Bang, and all the atoms just happened to come together to create life, with no help from God. How smart is that? I'll tell you how smart it is: it's so smart, it'll send you to straight to hell. You're part of the War on Faith, you and your godless theories. You people want to abandon the Christian nation built up by our Founding Fathers and turn the country into a temple to feel-good secular humanism, where anything goes—homosexuality, abortion, drugs, premarital sex, pornography. But now you're reaping what you've sown. Already there's been a suicide. That's where blasphemy and hatred of God lead you. *Suicide*. And God will visit his divine wrath on you again, Hazelius. *'Vengeance is mine; I will repay, sayeth the Lord.'*"

Eddy halted, breathing hard. The scientist gazed at him strangely, his eyes glittering like a pair of frozen steel bearings.

In a curiously strangled voice, Hazelius said, "It's now time for you to leave."

Eddy didn't answer. The beefy security guard stepped forward. "Come this way, pal."

"That's not necessary, Tony. Russ here has recited his little speech. He knows it's time to go."

The security guard took another step toward him anyway.

"Don't worry about me," Eddy said hastily. "I can't wait to get out of this godless place."

As the screen door shut behind him, Eddy heard the calm voice say, "The germ extends its flagellum to depart."

He turned, pressed his face against the wire mesh, and called, " *'Ye shall know the truth, and the truth shall make you free.'* John 8:32."

He spun around and walked stiffly to his truck, the left side of his face twitching from humiliation and boundless, fulminating anger.

24

FORD WATCHED THE SKINNY FIGURE OF the pastor striding across the parking area toward an old beater of a pickup truck. A man like that, if he had a following, could do a lot of damage to the Isabella project. He was very sorry Hazelius had provoked him, and he felt that they hadn't heard the end of this—not by a long shot.

When he turned back, Hazelius was checking his watch as if nothing had happened.

"We're late," the scientist said briskly, plucking his white lab coat from the hook. He glanced around. "Let's go." His eye fell on Ford. "I'm afraid you'll be on your own for the next twelve hours."

"Actually," said Ford, "I'd like to see a run."

Hazelius pulled on his coat and picked up his briefcase. "I'm so sorry, Wyman, that just won't be possible. When we're down in the Bunker on a run, everyone has his or her assigned role and it's very tight. We just can't have any extra people around. I hope you understand."

"I'm sorry, too, Gregory, because I feel that in order to do my job, I have to be present at a run."

"All right, then, but I'm afraid it can't be this particular run. We're having a lot of problems, we're all under stress, and until we solve these technical issues, we can't have extraneous people on the Bridge."

Ford said quietly, "I'm afraid I have to insist."

Hazelius paused. An awkward silence fell. "Why do you need to see a run in order to do your job?"

"I've been hired to assure the local people that Isabella is safe. I'm not going to assure anyone of anything until I'm sure of it myself."

"Do you actually *doubt* the safety of Isabella?"

"I'm not going to take someone else's word for it."

Hazelius shook his head slowly.

"I have to be able to tell the Navajos that I'm part of every aspect of the project, that nothing's being kept from me."

"As the senior intelligence officer," said Wardlaw suddenly, "I would like to inform Mr. Ford that, for security purposes, he is denied access to the Bunker. End of discussion."

Ford turned to Wardlaw. "I don't think you want to take us down that particular road, Mr. Wardlaw."

Hazelius shook his head. "Wyman, I understand what you're saying. I really do. The problem is—"

Kate Mercer interrupted. "If you're worried about him finding out about the malware in the system, don't bother. He already knows about it."

Everyone stared at her. A shocked silence settled over the group.

"I told him everything," said Mercer. "I felt he should know."

"Oh, now that's just great," said Corcoran, looking up at the ceiling.

Kate turned on her. "He's a member of the team. He's got a right to know. I can vouch for him one hundred percent. He won't reveal our secret."

Corcoran's face flushed. "I think we can all read between the lines of *that* little speech."

"It's not what you think," said Mercer coldly.

Corcoran smirked. "And what is it that I think?"

Hazelius cleared his throat. "Well, well." He turned to Ford and laid a not-unkindly hand on his shoulder. "So Kate explained everything."

"She did."

He nodded. "All right . . ." He seemed to be thinking. Then he turned and smiled to Kate. "I respect your judgment. I'm going to trust you on this one." He turned to Ford. "I know you're an honorable man. Welcome to the group—for real, this time. You're now privy to our little secret." His blue eyes were disconcertingly penetrating.

Ford tried to stop the flush from mounting into his

197

face. He glanced at Kate and was startled by her expression—of what, hope? Anticipation? She didn't seem angry that he'd pushed the issue.

"We will speak of this later, Wyman." Hazelius let the hand slide off Ford's shoulder and he turned to Wardlaw. "Tony, it looks like Mr. Ford will be part of the next run after all."

The SIO didn't answer. His face remained utterly stolid and expressionless, his eyes straight ahead.

"Tony?"

"Yes, sir," came the strained answer. "I understand, sir."

Ford made a point of looking at Wardlaw as he passed by. The man returned the look with cold, empty eyes.

25

KEN DOLBY WATCHED THE GREAT TITANIUM door to the Bunker drop down and seal itself with a hollow boom. A damp movement of air played over his face, smelling of caverns, wet stones, warm electronics, machine oil, and coal dust. He inhaled. It was a heady smell, a rich smell—the smell of Isabella.

The scientists filed past on their way to the Bridge. Dolby caught Hazelius as he passed.

"There's a red light on Magnet 140," he said. "I got a squelch warning on it. Nothing serious. I'm going to check it out."

"How long do you think it'll take?" Hazelius asked.

"Less than an hour."

Hazelius gave him an affectionate pat on the back. "You do that, Ken, and report back. I won't turn on Isabella until we hear from you."

Dolby nodded. He stood in the vast cavern while the others disappeared into the Bridge. The door closed with a clang that reverberated through the hangarlike space.

Silence gradually returned. Dolby breathed once again the fragrant air. He had led the design team for Isabella—directing a dozen Ph.D. engineers and almost a hundred contractor-designers who were blueprinting specific subsystems and the supercomputer. Despite the many people involved, he had been firmly in charge, his hand in everything. He knew every square inch of Isabella, every quirk and foible, every curve and hollow. Isabella was his creation—his machine.

The oval opening to Isabella's tunnel—like a slice taken off the side of doughnut—glowed in soft blue light. Condensation snaked out of the portal in sinuous tracks that crawled this way and that before evaporating. Inside the tunnel, just beyond the opening, Dolby could see the massive blue-gray wall of depleted uranium shielding—behind which was CZero, the beating heart of Isabella.

CZero. Coordinate Zero. This was the tiny place, no bigger than a pinhead, where the beams of matter and antimatter were brought together at the speed of light to annihilate themselves in a burst of pure energy.

When Isabella was running at 100 percent full power, it was the hottest, brightest place in the entire universe—one trillion degrees. Unless, thought Dolby with a smile, there was an intelligent race of beings out there with a particle accelerator bigger than his.

He was inclined to think not.

Most of the energy of the matter–antimatter explosion at CZero was instantly converted back to mass, according to Einstein's famous formula, $E=mc^2$, and became an awesome spray of exotic subatomic particles, some not seen since the very creation of the universe in the Big Bang, 13.7 billion years ago.

He closed his eyes and imagined himself as one of the protons circulating in the ring, going round and round, being accelerated by the supermagnets to 99.999 percent the speed of light. He made the forty-seven-mile circuit four thousand times per second, round and round. He saw himself plunging down the curving tunnel at unimaginable speed, getting a kick in speed from each magnet, more than three million kicks per second, faster and faster . . . it thrilled him to imagine it. And ripping along just half an inch from him in the pipe was the beam of antiprotons, circulating in the opposite direction, whipping by him at the same incredible speed.

He imagined the moment of contact. His beam was forced into the oncoming beam. Into a head-on collision at CZero. Matter striking antimatter at the speed of light. Riding the particle into CZero, he felt the collision—the pure, absolute, thrilling annihilation of it. He felt his rebirth into strange new particles spraying outward in all directions, ripping into the many layers of detectors that logged, counted, and examined each particle.

Ten trillion particles per second.

DOLBY OPENED HIS EYES, RETURNING FROM his reverie, feeling slightly foolish. Checking his pockets for loose change or other ferromagnetic items, he walked across the staging area toward the row of electric golf carts. Isabella's superconducting magnets were thousands of times more powerful than the ones used in medical MRI machines. They could pull a nickel right through your body or gut you with your own belt buckle.

Isabella was dangerous and demanded respect.

He climbed in behind the wheel. Pressing a button, he engaged the clutch and eased the cart into first gear.

He had designed it himself, and it was one sweet little cart. Although it could do only twenty-five miles an hour, it had cost almost as much as a Ferrari Testarossa, mostly because it had to be built entirely out of nonmagnetic materials—plastics, ceramics, and low-diamagnetic metals. It came with a communications system, a built-in computer, radar warning sensors and controllers front, side, and back, radiation sensors, ferromagnetic alarms, and a special vibration-damped bay for transporting delicate scientific instruments.

He sped across the concrete floor and entered the oval opening to the Isabella tunnel. The turn was tight and he came to a full stop.

"Hello, Isabella."

He eased onto the concrete track that ran along the bottom of the tunnel, next to the curving bundle of pipes. Once on the track, he accelerated, the wheels staying in their grooves. Everything was bathed in greenish-blue light from a double row of fluorescent tubes overhead. As he whipped along, he glanced at the biggest pipe, gleaming 7000 aluminum-alloy construction, flanged and bolted every six feet. Inside was a vacuum harder than that found on the surface of the moon. It had to be tight: one loose atom wandering into CZero would be like a horse straying onto the racetrack at Daytona. Crash and burn.

He accelerated to top speed. The rubber wheels whispered in their grooves. Every hundred feet he passed a magnet wrapped around the pipe like a big doughnut. Each magnet, supercooled to four and a half degrees above absolute zero, wept a fog of condensation. Dolby blew through each cloud, leaving behind a whirl of eddies, the pipes racing past.

Periodically he passed a steel door on the left side of the tunnel, an opening into the old coal tunnels. Emergency exits, in case something happened. But nothing would happen. This was Isabella.

Magnet 140 was eight miles down the tunnel. . . . A twenty-minute drive. It wasn't anything serious.

Dolby was almost glad about it—he liked having time alone with his machine.

"Pretty good," he said out loud, "for the son of a grease monkey from Watts, eh, Isabella?"

He thought of his dad, who could rebuild any car engine on earth. Never made more than the barest of livings—it was almost a crime that a fine mechanic like him never had a chance. Dolby was determined to make up for it—and he did. When Dolby was seven, his father gave him a radio kit. It seemed like a miracle, to screw and solder together a bunch of plastic and metal crap and have a voice come out. By the time he was ten, Dolby had built his first computer. Then he built a telescope, threw in a couple of CCD chips, hooked it to the computer, and began tracking asteroids. He built a tabletop accelerator using an old electron gun from a TV set. With that he achieved the alchemist's dream, something that had eluded even Isaac Newton himself: he'd smashed a piece of lead foil with electrons, turning maybe a few hundred atoms to gold. His poor father, God rest his kindly soul, had spent every free dollar from his meager paychecks buying him kits, equipment, and parts. Ken Dolby's dream was to build the biggest, shiniest, most expensive machine ever.

And now he had done it.

His machine was perfect, even if some bastard had hacked into the computer software.

Magnet 140 came into view and he braked hard and came to a halt. He pulled a special laptop out of the instrument bay and jacked it into a panel on the side of the magnet. Sitting on his heels, he worked on the laptop, talking to himself. He unscrewed a metal plate on the side of the magnet's case, clipped a device with two wires—one red, one black—to terminals in the magnet.

He consulted the computer, his face darkening. "Well, damn you, bitch." The cryogenic pump that was part of the insulating system was failing. "I'm glad I caught you early."

Silently he repacked the tools, shoved the laptop back into its neoprene carrying case, and got behind the wheel of the cart. He unhooked a radio from the dashboard, pressed a button.

"Dolby calling the Bridge."

"Wardlaw here," came a tinny voice from the speaker.

"Lemme talk to Gregory."

After a moment Hazelius came on.

"You can start Isabella."

"The high-temperature alarm is still red on the board."

A silence. "You know I'd never risk my machine, Gregory."

"Fine. I'll start her up."

"We're going to have to install another cryogenic pump, but we've got plenty of time. It'll last at least another two runs."

Dolby signed off, put his hands behind his head, and kicked back, propping his feet up on the dashboard. In what at first felt like utter silence, Dolby began to make out faint sounds—the whisper of the forced-air system, the humming of the cryogenic pumps, the hiss of liquid nitrogen moving through the outer jackets, the faint creakings of the golf cart engine as it continued to cool, the cricks and ticks of the mountain itself.

Dolby closed his eyes and waited, and then he heard a new sound. It was like a low, low singing, a humming, rich and dark.

Isabella had been turned on.

He felt that ineffable shiver of wonder, of awe that he had designed a machine that could peer into the moment of creation—a machine that actually *re-created* the moment of creation.

A God machine.

Isabella.

26

FORD DRAINED THE BITTER DREGS FROM his coffee mug and checked his watch: close to midnight. The run had been one long bore, endless adjustments and tinkerings stretched out over hours and hours of time. As he watched everyone work, he wondered: Was one of them the saboteur?

Hazelius strolled over. "We're bringing the two beams in contact. Keep your eye on the Visualizer—that screen in front."

The physicist murmured a command and, after a

moment, a bright point of light appeared in the center of the screen, followed by a flickering of colors that radiated outward.

Ford nodded at the screen. "What do all those colors represent?"

"The computer translates the particle collisions at CZero into pictures. Each color represents a type of particle, the bands represent energy levels, and the radiating shapes are the particles' trajectories as they exit CZero. It's a way for us to see at a glance what's going on, without having to crunch a bunch of numbers."

"Clever."

"It was Volkonsky's idea." Hazelius shook his head sadly.

Ken Dolby's voice tolled out, "Ninety percent power."

Hazelius held up his empty coffee mug. "Get you another?"

Ford winced. "Why don't you get a decent espresso machine in here?"

Hazelius went off with a low chuckle. Everyone else in the room was quiet, focused on various tasks, except for Innes, who paced the room with nothing to do, and Edelstein, who sat in a corner reading *Finnegans Wake*. The boxes from the frozen pizzas they'd eaten for dinner spilled out of the trash bin by the door. Coffee rings marked various white surfaces. The bottle of Veuve Clicquot still lay by the wall.

It had been a long twelve hours—long stretches of crushing boredom, punctuated by brief bursts of manic activity, and then more boredom. "Beam steady, collimated, luminosity fourteen point nine TeV," said Rae Chen, hunched over a keyboard, her glossy black hair spilling in an unruly curtain over the keys.

Ford strolled along the raised part of the Bridge. As he passed Wardlaw, who was at his own monitoring station, he caught a faintly hostile glance, and smiled coldly back at it. The man was waiting and watching.

He heard Hazelius's quiet voice. "Bring it to ninety-five, Rae."

The faint clicking of a keyboard sounded in the hushed room.

"Beam holding steady," said Chen.

"Harlan? How's the power?"

St. Vincent's leprechaun-like face popped up. "Coming in like a tidal bore: smooth and strong."

"Michael?"

"So far so good. No anomalies."

The murmured catechism went on, Hazelius asking for a report from everyone in turn, then repeating the process. It had been going on like this for hours, but now Ford could feel the anticipation finally beginning to build.

"Ninety-five percent power," said Dolby.

"Beam steady. Collimated."

"Luminosity seventeen TeV."

"Okay, folks, we're verging into unknown territory," said Chen, her hands on a set of controllers.

"Here there be monsters," intoned Hazelius.

The screen was awash in color, like a flower forever blooming. Ford found it mesmerizing. He glanced over at Kate. She had been working quietly on a networked Power Mac to one side, running a program he recognized as Wolfram's Mathematica. The screen displayed a complicated infolded object. He went over and looked over her shoulder.

"Am I interrupting?"

She sighed, turned. "Not really. I was going to shut this down and watch the final run-up anyway."

"What is it?" He nodded at the screen.

"A Kaluza-Klein eleven-dimensional space. I've been running some calculations on mini black holes."

"I hear that Isabella will investigate the possibility of power generation using mini black holes."

"Yes. That's one of our projects—if we can ever get Isabella online."

"How would that work?"

He saw a nervous glance back at Hazelius. Their eyes met for just a moment.

"Well, it turns out Isabella might be powerful enough to create miniature black holes. Stephen Hawking showed that mini black holes evaporate after a few trillionths of a second, releasing energy."

"You mean, they blow up."

"Right. The idea is that maybe we can harness the energy."

"So there's a possibility of Isabella creating a black hole that will blow up?"

Kate waved her hand. "Not really. The black holes Isabella might create—if any get created at all—would be so small that they would evaporate in a trillionth of a second, releasing a lot less energy than, say, the bursting of a soap bubble."

"But the explosion might be bigger?"

"Highly unlikely. I suppose it's possible that if the mini black hole lasted, say, a few seconds, it might knock around long enough to acquire more mass and . . . then blow up."

"How big an explosion?"

"Hard to say. The size of a small nuke, perhaps."

Corcoran glided over, sidling up to Ford. "But that's not even the scariest scenario," she said.

"Melissa."

She arched her eyebrows at Kate, putting on an innocent look. "I thought we weren't going to hide anything from Wyman." She turned to Ford. "The really scary possibility is that Isabella will create a mini black hole that might be *completely* stable. In which case, it would drift down to the center of the earth and hang out there, swallowing up more and more matter until . . . *krrrrch!* Good-bye Earth."

"There's a chance that might happen?" Ford asked.

"No," said Kate irritably. "Melissa's just teasing you."

"Ninety-seven percent," intoned Dolby.

"Luminosity at seventeen point nine two TeV."

Ford lowered his voice. "Kate . . . Don't you think even the smallest possibility is too high? We're talking about the destruction of the earth."

"You can't shut down science on outlandish possibilities."

"Don't you care?"

Kate flared up. "Damn it, Wyman, of course I care. I live on this planet, too. You think I'd risk that?"

"If the probability isn't exactly zero, you *are* risking it."

"The probability *is* zero." She swiveled her chair, roughly turning her back on him.

Ford straightened up and noticed Hazelius still looking at him. The physicist rose from his chair and strolled over with an easy smile.

"Wyman? Let me reassure you with this little fact: if miniature black holes were stable, we'd see them everywhere, left over from the Big Bang. In fact, there'd be so many that they would have swallowed up everything by now. So the fact that we exist is proof that mini black holes are unstable."

Corcoran smirked at the sidelines, pleased at the effect of her words.

"Somehow I'm not completely reassured."

Hazelius placed a reassuring hand on his shoulder. "It's *impossible* that Isabella will create a black hole that will destroy the earth. *It simply can't happen.*"

"Power steady," said St. Vincent.

"Beam collimated. Luminosity eighteen point two TeV."

The murmuring in the room had increased. Ford heard a new sound—a faint, distant singing.

"You hear that?" Hazelius said. "That's a sound generated by trillions of particles racing around Isabella. We're not sure why there's a sound at all—the beams are in a vacuum. Somehow they set up a sympathetic vibration transmitted by the intense magnetic fields."

The atmosphere on the Bridge was thickening with tension.

"Ken, take it up to ninety-nine and hold," said Hazelius.

"Will do."

"Rae?"

"Luminosity just over nineteen TeV and rising."

"Harlan?"

"Steady and cool."

"Michael?"

"No anomalies."

Wardlaw spoke from his security station across the room. His voice was very loud in the hushed atmosphere. "I've got an intruder."

"What?" Hazelius straightened up, astonished. "Where?"

"At the perimeter fence up top, around the elevator. I'm focusing in."

Hazelius strode over, and Ford quickly joined him. A greenish image of the fence materialized on one of

Wardlaw's screens, seen from the perspective of a camera mounted high up on a mast above the elevator. It was of a man, pacing restlessly along the fence.

"Can you zero in?"

Wardlaw hit a switch, and a different view sprang into focus from the level of the fence.

"It's that preacher!" said Hazelius.

The form of Russ Eddy, as gaunt as a scarecrow, paused in his pacing and hooked his fingers into the chain links, peering in with a suspicious scowl on his face. Behind him, the moon cast a greenish glow across the barren mesa.

"I'll take care of it," said Wardlaw, rising.

"You'll do nothing of the sort," said Hazelius.

"He's trespassing."

"Leave him be. He's harmless. If he tries to climb the fence, then you can speak to him over the loudspeakers and tell him to scram."

"Yes, sir."

Hazelius turned. "Ken?"

"Holding at ninety-nine."

"How's the supercomputer, Rae?"

"So far, so good. Keeping up with the flow of particles."

"Ken, take it up a tenth."

The flower on the screen flared, flickering and spreading, running through all the colors of the rainbow. Ford stared at the screen, mesmerized by the image.

"I'm starting to see the very lowest end of that resonance," said Michael Cecchini. "It's a powerful one."

"Take it up another tenth," said Hazelius.

The writhing flower on the screen grew more intense, and two faint, shimmering lobes appeared on either side of the central point, darting outward again and again, like a grabbing hand.

"All power systems go," said St. Vincent.

"Up a tenth," said Hazelius.

Chen hit the keyboard. "I'm starting to see it—extreme space-time curvature at CZero."

"Up a tenth." Hazelius's voice was calm, steady.

"There it is!" said Chen, her voice resonating across the Bridge.

"You see?" said Kate to Ford. "That black dot right at CZero. It's as if the spray of particles was just briefly passing out and then back into our universe."

"Twenty-two point five TeV." Even the laid-back Chen sounded tense.

"Steady at ninety-nine point four."

"Up a tenth."

The flower writhed, twisted, throwing off veils and sprays of color. The dark hole in the center increased, its edges flickering raggedly. The resonance suddenly lunged outward, right off the sides of the screen.

Ford saw a drop of sweat crawl down Hazelius's cheek.

"That's the source of the charged jet at twenty-two

point seven TeV," said Kate Mercer. "We seem to be tearing the 'brane at that point."

"Up a tenth."

The hole grew, pulsating strangely, like a beating heart. In the middle it was black as night. Ford stared, drawn in.

"Infinite curvature at CZero," said Chen.

The hole had grown so large, it swallowed most of the center of the screen. Ford suddenly saw flashes in its depths, like a school of fish darting about in deep water.

"How's the computer?" Hazelius asked sharply.

"Flaky," said Chen.

"Up a tenth," said Hazelius, his voice low.

The flecks increased. The singing noise, which had been steadily rising, added a hissing, snakelike overtone.

"Computer's getting funkier," said Chen, her voice tight.

"How so?"

"Take a look."

Everyone was now standing before the big screen—everyone but Edelstein, who continued reading. Something was materializing in the central hole, with little bits and flashes of color, swarming faster, coming up from infinite depths, shimmering, taking shape. It was so strange, Ford wasn't sure if his brain was interpreting it right.

Hazelius pulled the keyboard over and rapped in a command. "Isabella's having trouble managing the bitstream. Rae, kill the checksum routines—that should free up CPU."

"Hold it," said Dolby. "That's our early warning system."

"It's a backup to a backup. Rae? Please do it."

Chen hammered in the command.

"Computer's still funky, Gregory."

"I'm with Ken—I think you should turn the checksum routines back on," said Kate.

"Not yet. Take it up a tenth, Ken."

A hesitation.

"Up a tenth."

"All right," said Dolby, his voice uncertain.

"Harlan?"

"Power's deep, strong, and clean."

"Rae?"

Chen's voice was high-pitched. "It's happening again. The computer's getting all glacky on me, just like it did with Volkonsky."

The shimmering intensified.

Cecchini said, "Beams still collimated. Luminosity twenty-four point nine. Tight and focused here."

"Ninety-nine point eight," said Chen.

"Up a tenth."

Dolby spoke, his usually laconic voice uncharacteristically tight. "Gregory, are you sure—?"

"Up a tenth."

"I'm losing the computer," said Chen. "I'm losing it. It's happening again."

"It can't be happening. Put it up a tenth!"

"Approaching ninety-nine point nine," said Chen, a slight tremble in her voice.

The singing had become louder, and it reminded Ford of the sound made by the monolith in the movie *2001*, a chorus of voices.

"Take it up to ninety-nine point nine five."

"It's gone! It won't accept any input!" Chen tossed her head, her hair sweeping back in an angry cloud of black.

Ford stood with the others, just behind Hazelius, Cecchini, Chen, and St. Vincent, all of whom were riveted to their own keyboards. The image, the thing in the center of the Visualizer, had taken solidity, and it was shimmering faster, with purple and deep red darts whipping in and out, a whirling hive of color, deep and three-dimensional.

It looked almost alive.

"My God," gasped Ford involuntarily. "What *is* that?"

"Slag code," said Edelstein dryly, not even looking up from his book.

Instantly the Visualizer went blank.

"Oh no. God no," Hazelius groaned.

A word popped up in the middle of the screen:
Greetings
Hazelius smacked the keyboard with his hand. "Son of a bitch!"

"Computer's frozen," said Chen.

Dolby turned to Chen, "Power down, Rae. Now."

"No!" Hazelius turned on him. "Up to one hundred percent!"

"Are you crazy?" Dolby screamed.

Suddenly, instantly, Hazelius became calm. "Ken, we've *got* to find the malware. It seems to be a bot program—it's moving around. It's not in the main computer. So where is it? The detectors have built-in microprocessors—*it's moving around in the detectors*. And that means we can find it. We can isolate the output from each detector and corner it. Am I right, Rae?"

"Absolutely. That's a brilliant idea."

"For God's sake," said Dolby, his face covered with sweat, "we're flying blind. If the beams decollimated, they could slice through here, blow the shit out of all of us—not to mention frying two hundred and fifty million dollars' worth of detectors."

"Kate?" said Hazelius.

"I'm with you all the way, Gregory."

"Take it to a hundred, Rae," Hazelius said coolly.

"Okay."

Dolby lunged for the keyboard, but Hazelius stepped into his way, blocking him.

"Ken," Hazelius said rapidly, "listen to me. If the computer's going to crash, it would have already happened. The controller software's still running in the background. We just can't see it. Give me ten minutes to trace this."

"No way."

"Five minutes, then. Please. This is not an arbitrary decision. My assistant director agrees with me. We're in charge."

"Nobody's in charge of my machine but me." Breathing hard, Dolby stared at Hazelius, stared at Mercer, then turned back, his arms at his side, fists clenched.

Without turning, Hazelius said, "Kate? We're going to try what you and I discussed earlier: type in a question—anything. Let's see if we can get it talking."

"What the hell's the point of asking it questions?" Dolby turned. "It's a chatterbot program."

"Maybe we can trace the output back to the source. Back to the logic bomb."

Dolby stared at him.

"Rae," said Hazelius, "if it outputs, you troll through the detectors looking for the signal."

"Gotcha." Chen jumped up from the console and went to another workstation, where she began typing.

The others stood almost paralyzed, as if in shock. Ford saw that Edelstein had finally put down his book to watch, a distant look of interest on his face.

Hazelius and Dolby continued their face-off, Hazelius blocking access to the power control board.

Greetings to you, too, Kate typed in.

The LED screen above the console flickered, went dark. Then an answer appeared:

I am glad to be speaking to you.

"It's responding!" Kate cried.

"Did you get that, Rae?" Hazelius shouted.

"I did," said Chen excitedly. "I've got a bead on the output stream. You were right, it *is* coming from a detector! This is it! We got it! Keep going!"

Glad to be speaking to you, too, Kate typed. "Jeez, what should I say?"

"Ask who it is," said Hazelius.

Who are you? Kate typed.

For lack of a better word, I am God.

A derisive snort from Hazelius. "Stupid-ass hackers!"

If you're really God, typed Kate, *then prove it.*

We don't have much time for proofs.

I'm thinking of a number between one and ten. What is it?

You are thinking of the transcendental number e.

Kate took her fingers off the keyboard and sat back.

"How's it going, Rae?" Hazelius called to Chen.

"I'm tracing it! Just keep typing!"

Kate straightened her shoulders and leaned forward to type again.

Now I'm thinking of a number between zero and one.

Chaitin's number: Omega.

At this, Kate stood up abruptly and stepped back from the keyboard, her hand over her mouth.

"What is it?" Ford asked.

"Keep typing!" Chen screamed from her hunched-over position.

Kate shook her head, her face pale, hand over her mouth, backing away from the machine.

"Why the hell isn't someone inputting!" Chen screamed.

Hazelius turned to Ford. "Wyman—you take over from Kate."

Ford stepped forward to the keyboard. *If you're God, then . . .* What could he ask? He quickly typed, *what's the purpose of existence?*

I don't know the ultimate purpose.

"I'm getting it!" Chen shouted. "That's it! Keep it going!"

That's a fine thing, Ford typed, *a god who doesn't know the purpose of existence.*

If I knew, existence would be pointless.

How so?

If the end of the universe were present in its beginning—if we are merely in the middle of the deterministic unfolding of a set of initial conditions—then the universe would be a pointless exercise.

"All right," said Dolby, in a low and menacing tone. "Your time's up. I want Isabella back."

"Ken, we need more time," said Hazelius.

Dolby tried to step past Hazelius, but the physicist blocked him. "Not yet."

"I've almost got it!" yelled Chen. "Give me just a minute more, for chrissakes!"

"No!" said Dolby. "I'm powering down now!"

"The hell you are," said Hazelius. "Damn it, Wyman, keep inputting!"

Explain, Ford hastily typed.

If you're at your destination, why make the journey? If you know the answer, why ask the question? That is why the future is—and must be—pro-

foundly hidden, even from God. Otherwise, existence would have no meaning.

That's a metaphysical argument, not a physical argument, Ford typed.

The physical argument is that no part of the universe can calculate things faster than the universe itself. The universe is "predicting the future" as fast as it can.

Dolby tried to step around Hazelius, but the physicist darted to the side, still blocking him.

"Keep it outputting, I'm almost there!" Chen screamed, hunched over the keyboard, typing maniacally.

What is the universe? Ford typed, plucking questions at random. *Who are we? What are we doing here?*

Dolby lunged forward, shoving Hazelius out of the way. Hazelius stumbled back, but he recovered quickly and flung himself on the engineer's back, pulling him away from the console with astonishing force.

"Are you crazy?" Dolby yelled, trying to shuck him off. "You're going to wreck my machine—!"

The two men wrestled, the diminutive physicist clinging like a monkey to the engineer's broad back—and they fell heavily to the floor, the chair overturning with a crash.

The others were frozen with shock at the brawl. Nobody knew what to do.

"You crazy bastard—!" Dolby yelled, rolling on the

floor, struggling to break free of the fiercely clinging physicist.

The logic bomb continued outputting to the Visualizer screen.

The universe is one vast, irreducible, ongoing computation, which is working toward a state that I do not and cannot know. The purpose of existence is to reach that final state. But that final state is a mystery to me, as it must be, for if I knew the answer, what would be the point of it all?

"Let me go!" Dolby cried.

"Somebody help me," Hazelius cried. "Don't let him touch that keyboard!"

What do you mean by computation? Ford typed. *We're all inside a computer?*

By computation I mean thinking. All of existence, everything that happens—a falling leaf, a wave upon the beach, the collapse of a star—it is all just me, thinking.

"I got it!" Chen cried triumphantly. "I've—wait! What the hell—?"

What are you thinking? Ford typed.

With a final wrench, Dolby broke away from Hazelius and threw himself on the console.

"No!" Hazelius screamed. "Don't shut her down! Wait!"

Dolby sat back, breathing hard. "Power-down sequence initiated."

The singing noise that filled the room attenuated, and the screen in front of Ford flickered, the words dissolving. He had just the briefest glimpse of some eldritch shape flurrying up and disappearing into a point in the center of the screen, and then it went dark.

Hazelius shrugged his shoulders, straightened his clothes, brushed the dust off his shoulders, and turned to Chen, his voice calm. "Rae? Did you get it?"

Chen stared back at him, her face blank.

"Rae?"

"Yeah," she said. "I got it."

"Well? What processor is it coming from?"

"None."

A silence settled in the room.

"What do you mean, *none?*"

"It was coming from CZero itself."

"What are you talking about?"

"Just what I said. The output was coming directly out of the space-time hole at CZero."

In the shocked silence, Ford looked around for Kate. He found her standing all alone and very still at the back of the Bridge. He quickly walked over to her and spoke to her in a low voice. "Kate? Are you all right?"

"It knew," she whispered, her face white. *"It knew."* Her hand sought his and closed around it, trembling.

27

EDDY EXITED HIS TRAILER, TOWEL OVER his shoulder, shaving kit in hand, and stared at the boxes of unsorted clothing that had arrived during the week. After his midnight trip up the mesa, he hadn't been able to sleep and he'd spent most of the night online, haunting the late-night Christian chat rooms.

He gave the pump a few pulls and caught the cold water with his hand, dashing it into his face, trying to shock himself into awareness. There was a humming noise in his head from lack of sleep.

He lathered up and shaved, swished the razor blade clean in the basin, and dumped out the water into the sand. He watched as it soaked in, leaving clots of foam on the surface. It suddenly reminded him of Lorenzo's blood. With a feeling of panic, he stamped down hard on the image. God had smote Lorenzo down—not him. It was not his fault—it was God's will. And God never did anything without a purpose. And that purpose involved the Isabella project—and Hazelius.

Hazelius. He found himself replaying in his mind the encounter of the day before. He flushed at the memory and his hands trembled. He kept rephrasing, again and again, what else he could have said; with each revision his speech grew longer, more eloquent, more full of righteous anger. In front of everyone, Hazelius had called him an insect, a germ—because he was a Christian. The man was an example of all that was wrong with America, a high priest in the temple of secular humanism.

Eddy's eye wandered over to the boxes that had arrived the day before. With Lorenzo gone, he had a lot more work to do. Thursday was "clothes day," when he distributed free clothes to the Indians. Through the Internet, Russ had worked out a deal with a half dozen churches in Arkansas and Texas to collect used clothing and ship it to him for distribution to needy families.

With his penknife, Eddy slit open the top of the first box and began sorting through the sorry pickings, pulling out a jacket here, a pair of jeans there, hanging them on racks or laying them out on plastic tables under the hay barn. He worked in the cool of the morning, sorting, racking, folding. The great form of Red Mesa rose up in the background, purple in the early light. His mind continued to orbit around Hazelius, replaying their scene. God had shown him what He would do to a blasphemer like Lorenzo. What more would He do against Hazelius?

He glanced up at the outline of the mesa rising above him, vaguely menacing, and remembered the darkness of the night before, the desolation, the emptiness. The humming and crackling of the power lines, the smell of ozone. He could *feel* the presence of Satan up there.

A telltale cloud of dust on the horizon indicated an approaching vehicle. He squinted into the rising sun, and soon a pickup materialized out of the dust, lurching and groaning along the potholed road. It came to a shuddering halt. A large Indian woman climbed out, followed by two boys. One carried a *Star Wars* gun, the other a plastic Uzi. They rushed off through the saltbush, pretending to shoot at each other. Russ followed them with his eyes, thinking of his own son growing up without him, and his internal rage increased.

"Hey, Pastor, how you doing?" asked the woman cheerfully.

"Greetings in Christ, Muriel," said Eddy.

"What you got today?"

"Help yourself." His eyes strayed back to the boys, who were shooting at each other from behind clumps of sagebrush.

The bell he had mounted on the outside of the trailer sounded to tell him the phone was ringing inside. He dashed in, searched for the receiver among piles of books.

"Hello?" he asked breathlessly. He almost never got calls.

"Pastor Russ Eddy?" It was Reverend Don Spates.

"Good morning, Reverend Spates. Christ be with—"

"I was wondering if you'd done any more looking around, like I asked."

"I did, Reverend. I went back up the mesa last night. The houses and village were completely deserted. The high-tension lines, all three of them, were *humming* with power. My hair was just about standing on end."

"Is that right?"

"Then around midnight, I heard like a vibration or a singing noise, coming from underground. It lasted about ten minutes."

"Did you get past the security fence?"

"I . . . I didn't dare."

Another grunt and a long silence. Eddy could hear more pickup trucks arriving and someone calling his name. He ignored it.

"Lemme tell you my problem," Spates said. "I'm doing my television talk show tomorrow evening at six—*Roundtable America*—and as my guest I've got a physicist from Liberty University. I've *got* to have something new on the Isabella project."

"I understand, Reverend."

"So like I told you the other day, you need to dig up something good. You're my man on the scene. This suicide's a start, but it's not enough. We need something to scare people. What are they *really* doing out there? Is radiation leaking out, like those rumors you told me about? Are they going to blow up the earth?"

"I wouldn't know. . . ."

"That's the point, Russ! Get in there and *find out*. Trespass a little, bend the laws of man to serve the Law of God. I'm *counting* on you!"

"Thank you, Reverend. Thank you. I'll do it."

After the call, Pastor Russ stepped back out into the bright sunlight and crossed over to where half a dozen people were sorting through clothes—mostly single mothers with children. He held up his hands. "Folks? I'm sorry, but we have to shut this down. Something's come up."

There was a murmur of disappointment, and Eddy felt bad—he knew some of the mothers had driven a long ways to get there, despite the price of gas.

After they'd gone, Russ hung up a notice that clothes day had been canceled and climbed into his pickup. He looked at the gauge: eighth of a tank, not enough gas to get up the mesa and back. Fishing out his wallet, he found three dollars. He already owed a couple hundred dollars at the filling station in Blue Gap and almost as much at Rough Rock. He'd have to pray he could make it to Piñon and fill up there, hoping they'd extend him credit. He was pretty sure they would—Navajos always let you borrow money.

It made no sense to go over to Isabella during the day—they'd see him. He would drive over after sunset, hide his pickup behind Nakai Rock, and poke around in the dark. In the meantime, he might be able to pick up some more information in Piñon about the suicide up on the mesa.

He took a deep, satisfying breath. God had finally called him. Gregory North Hazelius, that bile-spewing Christ hater, had to be stopped.

28

FORD, ENSCONCED IN AN OLD LEATHER chair in the corner of the rec room, watched as the rest of the team arrived from the Bunker, exhausted and demoralized. The first rays of the sun angled down from the horizon and blasted in through the building's eastern windows, filling the room with a golden light. People sank silently down into chairs, their eyes unfocused. Hazelius was the last to enter. He went to the fireplace and lit the kindling beneath a prelaid fire. Then he, too, sank into a chair.

For a while they sat in silence, the only sound the crackling of the fire. Finally Hazelius rose slowly to his feet. All eyes turned to him. He looked from person to person, his blue eyes rimmed with the pink of fatigue, his lips white with tension. "I have a plan."

This announcement was greeted with silence. A sap pocket burst in a log, causing everyone to jump.

"Tomorrow, at noon, we ramp up for another run," Hazelius continued, "at one hundred percent power. Here's the important thing: *we stick with the run until we've traced the slag code to its source.*"

Ken Dolby took out a handkerchief and wiped his face. "Look, Gregory, you almost wrecked my machine. I can't let that happen again."

Hazelius bowed his head. "Ken, I owe you an apology. I know I push too hard sometimes. I was angry and frustrated. I acted like a madman. Forgive me." He offered his hand.

After a moment Dolby took it.

"Friends?"

"Okay, sure," said Dolby. "But that doesn't change the fact that I'm not going to allow any more runs at one hundred percent power until we fix the hacker problem."

"And how do you propose we fix the problem without runs at one hundred percent?"

"Maybe the time has come to admit failure and report this back to Washington. Let them handle it."

A long silence followed, until Hazelius said, "Anyone else have an opinion?"

Melissa Corcoran turned to Dolby. "Ken, if we admit failure now, we'll be flushing our careers down the toilet. I don't know about the rest of you, but this was the chance of a lifetime for me. No way in hell am I going to let it go."

"Any other thoughts?" asked Hazelius.

Rae Chen stood up, her diminutive form hardly taller than those who were sitting. But the formal gesture of rising added weight. "I've got an opinion."

Her black eyes circled the table.

"I grew up in the back of a Chinese restaurant in Culver City, California. My mother worked herself half to death to send me to college and graduate school. She's proud of me because I made it in this country. And now I'm here. The whole world's watching us." Her voice began to break. "I'd rather die than give up. That's what I have to say. *I'd rather die.*"

She sat down abruptly.

Into the uncomfortable silence, Wardlaw spoke. "I know how things work at the DOE. If we report this now, we'll be charged with a cover-up. There could be criminal charges."

"Criminal charges?" said Innes from the back of the room. "For God's sake, Tony, let's not be absurd."

"I'm quite serious."

"That's sheer alarmism." Innes's pale face belied his dismissive tone. His eyes darted around the table. "And even if it were true, I'm only the team psychologist. I had nothing to do with the decision to withhold information."

"Yeah, but you didn't report it either," said Wardlaw, narrowing his eyes. "Don't kid yourself, you'll be in the dock with the rest of us."

The twittering of birds came in through the silence.

"Anyone in agreement with Ken?" Hazelius asked finally. "That we throw in the towel and report the problem to Washington?"

No one was in agreement.

Dolby looked around. "Think of the *risk!*" he cried. "We could wreck Isabella! We can't just power up Isabella and run it blind!"

"That's right, Ken," said Hazelius. "My plan takes that into account. Would you like to hear it?"

"Hearing isn't agreeing," said Dolby.

"Understood. As you know, the Isabella project facilities are run by three state-of-the-art IBM p5 595 servers. You specked them out yourself, Ken. They control telecommunications, e-mail, the LAN, and a bunch of other stuff. It's computational overkill—those servers are powerful enough to run the Pentagon. My idea is, let's reconfigure them as a backup system to Isabella." He turned to Rae Chen. "Possible?"

"I think so." She glanced at Edelstein. "Alan, what do you think?"

He nodded slowly.

"Just how do you propose doing this?" Dolby asked.

"The biggest problem is the firewall," Chen said. "We'll have to disable all links to the outside. Including telecommunications. Our landlines and cell phones would go down. Then we gang the servers, link them directly to Isabella. It's doable."

"No outside communications at all?"

"None, as long as Isabella is engaged. The firewall's unbreakable. If the software running Isabella senses any link to the outside, it shuts down for security purposes. That's why we have to cut all communications."

"Ken?"

Dolby drummed his fingers on the table and frowned.

Hazelius looked around the room. "Anyone else?" His eye fell on Kate Mercer, who was sitting in the back, disengaged from the discussion. "Kate? Any thoughts?"

Silence.

"Kate? Are you all right?"

Her voice was barely audible. "It *knew.*"

More silence. Then Corcoran said briskly, "Well, that may not be as amazing as it seems. Obviously we're dealing with an Eliza-like program—anyone remember Eliza?"

"That old FORTRAN program back in the eighties, talked to you like a psychoanalyst?" said Cecchini.

"That's the one," said Corcoran. "The program was simple—it turned everything you said into another question. You'd type, *My mother hates me,* and Eliza would answer, *Why do you say your mother hates you?* A little programming went a long way."

"This was no Eliza," said Kate. "It *knew* what I was thinking."

"It's actually quite elementary," said Melissa, giving her a breezy, superior look. "The hacker who created this logic bomb knows we're a bunch of egghead scientists, right? He knows we don't think like ordinary people. So when you said, 'I'm thinking of a number between one and ten,' the hacker had already anticipated someone asking a question like that. He figured you wouldn't necessarily be thinking of a whole number or even a rational number—no, he assumed you'd be thinking of *all* the numbers between one and ten. And what's the most interesting number between one and ten? Either pi or *e.* But of the two, e is the more mysterious." She looked around brightly.

"How about the next one it got?"

"Same rule applies. What's by *far* the weirdest frigging number between zero and one? Easy: Chaitin's halting-probability number—Omega. Right, Alan?"

Alan Edelstein dipped his head.

Melissa turned a radiant smile on Kate. "See?"

"Bullshit."

"Oh, so you think we're talking to God?"

"Don't be an ass," Kate said irritably. "All I'm saying is, it *knew*."

Rae Chen spoke up. "Look, I don't want to get all woo-woo here, but I traced that output right into the center of CZero. It was *not* coming from a detector or from any hardware. It was coming out of that weird data cloud inside the tear in space-time at CZero."

"Rae," said Hazelius, "you *know* that can't be true."

"I'm telling you what I saw. That data cloud was spewing out binary code directly into the detectors. On top of that there was an energy surplus—more energy was coming out of CZero than was being pumped in. The calculation's right here." She pushed a folder of papers in Hazelius's direction.

"Impossible. Can't happen."

"Yeah, well then *you* run the calculations." Chen spread her hands.

"That's why we need to do this again," said Hazelius, "not under pressure, not under some deadline. We need to do another run that'll give Rae all the time she needs to *really* track down that logic bomb."

Edelstein spoke. "I was tied up at Console Three during the exchange. Does anyone have a transcript? I'd like to read what the malware actually outputted."

"What does it matter?" Hazelius said.

Edelstein shrugged. "Just curious."

Hazelius looked around. "Anyone keep a record?"

"I've got it somewhere," said Chen. "It printed out with the data dump." She shuffled through some papers, pulled one out. Hazelius took it.

"Read it out loud," said St. Vincent. "I didn't catch most of it either."

"Me neither," said Thibodeaux. The others concurred.

Hazelius cleared his throat and read in a matter-of-fact tone:

Greetings

Greetings to you, too.

I am glad to be speaking to you.

Glad to be speaking to you, too. Who are you?

For lack of a better word, I am God.

Here Hazelius paused. "When I get my hands on the son of a bitch who dropped this logic bomb into the system, I'm going to rip his nuts off."

Thibodeaux laughed nervously.

"How do you know it wasn't a woman?" asked Corcoran.

After a moment, Hazelius continued.

If you're really God, then prove it.

We don't have much time for proofs.

235

I'm thinking of a number between one and ten. What is it?

You are thinking of the transcendental number e.

Now I'm thinking of a number between zero and one.

Chaitin's number: Omega.

If you're God, then what's the purpose of existence?

I don't know the ultimate purpose.

That's a fine thing, a god who doesn't know the purpose of existence.

If I knew, existence would be pointless.

How so?

If the end of the universe was present in its beginning—if we are merely in the middle of the deterministic unfolding of a set of initial conditions—then the universe would be a pointless exercise.

Explain.

If you're at your destination, why make the journey? If you know the answer, why ask the question? That is why the future is—and must be—profoundly hidden, even from God. Otherwise, life would have no meaning.

That's a metaphysical argument, not a physical argument.

The physical argument is that no part of the universe can calculate things faster than the universe itself. The universe is "predicting the future" as fast as it can.

What is the universe? Who are we? What are we doing here?

The universe is one vast, irreducible, ongoing computation, which is working toward a state that I do not and cannot know. The purpose of existence is to reach that final state. But that final state is a mystery to me, as it must be, for if I knew the answer, what would be the point of it all?

What do you mean by computation? We're all inside a computer?

By computation I mean thinking. All of existence, everything that happens—a falling leaf, a wave upon the beach, the collapse of a star—it is all just me, thinking.

What are you thinking?

Hazelius lowered the paper. "And that's all she wrote."

Edelstein murmured, "That is truly extraordinary."

"It strikes me as being a lot of New Age claptrap," said Innes. "*It is all just me, thinking.* I find the sentiments to be puerile. They are just what you might expect from a socially underdeveloped computer hacker."

"You think so?" Edelstein said.

"I certainly do."

"Then may I point out that this malware has—at least so far—passed the Turing test?"

"The Turing test?"

Edelstein squinted at him. "Surely you're aware of it."

"I apologize for being a mere psychologist."

"The seminal paper on the Turing test was published in the psychological journal *Mind*."

Innes's face shifted into professional blandness. "Perhaps you should consider, Alan, why it is that you feel such a strong need for self-validation."

"Turing," said Edelstein, "was one of the great geniuses of the twentieth century. He invented the idea of the computer back in the thirties. During World War Two he cracked Germany's Enigma code. After the war, he was horribly mistreated for being a homosexual and committed suicide by eating a poisoned apple."

Innes frowned. "A seriously unstable individual."

"You're saying homosexuals are unstable?"

"No, not at all, of course not," Innes said hastily. "I was referring to his method of suicide."

"Turing saved England from the Nazis—the British would have lost the war otherwise—and England thanked him with ruthless persecution. Under the circumstances, I should think suicide would not be . . . *illogical*. As for his method, it was clean, efficient, and eloquent in its symbolism."

Innes's face flushed. "I'm sure we would all appreciate it, Alan, if you would get to the point."

Edelstein continued smoothly. "The Turing test was an attempt to answer the question, 'Can a machine think?' Turing's proposal was this: a human judge engages in a written conversation with two entities he can't see—one human and the other machine. If, after a long exchange, the judge can't tell the human from the machine, then the machine is said to be 'intelligent.' The Turing test became the standard definition of artificial intelligence."

"All very interesting," said Innes, "but what does that have to do with our problem?"

"Since we haven't achieved anything close to artificial intelligence, even with the most powerful super-computers, I find it astonishing that a mere piece of malware—a few thousand lines of slag code, presumably—could pass the Turing test. And on such an abstract subject as God and the meaning of life." He pointed at the transcript. "That is why this is *not* puerile—not at all." He folded his arms and looked around.

"Which is why we have to do another run," said Hazelius. "We have to keep it talking so Rae can trace it back to its source."

People sagged in their chairs. No one spoke.

"Well?" said Hazelius. "I've made a proposal. We've talked about it. Let's take a vote: Tomorrow, do we run this logic bomb to ground or not?"

Halfhearted nods and sounds of vague assent went around the room.

Ford said, "Tomorrow is the day of the protest ride."

"There's no way we can delay this any longer," said Hazelius. He looked fiercely from face to face. "Well? Raise your hands!"

One by one, the hands rose. After a hesitation, Ford raised his with the others. Only Dolby's remained down.

"We can't do it without you, Ken," Hazelius said quietly. "Isabella's your baby."

A pause, then Dolby swore. "All right, damn it, I'm in."

"Unanimous," said Hazelius. "We'll begin the run at noon tomorrow. If all goes well, by nightfall we'll be at one hundred percent power. Then we'll have all night to track down and kill this malware. And now— let's get some sleep."

As Ford headed back across the field, Kate's phrase kept ringing through his head: *It knew. It knew.*

29

AS FORD WALKED TOWARD HIS CASITA, he heard someone speak his name and turned. The short, slim figure of Hazelius came striding across the field toward him.

"The events of last night must have been quite a shock to you," the director said, falling into step next to him.

"They were."

"What do you think?" Hazelius tilted his head slightly and looked at Ford sideways. His gaze was like a microscope.

"I think by not reporting it right away, you painted yourselves into a corner."

"What's done is done. I'm relieved that Kate told you about it. I didn't like deceiving you. I hope you understand why we didn't level with you before."

Ford nodded.

"I know you assured Kate you would keep this to yourself." He paused significantly.

Ford didn't dare speak. He no longer trusted himself to be a good liar.

"Do you have a moment?" Hazelius asked. "I'd like to show you the Indian ruin up the valley that's causing the controversy. It would give us a chance to chat."

They crossed the road and followed a path through the cottonwoods, moving rapidly up the dry bed of an arroyo that branched off from Nakai Wash. Ford could feel his body and his senses revving up after the exhausting night. The sandstone walls on either side of the wash narrowed, until the ripples and twists carved in the soft stone by ancient floods were close enough to touch. A golden eagle came gliding over the rim, its wingspan as wide as Ford was tall, and they paused to watch it. After it spiraled out of sight, Hazelius touched his shoulder and pointed upcanyon. About fifty feet up the canyon's sloping sandstone wall stood a small Anasazi ruin, wedged into an alcove. An ancient trail, pecked into the rock, led to it.

"When I was younger," Hazelius said, speaking softly, "I was an arrogant little prick. I thought I was smarter than everyone else. I believed that made me a better person, more worthy than those born with normal intelligence. I didn't know what I believed in and I didn't care. I churned along with my life, collecting proofs of my worth—a Nobel, the Fields, honorary degrees, accolades, buckets of money. I saw other people as props in the movie starring me. And then I met Astrid."

He paused as they reached the bottom of the ancient trail up the rock.

"Astrid was the only person on earth I ever truly loved, who took me out of myself. Then she died. Young and vital, struck down in my arms. After she was gone, I thought the world had ended."

He stopped. "It's hard to describe to someone who's never been through it."

"I have been through it," Ford said, almost before meaning to. The awful coldness of loss wrapped itself again around his heart and squeezed.

Hazelius leaned an arm on the sandstone. "You lost your wife?"

Ford nodded. He wondered why he was talking about this with Hazelius when he wouldn't even open up with his own shrink.

"How did you deal with it?"

"I didn't. I ran away to a monastery."

Hazelius drew closer. "Are you religious?"

"I . . . don't know. Her death shook my faith. I needed to find out—where I stood. What I believed in."

"And?"

"The more I tried, the less I was certain. It was good to discover that I never would be sure. That I wasn't born a true believer."

"Perhaps no rational, intelligent person can ever be absolutely sure of his faith," said Hazelius. "Or in my case, sure of my lack of faith. Who knows, maybe Eddy's God really is up there—vengeful, sadistic, genocidal, ready to burn everyone who doesn't believe in him."

"When your wife died . . . ," Ford asked, "how did you deal with it?"

"I decided to give something back to the world. And so, being a physicist, I came up with the idea for Isabella. My wife used to say, 'If the smartest person on earth can't figure out how we got here, then who can?' Isabella is my attempt to answer that question—and many others. It's my statement of faith."

In a small patch of sunlight, Ford noticed a baby lizard gripping the wall of stone. Somewhere overhead, the golden eagle still circled, its high-pitched cry echoing off the cliffs.

"Wyman," Hazelius went on, "if this hacker business got out, it would destroy the Isabella project, ruin our careers, and set back American science by a generation. You know that, don't you?"

Ford said nothing.

"I'm asking you with all my heart to please not divulge this problem until we have a chance to fix it. It would destroy all of us—Kate included."

Ford looked at him sharply.

"Yes, I can see there's something between you two," Hazelius continued. "Something good. Something sacred, if I may use that word."

If only it were true, Ford thought.

"Give us forty-eight more hours to solve this problem and save the Isabella project. I beg you."

Ford wondered if this intense little man knew, or had guessed, his real mission. It almost seemed as if he had.

"Forty-eight hours," Hazelius repeated softly.

"All right," Ford said.

"Thank you," said Hazelius, his voice hoarse with emotion. "Now, let's climb up."

Ford put his hands in the steps above him and followed Hazelius slowly up the treacherous trail. Weather had worn and softened the steps, and it was hard for his fingers and feet to keep their grip.

When they reached the small ruin, they paused on the ledge in front of the doorway to catch their breath.

"Look." Hazelius gestured to where an ancient inhabitant of the house had smoothed an outer layer of mud plaster across the stone wall. Most of this plaster had eroded away, but near the wooden lintel, handprints and streaks remained in the dried mud.

"If you look closely, you can see the whorls in the fingerprints," said Hazelius. "They're a thousand years old, but this is all of that person that remains."

He turned his face toward the blue horizon. "That's how it is with death. One day, bang. Everything's gone. Memories, hopes, dreams, houses, loves, property, money. Our family and friends shed a tear, hold a ceremony, and go on with their lives. We become a few fading photographs in an album. And then those who loved us die, and those who loved them die, and soon even the memory of us is gone. You've seen those old photo albums in antique shops, filled with people in nineteenth-century dress—men, women, children. Nobody knows who they are anymore. Like the person who left this handprint. Gone and forgotten. To what purpose?"

"I wish I knew," said Ford.

Despite the growing warmth of the day, Ford felt a shiver as they descended, touched to the core by a sense of his own mortality.

30

WHEN FORD REACHED THE CASITA, HE locked the door, drew the curtains, pulled his briefcase from the file cabinet, and dialed in the combination.

Sleep, you fool, sleep, his body screamed. Instead he extracted the laptop and Volkonsky's note from the briefcase. It was the first free moment he'd had to try to decrypt the note. He settled cross-legged on the bed with his back against the wooden headboard and pulled the computer into his lap. He called up a hex editor and began to type in the numbers and letters into a data file. The hexadecimal code of the mysterious note had to be in the machine before he could work with it.

The code could be anything at all: a short computer program, a data file, a text file, a small picture, the first few notes of Beethoven's Fifth. It might even be an RSA private key—and useless, since the FBI had carried off Volkonsky's personal computer.

Ford nodded off and slumped forward, knocking the laptop off his legs. He roused himself and went to the kitchen to make coffee. He hadn't slept in almost forty-eight hours.

He was measuring the final scoop into the filter when he felt a stab in his belly and thought of all the coffee he'd been pumping into his system for days. He shoved the coffee machine aside and rummaged in the cupboard, finding a box of organic green tea way in the back. Two bags, steeped ten minutes—and he returned to the bedroom with a mug of the green liquid. As he typed in more code, he gulped the hot, bitter tea.

He wanted to finish quickly so he could nap before riding down to Blackhorse to talk to Begay one final time before the protest ride, but his eyes blurred as they moved back and forth from the screen to the paper, and he kept catching mistakes.

He forced himself to slow down.

By ten thirty he was finished. He sat back and checked the data file against the note. It looked clean. He saved the file and hit the hex-binary convert module.

Instantly the hex code showed up as a binary file— a large block of zeros and ones.

On a hunch, he activated the binary-ASCII convert module, and to his surprise, a plain-text message appeared on the screen.

Congratulations, whoever you are. Ha ha! You have IQ slightly better than normal human idiot.

So. I take my skinny ass the hell out of this nuthouse and go home. I park myself in front of TV with bottle of ice-cold vodka and doobie and watch apes in monkey house beat on bars. Ha ha! And maybe I write long letter to Aunt Natasha.

I know the truth, you fool. I saw through the madness.

To prove it, I give you a name only: Joe Blitz.

Ha ha!

P. Volkonsky

Ford read the note twice and sat back. It had the rambling, manic tone of someone growing deranged. What madness had he meant? The malware? Isabella? The scientists themselves? Why did he conceal the message in code, instead of simply leaving a note?

And Joe Blitz?

Ford Googled the name and got back a million hits. He paged through the top ones, seeing no obvious connections.

He pulled the satellite phone out of the briefcase and stared at it. He'd misled Lockwood. No, he'd lied to him. And now he'd promised Hazelius he wouldn't mention the malware.

Damn it to hell. Why had he imagined that after two

years in the monastery, he could just slide back into the same old lying and deception of his CIA years? At least he could tell Lockwood about the note. Perhaps Lockwood might even have an idea about this mysterious Joe Blitz. He entered his number.

"It's been more than twenty-four hours," Lockwood answered the phone testily, not bothering with the usual salutations. "What have you been doing?"

"I found a note at Volkonsky's the other night I thought you'd want to know about."

"Why didn't you mention it yesterday?"

"It was just a piece of torn paper with some computer code on it. I didn't know it was significant. But then I was able to decode it."

"Well? What did it say?"

He read the note into the phone.

"Who the hell's Joe Blitz?" Lockwood asked.

"I was hoping you might know."

"I'll get my staff on it. And also this Aunt Natasha."

Ford slowly hung up the phone. There was one other thing he'd noticed: the note did not at all strike him as being written by a man on the verge of suicide.

31

AFTER A QUICK NAP AND A late lunch, Ford walked over to the stables. He had some important business to take care of with Kate: she had leveled with him, and now it was his turn to tell her the truth.

He found her filling up the horse troughs from a hose. She glanced at him. Her face was still pale, almost translucent, with worry.

"Thanks for vouching for me back there," Ford said. "I'm sorry I put you in an awkward position."

She shook her head. "Never mind. I'm just relieved I don't have to hide anything from you anymore."

He stood in the doorway, trying to screw up the courage to tell her. She was not going to take it well—not at all. His courage failed. He would tell her later, on the ride.

"Thanks to Melissa, everyone thinks we're sleeping together." Kate looked at him. "She's impossible. First she was chasing Innes, and then Dolby, and now you. What she really needs is a good shagging." She managed a wan smile. "Maybe you guys should get together and draw straws."

"No thanks." Ford eased himself down on a bale. It was cool in the barn and motes drifted in the air. Blondie was playing again on the boom box.

"Wyman, I'm sorry I wasn't very welcoming when you arrived. I want to tell you that I'm glad you're here. I never liked how we broke things off."

"It was pretty nasty."

"We were young and stupid. I did a lot of growing up since then—I mean, a *lot*."

Ford wished he hadn't read her dossier, knowing the pain she must have gone through in the intervening years.

"Me, too."

She lifted her arms and let them drop. "And so here we are. Again."

She looked so hopeful, standing there in dusty barn, hay in her hair. And so breathtakingly pretty. "Want to go for a ride?" he asked. "I'm going to pay another visit to Begay."

"I've got a lot to do. . . ."

"We made a pretty good team last time."

She brushed back her hair and looked at him—searchingly, for a long time. Finally she spoke. "All right."

They saddled up and set off southwestward toward the sandstone bluffs along the edge of the valley. Kate rode ahead, her slim body fitted confidently to her horse, swaying with it, in a rhythmic, almost erotic motion. A battered Australian cowboy hat was crammed on her head, and her black hair stirred in the wind.

God, how am I going to tell her?

As they approached the edge of the mesa where the Midnight Trail plunged down through a cut in the rock, Ford moved his horse up alongside her. They stopped twenty feet from the edge of the cliffs. She was staring across toward the horizon, a troubled look on her face. The wind blew up in uneven gusts from below, bringing with it an invisible cloud of grit. Ford spat and shifted in the saddle. "Are you still thinking about what happened last night?" he asked.

"I can't *stop* thinking about it. Wyman, how could it guess those numbers?"

"I don't know."

She gazed out over the vast red desert unrolling to blue mountains and cloud-castled infinities. "Looking at this," she murmured, "it's not hard to believe in God. I mean, who knows? Maybe we *are* talking to God."

She brushed back her hair and smiled ruefully at him.

Ford was astonished. This was a very different Kate from the strident atheist he had known in graduate school. He wondered once again what had happened in those missing two years.

32

BOOKER CRAWLEY STUCK THE CHURCHILL IN his mouth while he lined up the snooker shot. Satisfied, he hit the cue ball with a decisive rap and watched the little balls do their thing.

"Nice," said his billiards companion, watching the three ball drop into the braided leather pocket.

Through a row of narrow windows, the sun glinted off the river. It was a pleasant Thursday morning at the Potomac Club, and most members were at work. Crawley was also at work, or so he considered it— entertaining a potential client who owned a barrier island near Cape Hatteras and wanted the government to pay twenty million dollars to build a bridge to it. A bridge like that would double, even triple his land investment. For Crawley, this was a no-brainer. The junior senator from North Carolina owed him a favor after that golfing trip to St. Andrews, and he was a man who could be counted on for his loyalty and the preservation of his perks. One phone call, an earmark slipped into an unrelated bill, and Crawley would make the developer millions while pocketing a seven-figure fee for himself. If Alaska could have its bridge to nowhere, North Carolina should have one, too.

He watched the developer lining up his shot. He came from that special tribe of southerners who sported three last names and a roman numeral. Safford was his name, Safford Montague McGrath III. McGrath came from fine old Scotch-Irish stock, a big, blond, trim specimen of southern gentility. In other words, he was as dumb as a cow in the rain. McGrath made a show of being savvy in the ways of Washington, but anyone could see he was walking around with a hayseed jammed in one of his big country ears. Crawley had a feeling the man was going to tussle over the fee like a pigskin at the two-yard line. He was the type who had to come away from a negotiation feeling like he'd beat the crap out of the other side, or he wouldn't be able to get it up at home.

"So how's Senator Stratham these days?" McGrath asked, as if he had once known the old bastard.

"Fine, just fine." No doubt these days the old boy was enjoying a lunch of Gerber's whirled peas and sipping Ensure through a straw. The reality was, Crawley had never worked with old Senator

Stratham; he'd bought the firm, Stratham & Co., when Stratham had retired. He had thereby acquired an aura of respectability, a link to the fine old days, which handily distinguished him from the other K Street lobbyists who had sprung up after the last election like mushrooms in a steaming pile after a rain.

McGrath's next shot grazed the corner, made a little jog in front of the pocket, and drifted off down the felt. The man straightened up, saying nothing, his lips tight.

Crawley could polish off the fellow with his eyes closed, but that wouldn't do. No—the best way was to stay just ahead until the very end, then lose. Close the deal on the man's flush of triumph.

He flubbed the next shot by a close enough margin to give it verisimilitude.

"Nice try," said McGrath. He took a long puff on his cigar, laid it in the marble ashtray, crouched, and sighted. Then he shot. He obviously considered himself a hotshot pool player, but he didn't have the finesse for snooker. Still, this was an easy one and the ball was well potted.

"Whew," said Crawley. "You're going to make me work, Safford."

An attendant entered carrying a silver tray that held a note. "Mr. Crawley?"

Crawley took the note with a flourish. The club management, he thought with a smile, still used a system whereby an army of old-time darkies went flitting around with notes on silver platters—very antebellum. Getting a note on a silver platter beat hell out of fumbling for a squealing cell phone.

"Excuse me, Safford." Crawley unfolded the note. It read, *Delbert Yazzie, Chairman, Navajo Nation, 11:35* A.M. *Please call a.s.a.p.* Then a number.

When courting a prospective client, Crawley liked to make it clear he had at least one client who was more important. People despised you if they thought they were your number one client.

"I'm terribly sorry, Safford, but I've got to take this call. In the meantime—order us a round of martinis."

He hustled off to one of the old oak phone booths that could be found on every floor, shut himself in, and dialed. In a moment he had Delbert Yazzie on the other end.

"Mr. Booker Crawley?" The Navajo's voice sounded faint, old, quavering, like it was coming all the way from Timbuktu.

"How are you, Mr. Yazzie?" Crawley kept his voice friendly but distinctly cool.

A silence. "Something unexpected seems to have come up. Have you heard of this preacher, Don T. Spates?"

"I certainly have."

"Well, that sermon of his caused quite a ruckus out here already, just among our own people. As you know, we have a lot of missionary activity on the Navajo Nation. Now I'm hearing it may be causing a problem in Washington, too."

"Yes," said Crawley. "It is."

"It seems to me this could be a serious challenge to the Isabella project."

"Absolutely." Crawley felt a swell of triumph. He had called Spates less than a week ago. This would go down as one of the masterstrokes of his career.

"Well, then, Mr. Crawley, what can we do about it?"

Crawley let a silence build. "Well, I don't know if there's anything I *can* do about it. I was under the impression you no longer required our services."

"Our contract with you isn't up for six weeks. We're paid up until November first."

"Mr. Yazzie, we're not a house rental. That isn't how things work in Washington. I'm sorry. Our work on the Isabella project has, most regretfully, come to a close."

Crackle, hiss. "Losing the government leasing payments for the Isabella project would be a great blow to the Navajo Nation."

Crawley held the receiver silently.

"I'm told Spates has a television program tomorrow night that's going to attack the Isabella project again. And there are rumors Isabella is having problems. One of the scientists committed suicide. Mr. Crawley, I'm going to consult with the Tribal Council and see about getting your contract renewed. We're going to need your help after all."

"I'm very sorry, Mr. Yazzie, but we've filled your slot with another client. Really, I'm *terribly* sorry— but, if you don't mind me saying so, I did mention this possibility. I can't tell you how much I regret

255

this, personally and professionally. Perhaps you could find some other firm to take up your case? I can recommend several."

The phone line spat noises into the silence. Crawley could hear a faint, ghostly conversation going on in the static. Christ, what kind of phone system did they have out there? Probably still using telegraph lines strung up by Kit Carson.

"Another firm would take too much time getting up to speed. We need Crawley and Stratham. We need you."

We need you. Oh God, was this music to his ears or what?

"I'm terribly sorry, Mr. Yazzie. This kind of work involves a lot of one-on-one staff time. Very intensive. And we're booked to the gills. To take this back on . . . It would mean hiring more staff, maybe even leasing more space."

"We would be glad—"

Crawley interrupted. "Mr. Yazzie, I'm truly extremely sorry, but you caught me just before an important luncheon engagement. Would you be kind enough to call me Monday afternoon, say at four, eastern time? I really want to help, and I promise I'll give it serious thought. Tomorrow night I'll watch Spates's show, and you and the Tribal Council should do the same, so we can get a better idea of what we're up against. We'll talk Monday."

He exited the little booth and paused to relight his cigar, inhaling deeply. It was like a sweet, heady perfume. The whole Tribal Council watching the show—what a trip. Spates had better put on a good one.

He swept back into the billiard room, trailing a stream of smoke and feeling seven feet tall, but when he saw Safford crouching at the table, examining all the angles, he felt a twinge of irritation. Time to cut bait.

It was Crawley's shot, and Safford had foolishly parked the cue ball where it could be snookered.

In five minutes, the game was over. Safford had lost—badly.

"Well," said Safford, taking up his martini and smiling gamely. "I'll think twice before playing billiards with you again, Booker." He mustered an artificial chuckle. "Now about your fee," he went on, his voice switching into *High Noon* mode. "There's no way we can even consider the level you mentioned in your letter. It's just not in our budget. Nor does it seem in line with the amount of work required, if I may speak frankly."

Crawley racked his cue and tossed the cigar into the sand bucket. He passed by his martini, not bothering to pick it up, and said, without looking back, "I'm afraid something's come up, Safford, that requires me to cancel our lunch."

He turned, then, to enjoy the expression on the developer's face. The man stood there—cue, cigar, martini, and all—looking like he'd been slapped upside the head.

"If you change your mind about our fee, give me a call," Crawley added as he strode out.

Safford Montague McGrath III wasn't going to get it up tonight, that was for sure.

33

FORD REACHED THE BOTTOM OF THE mesa and rode down the wash in the direction of Blackhorse, Kate coming up and riding alongside him. Halfway down the wash he heard a horse nicker and turned. "Someone's behind us," he said, pulling Ballew to a stop.

Through a thicket of tamarisk came the sound of hooves, and a moment later a tall man pushed through on a big quarterhorse. It was Bia. The Tribal Police lieutenant halted and touched his hat brim. "Out for a pleasure ride?" he asked.

"We're on our way to Blackhorse," said Ford.

Bia smiled. "Nice day for it, not too hot, bit of a breeze." He rested his hands on the saddlehorn. "Paying a visit to Nelson Begay, I imagine."

"That's right," said Ford.

"He's a good man," Bia said. "If I thought there'd be trouble on this protest ride, I'd offer you a Tribal Police presence. But I think that might be counter-productive."

"I agree," said Ford, grateful for the man's insight.

"Better to let them do their thing. I'll keep an eye on them—discreetly."

"Thank you."

Bia nodded and leaned forward. "Long as you're here, mind if I ask a question or two?"

"Shoot away," said Ford.

"This Peter Volkonsky—did he get along with everyone?"

Kate answered. "Mostly."

"No personality clashes? Disagreements?"

"He was a little high-strung, but we were cool with that."

"Was he an important member of the team?"

"One of the most important."

Bia tugged on his hat. "The man throws some clothes in a suitcase and leaves. It's nine o'clock, give or take an hour, moon's already up. Drives about ten minutes, then leaves the road and drives about a quarter mile across the desert. Comes to a deep ravine. Stops the car on an incline near the brink, pulls the emergency brake, turns off the engine, and puts the car in neutral. Then he puts a gun to his head with his right hand, releases the brake with his left hand, fires a bullet into his right temple, and the car rolls over the edge."

He paused. The bar of shade under his hat hid his eyes.

"Is that what you think happened?" asked Kate.

"That's the FBI reconstruction."

"But you don't buy it," said Ford.

From the stripe of heavy shadow beneath his hat, Bia seemed to be looking at him intently. "Do you?"

"I find it a little strange that he rolled his car off a cliff after shooting himself," Ford countered. He thought of the letter. Should he tell Bia? Better to let Lockwood handle it at his end.

"Actually," said Bia, "that to me is a believable element."

"Are you puzzled that he packed a suitcase?"

"Some suicides do that sort of thing. Suicide is often spontaneous."

"So where do you see a problem?"

"Mr. Ford, how'd you know there was a car out there?"

"I saw the fresh tire tracks and the crushed sagebrush—and then there were the buzzards."

"But you didn't see the ravine."

"No."

"Because it isn't visible from anywhere along the road—I checked. How'd Volkonsky know it was there?"

"He was distraught, drove off into the desert to shoot himself, came across the ravine, and decided to make it even more certain." Ford didn't quite believe it himself; he wondered if Bia would.

"That's exactly what the FBI thinks."

"But not what you think."

Bia straightened up and touched his hat. "Be seeing you."

"Wait," said Kate.

Bia paused.

"You don't think one of *us* might have killed him?" Kate asked.

Bia brushed a broken tamarisk twig off his thigh. "Let me put it this way: if it's not suicide, it was a very, very intelligent murder."

With this, he touched his hat brim again, nudged the flanks of his horse with his heels, and passed them by.

Ford thought: *Wardlaw.*

34

BLACKHORSE LOOKED EVEN BLEAKER THAN IT had when Ford had first seen it on Monday—a lonely collection of dust-covered trailers huddled between the flanks of Red Mesa and some low yellow hills. There was the smell of snakeweed in the air. In the patch of dirt where the children had been playing last time, a swing rocked emptily in the wind. Ford wondered where the school was—probably Blue Gap, thirty miles away.

What a place to grow up. And yet, there was a kind of monastic-like emptiness to a Navajo settlement that Ford found appealing. Navajos did not accumulate property the way other people did. Even their houses were spare.

As they rode toward the corrals, Ford spotted Nelson Begay shoeing a sorrel horse snubbed to a cedar post. He was cold-shaping a horseshoe on an anvil with a series of well-aimed blows of a hammer. The blows echoed off the mesa.

Begay laid the hammer and shoe down with a clatter and straightened up, watching them approach.

Ford and Kate halted, dismounted, and tied their horses to a corral fence. Ford raised his hand in greeting, and Begay motioned them over.

"This is Dr. Kate Mercer, assistant director of the Isabella project."

Begay lifted his hat brim to Kate. She stepped over and shook his hand.

"You a physicist?" Begay asked, eyeing her skeptically.

"Yes."

Begay's eyebrows rose slightly. With great deliberation he turned his back, put his shoulder into the horse's flank, pulled up the hind leg, and began matching the shoe to the hoof. Then he placed it on the anvil and gave it a few more whacks.

As Ford stood there pondering Navajo cultural sensitivities, Kate said to Begay's blue plaid back, "We were hoping to talk to you."

"Then talk."

"I'd prefer not to talk to a man's back."

Begay dropped the hoof and straightened up. "Well, now, ma'am, I didn't ask you to come, and right now I happen to be busy."

"Don't 'ma'am' me. I've got a Ph.D."

Begay coughed, laid down his tools, and faced her without expression.

"Well?" she said. "Are we going to stand here in the hot sun or are you going to invite us in for coffee?"

Exasperation mingled with amusement spread across Begay's face. "All right, all right, come on in."

Once more Ford found himself in the spare living room with the military photographs on the walls. As Begay poured coffee, Ford and Kate sat down on the brown sofa. When their mugs were full, Begay settled into the broken Barcalounger. "Are all lady scientists like you?"

"Like what?"

"Like my grandmother. You don't take no for an answer, do you? You could be Diné yourself. In fact"—he leaned forward, scrutinizing her face—"you aren't—?"

"I'm half Japanese."

"Right." He leaned back. "All right. Here we are."

Ford waited for Kate. She always had a knack with people, as she was already proving with Begay. He was curious to see how she'd handle him.

"I've been wondering," Kate said, "what, exactly, is a medicine man?"

"I'm a kind of doctor."

"How so?"

"I perform ceremonies. I cure people."

"What kind of ceremonies?"

Begay didn't answer.

"I'm sorry if I seem nosy," Kate said, giving him a dazzling smile. "It's sort of my profession."

"Well, I don't mind the question, as long as it isn't idle curiosity. I perform several ceremonies—the Blessing Way, the Enemy Way, and the Falling Star Way."

"What do the ceremonies do?"

263

Begay grunted, sipped his coffee, eased back. "The Blessing Way restores balance and beauty in a person's life—after troubles with drugs or alcohol, time in jail. The Enemy Way is for soldiers returning from war. It's a ceremony that removes the taint of killing. Because when you kill, a little bit of that evil clings to you, even though it's war and you did it lawfully. If you don't do an Enemy Way, that evil will eat you up."

"Our doctors call it posttraumatic stress disorder," said Kate.

"Yes," said Begay. "Like my nephew, Lorenzo, who went to Iraq . . . He'll never be the same."

"Does the Enemy Way cure PTSD?"

"In most cases."

"That's extremely interesting. . . . And the Falling Star Way?"

"That's a ceremony we don't speak about," said Begay curtly.

"Would you ever consider doing a ceremony for a non-Navajo?"

"Why, you need one?"

Kate laughed. "I could use a good Blessing Way."

Begay looked offended. "This is not something you do lightly. There's a lot of preparation involved and you have to *believe* in it for it to work. A lot of *Bilagaana* have trouble believing things they can't see with their own eyes. Or they're New Agers who don't like the hard preparation—the sweat lodge, fasting, sexual abstinence. But I wouldn't deny the ceremony to a *Bilagaana* just because they're white."

"I didn't mean to sound flippant," she said. "It's just . . . For a long time, I've been wondering what the point of it all is. What we're doing here."

He nodded. "Join the club."

After a long silence Kate said, "Thank you for sharing that with us."

At this Begay leaned back and rested his hands on his jeans. "In Diné culture, we believe in exchanging information. I've told you something about my work. Now I'd like to hear something of yours. Mr. Ford here tells me that over there at the Isabella project, you're investigating something called the Big Bang."

"That's right."

"I been thinking about that. If the universe was created in a Big Bang, what came before?"

"Nobody knows. Many physicists believe there was nothing. In fact, there wasn't even a 'before.' Existence itself began with the Big Bang."

Begay whistled. "So what caused the Bang?"

"That's a difficult question to explain to a non-physicist."

"Try me."

"The theory of quantum mechanics says things can *just happen,* without a cause."

"You mean you don't know the cause."

"No, I mean there *is* no cause. The sudden creation of the universe from nothing may not violate any laws or be unnatural or unscientific in any way. Before, there was absolutely nothing. No space, no time, no existence. And then, it just *happened*—and existence came into being."

Begay stared at her, then shook his head. "You're talking like my nephew, Lorenzo. Smart boy, full scholarship to Columbia University, studied mathematics. It screwed him up—the whole *Bilagaana* world messed up his head. Dropped out, went to Iraq, came back believing in nothing. And I mean *nothing*. Now he sweeps out a damn church for a living. Or at least he used to, till he ran off."

"You blame science for that?" Kate said.

Begay shook his head. "No, no, I'm not blaming science. It's just that hearing you talk about how the world came into being out of nothing, it sounded like the kind of nonsense he spouts. . . . How could the Creation *just happen?*"

"I'll try to explain. Stephen Hawking proposed the idea that before the Big Bang, time didn't exist. Without time, there can't be any kind of definable existence. Hawking was able to show mathematically that nonexistence still has some kind of spatial potential, and that under certain weird conditions space can turn into time and vice versa. He showed that if a tiny, tiny bit of space morphed into time, the appearance of time would trigger the Big Bang—because suddenly there could be movement, there could be cause and effect, there could be real space and real energy. Time makes it all possible. To us, the Big Bang looks like an explosion of space, time, and matter from a single point. But here's the really weird part. If you peer into that first

266

tiny fraction of a second, you'll see there wasn't a beginning at all—time seems to have always existed. So here we have a theory of the Big Bang that seems to say two contradictory things: first, that time did not always exist; and second, that time has no beginning. Which means that time is eternal. Both are true. And if you *really* think about it, when time didn't exist, there could be no difference between eternity and a second. So once time came into existence, it had always existed. There was never a time when it didn't exist."

Begay shook his head. "That's just plain crazy."

An awkward silence settled in the shabby living room.

"Do the Navajo have a creation story?" Kate asked.

"Yes. We call it the Diné Bahané. It's not written down. You have to memorize it. It takes nine nights to chant it. That's the Blessing Way I told you about— it's a chant that tells the story of the creation of the world. You chant it in the presence of a sick person and the story heals them."

"You memorized it?"

"Sure did, my uncle taught it to me. Took five years."

"About the same as my Ph.D.," said Kate.

Begay looked pleased by the comparison.

"Will you chant a few lines?"

Begay said, "The Blessing Way shouldn't be chanted casually."

"I'm not sure we're having a casual conversation."

He looked at her intently. "Yes, maybe so."

Begay closed his eyes. When he opened his mouth, his voice quavered and was pitched high, as he chanted in a strange five-tone scale. The non-Western harmonics and the sounds of the Navajo words—a few still familiar, but most not—filled Ford with a longing for something he had no name for.

After about five minutes, Begay stopped. His eyes were damp. "That's how it begins," he said quietly. "It's the most beautiful poetry ever written, at least in my opinion."

"Can you translate it for us?" asked Kate.

"I was hoping you wouldn't ask me that. Well, here goes." He took a deep breath.

Of it he is thinking, he is thinking.
Long ago of it, he is thinking.
Of how darkness will come into being, he is thinking.
Of how Earth will come into being, he is thinking.
Of how blue sky will come into being, he is thinking.
Of how yellow dawn will come into being, he is thinking.
Of how evening twilight will come into being, he is thinking.
Of dark moss dew he is thinking, of horses he is thinking.
Of order he is thinking, of beauty he is thinking.
Of how everything will increase without decreasing, he is thinking.

He stopped. "It doesn't sound good in English, but that's sort of how it goes."

"Who is this 'he'?" Kate asked.

"The Creator."

Kate smiled. "Tell me, Mr. Begay: Who created the Creator?"

Begay shrugged. "The stories don't tell us that."

"What came before Him?"

"Who knows?"

Kate said, "It seems that both of our creation stories have origin problems."

From the kitchen sink, a drip of water splatted into the silence, then another, and another. Finally Begay rose and limped over to turn it off. "This was an interesting conversation," he said, returning. "But there's a real world out there, and in it is a horse who needs new shoes."

They stepped out into the brilliant sun. As they walked back to the corrals, Ford said, "One of the things we wanted to tell you, Mr. Begay, is that tomorrow we're doing a run of Isabella. Everyone will be underground. When you and your riders arrive, I'll be the only one there to meet you."

"We aren't doing a 'meet and greet.'"

"I didn't want you to think we were being disrespectful."

Begay patted his horse and stroked his flank. "Look, Mr. Ford, we got our own plans. We're going to set up a sweat lodge, do some ceremonies, talk to the ground. We'll be peaceful. When the police come to arrest us, we'll go quietly."

"The police aren't going to come," said Ford.

Begay looked disappointed. "No police?"

"Should we call them?" Ford asked dryly.

Begay smiled. "I suppose I had a fantasy of being arrested for the cause." He turned his back and plucked up the horse's leg with one hand, the paring knife with the other. "Easy, boy," he murmured, as he began to pare and trim.

Ford glanced at Kate. On the ride back, he would come clean.

35

BY THE TIME FORD AND KATE reached the top of the mesa, the sun was so low, it seemed to wobble at the horizon. As they rode quietly through the blooming snakeweed, Ford tried for the hundredth time to frame what he wanted to say. If he didn't start talking, they'd be back at Isabella—and he'd have missed his chance.

"Kate?" he began, riding up alongside her.

She turned.

"I asked you on this ride for another reason besides visiting Begay."

She gazed at him, her hair like black gold in the sunlight, her eyes already narrowing in suspicion. "Why do I have a feeling this is something I'm not going to like?"

"I'm here partly as an anthropologist, and partly for another reason."

"I should've guessed. So what's the mission, Secret Agent Man?"

"I . . . was sent here to investigate the Isabella project."

"In other words, you're a spy."

He took a deep breath. "Yes."

"Does Hazelius know?"

"Nobody knows."

"I see . . . And you *befriended* me because I was a quick route to the information you needed."

"Kate—"

"No, wait—it's worse: they *hired* you knowing of our past relationship, in the hopes that you could blow on those old coals and coax the information out of me."

As usual, Kate had figured it all out even before he could finish.

"Kate, when I agreed to this assignment, I didn't realize . . ."

"Didn't realize what? That I'd be such a sucker?"

"I didn't realize . . . that there'd be a complication."

She tugged her horse to a halt and stared at him. "Complication? What do you mean?"

Ford's face burned. Why was life suddenly so incomprehensible? How could he answer her?

She tossed her hair and brushed her cheek roughly with a gloved hand. "You're *still* in the CIA, aren't you?"

"No. I quit three years ago when my wife . . . My wife . . ." He couldn't say it.

"Yeah, *sure* you quit. So—did you tell them our secret?"

"No."

"Bullshit. Of course you told them. I trusted you, opened up to you—and now we're all screwed."

"I didn't tell them."

"I wish I could believe you." She gave her horse a jab and trotted away.

"Kate, please listen—" Ballew broke into a trot, too. Ford bounced up and down, one hand gripping the saddlehorn.

Kate gave her horse another nudge and it began to canter. "Get away from me."

Ballew broke into a canter, unasked. Ford clutched the saddlehorn, his body joggling around like a rag doll's. "Kate, *please*—slow down, we need to talk—"

She kicked her horse into a gallop, and again Ballew thundered after her. The two horses whipped along the mesa top, hooves pounding the ground. Ford held on for dear life, terrified.

"Kate!" he shouted. A rein slipped from his hand. He lunged forward to snag it, but Ballew stepped on the dragging rein and jerked up short. Ford cartwheeled off the back of the horse and landed on a carpet of snakeweed.

When he came to, he was staring at the sky, wondering where the hell he was.

Kate's face loomed into his field of view. Her hat was gone and her hair was wild, her face in an agony of concern.

"Wyman? My God, are you all right?"

He gasped and coughed as air returned to his lungs. He tried to sit up.

"No, no. Lie down." When he sank back, he felt his head settling into her hat and realized she must have folded it up for a pillow. He waited for the stars to clear from his eyes and memory to return.

"Oh my God, Wyman, for a moment there I thought you were dead."

He couldn't gather his thoughts. He breathed in, out, in again, sucking in air.

She had taken off her glove, and her cool hand patted his face. "Did you break anything? Do you hurt? Oh, you're bleeding!" She slipped off her bandanna and dabbed at his forehead.

His head began to clear. "Let me sit up."

"No, no. Stay still." She pressed the bandanna firmly against his skin. "You hit your head. You might have a concussion."

"I don't think so." He groaned. "What an idiot I must seem. Falling off a horse like a sack of potatoes."

"You don't know how to ride, that's all. It was my fault. I never should have run off like that. You just make me so *mad* sometimes."

The throbbing in his head began to subside. "I didn't betray your secret. And I'm not going to."

She looked at him. "Why? Isn't that what you were hired to do?"

"Screw what I was hired to do."

She dabbed at his cut. "You need to rest a little more."

He lay still. "Aren't I supposed to get back on the horse?"

"Ballew took off for the barn. Don't be embarrassed—everyone falls off eventually."

Her hand rested on his cheek. He lay still for a moment longer, and then slowly sat up. "I'm sorry."

After a moment, she said, "You mentioned something about a wife. I . . . didn't know you were married."

"Not anymore."

"Must be hard to be married to the CIA."

He said quickly, "It wasn't that. She died."

Kate covered her mouth. "Oh—I'm *sorry*. What a stupid thing for me to say."

"It's all right. We were partners in the CIA. She got killed in Cambodia. Car bomb."

"Oh my God, Wyman. I'm *so* sorry."

He hadn't thought he'd be able to tell her. But it came out so easily. "So I left the CIA and went into a monastery. I was looking for something; I thought it was God. But I didn't find Him. I wasn't cut out to be a monk. I left and had to earn a living, so I hung out my shingle as a PI, got hired for this job. Which I never should have taken. End of story."

"Who are you working for? Lockwood?"

He nodded. "He knows you're hiding something and he wanted me to find out what it is. He says he's going to pull the plug on Isabella in two days."

"Jesus." She laid that cool hand again on his face.

"I'm sorry I lied to you. If I'd known what I was getting into, I never would have taken this assignment. I didn't count on . . ." His voice trailed off.

"What?"

He didn't answer.

"You didn't count on what?" She leaned over him, her shadow crossing his face, her faint scent drifting in.

Ford said, "On falling in love with you again."

In the distance, an owl hooted in the dimming light.

"You're serious?" she said finally.

Ford nodded.

Slowly, Kate brought her face closer to his. She didn't kiss him—she just looked. Astonished. "You never said that to me when we were going out."

"I didn't?"

She shook her head. "The word 'love' wasn't in your vocabulary. Why do you think we broke up?"

He blinked. *That* was the reason? "What about me going into the CIA?"

"I could've lived with that."

"You want . . . to try again?" Ford asked.

She looked at him, the golden light all around her. She had never looked so beautiful. "Yes."

Then she kissed him, slowly, lightly, deliciously. He leaned forward to kiss her but she stopped him with a gentle hand on his chest. "It's almost dark. We've got a ways to walk. And . . ."

"And what?"

She continued looking down at him, smiling. "Never mind," she said, leaning down to kiss him again, and then again, her soft breasts settling against him. Her hand strayed to his shirt, and she began unbuttoning it, one button at a time. She slid the shirt open and began unbuckling his belt, her kisses becoming deeper and softer, as if her mouth was melting into his, while the shadows of evening grew ever longer on the desert floor.

36

PASTOR RUSS EDDY COAXED HIS TRUCK off the mesa road and drove toward a fin of sandstone, behind which he could hide the vehicle. It was a clear night, with a gibbous moon and a scattering of stars speckling the night sky. The truck lurched and rattled across the barren rock, a loose fender banging with each heave. If he didn't borrow the arc welder at the service station in Blue Gap one of these days, the fender would fall off, but it made him feel so ashamed, always borrowing the Navajos' tools and wheedling gas out of them. He kept having to remind himself that he was bringing these people the greatest gift of all, salvation—if only they would accept it.

All day he'd been thinking about Hazelius. The more he listened to the man's words playing over and over in his head, the more verses from the First Epistle of John seemed to apply: *"Ye have heard that antichrist shall come. . . . He is antichrist, that denieth the Father and the Son. . . . This is that spirit of antichrist. . . ."*

The memory of Lorenzo, sprawled on the ground, flashed into his head, the clots of living blood that wouldn't sink into the sand . . . He winced—why did that hideous image keep popping up? He forced it out with an audible groan.

He eased the truck behind the fin of sandstone until it was well hidden from the road. The engine died with a cough. He yanked on the emergency brake and blocked the wheels with loose rocks. Then he pocketed the keys, took a deep breath, and set off walking down the road. The moon was bright enough that he could see where he was going without the flashlight.

He felt a stronger sense of purpose than ever before. God had called him and he had said *yes.* Everything until now, all the troubles in his life, had been mere prelude. God had been testing him and he had passed. The final test had been Lorenzo. It had been God's sign to him that he was readying him for something big. Very big.

The Lord had guided him in Piñon that afternoon. First a full tank of gas—free. Next, a turned-around tourist trying to find Flagstaff thanked him with a ten-dollar bill. Then he learned from the gas station clerk that Bia was investigating the death at the Isabella project as a murder—not a suicide. Murder!

A coyote howled in the distance, answered by another even farther away. They sounded like the lonely, lost cries of the damned. Eddy reached the

277

edge of the bluffs and scrambled down the trail into Nakai Valley. The dark hump of Nakai Rock rose on his right like a hunchbacked demon. Below, a scattering of lights marked the village; the windows of the old trading post cast boxes of light into the darkness.

Keeping close to the rocks and junipers, he moved toward the trading post. He did not know what he was looking for, or how he would find it. His only plan was to wait for a sign from God. God would show him the way.

The faint sound of piano music drifted through the desert night. He reached the valley floor, easing through the shadows of the cottonwoods, and sprinted across the grass to the back wall of the trading post. Through the old logs, chinked with plaster, he could hear muffled conversation. With infinite care he approached a window and peeked inside. Some scientists sat around a coffee table, talking intensely, as if arguing. Hazelius sat playing the piano.

At the sight of the man who might be the Antichrist, Russ felt a rush of fear and rage. He hunkered beneath the window and tried to hear what people were saying, but the man was playing so loudly, Eddy could hear almost nothing. Then, over the piano notes, through the double-paned window, down through the chilly autumn air to where Russ huddled on the grass, burst a single word, in the voice of one of the scientists: *God.*

Again, in a different voice: *God.*

The screen door banged, and two voices drifted around the corner and into his ears: one high and tense, the other slow, careful.

His heart pounding, Eddy crawled forward in the dark until he was just around the corner from the front door. He listened, hardly breathing.

". . . one thing, Tony, I wanted to ask you—sort of confidentially . . ." The man lowered his voice. Eddy didn't catch the rest, but he could not risk moving closer.

". . . we're the only two nonscientists here . . ."

They walked out into the darkness. Eddy shrank back, and the voices dissolved into indistinctness. He could see the two dark shapes, strolling down the road. He waited, and then darted across the road and into the trees, where he pressed himself against the gnarly trunk of a cottonwood.

Air brushed past his face. It could have been the Holy Ghost, changing itself into a breeze in order to carry the voices of the shadow figures toward him.

". . . about these criminal charges, but I don't have anything to do with the operation of Isabella."

The deeper voice answered, "Don't kid yourself. Like I said before, you'll take the fall with the rest of us."

"But I'm just the psychologist."

"You're still part of the deception . . ."

Deception? Eddy moved through the darkness to another position.

". . . how in hell did we get into this mess?" said the high voice.

The answer was too low for Eddy to hear.

"I can't believe the damn computer is claiming to be God. . . . It's like something out of a science-fiction novel. . . ."

Another low reply. Eddy was trying so hard to listen and understand that he held his breath.

The men walked into the scattering of lights that marked the living quarters. Eddy scuttled forward like a spider as their phrases rose and fell with the breeze.

". . . God in the machine . . . driving Volkonsky over the edge . . ." The high voice again.

". . . waste of time speculating . . . ," came the gruff answer.

The conversation continued more softly. Eddy thought he would go crazy not being able to hear. He took a risk and scurried closer. The two men had halted at the end of a driveway. In the soft yellow light the bigger one looked impatient, as if trying to get away from the nervous one. The voices were clearer now.

". . . saying things like no God I ever heard of. It's a lot of New Age bullshit. 'Existence is me thinking'— give me a break. And Edelstein buying it. Well, he's a mathematician—he's by definition a weirdo. I mean, the fellow keeps rattlesnakes as pets. . . ." The high-pitched voice rose, as if by talking more loudly, he could keep the big guy from moving on.

The big guy shifted, so that Eddy could see his face. It was the security man.

The man's low voice said something that sounded like "check around before hitting the sack." A handshake, and the little guy walked down the driveway toward his house, while the security guy stared down the road one way, then the other, then toward the cottonwoods, as if scouting the scene, deciding which way to begin his patrol.

Please, Lord, please. Eddy's heart was beating so strongly, he could hear the pulse of his own blood whooshing in his ears. Finally the man walked down the road in the other direction. Moving with exquisite caution to keep from crunching fallen twigs, Eddy passed slowly through the cottonwoods and felt his way up the dark trail and out of the valley.

Only when he was driving back down the Dugway did he permit himself to whoop out loud with giddiness. He had exactly what Reverend Spates needed. It would be the middle of the night in Virginia, but surely the reverend wouldn't mind being woken up for this. Surely not.

37

ON FRIDAY, AT THE BREAK OF dawn, Nelson Begay leaned against the doorframe of the chapter house and watched the first horse trailers arrive. The horses were stirring the dust up into golden fireclouds, the riders unloading their horses and sad-

281

dling up amid the jingling of spurs and slapping of leather. Begay's own horse, Winter, was already saddled and ready to ride, tied in the shade of the only live piñon in sight, eating from a morral. Begay wished he could blame the *Bilagaana* for all the dead piñons, but as far as he could tell, the television news was right: bark beetles and drought hadn't needed any help.

Maria Atcitty, the chapter president, came up. "Nice turnout," she said.

"Better than I thought. You coming?"

Atcitty laughed. "Anything to get me out of the office."

"Where's your horse?"

"Are you nuts? I'm driving."

Begay went back to watching the motley collection of horseflesh gathering for the protest ride. Aside from a couple of fine quarterhorses and an Arab, they were mostly reservation canners, unshod, skinny, white-eyed. The scene reminded him of his uncle Silvers's place over at Toh Ateen. Silvers had taught him the Blessing Way, but he'd also been a bronc rider, working the Santa Fe–Amarillo rodeo circuit until he busted his back. Afterward he kept a ragged bunch of horses for the kids to ride; that's where Begay had learned all he knew about horses.

He shook his head. It seemed like such a long time ago. Uncle Silvers was gone, the old ways were dying, and the kids nowadays couldn't ride or speak the language. Begay was the only one old Uncle Silvers had been able to talk into learning the Blessing Way.

The ride was more than a protest about the Isabella project; it was about recapturing a way of life that was rapidly disappearing. It was about their traditions, their language, and their land, about taking responsibility for their destiny.

A decrepit Isuzu pickup pulled up, pulling a stock trailer too big for it. With a whoop, a rangy man hopped out, wearing a shirt with the sleeves cut off. He pumped one skinny arm into the air, hollered again, and went around to unload the horse.

"Willy Becenti's here," said Atcitty.

"Hard to miss Willy."

The horse, already saddled, stepped down onto the dirt. Becenti brought him around and tied him to the tongue of the trailer.

"He's packing."

"I see it."

"You going to let him bring that?"

Begay considered that for a moment. Willy was excitable, but he had a good heart and was solid as a rock when he wasn't drinking. There'd be no liquor on this ride—that was one rule Begay was going to enforce.

"Willy'll be all right."

"What if things get nasty?" asked Maria.

"Things aren't going to get nasty. I met a couple of the scientists yesterday. Nothing's going to happen."

Atcitty said, "Which ones did you meet?"

"That one who calls himself an anthropologist, Ford, and the assistant director, a woman named Mercer."

Atcitty nodded. "Same ones I met." A moment passed and she said, "You sure this is a good idea, this protest ride?"

"I guess we'll find out, won't we?"

38

KEN DOLBY LOOKED AT HIS WATCH. Six o'clock P.M. He turned back to the screen and checked the temperature on the bad magnet. It was holding steady, well within the tolerance range. He moused through several pages of software controls for Isabella. All systems were go, everything running perfectly. Power was at 80 percent.

It was a perfect night for a run. With Isabella diverting a large percentage of the megawattage of the RM-West Grid for its own use, even the smallest disruption—a lightning strike, blown transformer, downed lines—could cause a cascade. But it was a cool evening over much of the Southwest, the ACs were turned off, there were no storms and little wind.

Dolby had a feeling in his gut—that tonight, they'd solve the problem. Tonight was the night Isabella would shine to perfection.

"Ken, bring it up to eighty-five," said Hazelius from his leather seat at the center of the Bridge.

Dolby glanced over at St. Vincent, monitoring the power flows. The leprechaun-like man gave him a thumbs-up and winked.

"Gotcha."

At the very edge of perceptibility he could feel the faint vibration that marked the immense flow of power. The two beams of protons and antiprotons, circulating in opposite directions at unimaginable speed, still had not been brought into contact. That would happen at 90 percent power. Once they were brought into contact, it took a lot more power, a lot more time, and an exquisite level of fine-tuning to bring the system up to 100 percent.

The power gauges rose smoothly to 85 percent.

"Lovely night for a run," said St. Vincent.

Dolby nodded, glad that St. Vincent was handling the power flows. He was a quiet, agreeable old fellow who seldom said a word, but he handled power the way a conductor handles a symphony orchestra, with exactness and great finesse. All without breaking a sweat.

"Eighty-five percent," Dolby said.

"Alan?" asked Hazelius. "How are the servers?"

"Everything fine over here."

Hazelius went around the room for perhaps the fiftieth time, soliciting answers from the team. So far, it was a textbook run.

Dolby reviewed his systems. Everything was working according to specs. The only glitch was the warm magnet, but by "warm" they were talking about only three one-hundredths of a degree warmer than it should be.

Isabella was settling in at 85 percent, while Rae Chen made tiny adjustments to the beams. Glancing idly around the room, Dolby thought about the group Hazelius had brought together. Take Edelstein, for example. Dolby suspected he might be even smarter than Hazelius—but a kind of weird-smart. Edelstein was a little scary, like his brain was half-alien. And what was it with the rattlesnakes? A weird frigging hobby. Then there was Corcoran, who looked like Darryl Hannah. She wasn't really his type, too tall and abrasive. Way too pretty and too blond to be as smart as she obviously was . . . It was a brilliant group, even the robot Cecchini, who always seemed to be on the verge of going postal. Except for Innes. He was an earnest guy who tried hard but didn't have the candlepower to illuminate much more than the well-trodden middle of the room. How could Hazelius take the man and his little rap sessions so seriously? Or was Hazelius just going along with DOE regs? Were all psychologists like Innes, spinning their neat little theories without a shred of empirical evidence? He was a man who saw everything and understood nothing. Innes reminded Dolby of that pop-psychology-spouting truck driver his mother had dated after his father's death, a decent guy who double-chinned you half to death with advice from the latest self-improvement bestseller.

Then there was Rae Chen. She was smart as hell but

totally laid-back about it. Someone had said she'd been a champion skateboarder as a kid. She looked like a Berkeley free-love type, fun, easy, uncomplicated. Or was she really uncomplicated? It was hard to tell with Asians. Either way, he'd love to get something going with her. He glanced over at her, bent over her console so intently, her black hair hanging down like a waterfall, and he imagined her without clothes. . . .

Hazelius's voice broke in.

"We're ready to go to ninety, Ken."

"Sure thing."

"Alan? When we've stabilized at ninety, I want you to be ready to switch over the p5 595s all at once, ganged and linked."

Edelstein nodded.

Dolby moved the sliders, watched Isabella respond. This was it. This was the night. Everything in his life had led up to this point. He felt the deep vibration of the power as it increased. It was like the whole mountain was energized. It purred like a Bentley. God, how he loved this machine. *His* machine.

39

FROM THE BACK BEDROOM OF HIS bungalow, Ford saw the first of the protest riders appear on the rim behind Nakai Rock, silhouetted against the sunset. He raised his binoculars and identified Nelson Begay astride a paint horse, with a dozen other riders.

He turned his head and felt a throb from his fall the evening before. Since then, he and Kate had hardly been able to exchange a word, she had been so busy getting ready for the run.

The light on his satellite phone blinked, right on schedule. He picked it up.

"News?" Lockwood asked.

"Nothing specific. Everyone's in the Bunker, starting another run of Isabella. I'm waiting to go meet the protest riders."

"I wish you could have headed that off."

"Trust me, it's better this way. Did you look into this Joe Blitz thing?"

"There are hundreds of Joe Blitzes out there—people, companies, places, what have you. I culled a list of some that struck me as being possibilities. I thought I'd run a few past you."

"Go ahead."

"First of all, Joe Blitz is the name of a GI Joe action figure."

"That could be an allusion to Wardlaw—Volkonsky hated him. What else?"

"Broadway producer of the forties who did *Garbage Can Follies* and *Crater Lake Cut-up*. Two musicals, one about tomcats, the other about a nudist colony. Both flops."

"Keep going."

"Joe Blitz, bankrupt Ford dealership in Ohio . . . Joe Blitz State Park, Medford, Oregon . . . Joe Blitz Memorial Hockey Rink, Ontario, Canada . . . Joe

Blitz, sci-fi writer in the thirties and forties . . . Joe Blitz, developer who built the Mausleer Building in Chicago . . . Joe Blitz, cartoonist."

"Tell me about the writer."

"A Joe Blitz published science fiction potboilers in several pulp magazines in the early forties."

"Titles?"

"A whole bunch of them. Let's see . . . 'Sea Fangs' and 'Man-Killers of the Air,' among others."

"Did he publish any novels?"

"As far as we could tell, just a lot of stories."

"What about Joe Blitz the cartoonist?"

"Did a syndicated strip in the late fifties about a fat slob and a toy poodle. Sort of like *Garfield*. Never a big success. Let's see . . . I've got about two hundred more, everything from the name of a funeral home to a recipe for smoking fish."

Ford sighed. "This is like looking for a needle in a haystack when we don't even know what the needle looks like. What about that Aunt Natasha?"

"Volkonsky had no Aunt Natasha. It might have been a kind of joke—you know, every Russian has an Aunt Natasha and an Uncle Boris."

Ford glanced out the window at the riders entering the valley. "Looks like the note's a dead end."

"Seems so."

"I've got to go—the riders are coming down into the valley."

"Call me as soon as the run's over," said Lockwood.

Ford put away the satellite phone, locked up the

289

briefcase, and went outside. He heard a distant engine, and a battered pickup appeared where the road entered the valley. It topped the rise and came down, followed by a white van with KREZ on the side and a satellite dish on top.

Ford walked over and stood in the trees at the edge of the fields, watching Begay and a dozen riders on lathered horses approach. The KREZ van stopped and a couple of television people got out and began setting up a shot of the riders. A large woman stepped out from the pickup—Maria Atcitty.

As the riders reached the fields, the cameraman started rolling tape. One rider broke away and galloped ahead, giving a whoop of triumph and whirling a bandanna in an upraised fist. Ford recognized Willy Becenti, the man who had lent him money. Some of the other riders urged their horses into a run, and Begay followed suit. They tore across the fields, whipping past the camera, and pulled up in the dirt parking lot outside the old trading post, not far from Ford.

When Begay dismounted, the reporter for KREZ came up, high-fived him, and started setting up the equipment for an interview.

Now the others were coming up. More high fives. The video lights went on, and the reporter began to interview Begay. The others stood around watching.

Ford strolled out from the trees and walked across the grass.

All eyes turned in his direction. The reporter approached him, holding out the mike.

"What is your name, sir?"

Ford could see the camera was rolling. "Wyman Ford."

"Are you a scientist?"

"No, I'm the liaison between the Isabella project and the local communities."

"You aren't liaising very well," said the reporter. "You got a big protest on your hands."

"I know it."

"So what do you think?"

"I think Mr. Begay here is right."

There was a brief silence. "Right about what?"

"A lot of what he's been saying—that Isabella is frightening local people, that its presence isn't the economic boon it was supposed to be, that the scientists have been too aloof."

Another brief, confounded silence. "So what are you going to do about it?"

"To start with, I'm going to listen. That's why I'm here right now. Then I'm going to do what I can to make things right. We got off to a bad start with the community, but I promise you, things will change."

"Bullshit!" came a cry—Willy Becenti, striding over from where he had staked out his horse in the field.

"Cut!" The reporter turned to Becenti. "Hey, Willy, I'm trying to do an interview here, do you mind?"

"He's full of bullshit."

"I can't air anything you say if you use words like that."

Becenti stopped short, staring at Ford. His face bloomed with recognition. "Hey—it's you!"

"Hello, Willy," said Ford, extending his hand.

Willy ignored it. "You're one of them!"

"Yes."

"You owe me twenty bucks, man."

Ford reached for his wallet.

Becenti flushed triumphantly. "You keep your money. I don't want it."

"Willy, I'm hoping we can solve these problems working together."

"Bull*shit*. You see up there?" Becenti pointed a skinny arm vaguely up the valley, exposing a tattoo. "There's ruins up there in those bluffs. Graves. You're desecrating our ancestors' graves."

The camera was rolling again. "Your response, Mr. Ford?" said the reporter, shoving the microphone back in his face.

Ford refrained from pointing out that they were Anasazi ruins. "If we could have some help identifying exactly where the graves are, we could protect—"

"They're all over! Everywhere! And the spirits of the dead are unhappy and wandering around. Something bad's going to happen. I can feel it. Can't you feel it?" Becenti looked around. "Can't you *feel* it?"

There were nods, murmurs.

"*Chindii* are all around, skinwalkers. Ever since Peabody Coal gouged out the soul of Red Mesa, it's been a bad, *bad* place."

"A bad place," people repeated.

"This is just one more example of the white man coming in and taking Indian land. That's what this is. Am I right?"

Louder murmurs, nods of agreement.

"Willy, you have every right to feel as you do," said Ford. "But let me say in our defense that part of the problem is, the Navajo tribal government made this deal without consulting the local folks."

"The Navajo tribal government is just a bunch of assholes hired by the *Bilagaana* to do the old step-and-fetch-it. We didn't have no *Navajo tribal government* before the *Bilagaana* came."

"You can't reverse that. Neither can I. But we can work together to make things better. How about it?"

"Yeah, well, my answer to that is screw you!" Becenti advanced threateningly. Ford held his ground, and they faced each other. Becenti breathed hard, his skinny rib cage heaved, his stringy arm muscles flexed.

Ford kept himself loose, relaxed. "Willy, I'm on your side."

"Don't patronize me, *Bilagaana!*" He was about two-thirds Ford's size and half his weight, but he looked like he might start swinging at any time. Ford glanced at Begay and saw from the medicine man's indifferent face that he would let the situation evolve on its own.

The camera continued filming.

Becenti swept his arm out across the grass. "Look

at this. You *Bilagaana* take away our mesa and drill thousands of feet through the rock so you can water your effing fields, while my aunt Emma has to drive thirty miles one way to haul water for her grandkids and sheep. How long do you think it will be before the wells in Blue Gap or Blackhorse go dry? And what about hantavirus? Everyone knows there was never any hantavirus until something happened over there at Fort Wingate."

Several riders called out their agreement to the old conspiracy theory.

"For all we know, something in Isabella is poisoning us already. Any day now, our kids might start dying." He jabbed a dusty finger into Ford's chest, just below the breastbone. "You know what that will make you, *Bilagaana*? A murderer."

"Let's keep it cool, Willy. Peaceful and respectful."

"Peaceful? Respectful? Is that why you people burned our hogans and cornfields? Why you raped our women? Is that why you sent us on the Long Walk to Fort Sumner—in order to be peaceful and respectful?"

Ford knew from Ramah that Navajos still talked about the Long Walk of the 1860s, even if, to the rest of the country, it was ancient history, long forgotten. "I wish to God there was some way to undo history," he said, with more feeling than he intended.

A cheap .22 appeared in Willy's hand from out of his jeans. Ford tensed, ready to move fast.

Begay stepped in at once. "Daswood, turn the camera off," he said sharply.

The reporter complied.

"Willy, put the gun away."

"Screw you, Nelson, I'm here to fight, not talk."

Begay replied in a low voice. "We're going to set up a sweat lodge in the field. We're going to be here all night, performing *peaceful* ceremonies. We're going to take back this land spiritually with our prayers. This is a time for prayer and contemplation, not confrontation."

"I thought this was a *protest,* not a damn squaw dance," Becenti said, but he nevertheless slipped the gun back into his pants pocket.

Begay pointed to the high-tension wires converging toward the edge of the mesa, a half mile away. "Our fight isn't with this man. It's with *that.*"

The power lines hummed and crackled, the sound faint but distinct.

"Sounds like your machine's up and running," said Begay, turning back to Ford, his eyes neutral. "I guess this would be a good time for you to leave us to do our thing."

Ford nodded, turned, and walked toward the Bunker.

"That's right, get out of here," Becenti yelled after him, "before I put a cap in your *Bilagaana* ass!"

As Ford approached the Isabella security gate, the crackling and humming of the powerlines got louder, and he felt a faint shiver run down his spine at the eerie noise, which seemed almost alive.

40

AT FIVE MINUTES TO EIGHT, BOOKER Crawley settled in front of the TV set in the cozy, cherry-paneled den of his house on Dumbarton Street, Georgetown, feeling an extraordinary sense of anticipation. When Spates had said he would give good value for his money, he wasn't kidding. The Sunday sermon had been a shotgun blast. Now the *Roundtable America* show would unload the second barrel. Amazing that all it had taken was a single phone call and a couple of cash payments. There wasn't even anything illegal about it, just charitable giving to a 501(c)(3)—tax deductible.

The lobbyist cupped a snifter in his hand, warming it, and took a sip of his customary after-dinner Calvados. With a blast of patriotic music, the logo of *Roundtable America* came on amid a digital swirl of American flags, eagles, and patriotic emblems. Then a cherry roundtable appeared, with an image of the Capitol in the background. At the roundtable sat Spates, with a serious, concerned expression. His guest sat across from him, a white-haired man in a suit, with a deep face, shaggy eyebrows, lips pursed as if pondering the very mystery of existence.

The music died down and Spates turned to the camera.

Crawley was amazed that this man, who was a complete ass in person, a cracker from the backwoods, could have such tremendous presence on television. Even the orange hair looked respectable, muted. Crawley congratulated himself again. What a brilliant stroke it had been to bring the preacher in.

"Good evening, ladies and gentlemen, and welcome to *Roundtable America*. I'm Reverend Don T. Spates, and I am delighted to have as my guest Dr. Henderson Crocker, Distinguished Professor of Physics at Liberty University in Lynchburg, Virginia."

The professor nodded sagely at the camera, his face the definition of gravitas.

"I've asked Dr. Crocker here to talk to us about the Isabella project—the subject of tonight's show. For those of you who don't know of Isabella, it is a scientific machine the government has completed in the Arizona desert at a cost of forty billion taxpayer dollars. A lot of people are concerned about it. That's why we've asked Dr. Crocker here, to help explain to us ordinary folks just what it's all about." He turned to his guest. "Dr. Crocker, you're a physicist and a teacher. Could you tell us what Isabella is?"

"Thank you, Reverend Spates. I certainly can. Essentially, Isabella is a particle accelerator—an atom smasher. It smashes atoms together at high speed to break them apart and see what they're made of."

"Sounds scary."

"Not at all. There are quite a few of them in the world. They were essential, for example, in helping America design and build nuclear weapons. And they helped lay the theoretical foundation for the nuclear power industry."

"Do you see a problem with this one, in particular?"

A dramatic pause. "Yes."

"And what is that?"

"Isabella is not like other particle accelerators. It is not being used as a scientific instrument. It is being *misused* to promote a particular agenda, a theory of creation promulgated by a hard-core cadre of atheistic and secular humanist scientists."

Spates raised his eyebrows. "That's quite a statement."

"I do not make it lightly."

"Elaborate."

"Gladly. This group of atheistic scientists have as their creed the theory that the universe created itself out of nothing, without any guiding hand or primum mobile. They call this theory the Big Bang. Now, most intelligent people, including many scientists like myself, know this theory is based on an almost complete lack of scientific evidence. The theory has its roots not in science, but in the deeply anti-Christian sentiment that pervades our nation today."

Crawley took another long, warm pull on the Calvados. Spates was coming through again. This was damn good stuff, demagoguery dressed up in sober, scientific language—and coming right out of the mouth of a physicist. Just the kind of claptrap a certain segment of the American people would eat up.

"Over the past decade, virtually every layer of our

government and university system has been taken over by atheists and secular humanists. They control the grant money. They decide what research is done. They choke off any dissenting voices. This scientific fascism cuts right across the board, from nuclear physics and cosmology to biology and, of course, evolution. These are the scientists who have given us the atheistic, materialistic theories of Darwin and Lyell, Freud and Jung. These are the people who insist that life does not begin with conception. These are the people who want to conduct ghastly experiments on stem cells—living human embryos. These are the abortionists and the so-called family planners."

The voice droned on, sounding like the very embodiment of reason. Crawley tuned it out to fantasize about the moment when he would sign up Yazzie at twice the retainer.

The show continued with more questions and answers, variations on a theme, then the usual appeal for money, more talk and more appeals. The voices went on and on, rising and falling like a chant. Repetition was the soul of Christian television, Crawley thought: pound it into their thick heads—and take their money to boot.

The camera tightened in on Spates as he took over the commentary. Crawley was only half-listening. Spates had put on a good show so far, and the thought of the Tribal Council watching it brought him great delight.

". . . God is clearly withdrawing his protective hand over America . . ."

Crawley sank into a state of warmth and relaxation. He couldn't wait for that four o'clock call Monday. He would extract millions from those apes. *Millions.*

". . . To the pagans and the abortionists, to the feminists and the homosexuals, the ACLU—all who are trying to secularize America—I point a finger in their face and say, 'When the next terror attack comes, it will be *your* fault . . .'"

Maybe he could even triple his fee. That would be something to tell his friends at the Potomac Club.

". . . And now they've built a Tower of Babel, this *Isabella,* to challenge God on His very throne. But God is no pansy: He will strike back. . . ."

As Crawley sank further into delicious reverie, a word jolted him awake. The word was "murder."

He sat forward. What was Spates talking about now?

"That's right," Spates said. "Through a confidential source, I have learned that four nights ago, one of the top scientists on the Isabella project, a Russian named Volkonsky, allegedly committed suicide. But my source indicates that some police investigators aren't so sure it was a suicide. It's looking more and more like murder—an inside job. A scientist killed by his fellow scientists. Why? To shut him up?"

Crawley sat forward, fully alert, watching keenly. What a stroke of genius to hold this bit of news for the end of the show.

"Maybe I can tell you why. I have another piece of news from my source that is truly shocking. I can hardly believe it myself."

With a manicured hand, in a slow, dramatic movement, Spates picked up a single piece of paper and held it up. Crawley recognized the trick—Joseph McCarthy had pioneered it back in the fifties—in which information, by virtue of being on paper, acquired the solidity of truth.

Spates gave the paper a little shake. "It's right here."

Another dramatic pause. Crawley sat up, his drink forgotten. Where was Spates going with this?

"Isabella was supposed to be online months ago. It isn't. There's a problem with it. Nobody knows why—except my source and me. And now *you.*"

Another dramatic shaking of the paper.

"This machine called Isabella has, as its brain, the fastest supercomputer ever built. And this Isabella is claiming to be . . ." He paused dramatically. *"God."*

He laid the paper down, his eyes straight at the camera. Even his guest seemed shocked.

The silence crawled on as Spates glared at the camera—the man knew the power of silence, especially on television.

Crawley sat at the edge of his seat, trying to fit this bombshell in. His exquisite internal radar for political trouble was illuminating something big and fast coming in out of nowhere. This was sheer craziness. Maybe it hadn't been so smart after all, passing the

301

ball to Spates and letting him run with it. Maybe he should have faxed Yazzie a new contract for a quick signature that morning.

Finally Spates spoke.

"My friends, I would not make such a statement if I wasn't absolutely sure of my facts. My source, a devout Christian and a pastor like myself, is onsite—and he got this information directly from the scientists themselves. That's right: this gigantic machine called Isabella is claiming to be God. You heard me: *claiming to be God.* If my information is wrong, *I challenge them to publicly refute me.*"

Spates rose from his chair, a gesture made all the more dramatic by expert camerawork. He towered over the viewers, a pillar of controlled fury. "I ask—I *demand*—that Gregory North Hazelius, the ringleader of this project, appear before the American people and explain himself. *I demand it.* We, the American people, have spent forty billion dollars building that infernal machine in the desert, a machine specifically created to prove God a liar. And now it is claiming to *be* God!

"O my friends! What blasphemy is this? *What blasphemy is this?*"

41

FORD ARRIVED ON THE BRIDGE AT eight o'clock. As he entered the room he glanced at Kate, at her workstation. Their eyes met. Not a word was exchanged, but the glance itself said a lot. The rest of the scientists were hunched over their various workstations, Hazelius directing the show from his swiveling captain's chair in the center. The machine hummed, but the Visualizer remained black.

The others noted his arrival with few nods and distracted greetings. Wardlaw gave him a long stare before turning back to his security board.

Hazelius beckoned him over. "How are things up top?" he asked.

"I don't think we'll have any problems."

"Good. You're just in time to see us make contact at CZero. Ken, how are we?"

"Holding steady at ninety percent," said Dolby.

"The magnet?"

"Still good."

"Then we're ready to roll," said Hazelius. "Rae? Take up your position at the detector control panel. As soon as the logic bomb goes off, I want you on top of it. Julie, back her up."

He turned. "Alan?"

Edelstein raised his head slowly from his workstation.

"Monitor the backup servers and the main computer simultaneously. At the first sign of instability, switch control of Isabella over to the three p5 595s. Don't wait for a full crash."

Edelstein nodded, gave a few sharp raps on the keyboard.

"Melissa, I want you monitoring that hole in space-time. If you see anything, I mean *anything,* that indicates a problem, an unexpected resonance, unknown superheavy or stable particles—especially stable singularities—sound the alarm."

A thumbs-up.

"Harlan? We're going to run at a hundred percent power for as long as it takes. It'll be your job to keep the juice coming in strong and clean—and to monitor the wider grid for third-party power issues."

"Sure thing."

"Tony, even if we switch over the three servers as backup, the security systems will remain online. Don't forget we've got some protesters up there, and they might do something stupid, like scale the perimeter fence."

"Yes, sir."

He looked around. "George?"

"Yes?" Innes said.

"Normally, you don't have much to do during a run. But this run's different. I want you to position yourself near the Visualizer so you can *read* the output from the logic bomb and analyze it psychologically. A human being wrote this slag code, and it may contain clues to its creator. Look for insights, ideas, psychological quirks—anything that might help us identify the perpetrator or nail this logic bomb."

"Excellent idea, Gregory, I certainly will."

"Kate? I'd like you at the control keyboard, typing in the questions."

"I—" Kate hesitated.

Hazelius arched an eyebrow. "Yes?"

"I'd rather not, Gregory."

The intense blue eyes studied her, then turned to Ford. "You've got nothing else to do. Would you like to ask the questions?"

"I'll be glad to."

"What you ask isn't important—just keep the malware talking. Rae's going to need a steady output to trace this thing. Don't get hung up asking long or complicated questions—keep them short. Kate, if Wyman falters or runs out of questions, you be ready to jump in. We can't waste a second."

Ford walked over to her workstation. She rose, offered him the seat. He laid a hand on her shoulder. He bent down, as if to examine the screen. "Hello," he whispered, taking her hand and squeezing it.

"Hi."

Kate hesitated, and then said, sotto voce, "Promise me, Wyman, that no matter what happens here—*no matter what*—we're going to start over again. You and me. Promise me that . . . what happened on our ride out there on the mesa wasn't just a one-time thing." Her face was intensely flushed. She bent down to hide it, her black hair hanging down like a curtain.

He gave her hand a squeeze. "I promise."

Hazelius had finished discussing various details with certain team members, and he returned to the center of the Bridge. He cast his flashing blue eyes across the group. "I've said it before; I'll say it again. We're sailing into unknown waters. I won't kid you: what we're about to do is dangerous. There's no alternative: our backs are against the wall. We're going to find this logic bomb and destroy it. Tonight."

In the long silence that followed, the singing of the machine rose and fell.

"We're going to be out of touch with the outside world for a few hours," he said. His fierce eye ranged about the room. "Any questions?"

"Um, I do." Julie Thibodeaux responded. Her face was slick with sweat, and the dark circles under her eyes seemed almost translucent. Her hair was long and stringy. It shook as she moved.

Hazelius gazed at her. "Yes?"

"I—" She faltered.

Hazelius arched his eyebrows, waiting. She pushed her chair back suddenly and rose. The rollers snagged on the carpet, causing her to stumble. "This is insane," she said, her voice loud. "We've got a warm magnet, an unstable computer, malware—and now we're going to pump a few hundred megawatts of power into the machine? You're going to blow the shit out of this whole mountain. You can count me out."

Hazelius's glance flickered briefly toward Wardlaw, then back to Thibodeaux.

"I'm afraid it's too late, Julie."

"What do you mean, too late?" she yelled. "I'm out of here."

"The Bunker doors are closed, locked, and sealed. You know the drill."

"Bullshit. Ford just came in."

"By previous arrangement. Now, no one can leave until dawn. Not even me. It's part of the security arrangement."

"Bullcrap. What if there were a fire, an accident?" She stood defiantly, her body quivering.

"The only person with the security codes who can open the door before dawn is Tony. It's his decision as SIO. Tony?"

"No one can leave," said Wardlaw stolidly.

"I refuse to accept that answer," she said, her voice rising in panic.

"I'm afraid you must," said Hazelius.

Tony. I want out, now, goddamn you." Her voice rode up toward the edge of a scream.

"I'm sorry," Wardlaw said.

She rushed at him, all five feet three inches of her. He let her come on. She raised her fists and he caught them neatly as she flung herself on him.

"Let me go, you bastard!" She twisted and turned helplessly.

"Easy, now."

"I'm not going to die for some machine!" She

slumped against him and began to sob.

Ford looked on incredulously. "If she wants out, let her out."

Wardlaw gave him a hostile stare. "It's against protocol."

"She's no security risk. Look at her—she's falling apart."

"The rules are there for a reason," said Wardlaw. "No one leaves Isabella during a run except in the case of a life-threatening emergency."

Ford turned to Hazelius. "This isn't right." He looked around. "Surely the rest of you agree." But instead of agreement, he saw uncertainty. Fear. "You *can't* keep her here against her will."

Until now he hadn't realized how much they had fallen under Hazelius's spell. "Kate?" He turned to her. "You know this is wrong."

"Wyman, we all signed on to the rules. Even her."

Hazelius walked over to Thibodeaux and nodded to Wardlaw. The SIO released her into Hazelius's arms. She tried to break free but he held her, firmly but gently. Her sobs began to subside to whimpers and gulps. He cradled her gently, almost lovingly. She leaned into his chest, crying softly, like a little girl. Hazelius patted and stroked the back of her head and brushed away her tears with a thumb, all the while murmuring into her ear. A few minutes passed and she calmed down.

"I'm sorry," she whispered.

He patted her, smoothing her hair, running his

hands sensually over her plump back. "We need you, Julie. *I* need you. We can't do it without you. You know that."

She nodded, sniffed. "I lost it. I'm sorry. I won't do it again."

He held her until she was quiet. When he released her, she stepped back, eyes on the floor.

"Julie, stay here with me. You'll be safe—I promise."

She nodded again.

Ford stared after her in amazement, until he noticed Hazelius looking at him with a sad, kind face. "Are we all right now, Wyman?"

Ford met the blue eyes and would not speak.

42

IN HIS TRAILER, PASTOR RUSS EDDY sat in front of the twenty-inch screen on his iMac. The live Webcast of *Roundtable America* had just ended. Eddy's brain was afire, his soul burning, the words of Reverend Spates still reverberating in his mind. He, Russell Eddy, was the "devout Christian on-site" who had exposed the Isabella project. "A pastor just like me," Reverend Spates had said to millions. It was Eddy who had gathered the critical information at great personal risk, guided by the invisible hand of the Lord. These were not normal times. The righteous wrath of the Lord, with all its immense power, was surely coming. Not even the rocks would hide the pagan scientists from the vengeance of the Almighty Lord.

Eddy sat before the quiet blue screen, his mind reeling with the glory of God. The grand design was starting to show its outlines. God's plan for him. It all started with the death of the Indian, struck down by God's own hand, a direct sign to Eddy of His coming fury. The end was upon them. *"For the great day of His wrath has come, and who shall be able to stand?"*

Slowly, Eddy's consciousness drifted back to the trailer. It was so quiet in the shabby bedroom—as if nothing had happened at all. Yet the world had changed. God's plan for him stood revealed. But what was the next step? What did God intend him to do?

A sign . . . he needed a sign. He clasped his Bible, his hands trembling with emotion. God would show him what to do.

He laid the book spine down and let it fall open where it would. The well-worn pages whiffled past until almost the end, where they settled flat, open to the book of Revelation. His eye fell randomly on a sentence: *"And there was given unto him a mouth speaking great things and blasphemies . . ."*

His spine seemed to contract with the chill. The passage was one of the clearest and most unambiguous references to the Antichrist in the entire Bible.

Confirmation.

43

EVEN WITH THE TENSION IN THE room, Ford thought, the run-up to the top of the power spectrum was even duller the second time around. By ten o'clock, Isabella reached 99.5 percent power. Everything was happening as before: the resonance, the hole in space-time, the strange image condensing in the center of the Visualizer. Isabella hummed; the mountain vibrated.

As if on schedule, the Visualizer went blank and the first words appeared.

We speak again.

"Go to it, Wyman," Hazelius said.

Ford typed, *Tell me all about yourself.* He could feel Kate leaning over behind him, watching him work.

I can no more explain to you who I am than you could explain to a beetle who you are.

"Rae?" Hazelius asked. "Are you getting it?"

"I'm trolling."

Try anyway, Ford wrote.

I will explain instead why you cannot understand me.

"George," said Hazelius, "are you following this?"

"I am," said Innes, delighted to be consulted. "It's clever—telling us we won't understand is a way of avoiding being tripped up by detail."

Go ahead, typed Ford.

You inhabit a world scaled midway between the Planck length and the diameter of the universe.

"Seems to be a bot program," said Edelstein, examining the output on a screen. "It copies itself to another location, erases the original and covers its tracks."

"Yeah," said Chen, "and I've got a bunch of hungry bot-wolves roaming Isabella, looking for it."

Your brain was exquisitely fine-tuned to manipulate your world—not to comprehend its fundamental reality. You evolved to throw rocks, not quarks.

"I'm on its trail!" Chen cried. She hunched over the keyboard, like a chef over a hot stove, working maniacally. Code was racing by on four flat panels in front of her.

"Main computer's crashing," said Edelstein calmly. "Switching control of Isabella over to the backup servers."

As a result of your evolution, you see the world in fundamentally erroneous ways. For example, you believe yourselves to occupy a three-dimensional space in which separate objects trace smoothly predictable arcs marked by something you call time. This is what you call reality.

"Switchover complete."

"Cut the power to the main computer."

"Wait," said Dolby sharply. "That wasn't the plan."

"We want to make sure the malware isn't in there. Pull the plug, Alan."

Edelstein smiled coldly and turned back to the computer.

"Jesus Christ, wait—!" Dolby leapt up, but it was too late.

"Done," Edelstein said, with a sharp rap on the keyboard.

Half the peripheral screens went blank. Dolby stood, swaying, uncertain. A moment went by. Nothing happened. Isabella continued to hum along.

"It worked," said Edelstein. "Ken, you can relax."

Dolby flashed him an annoyed look and settled back down to his workstation.

Are you saying, Ford typed, *that our reality is an illusion?*

Yes. Natural selection has given you the illusion that you understand fundamental reality. But you do not. How could you? Do beetles understand fundamental reality? Do chimpanzees? You are an animal like them. You evolved like them, you reproduce like them, you have the same basic neural structures. You differ from the chimpanzee by a mere two hundred genes. How could that minuscule difference enable you to comprehend the universe when the chimpanzee cannot even comprehend a grain of sand?

"I swear," Chen cried, "the data's streaming out of CZero again!"

"Impossible," said Hazelius. "The malware's hiding in a detector. Force-quit and restart the detector processors, one at a time."

"I'll try."

If our conversation is to be fruitful, you must abandon all hope of understanding me.

"More clever obfuscation," said Innes. "It's basically saying nothing."

Ford felt a gentle hand on his shoulder. Kate asked, "May I take over for a moment?"

He dropped his hands from the keyboard and moved over. Kate sat down.

What are our illusions? she typed.

You evolved to see the world as being made up of discrete objects. That is not so. From the first moment of creation, all was entangled. What you call space and time are merely emergent properties of a deeper underlying reality. In that reality, there is no separateness. There is no time. There is no space. All is one.

Explain, Kate typed.

Your own theory of quantum mechanics, incorrect as it is, touches on the deep truth that the universe is unitary.

All well and good, Kate typed, *but how does this matter in our own lives today?*

It matters a great deal. You think of yourself as an "individual person," with a unique and separate mind. You think you are born and you think you die. All your life you feel separate and alone. Sometimes desperately so. You fear death because you fear the loss of individuality. All this is illusion. You, he, she, those things around you living or not, the stars and galaxies, the empty space in between—these are not

distinct, separate objects. All is fundamentally entan-
gled. Birth and death, pain and suffering, love and
hate, good and evil, are all illusive. They are atavisms
of the evolutionary process. They do not exist in
reality.

So it's just like the Buddhists believe, that all is illu-
sion?

Not at all. There is an absolute truth, a reality. But
a mere glimpse of this reality would break a human
mind.

Suddenly Edelstein, who had abandoned his computer console, appeared behind Ford and Mercer.

"Alan, why are you leaving your station—?"
Hazelius began.

"If you're God," said Edelstein with a half smile on
his face, hands clasped behind his back, strolling
along in front of the Visualizer, "let's dispense with
the typing. You should be able to hear me."

Loud and clear, came the response on the Visualizer.

"We've got a hidden mike in here," said Hazelius.
"Melissa, get on it. Hunt it down."

"You bet."

Edelstein went on, unperturbed. "You say, 'all is
unitary'? We have a numbering system: one, two,
three—and in this way I refute your statement."

One, two, three . . . Another illusion. There is no
enumerability.

"This is mathematical sophistry," said Edelstein,
growing annoyed. "No enumerability—I just dis-

proved it by counting." He held up his hand. "Another disproof: I give you the integer five!"

You give me a hand with five fingers, not the integer five. Your number system has no independent existence in the real world. It is nothing more than a sophisticated metaphor.

"I'd like to hear your proof of that ridiculous conjecture."

Pick a number at random on the real number line: with probability one you have picked a number that has no name, has no definition, and cannot be computed or written down, even if the whole universe were put to the task. This problem extends to allegedly definable numbers such as pi or the square root of two. With a computer the size of the universe running an infinite amount of time, you could not calculate either number exactly. Tell me, Edelstein: How then can such numbers be said to exist? How can the circle or the square, from which these two numbers derive, exist? How can dimensional space exist, then, if it cannot be measured? You, Edelstein, are like a monkey who, with heroic mental effort, has figured out how to count to three. You find four pebbles and think you have discovered infinity.

Ford had lost the thread of the argument, but he was startled to see Edelstein's face pale, shocked into silence, as if the mathematician had understood something that staggered him.

"Is that so?" cried Hazelius, stepping down from the Bridge and brushing Edelstein aside. He placed himself squarely in front of the screen. "You talk a fine streak, you boast that even the word 'God' is inadequate to describe your greatness. All right, then—prove it. Prove you're God."

"Don't," said Kate. "Don't ask that."

"Why the hell not?"

"You just might get what you ask for."

"Fat chance." He turned back to the machine. "Did you hear me? *Prove you're God.*"

There was a silence, and then the answer appeared on the screen: *You construct the proof, Hazelius. But I warn you, this is the last test to which I will submit. We have important business and very little time.*

"You asked for it."

"Wait," said Kate.

Hazelius turned to her.

"Gregory, if you have to do this, do it right. *Make it count.* There can't be any room for doubt or ambiguity. Ask it something that only you know—*only* you, and no one else in the entire world. Something personal. Your deepest, most private secret. Something only God—the *real* God—could possibly know."

"Yes, Kate. That's quite right." He thought for a long minute, and then spoke quietly. "All right. I've got it."

Silence.

Everyone had stopped their tasks.

Hazelius turned toward the Visualizer. He spoke calmly and quietly. "My wife, Astrid, was pregnant when she died. We had just found out. Nobody else knew of her pregnancy. *Nobody.* Here is your test: tell me the name we chose for our child."

Another silence, filled only by the ethereal singing of the detectors. The screen remained blank. The seconds crawled by.

Hazelius snorted. "Well, that settles it. If anyone had any doubts."

And then, as if from a great distance, a name swam into focus on the screen.

Albert Leibniz Gund Hazelius, if it was a boy.

Hazelius remained still, his face expressionless. Everyone stared at him, awaiting a denial that did not come.

"And if it was a girl?" Edelstein cried, stepping toward the screen. "What if it was a girl? What would the name have been?"

Rosalind Curie Gund Hazelius.

Ford stared in utter astonishment as Hazelius folded to the floor, as slowly and gently as if he had fallen asleep.

44

BY THE TIME STANTON LOCKWOOD REACHED the Oval Office for the emergency meeting, the president was pacing the center of the room like a caged lion. Roger Morton, his chief of staff, and the ubiquitous campaign chief Gordon Galdone were standing on either side of his pacing ground, like referees. His ever-silent secretary, Jean, clutched her steno book primly. Lockwood was surprised to see the president's National Security Advisor in video conference, split-screened on a flat panel display with Jack Strand, the Director of the FBI.

"Stanton." The president came over and grasped his hand. "Glad you could get here at such short notice."

"Of course, Mr. President."

"Have a seat."

Lockwood sat while the president continued to stand. "Stan, I called this little meeting because we've got some shit going on down there in Arizona with the Isabella project that Jack's just brought to my attention. Around eight o'clock Mountain Daylight Time all communications to and from Isabella were cut off. From all of Red Mesa, even. The DOE Offsite Project Manager tried to raise them on the secure lines, by open cell lines, even by regular landlines. No luck. Isabella is running at full power and it seems the team is below, in the Bunker, totally cut off. The situation was vetted up the ladder and just came to the attention of Director Strand—who informed me."

Lockwood nodded. This was very strange. There were backup systems to the backup systems. It shouldn't happen. Couldn't happen.

"Look, it's probably some glitch," said the president, "power failure maybe. I don't want to make a big deal out of it—not at this sensitive time."

"Sensitive time," Lockwood knew, was the president's euphemism for the upcoming election.

The president paced. "And that's not the *only* problem." He turned to his secretary. "Jean? Roll it."

A screen dropped from the ceiling. Static hissed; then the image of Reverend Don T. Spates filled the screen at his cherrywood roundtable, speaking to an eminence grise. His voice rolled from the sound system like thunder. The segment had been edited down to eight minutes of the high points of the show—sound bullets. When the tape ended, the president stopped pacing and faced Lockwood. "*That's* the second problem."

Lockwood took a deep breath. "Mr. President, I wouldn't be too concerned. This is crazy stuff. Only the fringe is going to buy this."

The president turned to his chief of staff. "Roger? Tell him."

Morton's spatulate fingers coolly adjusted his tie, his gray eyes on Lockwood. "Before *Roundtable America* had even ended, the White House had received almost one hundred thousand e-mails. We hit two hundred thousand a half hour ago. I don't have the latest tally, because the servers crashed."

Lockwood felt a thrill of horror.

"In all my years in politics," said the president, "I've never seen anything like it. And wouldn't you know it, right at this very moment the goddamn Isabella project goes silent!"

Lockwood glanced at Galdone, but as usual the lugubrious campaign chief was reserving counsel.

"Could you send someone out there," Lockwood asked, "to check it out?"

The FBI Director spoke. "We're considering it. Perhaps a small team . . . in case there's a . . . situation out there."

"A situation?"

"It's not beyond the bounds of possibility that we may be dealing with terrorists or some kind of internal mutiny. A *very* remote possibility. But we do have to consider it."

Lockwood felt a spiraling sense of unreality.

"So, Stanton," said the president, clasping his hands behind his back. "You're in charge of Isabella. What the hell's going on?"

Lockwood cleared his throat. "All I can say is, this is extremely unusual. It's way outside the protocols. I can't begin to understand it, unless . . ."

"Unless what?" the president asked.

"The scientists deliberately shut down the communications system."

"How can we find that out?"

Lockwood thought for a moment. "There's a guy named Bernard Wolf up at Los Alamos. He was the right-hand man to the chief engineer, Ken Dolby, who designed Isabella. He knows the whole layout, the systems, the computers, how it all works together. And he'll have a full set of blueprints."

The president turned to his chief of staff. "Get him up and ready to roll."

"Yes, Mr. President." Morton sent his assistant scurrying from the room on the task. Morton walked to the window and turned. His face was red, and the veins in his neck pulsed faintly. He looked directly at Lockwood. "For weeks, Stan, I've been *repeatedly* expressing to you my concern about the lack of progress with the Isabella project. What the *hell* have you been *doing?*"

Lockwood was stunned by his tone. Nobody had talked to him that way in years. He kept his voice under rigid control. "I've been working on it day and night. I even put a man on the inside."

"A man on the inside? Sweet Jesus. Without running it by me?"

"I authorized it," said the president sharply. "Let's stay focused on the problem at hand and stop bickering."

"What, exactly, is this man supposed to be doing?" said Morton, ignoring the president.

"He's looking into the delay, trying to figure out what's behind it."

"And?"

"I expect results tomorrow."

"How are you in contact with him?"

"By secure sat phone," said Lockwood. "Unfortunately, if he's in the Bunker with the rest, it doesn't work underground."

"Try it anyway."

With a shaking hand, Lockwood wrote the number on a piece of paper and handed it to Jean.

"Put it on speaker," said Morton.

The phone rang five times, ten, fifteen.

"Enough," said Morton, staring hard at Lockwood. Then he slowly turned to the president. "Mr. President, may I respectfully suggest that we move this meeting to the Situation Room? Because I have the feeling it's going to be a long night."

Lockwood stared at the Great Seal on the carpet. It all seemed so unreal. Was it possible they had gotten to Ford and turned him, too?

45

HAZELIUS LAY SPRAWLED ACROSS THE LINOLEUM floor. Ford rushed over to where he was stretched out and the other members of the team crowded around. Ford knelt and felt the pulse in his neck. It was strong, rapid, and steady. Kate grasped his hand, patting it. "Gregory? Gregory!"

"Get me a flashlight," said Ford.

Wardlaw handed him a flashlight. Ford thumbed

Hazelius's eyelid open and shined the light in. The pupil contracted strongly.

"Water."

A styrofoam cup was thrust into his hands. Ford took out his handkerchief, dipped it in the water, and patted it on Hazelius's face. The scientist's shoulders moved slightly, and both eyes fluttered open. They darted around, full of alarm and confusion.

"What—?"

"It's all right," said Ford. "You just fainted."

Hazelius stared around uncomprehendingly. Realization crept back into his eyes. He struggled to sit up.

"Take it easy," said Ford, gently keeping him down. "Wait for your head to clear."

Hazelius lay back, staring at the ceiling. "Oh my God," he groaned. "This can't be real. This can't be happening."

The smell of hot electronics hung heavy in the stifling atmosphere. Isabella moaned, the sound coming from all directions, as if the mountain itself were keening.

"Help me into my chair," Hazelius gasped.

Kate took one arm, Ford took the other, and they helped him to his feet and walked him to the center of the Bridge, letting him settle into the captain's chair.

Hazelius steadied himself on the arms of the chair and looked around. Ford had never seen his eyes such an eerie blue.

Edelstein spoke fiercely. "Is it true? The names? *I must know.*"

Hazelius nodded.

"There's an explanation, of course."

Hazelius shook his head.

"Obviously, you told someone," Edelstein said. "Someone found out."

"No."

"The doctor who gave your wife the news. He learned the names."

"It was a home kit," Hazelius said hoarsely. "We only found out . . . an hour before she died."

"She called someone. Her mother, perhaps."

Again, a vigorous shake of the head. "Impossible. I was with her the whole time. We did the test and talked about the names. That was it. Sixty minutes. We didn't go anywhere, we didn't talk to anyone. She was so happy. That's what burst the aneurysm—the sudden rush of happiness from the news spiked her blood pressure. Cerebral hemorrhage."

"There's a fraud in here somewhere," said Edelstein.

Chen shook her head, setting her long black hair awhirl. "Alan, the data is coming out of that hole in space-time. It's not coming from anywhere in the system. I traced it once, I traced it again, I force-quit the processors in each detector, I did every test I could think of. It's *real*."

Hazelius drew a shuddering breath. "It knew my thoughts. Just like it knew Kate's. There's no getting around it, Alan. There's no way it could have guessed. *Whatever it is, it knows our innermost thoughts.*"

Nobody moved. Ford tried to wrap his mind around it, find a rational explanation. Edelstein was right: it had to be some kind of deception.

When Hazelius spoke again, his voice was calm, matter-of-fact. "The machine's running unattended. All of you, back to your stations."

"We aren't . . . going to power down?" Julie Thibodeaux asked, her voice quavering.

"Absolutely not."

Isabella continued to hum on autopilot with the immense flow of power. The screens hissed with snow. The detectors sang their strange song. The electronics crackled—as if the tension of the scientists had infected the computer and taken the machine itself to the edge.

"Alan, get back on the p5s, keep everything steady. Kate, I want you to do some calculations on the geometry of that space-time hole. Where does it go? What does it open into? Melissa, I want you to work with Kate and get on that data cloud. Analyze it at all frequencies—find out what the hell it is."

"What about the malware?" Dolby asked, as if unable to comprehend what had happened.

"Ken, don't you get it? There is no malware."

Dolby looked stupefied. "You think it's . . . God?"

Hazelius returned the man's look with an unreadable gaze of his own. "I think Isabella's in communication with something real. Whether it's actually God—whatever the hell that word means—we don't have enough data yet. And that's why we have to keep going."

Ford looked around. The shock of what had happened was still sinking in. Wardlaw's face was dripping sweat. Kate and St. Vincent looked pale as death.

He took Kate's hand. "Are you all right?"

She shook her head. "I'm not sure."

Hazelius spoke to Dolby. "How long can we keep it going?"

"It's dangerous to keep running at full power."

"I didn't ask you if it was dangerous. I asked you *how long*."

"Two, three hours."

"Wait," said Innes, "Let's not be rash. We need to stop and consider what's happened here. This is . . . unprecedented."

Hazelius faced Innes. "George, if God spoke to you, would you turn and walk away?"

"Come now, Gregory! You can't seriously believe we're speaking to God!"

"I merely asked *if*."

"I refuse to answer absurd hypotheticals."

"George, *if* we've made contact with some kind of universal intelligence, we can't turn away. Because the opportunity is here. It's now. It won't last."

"This is crazy," said Innes weakly.

"No, George, it isn't crazy. The thing gave us the

proof we asked for. Twice. It may be God, it may be something else. I don't know. What I *do* know is: I'm riding this train to the last station." He looked around fiercely. "What about it? Are you all with me?"

The singing of Isabella filled the room. The screens flickered. Nobody spoke. But Ford could see the *yes* in all their faces.

46

IN THE BACK BEDROOM OF HIS Oakwood, Pastor Russell Eddy closed his Bible and placed it on one of the tottering heaps of books stacked on his desk. He shoved the piles of books away from his sleeping Mac, clearing himself a space to work. Then he woke the machine up, the monitor bathing the room in cool blue. It was nine o'clock in the evening.

His head felt clearer than it had ever felt before. God had answered his prayers. God had told him exactly what he must do.

For a few minutes, he stared at the empty screen, collecting his thoughts. Outwardly his body was still. Inwardly his heart pounded with the zeal of the Holy Spirit. There was a reason he had ended up running a shabby mission church at the edge of the world. There was a reason why Lorenzo had died. Russell Eddy had been placed here as God's sentry. God had selected him to play a crucial role in the coming End of Days.

For a half hour he sat very still, thinking intensively

about the letter he must write. His mind remained preternaturally clear and sharp as he composed the letter, word by word, in his head.

He was ready. He bowed his head, uttered a short prayer, and placed his fingers on the computer keyboard.

My Friends in Christ,

Many of you watched the show *Roundtable America* earlier tonight, hosted by the Reverend Don T. Spates. You heard him speak of the Isabella project. You heard Rev. Spates mention a secret source, a "devout Christian on-site" from whom he got his information.

I am that secret source. God has asked me to reveal to you what I know. What you do with it is between you and the Lord.

My name is Russell Eddy, pastor of the Gathered in Thy Name Mission on the Navajo Indian Reservation. Ours is a very simple and remote Christian mission located in the desert of Arizona at the foot of Red Mesa, not ten miles from the Isabella project.

My friends, I bring you news—extraordinary, terrifying, yet joyous news. *The event for which Christians have been waiting for two thousand years is happening, right now, even as I write this e-mail.*

The End Days have arrived. The Apocalypse and Rapture are at hand, now, this very night. You read about it in the *Left Behind* series. Well, now it's no longer fiction. It's happening. For real.

I know many of you have heard claims like this before. Many false prophets have made this very claim in the past. You are skeptical, and rightly so. All I ask is that you hear me out. *"He that hath ears to hear, let him hear."*

Don't make the mistake of deleting this e-mail. By doing so, you may forfeit your place at the right hand of Jesus Christ on the Day of Judgment. Read what I have to say. Pray. Then decide.

I begin with two announcements. The first is this: **the Antichrist is here amongst us. I have met him.** I have spoken to him. He is real. His long-laid schemes and plans have reached fruition. As God is my witness, right in front of me he took off his mask and revealed himself.

My second announcement is even more

important: **The Apocalypse is now. It begins this very night.**

Naturally, you are skeptical. You say, right now? The Apocalypse? With my kids upstairs, sleeping? With my wife in bed? Impossible! But consider what the Apostle Matthew said: *"In such an hour as you think not, the Son of man cometh."* This is that hour. It is here. Now.

And now I will give you proof of what I say. The key is Revelation 13:1 and nearby passages.

"And I stood upon the sand of the sea, and saw a beast rise up out of the sea, having seven heads and ten horns, and upon his horns ten crowns, and upon his heads the name of blasphemy."

The "sand of the sea" is the Arizona desert. Isabella is exactly seven leagues in diameter. Isabella has ten different detectors, each one recording ten different particles. Some of the detectors are actually called "horns." If you think I'm making this up, check the Isabella Web site, www.theisabellaproject.org. It's all there.

"The dragon gave him his power, and his seat, and great authority."

And who is the Antichrist running the show? **He is a man named Gregory North Hazelius.** He is the one who proposed the Isabella project, who got the money for it, and who now leads the team. *The New York Times* calls Hazelius the "smartest man on earth." Hazelius himself has made many boasts. He once said "everyone is beneath me intellectually" and called human beings a "race of morons." That's right, my friends. But now his true nature is revealed: Gregory North Hazelius is the Antichrist. You doubt me? I met him. I spoke to him, face-to-face. I listened to his blasphemy, his vomiting of bile about our Savior. I listened to him curse Christians as "insects" and "bacteria." But don't believe me: believe the Bible. Here's more from Revelation 13.

"And they worshipped the beast, saying, Who is like unto the beast? And there was given unto him a mouth speaking great things and blasphemies. . . . And he opened his mouth in blasphemy against God, to blaspheme his name, and his tabernacle, and them that dwell in heaven."

As you heard on *Roundtable America*, the Isabella machine is claiming to be God. But they're not talking to God, my friends. They're talking to *Satan*.

"Woe to the inhabiters of the earth and of the sea! for the devil is come down unto you, having great wrath, because he knoweth that he hath but a short time."

Satan is backed into a corner. He's making his last stand—and he's never been more dangerous.

You may ask: Where's the proof? Listen, and you shall hear.

Consider this statement, which I have taken directly from the Isabella project Web site: "Running at full power, Isabella re-creates at CZero the temperature of the universe as it was in the first millionth of a second of the Big Bang, a temperature of over one trillion degrees Fahrenheit." And now consider Revelation 13:13.

"And he [the beast] doeth great wonders, so that he maketh fire come down from heaven on the earth in the sight of men."

Once again is the prophecy of the Apostle John fulfilled.

Here's another statement from the Isabella project Web site: "The supercomputer controlling Isabella is the most powerful calculating machine on the planet. It runs at a top speed of fifteen petaflops (fifteen quadrillion calculations per second). This is finally closing in on the estimated speed of the human brain." Now compare this to Revelation:

"And he [the Antichrist] had power to give life unto the image of the beast, that the image of the beast should both speak and cause that as many as would not worship the image of the beast should be killed."

Are you willing to go to bed tonight, knowing the Antichrist will kill you?

Finally, my friends, I give you the ultimate passage in Revelation, the one that lies at the very heart of the vision of the Apostle John:

"Let him that hath understanding count the number of the beast: for it is the number of a man; and his number is Six hundred threescore and six."

This is how the Bible tells us we will recognize the Antichrist—by the number 666. The first language of the Apostle John was Hebrew. He knew that every Hebrew letter has a numeric equivalent. Gematria is the process of looking for hidden numbers in a Hebrew name or text. So let's see what happens when we apply gematria to Isabella and its location, Arizona. If we turn the Roman letters into their Hebrew equivalents and assign each Hebrew letter its proper number, we get:

A	Aleph	1
R	Resh	200
I	Yodh	14
Z	Shin	300
O	Ayin	100
N	Nun	50
A	Final Aleph	1
Total		666

Still don't believe me? Consider this:

I	Yodh	14
S	Shin	300
A	Aleph	1
B	Bet	2
E	He	88
L	Lamed	130
L	Lamed	130
A	Final Aleph	1
Total		666

My friends, is this not the proof we have been waiting for?

Now, consider this passage from Revelation:

"And he gathered them together in a place called in the Hebrew tongue Armageddon."

Armageddon is where Satan makes his last stand against God's appointed King, Jesus. The word Armageddon is derived from the Hebrew words Har Megido, meaning "Mountain of Megido." But this "Mountain" has never been found in the Holy Land and the word "Megido" is really only an ancient form of the Hebrew word for reddish-colored earth. So you see that the word "Armageddon" in Revelation actually refers to a place called "Red Mountain." My friends, the Isabella project is situated on a place called Red Mesa in Arizona. The Navajo Indians call it Dzilth Chíí, which in the Navajo language literally means "Red Mountain"—Armageddon.

These are the proofs, my friends. And now the ball is in your court. What will you do with this information? *The ultimate moment in your life as a Christian has just happened, **RIGHT NOW**, as you read this e-mail.*

WHAT WILL YOU DO?

Will you stay at home? Will you hesitate, wondering if I am just another nutcase? Will you remain seated at your computer, not knowing where Red Mesa is or how to get there in the middle of the night? Will you decide to put it off until tomorrow? Will you wait for proof, for a sign?

Or will you answer the call *right now* and become a foot soldier in the Army of God? Will you drop everything *right now,* will you rise from your computer *right now,* leave your home, and come to Red Mesa to join me in *"the battle of that great day of God Almighty"*? Will you fight alongside me **right now,** shoulder to shoulder, brothers in Christ, in the final battle against Satan and his Antichrist?

THE CHOICE IS YOURS.

In Christ,
Pastor Russ Eddy
Gathered in Thy Name Mission
Blue Gap, Arizona
This original e-mail was sent
Sept. 14, at 9:37 P.M. MDT.

POST AND FORWARD THIS E-MAIL TO ALL YOUR CHRISTIAN FRIENDS—

THEN COME TO RED MESA AND JOIN ME!

When Eddy finished, he sat back in a sweat, his hands trembling. He didn't even read it over. God had been guiding his hand, and that meant it was perfect.

He went to the subject line and typed in:

Red Mesa=Armageddon

He checked the list of e-mail addresses he'd been developing in hopes of raising money for the mission. He'd culled some from churches and Christian mailing lists; others were contacts from Christian bulletin boards, newsgroups, chat rooms, and Usenet discussion sites.

Two thousand one hundred and sixteen names. Of course, most wouldn't respond. That's what the Bible said would happen—*"Many are called, but few are chosen."* But two thousand was a start. Of those, a few dozen might forward the e-mail and make the journey to Red Mesa. A few hundred might respond to the next round, and a few thousand to the next. The letter would be posted at hundreds of Christian Web sites. Christian bloggers would pick it up; and in that way the message would grow. Eddy had spent enough time on the Internet to know that the mathematics were in his favor.

He pasted his entire address book into the *To:* field

and moved the cursor to the little paper airplane button. He took a deep breath, then clicked the mouse. With a *whoosh!* the e-mail blasted into the electronic ether at the speed of light.

It is done.

He sat back, trembling. All was silent. But the world was changed.

He remained seated for five minutes. And then, his breathing under control, he rose, steadying himself. After a long hesitation he fished the keys out of his pocket and unlocked the filing cabinet next to his desk and took out the Ruger .44 Magnum Blackhawk revolver his father had given him for his eighteenth birthday. It was a limited edition, Old West replica gun, but updated and reliable. He had spent a few days at the firing range with it many years ago, and he had always kept it well oiled and in good working order.

Eddy had no illusions. This was going to be war—*real* war.

He loaded the revolver with Remington 240-grain jacketed soft points. He put the gun and two boxes of extra rounds into a knapsack, added a water bottle, a flashlight, extra batteries, binoculars, his Bible, a notebook and pencil. He hunted down the spare fuel bottle he kept filled with kerosene in case of black-outs. That went in, too.

He slung the knapsack over his shoulder, stepped out into the night air, and looked up at Red Mesa, a dark mass silhouetted against the night sky. A single, faint light marked the Isabella project, perched at the edge of the dark island of stone.

He tossed his knapsack into the cab of the pickup and got in beside it. He had barely enough gas to reach the top of the mesa. But why would that matter? God, who had led him this far, would bring him home and reunify him with his children, if not in this earthly life, then in the one to come.

47

"EVERYONE, BACK TO YOUR PLACES," HAZELIUS ordered, his voice gaining strength. He turned toward the Visualizer and spoke to it. "All right, let's start again from the top. What the hell are you—really?"

Ford stared at the screen, transfixed, waiting for the answer to appear. He felt himself being drawn in almost against his will.

For reasons I have already explained, you cannot know what I am. The word "God" comes close, but it remains a highly impoverished description.

"Are you part of the universe, or separate from it?" Hazelius asked.

There is no separateness. We are all one.

"Why does the universe exist?"

The universe exists because it is simpler than nothing. That is also why I exist. The universe cannot be simpler than it is. This is the physical law from which all others flow.

"What could be simpler than nothing?" Ford asked.

"Nothing" cannot exist. It is an immediate paradox. The universe is the state closest to nothing.

"If everything is so simple," Edelstein asked, "why is the universe so complex?"

The intricate universe you see is an emergent property of its simplicity.

"So what is this profound simplicity at the heart of everything?" Edelstein asked.

That is the reality that would break your mind.

"This is getting tiresome!" Edelstein cried. "If you're so smart, you should be able to explain it to us poor, benighted human beings! Do you mean to say that we're so ignorant of reality that our physical laws are a sham?"

You constructed your physical laws on the assumption of the existence of time and space. All your laws are based on frames of reference. This is invalid. Soon your cherished assumptions about the real world will crash and burn. From the ashes you will build a new kind of science.

"If our physical laws are false, how is it that our science is so spectacularly successful?"

Newton's laws of motion, while false, were adequate to send people to the moon. Just so with your laws: they are workable approximations that are fundamentally incorrect.

"So how do you construct the laws of physics without time and space?"

We are wasting time bandying about metaphysical concepts.

"So what should we be discussing?" Hazelius asked, cutting off Edelstein.

The reason I have come to you.

"What is that?"

I have a task for you.

The singing sound of Isabella yawed suddenly, like a Doppler-shifted train going by. There was a rumble somewhere in the mountain, a vibration of the very backbone of the mesa. The screen flickered and a hiss of snow whipped across it, obliterating the words.

"Shit," breathed Dolby. "Shit." He struggled to adjust the software controls, his fingers pounding the keyboard.

"What the hell's happening?" Hazelius cried.

"Decollimation of the beam," Dolby said. "Harlan, damn it, you have power-flow alarms going off! Alan! Get back on your servers! What the hell are all of you doing standing around, for chrissakes!"

"Back to your stations!" Hazelius said.

Another rumble shook the Bunker. Everyone rushed back to their workstations. A new message hung on the screen, unread.

"Stabilizing," St. Vincent said.

"Collimated again," said Dolby. A sweat stain was spreading across the back of his T-shirt.

"Alan, the servers?"

"Under control."

"What about the magnet?" asked Hazelius.

"Surviving" said Dolby, "but we don't have much longer. That was damn close."

"Well, then." Hazelius turned back to the Visualizer. "Why don't you tell us what this task is?"

48

THE PICKUP RAN OUT OF GAS just beyond the top of the Dugway. Eddy used the last bit of momentum to coast off the road into the sagebrush, where the truck came to a bumpy halt. Above the skeletons of the piñons, a faint glow of light in the night sky marked the Isabella project, three miles to the east.

He climbed out of the truck, pulled out his knapsack, shrugged into it, and began walking down the road. The moon had not yet risen. While he could see the stars from his trailer, tonight, on top of the mesa, they seemed unnaturally bright, pools and swirls of phosphorescence that filled the dome of the sky. In the distance, faintly silhouetted against the firmament, a line of high-tension towers headed for Isabella.

He could feel every thump of his heart. He could hear the blood singing in his ears. He had never felt so alive. He hiked at a rapid pace, and in twenty minutes he had reached the turnoff to the old Nakai Rock Trading Post. Here he paused, and then decided to scout out the valley. In a few minutes he had reached the edges of the bluffs where the road dropped down into the valley. He focused his binoculars on the settlement.

A large tipi sat in the middle of the field, aglow from the flickering light of a fire inside. Nearby stood a helter-skelter structure, a dome of branches leaning together, covered with canvas tarps held down with rocks. Beyond it, a bonfire was burning down to coals, exposing inside a pile of cherry-red rocks.

He had seen this before: a Navajo sweat lodge.

The faint sounds of chanting and a rapidly beating drum drifted up on the dry, quiet air. How odd. The Navajos were having a ceremony. Had they sensed it, too—this great and powerful thing that was about to happen? Had they felt the coming wrath of God? But they were idolaters, worshipping false gods. He shook his head in sadness: *"Strait is the gate, and narrow is the way, which leadeth unto life, and few there be that find it."*

The sweat lodge and the tipi were one more sign that the End Days were fully come, that the devil walked among them.

Aside from the Navajos, the valley looked deserted, the scattered houses dark. Eddy looped around and bypassed the settlement, and in another ten minutes he came to the airstrip. Deserted, too, were the hangars against the night sky. The Antichrist and his disciples had gathered at Isabella, deep down in the mountain—he was sure of that.

He approached the chain-link fence around the security area, taking care not to get close enough to set off the alarms he assumed were there. It gleamed in the harsh sodium lights that illuminated the area.

The elevator down to Isabella stood a few hundred yards away, a tall, ugly, windowless building topped with clusters of antennae and satellite dishes. He could feel the ground vibrate from deep within; he could hear the hum of Isabella. *"And they had a king over them, which is the angel of the bottomless pit, whose name in the Hebrew tongue is Abaddon."*

His mind and spirit burned, as if in a fever. He looked up at the hulking steel towers that brought in the electricity to run the machine, and his flesh crawled. They could have been the devil's very own army, striding through the night. The high-tension wires crackled and hummed like hair charged with static. He reached into his bag and grasped the warm leather of his Bible, feeling its reassuring solidity. Bracing himself with a short prayer, he walked toward the nearest tower, a few hundred yards away.

He stopped beneath the tower. The gigantic struts disappeared upward into the night, visible only by the lines of blackness they painted across the stars. The power lines spit and hissed like serpents, the sound mingling with the moaning of the wind through the struts, a symphony of the damned. Eddy shivered to the roots of his soul.

The phrase from Revelation came into his mind again: *". . . to gather them to the battle of that great day of God Almighty."* They would be coming—he was sure of that. They would answer his appeal. He needed to be ready. He needed a plan.

He began scouting the area, making notes of the

topography and terrain, the roads, access points, fences, towers, other structures.

Above him, the high-tension lines hissed and spit. The stars winked. The earth turned. Russell Eddy moved through the dark, for the first time in his life supremely sure of himself.

49

LOCKWOOD WAS SURPRISED AT HOW SHABBY and bare-bones-functional the White House Situation Room was. It smelled like a basement rec room that needed airing out. The walls were painted ochre. A mahogany table dominated the center, with micro-phones strung down the middle. Flat-panel screens lined the walls. Chairs lined the two long walls, shoulder to shoulder.

The ugly, institutional clock at the end of the table read midnight, exactly.

The president strode in, looking crisp in his gray suit and mauve tie, white hair swept back. He turned to the Navy rating who evidently ran the electronics. "I want you to patch in the Chairman of the Joint Chiefs, my National Security Advisor, DDHS, DFBI, and DCI."

"Yes, Mr. President."

"Oh, and don't forget the head of the Senate Intelligence Committee so he won't bitch later about being out of the loop."

He took a seat at the head of the table. Roger

Morton, the chief of staff, patrician and cautious, took the seat to his right. Gordon Galdone, the campaign manager, as large and disheveled as an unmade bed, wearing a brown Wal-Mart suit, took the seat on the other side of the president. Jean occupied a chair against the wall in the corner, behind the president, primly perched with her steno pad at the ready.

"Let's just go ahead—the others will join us when they join us."

"Yes sir."

Some of the flat panels were already lighting up with attendees. Jack Strand, the FBI director, was the first. He sat in his office over in Quantico, a giant FBI seal behind him, his square-jawed cop's face touched with old acne scars staring relentlessly into the screen—a man to inspire confidence, or at least trying to.

The Secretary of DOE, a man named Hall, popped up next from his office on Independence Avenue, the man ostensibly in charge of Isabella. But he had never taken control—he was a genial delegator—and now he was a mess, his plump face covered with a sheen of sweat, his light blue tie knotted so tight it looked like he'd just tried to hang himself with it.

"All right," said the President, clasping his hands on the table in front. "Secretary Hall, you're the man in charge, what the hell's going on out there?"

"I'm sorry," Hall stammered, "Mr. President, I have no idea. This is unprecedented. I don't know what to say—"

The president cut him off, turning to Lockwood. "Who was the last to be in contact with the Isabella team? Stan, do you know?"

"It was probably me. I spoke to my inside man at seven MDT, and he said everything was fine. He said a run was planned and that he'd go down and join them at eight. He gave no indication that anything was out of the ordinary."

"Got any theories about what's going on?"

Lockwood's mind had been racing through the possibilities, none of which made sense. He controlled the panic welling inside, keeping his voice steady and calm. "I'm not sure I've got a clear handle on it."

"Could we be dealing with some kind of internal mutiny? Sabotage?"

"It's possible."

The President turned to the Chairman of the Joint Chiefs, sitting in his office in the Pentagon, wearing his rumpled field uniform. "General, you're in charge of the rapid response units, where's the closest one?"

"Nellis AFB, in Nevada."

"National Guard Unit?"

"Flagstaff."

"FBI? Where's the closest field office?"

Jack Strand, the FBI Director, answered from his screen. "Also Flagstaff."

The president thought, his brow furrowed, tapping his finger on the table. "General, have them send out the closest chopper to investigate."

At this, Gordon Galdone, the campaign chief,

shifted his bulk, sighed, and pressed a finger to his soft lips.

The oracle speaks, thought Lockwood sourly.

"Mr. President?" The man had an orotund voice, not unlike Orson Welles in his obese years.

"Yes, Gordon?"

"May I point out that this is not just a scientific or even military problem? It's a *political* problem. For weeks the press and others have been asking why Isabella isn't online. The *Times* ran an editorial last week. Four days ago a scientist committed suicide. We've got a firestorm among the Christian fundamentalists. Now the scientists won't answer their telephones. On top of that, we have a science adviser who is freelancing as a spy."

"Gordon, I *approved* it," said the president.

Galdone continued unperturbed. "Mr. President, we are heading into a public relations disaster. You supported the Isabella project. You're identified with it. You're going to take a big hit—unless we solve this problem right away. Sending out a chopper to investigate is too little, too late. It'll take all night and things will still be a mess in the morning. God help us when the media gets hold of this."

"So what do you propose, Gordon?"

"To *fix* the problem by tomorrow morning."

"How?"

"Send in a team equipped to take control of Isabella and shut it down—and escort the scientists off the premises."

"Just a minute," the president said. "The Isabella project is the best thing I've done. I'll be damned if I'll shut it down!"

"You shut it down or it will shut you down."

Lockwood was shocked to hear an adviser address the president so rudely.

Morton spoke. "Mr. President, I agree with Gordon. We're less than two months from the election. We don't have the luxury of time. We've got to shut down the Isabella project tonight. We can sort it all out later."

"We don't even know what the hell's going *on* out there," the president said. "How do you know we're not dealing with some kind of terrorist attack or hostage situation?"

"Perhaps we are," said Morton.

A silence. The president turned to his National Security Advisor, on a flat panel. "You got a hint of something going down anywhere in national intelligence?"

"Nothing that we're aware of, Mr. President."

"All right, let's send in a team. Armed and ready for any level of conflict. But no big mobilization, nothing that would alert the press or make us look stupid later. A small, elite, SWAT-type team, highly trained—to get in there, secure the damn place, shut it down, and escort the scientists out. The operation to be completed by dawn." He sat back. "Okay: Who can do it?"

The Director of the FBI spoke. "The Rocky Mountain Hostage Rescue Team is based in Denver, less than four hundred miles from the Isabella project. Eleven highly capable men, all ex-Delta, specifically trained to operate on American soil."

"Yes, but here at the CIA—," began the DCI.

"Great." The president cut him off and turned to Lockwood. "Stan? What do you think?"

Lockwood struggled to keep his voice calm. "Mr. President, in my opinion this talk of a commando raid is premature. I strongly agree with what you said earlier—we should find out what's going on first. I'm sure there's a reasonable explanation. Send a helicopter out there with some people to knock on the door, so to speak."

Morton spoke in a crisp voice. "Tomorrow morning, every TV news station in the country will be out there. We'll be operating under a media microscope. Our freedom of action will be gone. If for some reason the scientists have barricaded themselves in there, it could be Waco all over again."

"Waco?" repeated Lockwood incredulously. "We're talking about twelve eminent scientists here led by a Nobel laureate. These are not a bunch of crazy cultists!"

The chief of staff turned to the president. "Mr. President, I can't emphasize strongly enough that this operation must be completed *without fail* by dawn. Everything will change when the media arrive. We don't have time to send someone out there to 'knock on doors.'" His voice rose with sarcasm.

"I absolutely concur," said Galdone.

"No alternative?" asked the president quietly.

"None."

Lockwood swallowed. He felt sick. He had lost the argument and now he would be forced to participate in the shutting down of Isabella. "The operation you propose may present some difficulties."

"Explain."

"You can't just cut power to Isabella. It could cause an explosion. The power flows are tricky and can only be controlled from within, by the computer. If for some reason the scientific team inside isn't . . . *cooperating,* you'll need to have someone along who can shut down Isabella safely."

"Who do you recommend?"

"That same man I mentioned earlier up at Los Alamos, Bernard Wolf."

"We'll send a chopper to fetch him. How about getting in?"

"The access door to the Bunker is hardened against external attack. All the forced air systems are highly secure. If the team won't or can't open the front doors, it may be difficult to reach them."

"There's no security override?"

"DHS felt an override might allow a point of entry for terrorists."

"How do we get in, then?"

God, how he hated this. "The best way would be straight in through the front door, with explosives. It's halfway down a sheer cliff. There's a large staging area in front, but much of it's recessed under the cliff and I'm sure you couldn't land a military helicopter in there. You'll have to land the team on top and rappel down, then breach the door. I'm describing a worst-case scenario. The scientists will probably just let the team in."

"How'd they get heavy equipment in there if there's no road?"

"They used the old coal-mine road, then dynamited it off the side of the mountainside when Isabella was complete. Again—security."

"I see. Tell me more about this entry door."

"It's a titanium honeycomb composite. *Very* hard to cut. Explosives would be the way to go."

"Get me the specs on it. And then?"

"Inside, there's a big cavern. Straight ahead is the Isabella tunnel. To the left is the control room, which we call the Bridge. Its door is one-inch stainless steel, a final defense against entry. I'll get you the blue-prints."

"That's it for security?"

"That's it."

"Are they armed?"

"The SIO, Wardlaw, carries a sidearm. No other firearms are allowed."

Morton turned to the president. "Mr. President, we need your order to go ahead with this operation."

Lockwood watched as the president hesitated, glanced at him, then looked over to the FBI Director. "Send in the FBI Hostage Rescue Team. Get the scientists out of the mountain and shut Isabella down."

"Yes, Mr. President."

The chief of staff slapped his briefing file shut with a smack, the sound like a slap to Lockwood's face.

50

A WHINING SINGSONG KEENED THROUGH THE Bunker. The screen flickered. Ford stood rooted before the Visualizer, Kate beside him. Somehow, he didn't remember when her hand had found his.

In response to Hazelius's question, more words appeared on the screen.

The great monotheistic religions were a necessary stage in the development of human culture. Your task is to guide the human race to the next belief system.

"Which is?"

Science.

"That's ridiculous—science can't be a religion!" said Hazelius.

You have already started a new religion—only you refuse to see it. Religion was once a way to make sense of the world. Science has now taken over this role.

"Science and religion are two different things," Ford broke in. "They ask different questions and require different kinds of evidence."

Science and religion both seek the same thing: truth. There can be no reconciliation between the two. The collision of worldviews is well under way and worsening. Science has already refuted most of the core beliefs of the world's historical religions, bringing those religions into a state of turmoil. Your task is to help humanity chart a path through the crisis.

"Oh, please!" Edelstein cried. "You think the fanatics in the Middle East—or the Bible Belt, for that matter—are going to roll over and accept science as the new religion? That's crazy."

You will offer the world my words and the story of what happened here. Do not underestimate my power—the power of truth.

"Where are we supposed to be going with this new religion? What's the point of it? Who needs it?" Hazelius asked.

The immediate goal of humankind is to escape the limits of biochemistry. You must free your mind from the meat of your bodies.

"The meat? I don't understand," said Hazelius.

Meat. Nerves. Cells. Biochemistry. The medium by which you think. You must free your mind from the meat.

"How?"

You have already begun to process information beyond your meat existence through computers. You will soon find a way to process it using quantum-state computing machines, which will lead you to harness the natural quantum processes in the world around you as a means of computation. No longer will you need to build machines to process information. You

*will expand into the universe, literally and figura-
tively, as other intelligent entities have expanded
before you. You will escape the prison of biological
intelligence.*

"Then what?"

*Over time, you will link up with other expanded
intelligences. All these linked intelligences will discover a way to merge into a third stage of mind that
will comprehend the simple reality that is at the heart
of existence.*

"And that's it? That's what it's all about?" Kate
asked.

No. That is merely a prelude to a greater task.

The Visualizer flickered, lines of snow shooting
across. Dolby labored at his workstation, hunkered
down and silent. The words rippled, as if reflected in
black water.

"Which is what?" Hazelius finally asked.

Arresting the heat death of the universe.

Ford felt Kate's hand instinctively tighten around
his.

51

BOOKER CRAWLEY TOOK THE CUP OF coffee into his
study and settled in his chair in front of the TV. Once
again he picked up the remote and flipped through the
news stations. Nothing. There didn't seem to be any
blowback from the wild accusations Spates had made
on his show. Still, Crawley couldn't shake the feeling

that something was about to happen. He glanced at the clock. It was thirty minutes past one, eastern daylight time—eleven thirty in Arizona. Or was it ten thirty?

He exhaled and swallowed a bitter mouthful of coffee. He was getting worked up over nothing. So far everything had gone as planned, and Spates's show, even if it was nutty, was sure to scare the crap out of the Navajo Tribal Council.

That thought made him feel better.

Still . . . It wouldn't hurt to check in with Spates and find out where the hell he had gotten that crazy information about Isabella claiming it was God.

He dialed Spates's office number first, on the off chance he might still be at work. Surprisingly, the line was busy. No voice mail, just busy. He waited several minutes and dialed again, then again, still without getting through.

Probably out of order.

He dialed Spates's cell number next, and got routed immediately to his voice mail. "You have reached the voice mailbox of Reverend Don T. Spates," a pleasant female voice said. "The mailbox is currently full. Please try later."

Crawley dialed the reverend's home phone. It, too, was busy.

Christ, it was stuffy in the study. He walked to the window, unlatched it, and slid it open. A stream of night air, fresh and lovely, washed in, swelling the lace curtains. He took a few deep breaths. He told himself again there was no reason for alarm. He sipped his coffee while staring into the darkened street, wondering what exactly had him spooked. A busy phone?

The reverend would have a Web site. Maybe there would be information posted there.

He sat down at his desk, booted up his laptop, and Googled:

Spates God's Prime Time

The first hit was indeed the televangelist's official Web site, www.godsprimetime.com. He clicked on the link and waited.

After a frustrating minute, an error message appeared.

```
        BANDWIDTH LIMIT EXCEEDED
   The server is temporarily unable to
service your request due to the site
owner reaching bandwidth limit. Please
try again later.
   Apache/1.3.37 Server at www.gods-
primetime.com Port 80
```

His uneasiness climbed a notch. Busy phones, server down . . . Could Spates's Web site be under a denial-of-service attack? Maybe other Christian sites would have posted something.

He Googled:

A bunch of unfamiliar Christian Web sites came up, with names like jesus-is-savior.com, rapture-ready.com, antichrist.com. He clicked on a link at random and immediately it opened to a document.

My Friends in Christ,

Many of you watched the show *Roundtable America* earlier tonight, hosted by the Reverend Don T. Spates. . . .

Crawley read the letter once. He read it again. A faint chill crawled up his spine. So this was Spates's source, a nutcase pastor out there in Navajoland. The note at the bottom indicated the crazy pastor had sent the letter just a few hours ago. From the list of hits it seemed to have been posted at a fair number of Web sites.

How many? There was a way to find out. He Googled the first sentence of the letter, enclosing it in quotation marks to retrieve only Web sites that had posted the exact text. A split second later the list of hits came up. The standard notation at the top indicated how many:

Results 1–10 of about 56,500 for **"Many of you watched the show *Roundtable America* earlier tonight, hosted by the Reverend Don T. Spates"**

For a long time Crawley sat in the silent George-town study. Could it be true that the letter had already been posted to over fifty thousand Web sites? Unthinkable. He breathed in and out, steadying himself. If his role behind Spates's attack on the Isabella project should become known, he'd fall harder than his old pal Jack Abramoff. The problem was, when he got down to it, he really didn't know much about Spates and his evangelical orbit. Crawley felt like a man who'd casually thrown a rock into a dark place and now could hear dozens of buzzing rattlesnakes. He rose again, walked to the window. Outside, Georgetown slept. The street was empty. The world was at peace.

As he stood, he heard his computer chime, indicating he had received an e-mail. He walked back to check it out. A little window popped up to give him the subject heading:

Fwd:Fwd: Red Mesa=Armageddon

He opened it up, began reading, and was shocked to find it was the exact same letter he had just read. Did someone know about his contact with Spates? Was this some kind of veiled threat? Had *Spates* sent this to him? But when he looked at the vast header over the e-mail, listing dozens of e-mail addresses, he realized he had not been singled out. Nor did he recognize the address of the sender. This was a scattershot e-mail, viral marketing as it were. Viral marketing for

Armageddon. And it had come into his mailbox by chance.

As he read the letter again in disbelief, trying to guess the probability of his getting that particular e-mail at that particular moment, his mail program chimed again and another e-mail appeared. It had the same subject heading—almost.

Fwd:Fwd:Fwd:Fwd: Red Mesa=Armageddon

Booker Crawley grasped the arms of his chair and rose unsteadily. As he made his way across the study, the computer chimed again, and again, as more e-mails hit it. He staggered into the bathroom at the far end of his study. Gripping the edge of the sink with one hand and holding his tie back with the other, he vomited.

52

BERN WOLF HUNKERED DOWN IN THE bay of the chopper, chewing nervously on a cud of gum and watching eleven heavily armed men dressed in black climb on board and settle silently into their seats. The only insignia on their uniforms was a small FBI shield on the breast. Wolf felt uncomfortable in his camouflage gear, flak jacket and helmet. He tried without success to adjust his gangly limbs into something reminiscent of comfort, shifted irritably, and crossed his arms. His ponytail stuck out from under the helmet and he didn't have to see himself in a mirror to know it looked ridiculous. His head was sweating and his ears rang from the first leg of the flight.

Once the men had buckled in, the helicopter took off, rising into the night sky, turned, and accelerated. A gibbous moon had risen, bathing the desert landscape below in a silvery sheen.

Wolf chewed and chewed. What the hell was going on? He'd been roused out of his house without explanation, dragged out to the Los Alamos airstrip, hustled into a chopper. Nobody would tell him a bloody thing. It was like the beginning of a bad film.

Through the window he could see the distant peaks of the San Juan Mountains in Colorado. The helicopter cleared the foothills, and Wolf glimpsed a faint ribbon of reflected starlight below: the San Juan River.

They followed the approximate course of the river, past patches of lights marking the towns of Bloomfield and Farmington, then on into the empty darkness. As the craft dipped south again, Wolf saw the dark hump of Navajo Mountain in the distance, and that was when he guessed their destination: the Isabella project.

He masticated his ball of gum, pondering. He'd heard rumors—everyone in the high-energy physics community had—about problems with Isabella. He'd been as shocked as anyone about the suicide of his former colleague, Peter Volkonsky. Not that he'd ever liked the Russian, but he had always respected the man for his programming skills. He wondered what was going on that required a black-clad goon squad to fix.

Fifteen minutes later the black outline of Red Mesa loomed dimly ahead. A bright patch of lights at its edge signaled the location of Isabella. The chopper swung down, raced along the mesa top, and slowed at an airfield illuminated by two long rows of blue lights, then turned and settled down on a helipad.

The rotors powered down and one of the team shifted out of his seat and opened the cargo door. Wolf's handler placed a hand on his shoulder and gestured for him to wait. The door slid open and the FBI team jumped out, one at a time, crouching and running in the rotor wash, like they were securing the landing zone.

Five minutes passed. Then the handler gestured him out. Wolf slung his pack over his shoulder and took his sweet time—he wasn't going to hustle and break his leg. He climbed down with excessive care and scuttled beyond the backwash. The handler touched his elbow lightly and pointed toward a Quonset hut. They walked over, and the handler opened the door for him. The hut smelled of fresh lumber and glue and was almost empty, except for a desk and a row of cheap chairs.

"Have a seat, Dr. Wolf."

Wolf dumped his backpack onto a chair near the desk and slumped down in the one next to it. He could hardly imagine a less comfortable seat, especially at this hour, so far from the pillow and bed where he belonged. He was still squirming when one of the men came in. The man extended his hand. "Special Agent in Charge Doerfler."

Wolf shook it halfheartedly, without getting up.

Doerfler sat down on the edge of the desk and tried to appear friendly and relaxed. It didn't succeed: the man was as wound up as the Energizer Bunny. "I bet you're wondering why you're here, Dr. Wolf."

"How did you guess?" He distrusted people like Doerfler, with their whitewall haircuts, southern accents, and smooth-talking language. He had dealt with too many of them during the design phase of Isabella.

Doerfler glanced at his watch. "We don't have much time, so I'll be brief. They tell me you're familiar with Isabella, Dr. Wolf."

"I should hope so," he said irritably. "I was assistant director of the design team."

"Have you been here before?"

"No. My work was all on paper."

Doerfler leaned over on his elbow, his face serious. "Something's happened out here. We don't exactly know what. The scientific team has sealed itself inside the mountain and turned off all external communications. They've shut down the main computer and they're running Isabella at full power using backup computer systems."

Wolf licked his lips. This was too far out to believe.

"We have no idea what's going on. It may be a hostage situation, it may be a mutiny, it may be an accident or some kind of unanticipated equipment or power failure."

"So what's my role?"

"I'll get to that in a moment. The men you flew in with are members of an FBI Hostage Rescue Team. It's like an elite SWAT team. That doesn't necessarily mean there are hostages, but we have to plan for that contingency."

"Are you talking about *terrorists?*"

"Perhaps. The HRT is going to enter the facility, perform hostage rescue if necessary, neutralize undesirables, isolate the scientists, and escort them from the premises."

"Neutralize undesirables—you mean shoot people?"

"If necessary."

"You're shitting me."

Doerfler frowned. "No, sir, I am not."

"You woke me up to join a commando raid? I'm sorry, Mr. Doerfler, but you've got the wrong Bern Wolf."

"You needn't be concerned in the slightest, Dr. Wolf. I've assigned you a handler. Agent Miller. Totally reliable. He'll be at your side, guiding you every step of the way. Once the facility is secure, he'll take you in and you'll perform your assignment."

"Which is?"

"Turn off Isabella."

● ● ●

FROM A PERCH AT THE TOP of the bluffs above Nakai
Valley, Nelson Begay scanned the Isabella complex
with a pair of old army binoculars. A chopper had
passed low over the tipi, its rotors drowning out their
Blessing Way ceremony and shaking the tipi like a
dust devil. Begay and Becenti had climbed up the
hillside for a better view, and they could see it had
landed at the airstrip, a mile away.

"They coming after us?" Willy Becenti asked.

"No idea," said Begay, watching. Men with guns
were piling out of the chopper. After breaking into a
hangar, they drove out two Humvees and began transferring gear into them.

Begay shook his head. "I don't think it has anything
to do with us."

"You sure?" Becenti sounded disappointed.

"I'm not sure. We better head over and take a closer
look." He glanced at Becenti, saw the eager restless-
ness in his eyes. Begay laid a hand on his shoulder.
"Just keep your cool, all right?"

53

STANTON LOCKWOOD LIFTED HIS CUFF TO peek at his
Rolex. Quarter to two in the morning. The president
had ordered in the FBI Hostage Rescue Team at midnight, and now the operation was in full swing. A few
minutes ago, the HRT had landed at the airstrip. They
were now transferring their gear to Humvees to take

them the half-mile to the secure zone at the cliff's edge, directly above the opening to the Bunker.

The atmosphere in the Oval Office was edgy. Jean, the president's secretary, was shaking the tension out of her writing hand.

"They've loaded the first Humvee," said the FBI Director, who had been giving the president a running commentary. "Still no sign of anyone. They're all down in the Bunker, as we thought."

"No luck contacting them?"

"None. All communications from the airstrip to the Bunker are turned off."

Lockwood shifted in his chair. He searched his mind for a logical explanation. There was none.

The situation room door opened, and Roger Morton entered carrying several sheets of paper. Lockwood followed him with his eyes. He had never liked the man, but now he detested him, with his horn-rimmed glasses, his immaculate suit, his tie that looked like it had been glued to his shirtfront. Morton was the quintessential Washington operator. With these sour thoughts in mind, he watched Morton conferring with the president, their heads together, scrutinizing the piece of paper. They waved Galdone over and all three took a long look.

The president looked up at Lockwood. "Stan, take a look at this."

Lockwood rose and joined the group. The president handed him the printout of an e-mail. Lockwood began to read:

"It's all over the Internet," said Morton, speaking even before he had finished. "And I mean *everywhere.*"

Lockwood shook his head and placed the letter on the table. "I find it depressing that in America in the twenty-first century, this kind of medieval thinking could still exist."

The president stared at him. "The letter is more than 'depressing,' Stan. It's calling for an armed attack on a U.S. government facility."

"Mr. President, I personally would not take this seriously. The letter has no directions, no plan of action, no meeting place. It's just hot air. Stuff like this circulates on the Web every day. Look how many people read that Left Behind series. You didn't see them taking to the streets."

Morton gazed at him with passive hostility. "Lockwood, this letter's been posted to tens of thousands of Web sites. It's circulating like mad. We've got to take it seriously."

The president heaved a sigh. "Stan, I wish I was as optimistic as you about this. But this letter, on top of that sermon . . ." He shook his head. "We need to prepare for the worst."

Galdone rumbled his throat clear to speak. "People who think the world is coming to an end might be liable to do something rash. Even resort to violence."

"Christianity is supposed to be a nonviolent religion," Lockwood said.

"We aren't impugning anyone's religious beliefs, Stan," the president said tartly. "All of us here need to realize that this is a sensitive area, in which people can easily take offense." He tossed the letter on the desk and turned to the Director of Homeland Security. "Where's the closest National Guard unit?"

"That would be Camp Navajo in Bellemont, just north of Flagstaff."

"How far is that from Red Mesa?"

"About a hundred and twenty-five miles."

"Mobilize them and chopper them down to Red Mesa. As a backup."

"Yes, sir. Unfortunately, half the unit's overseas and their equipment and their rotary wing aircraft are not what one might wish for an operation of this sort."

"How quickly could you bring the unit up to full strength?"

"We could bring up assets and personnel from Phoenix and Nellis AFB. It might take three to five hours, pushing it."

"Five is too long. Do what you can in three. I want them in the air by four forty-five A.M."

"Four forty-five A.M.," repeated the DNS. "Yes, Mr. President."

"Put out a quiet word to the Arizona State Police to double their patrols and report any unusual traffic on the interstates and secondary roads around the Navajo

Indian Reservation. And be ready to throw up road-blocks at short notice."

"Yes, Mr. President."

Lockwood spoke. "There's a small Navajo Tribal Police station in Piñon, only twenty miles from Red Mesa."

"Excellent. Have them send a patrol out to the Red Mesa road, to check it out."

"Very good, sir."

"I want all this done *quietly*. If we overreact, the Christian right will kick us around like a football. They'll accuse us of being anti-Christian, Jesus haters, godless liberals—those people will say anything." The president looked around the room. "Any other recommendations?'

There were none.

He turned to Lockwood. "I hope you're right. God knows, we might have ten thousand idiots heading to Red Mesa right now."

54

FORD FELT THE SWEAT TRICKLING DOWN his scalp. The heat was climbing in the Bridge, despite the air-conditioning system running at full power. Isabella hummed and sang, the walls vibrating. He glanced at Kate, but her attention was fully fixed on the Visualizer screen.

When the universe reaches a state of maximum entropy, which is the heat death of the universe, then will the universal computation come to a halt. I will die.

"Is this inevitable or is there some way to prevent it?" Hazelius asked.

That is the very question you must determine.

"So that's the ultimate purpose of existence?" asked Ford. "To defeat this mysterious heat death? Sounds like something out of a science fiction novel."

Circumventing the heat death is merely a step on the way.

"The way to what?" Hazelius asked.

It will give the universe the fullness of time it needs to think itself into the final state.

"What's this final state?"

I do not know. It will be like nothing you or even I could possibly imagine.

"You mentioned the 'fullness of time,'" said Edelstein. "How long is that, exactly?"

It will be a number of years equal to ten factorial raised to the ten factorial power, that number raised to the ten factorial power, that number raised to the ten factorial power, this power relation repeated 10^{83} times, and then the resulting number raised to its own factorial power 10^{47} times, as above. Using your mathematical notation, this number—the first God number—is:

$$(10!\uparrow\uparrow10^{83})^{[(10!\uparrow\uparrow10^{83})!\uparrow\uparrow10^{47}]}$$

This is the length of time in years it will take for the universe to think itself into the final state, to arrive at the ultimate answer.

"That's an absurdly large number!"

It is but a drop in the great ocean of infinity.

"Where is the role of morality, of ethics, in this brave new universe of yours?" Ford asked. "Or salvation and the forgiveness of sins?"

I repeat again: separateness is but an illusion. Human beings are like cells in a body. Cells die, but the body lives on. Hatred, cruelty, war, and genocide are more like autoimmune diseases than the product of something you call "evil." This vision of connectedness I offer you provides a rich moral field of action, in which altruism, compassion, and responsibility for one another play a central role. Your fate is one fate. Human beings will prevail together or die together. No one is saved because no one is lost. No one is forgiven because no one is accused.

"What about God's promise to us of a better world?"

Your various concepts of heaven are remarkably obtuse.

"Excuse me, but salvation is anything but obtuse!"

The vision of spiritual completion I offer you is immeasurably grander than any heaven dreamed on earth.

"What about the soul? Do you deny the existence of the immortal soul?"

"Wyman, please!" Hazelius cried. "You're wasting everyone's time with these ridiculous theological questions!"

"Excuse me, but I think they're vital questions,"

said Kate. "These are the questions people will ask—and which we better be able to answer."

We? Ford wondered who Kate meant.

Information is never lost. With the death of the body, the information created by that life changes shape and structure, but it is never lost. Death is an informational transition. Do not fear it.

"Do we lose our individuality at death?" Ford asked.

Do not mourn the loss. From that powerful sense of individuality, so necessary for evolution, flows many of the qualities that haunt human existence, good and bad: fear, pain, suffering, and loneliness, as well as love, happiness, and compassion. That is why you must escape your biochemical existence. When you free yourselves from the tyranny of the flesh, you will take the good—love, happiness, compassion, and altruism—with you. You will leave behind the bad.

"I don't find much uplift in the idea that the little quantum fluctuations my existence has generated will somehow give us immortality," said Ford sarcastically.

You should find great solace in this view of life. Information in the universe cannot die. Not one step, not one memory, not one sorrow in your life is ever forgotten. You as an individual will be lost in the storm of time, your molecules dispersed. But who you were, what you did, how you lived, will always remain embedded in the universal computation.

"Forgive me, but it still sounds so mechanistic, so

soulless, this talk of existence as 'computation.' "

Call it dreaming, if you prefer, or desiring, willing, thinking. Everything you see is part of an unimaginably vast and beautiful computation, from a baby speaking its first words to a star collapsing into a black hole. Our universe is a gorgeous computation that, starting with a single axiom of great simplicity, has been running for thirteen billion years. We have hardly begun the adventure! When you find a way to shift your own meat-limited process of thinking to other natural quantum systems, you will begin to control the computation. You will begin to understand its beauty and perfection.

"If everything is a computation, then what is the purpose of intelligence? Of mind?"

Intelligence exists all around you, even in nonliving processes. A thunderstorm is a computation vastly more sophisticated than a human mind. It is, in its own way, intelligent.

"A thunderstorm has no consciousness. A human mind has awareness of self. It's conscious. That's the difference, and it isn't trivial."

Did I not tell you that the very consciousness of self is an illusion, an artifact of evolution? The difference is not even trivial.

"A weather system isn't creative. It doesn't make choices. It can't think. It's merely the mechanistic unfolding of forces."

How do you know you are not the mechanistic unfolding of forces? Like the mind, a weather system contains complex chemical, electrical, and mechanical properties. It is thinking. It is creative. Its thoughts are different from your thoughts. A human being creates complexity by writing a novel on the surface of paper; a weather system creates complexity by writing waves on the surface of an ocean. What is the difference between the information carried in the words of a novel and the information carried on the waves of the sea? Listen, and the waves will speak, and someday, I tell you, you will write your thoughts on the surface of the sea.

"So what's the universe computing?" Innes continued angrily. "What's this great problem it's trying to solve?"

That is the deepest and most wonderful mystery of all.

"Perimeter alarms," said Wardlaw. "We have an intruder."

Hazelius turned. "Don't tell me that preacher's back."

"No, no . . . God, no. Dr. Hazelius, you better come look."

Ford and the rest followed Hazelius over to the security station. They peered over Wardlaw's shoulder at the wall of screens.

"What the hell?" Hazelius asked.

Wardlaw punched a series of buttons. "I shouldn't have been paying attention to whatever the hell that crazy thing on the screen was saying. Look, I'm rewinding. Here's where it starts. A chopper . . . a military Black Hawk UH-60A, landing at the air-field."

They all stood and watched—astonished. Ford could see men in dark jumpsuits, carrying weapons, tumbling from the chopper.

"They're breaking into the hangars," Wardlaw went on, "taking our Humvees. Loading them up . . . Now they're bashing down the gates to the security zone. . . . That's what set off the alarm. Okay, real time begins right here."

Ford watched as the soldiers, or whatever they were, jumped from the Humvees and fanned out, weapons at the ready.

"What's going on? What the hell are they doing?" cried Hazelius, his voice full of alarm.

"They're establishing a classic assault perimeter," said Wardlaw.

"Assault? On what?"

"On us."

55

RUSS EDDY CROUCHED BEHIND A JUNIPER tree and peered out into the fenced security area. The men in black had bashed down the security fence and were busy setting up lights and unloading equipment from a pair of Humvees. He had no doubt these men had been sent to protect the Isabella project in response to his letter. It was too much of a coincidence to be otherwise. Paramilitary forces of the New World Order who had arrived in black helicopters, just as Mark Koernke predicted.

Eddy knew that his letter had reached those in power.

He made careful note of how many there were, what weapons and equipment they carried, jotting everything down in his notebook.

The soldiers finished rigging up a string of portable lights and the area was bathed in brilliant white light. Eddy shrank back in the shadows and retreated to the road. He had seen enough. The army of God would soon begin arriving—and he needed to organize them.

As he walked back toward the far edge of the mesa, where the Dugway came up on top, that plan began to take shape. First, they would need a parking and staging area far enough away from Isabella so they could amass without being seen. They had to group themselves, organize, then attack. And, in fact, right at the top of the Dugway, about three miles from Isabella, was a vast open area of slickrock that would make a good location.

He glanced at his watch: eleven forty-five. It had been two hours since he sent the e-mail. People would begin arriving at any moment. He began to jog down the center of the road, to intercept any arriving traffic.

About a half mile from the Dugway, he heard the rumble of a bike engine. A single light appeared over the top of the mesa, moving rapidly toward him. The light slowed as the beam illuminated Eddy, and a dirt bike stopped in front of him, driven by a muscular man with long blond hair tied in a ponytail, wearing an unbuttoned denim jacket, sleeves torn off, and no shirt. He had a striking face, craggy, movie-star handsome, with the physique of a god. A heavy iron cross dangled from his neck on a metal chain, nestled on his hairy chest.

As the bike came to a stop he extended two leather-booted legs, steadied the bike, and grinned. "Pastor Eddy?"

His heart hammering, Eddy stepped forward. "Greetings in the name of Jesus Christ."

The man kicked down the kickstand, rose from his bike—he was enormous—and walked toward Eddy with his arms thrown wide. He enveloped Eddy in a dusty embrace, his body odor overpowering, and then stepped back, gripping him affectionately by his shoulders. "Randy Doke." He gave Eddy another hug. "Oh, man, am I really the first?"

"You are."

"I can't believe I made it. When I saw your letter, I hopped on my Kawasaki and came up from Hol-brook. Cross-country, over the desert, cutting fences and riding like hell. Woulda been here sooner, but I took a spill back near Second Mesa. I can't believe I'm here. Oh, man, I can't believe it."

Eddy felt a rush of faith, an inpouring of energy.

The man looked around. "So—what now?"

"Let's pray." He clasped Doke's rough hands, and

they bowed their heads. "Lord God Almighty, please surround us with Thine angels, wingtip to wingtip, with their swords drawn to protect us, so that they can lead us, Thy servants, into victory against the Antichrist. In the name of Jesus Christ our Lord. Amen."

"Amen, brother."

The man had a deep, resonant voice that Eddy found reassuring, magnetic. Here was the kind of man who knew what to do.

Doke went back to his bike, pulled a rifle out of a leather scabbard hanging off the seat, and slung it over his back. Hauling out a bandolier packed with rounds, he tossed it over the other shoulder, which gave him the look of an old-time guerrilla warrior. He shot Eddy a grin and saluted. "Brother Randy, reporting for service in God's army!"

More headlights approached—slowly, uncertainly. A dusty Jeep, top down, stopped next to them. A man and a woman in their thirties climbed out. Eddy opened his arms and took them in, first the man, then the woman. They both began to cry, their tears making tracks down their dusty faces.

"Greetings in Christ."

The man was wearing a business suit covered in dust. He carried a Bible. Tucked into his belt was a big kitchen knife. The woman had pinned little pieces of paper to her blouse, which fluttered as she walked. Eddy saw they were Bible verses and slogans: *Trust and obey. . . . Go ye into all the world. . . . For lo, I am*

379

with you always, even unto the end of the earth. . . .
"Grabbed them off the refrigerator," she said. She reached into the Jeep and fetched out a baseball bat.

"We prayed and prayed, but we couldn't decide," the man said. "Did God mean us to fight with His Word, or did He mean us to use real weapons?"

They stood in front of Eddy, awaiting for orders.

"No mistake about it," Eddy said. "This is going to be a battle. A *real* battle."

"I'm glad we brought these."

"A lot of people are going to be coming down that road," Eddy continued. "Thousands, probably. We need a place to gather everyone together, to prepare. A staging ground. That'll be that area, off to the right." He gestured toward the vast expanse of slick-rock and sand, pale in the light of the lopsided moon rising over the lip of the mesa. "Randy, God brought you to me first for a reason. You're my right-hand man. My general. You and I will gather everyone over there and plan our . . . our assault." It was hard to say the word, now that it was actually happening.

Randy nodded sharply, without speaking. Eddy noticed wetness around his eyes, too. He felt profoundly moved.

"You two need to block this road with your Jeep to prevent anyone from going on to Isabella. We need the element of surprise. Direct everyone off the road and have them park in that open area over there. Randy and I will be on that hill. Waiting. We're not moving on Isabella until we have sufficient force."

More sets of headlights appeared at the lip of the Dugway.

"Isabella is about three miles down that road. We want to keep quiet until it's time to move. Make sure no one jumps the gun or goes off halfcocked. We don't want the Antichrist knowing we're coming until we've got strength in numbers."

"Amen," they said.

Eddy smiled. *Amen.*

56

AT 2:00 A.M., THE REVEREND DON T. SPATES sat at the desk in his office behind the Silver Cathedral. Several hours earlier he had called Charles and his secretary at their homes and asked them to come in to handle all the calls and e-mails. In front of him stood a stack of e-mails Charles had culled out before his mail server crashed. Next to them was a stack of phone messages. He could hear the phone ringing incessantly in the outer office.

Spates was trying to absorb the momentous thing that was happening.

A light tap on the door, and his secretary entered with fresh coffee. She placed it on the table, along with a china plate with a macadamia-nut cookie.

"I don't want the cookie."

"Yes, Reverend."

"And stop answering the phone. Take it off the hook."

"Yes, Reverend." Plate and cookie disappeared with the secretary. With irritation, he watched her retreat; her hair wasn't as bouffant and sparkly as usual, her dress was wrinkled, and without makeup her true frumpiness showed plainly. She must have been in bed when he called, but still, she should have made a better effort.

When the door closed, he slipped a bottle of vodka from a locked drawer and splashed some into the coffee. Then he turned back to his computer. His Web site had also crashed under the weight of traffic, and now it seemed the whole Web was getting sluggish. With difficulty he trolled slowly through the familiar Christian sites. Some of the big ones, like rapture-ready.com, had also crashed. Others were as slow as molasses in Alaska. The uproar Eddy's letter had generated was astonishing. What few Christian chat rooms were still functioning were jammed with hysterical people. Many said they were leaving to respond to the call.

Spates sweated heavily, despite the coolness of the room, and his collar itched. Eddy's letter, which he must have read twenty times now, had frightened him. The letter was an incitement to a violent attack on a U.S. government installation and he had named Spates in the letter. Naturally, they would blame him. On the other hand, Spates reasoned, this immense display of Christian power, of Christian outrage, might be for the good. For too long, Christians had been discriminated against in their own country, ignored, sidelined, and mocked. Right or wrong, this uproar would be a wake-up call to America. The politicians and the government would finally see the power of the Christian majority. And he, Spates, had set the revolution in motion. Robertson, Falwell, Swaggart—in all their years of preaching and with all their money and power, none of them had pulled off anything like this.

Spates surfed the Web, looking for information, but all he could find was vitriol, outrage, and hysteria. And thousands of copies of the letter.

A new and disturbing idea suddenly infiltrated his mind as he glanced through the letter yet again.

What if Eddy is right?

He felt a sudden chill. He wasn't ready to let go of this life. He couldn't bear the thought that all his money, his power, his cathedral, his teleministry might be coming to an end—that it would all be over, before it had hardly begun.

An even more unsettling thought came hard on the heels of this one: in that great and glorious day of the Lord, how would he be judged? Was he truly right with God? All Spates's sins lurched forward to haunt him. The lies, the binges, the betrayals, the women and the flashy gifts he had bought for them with contributions from the faithful. Most horrifying of all, he recalled the way he'd more than once caught himself lusting after a boy in the street. All those sins—large and small—pushed in from the edges of his mind, shouting to be seen and reexamined.

Fear, guilt, and despair swept over him. God saw everything. Everything. *Please, Lord, please, forgive me, Thy unworthy servant,* he prayed, over and over, until, with a violent mental effort, he shoved his sins back into some dark cave in his brain. God had already forgiven him—why was he concerned?

And anyway, this couldn't be the Second Coming. What the hell was he thinking? Eddy was a nutcase. Of course he was. Spates had known it from the moment he first heard that high, cracked voice on the phone. Anyone who would live in the middle of the desert with a bunch of Indians, a hundred miles from a decent restaurant, was by definition crazy.

He read the man's letter again, looking for signs of insanity, and a fresh wave of dread hit him. The letter made sense. It was powerful. These were not the ravings of a madman. And this business of "ARIZONA" and "ISABELLA" each adding up to 666 was the most unsettling of all.

God, how he was sweating.

He opened the glass doors of the cherrywood bookcase, removed a thick book, and flipped through to the gematria tables. He looked up the Hebrew letters and jotted their numbers on a piece of paper. As he worked, he saw that Eddy had gotten some of his Hebrew letters wrong and misnumbered others.

He applied the correct numbers and added them up with a shaking hand. Neither word came to 666.

He sat back, gasping with relief. The whole thing was a farce, just as he'd thought. He felt as if an angel had swooped down and lifted him out of the burning lake. Jerking a linen handkerchief from his pocket, he mopped the sweat off from around his eyes and forehead.

Apprehension returned. God might have spared him. But would the media? Would the government? Could he be charged with incitement to violence? Or worse? He'd better pull his lawyer out of bed while he still could. There had to be a way to push the blame onto Crawley. It was Crawley, after all, who had started it.

He pulled at his collar, trying to get some air down his hot, sticky neck. It had been a mistake to bring in that damn cracker, Pastor Eddy. The guy was a loose cannon. Stupid, stupid, stupid.

He pressed the button on his intercom. "Charles, I need you."

The usually prompt young man did not appear.

"Charles? I *need* you."

His secretary opened the door instead. She looked more haggard than he had ever seen her.

"Charles left," she said in a flat voice.

"I certainly didn't give him leave to go."

"He went to Isabella."

Spates stared up at her from his chair. He couldn't believe it. *Charles?*

"He left about ten minutes ago. He said he'd been called by God. Then he walked out."

"For crying out loud!" Spates slammed his hand on the desk. Then he noticed she was wearing her coat and had her purse. "Don't tell me you're also going off to follow that jackass!"

"No," she said. "I'm going home."

"I'm sorry, but that won't be possible. I need you here for the rest of the night. Get my lawyer, Ralph Dobson, on the phone. Tell him to get down here pronto. I've got a problem on my hands, in case you hadn't noticed."

"No."

"No? 'No' what? What's that supposed to mean?"

"It means I don't care to work for you any longer, Mr. Spates."

"What are you talking about?"

She clasped her purse in two hands in front of her midriff as if for protection. "Because you're a despicable human being." She turned stiffly and left.

Spates heard the faint sound of a door being closed carefully—then silence.

He sat behind his desk, alone, streaming sweat—and very, very frightened.

57

THE WORD "ASSAULT" HUNG HEAVY IN the air. The others crowded in and watched the main security screen. It was a live feed from a high-angle camera mounted on top of the elevator and it gave a bird's-eye view of what was going on. At the edge of the cliffs above Isabella, Ford could make out a group of black-suited men setting up fixed ropes and stacking equipment and weapons. They were clearly getting ready to rappel down. Kate moved next to him, and took his hand again. Hers was sweaty, trembling.

George Innes broke the horrified silence. "Assault? What the hell for?"

"They couldn't contact us," said Wardlaw. "And this is their response."

"This is an absurd overreaction!"

Wardlaw turned to Dolby. "Ken, we need to restore communications right away and call this off."

"I can't do that without shutting down Isabella. As you well know, Isabella is totally firewalled to the outside. The programming simply won't let us turn on the communications system until Isabella is shut down."

"Restart the main computer and transfer control from the servers."

"It would take at least an hour to boot up and reconfigure the mainframe."

Wardlaw swore. "All right, then, I'll go up top, explain the situation in person." He turned toward the door.

"You'll do no such thing," said Hazelius.

Wardlaw stared at him. "Sir, I don't understand."

Hazelius pointed mutely away from Wardlaw's station toward the screen overhead. A new message had materialized.

We have very little time. What I have to say to you now is of the utmost importance.

387

Wardlaw looked at Hazelius in panic. His eyes swiveled to the security screens and back again. "We can't keep them out, sir. I've got to open the security door."

"Tony," said Hazelius, his voice low and urgent, "think for just a moment about what's going on here. You open that door and this conversation with . . . God or whatever it is comes to an end."

Wardlaw's Adam's apple bobbed as he swallowed. "God?"

"That's right, Tony. *God.* It's a very real possibility. We've made contact with God, except it's a God who's a whole lot bigger and more unknowable than anything dreamed up by humanity."

Nobody spoke.

Hazelius went on. "Tony, we can buy ourselves a little time, and it won't cost us. We'll tell them the door wasn't functioning, the communications systems were down, the computer crashed. We can finesse this. We can keep the doors shut and still come out of this without serious charges."

"They'll have a demolition kit. They'll blow the door," said Wardlaw, his voice high and tense.

"Let them," said Hazelius. He grasped Wardlaw's shoulder gently, gave it an affectionate shake, as if to wake him up. "Tony, Tony. *We might be talking to God.* Don't you understand?"

Wardlaw said, after a moment, "I understand."

Hazelius looked around. "Are we all in this together?" His eyes traveled around the room and locked on Ford. He must have seen the skepticism in Ford's eyes. "Wyman?"

Ford said, "I'm astonished you think there's a possibility we may be talking to God."

"If not God, then who is it?" Hazelius asked.

Ford glanced around at the others. He wondered who else could see that Hazelius was finally losing it. "Just what you've said all along. A fraud. Sabotage."

Melissa Corcoran suddenly spoke up. "If that's what you still think, Wyman, then I'm sorry for you."

Ford turned to her, astonished. There was a new look in her face that stopped him. Gone was the insecure young woman restlessly seeking affection. She looked radiantly serene, her eyes flashing with self-confidence.

"You think this is God?" Ford asked incredulously.

"I don't know why you're so surprised," she said. "Don't you believe in God?"

"Yes, but not *this* God!"

"How do you know?"

Ford faltered. "Come on! God would never contact us in this crazy way."

"You think it's less crazy for God to impregnate a virgin who produces a son who then brings the message to Earth?"

Ford could hardly believe his ears. "I'm telling you, this is *not* God."

Corcoran shook her head. "Wyman, don't you realize what's happened here? Don't you get it?

389

We've made the greatest scientific discovery of all time: *We've discovered God.*"

Ford looked about the group. His eyes ended up locked into Kate's, standing next to him. For a long moment they looked at each other. He could hardly believe what he saw: her eyes were brimming with emotion. She squeezed his hand, dropped it, and smiled. "I'm sorry, Wyman. You know Melissa and I don't always see eye to eye. But now . . . well." She reached out and clasped Corcoran's hand. "I agree with her."

Ford stared at the two adversaries suddenly together. "How could a rational human being possibly think that . . . *thing*"—he pointed at the screen—"is God?"

"What surprises me," Kate said, her voice calm, "is that you *don't* see it. Review the evidence. The space-time hole. It's real. I did the calculations. It's a wormhole or a flux tube into a parallel universe—a universe that exists right next to ours, incredibly close, almost but not quite touching, our two universes like two sheets of paper that have been balled up together. All we did was poke a hole through our piece of paper to expose a tiny piece of the one next to us. And that parallel universe is where . . . God lives."

"Kate, you can't be serious."

"Wyman, forget everything else and just listen to the words. *Just the words*. This is the first time in my life that I've actually heard the simple truth spoken. It's like the pealing of bells after years of silence.

What this . . . what *God* is saying is just so incredibly *true*."

Ford looked around the circular room and fixed on Edelstein. Edelstein, the ultimate skeptic. The man's dark, triumphant eyes returned the look.

"Alan, help me out here."

"I've never shopped around for God," Edelstein said. "I've been a resolute atheist all my life. I don't need God—never have, never will."

"At least someone agrees with me," said Ford with relief.

Edelstein smiled. "Which makes my conversion all the more telling."

"Your conversion?"

"That's correct."

"You . . . *believe?*"

"Of course. I'm a mathematician. I live and die by logic. And by logic, this thing speaking to us is some higher power. Call it God, call it the primum mobile, call it the Great Spirit, it doesn't matter."

"I call it a fraud."

"Where's your evidence? No programmer has ever written code that survived the Turning test. Nor is there a computer built—not even Isabella's super-computer brain—capable of true AI. You cannot explain how it knew Kate's numbers or Gregory's names. Most importantly, I, like Kate, recognize the profound truth it propounds. If not God, it's a highly intelligent entity from this or another universe, and therefore preternatural. Yes, I take it at face value.

The simplest explanation obtains. Occam's razor."

"Besides," said Chen, "that output was coming straight from CZero. How do you explain that?"

Ford looked at the others, from Dolby's fine ebony face, wet with tears, to the shaking delirium that seemed to be taking hold of Julie Thibodeaux's body. . . . *Unbelievable,* thought Ford. *Look at them all. They all believe it.* Michael Cecchini, his normally dead face suddenly alive, radiant . . . Rae Chen . . . Harlan St. Vincent . . . George Innes . . . all of them. Even Wardlaw, who in this impossible security crisis ignored his security feeds and instead gazed on Hazelius with slavish, sycophantish adoration.

Clearly he'd missed a dark and alarming dynamic in the team all along. Even in Kate, *especially* Kate.

"Wyman, Wyman," said Hazelius soothingly. "You're emoting. *We* are thinking. That's what we do best."

Ford took a step backward. "This isn't about God. It's just some hacker telling you what you want to hear. And you're falling for it."

"We're falling for it *because it's the truth,*" said Hazelius. "I know it in my intellect and in my bones. Look at us: me, Alan, Kate, Rae, Ken—all of us. Could we *all* be wrong? Scientific skepticism is in our blood. We're steeped in it. No one can accuse us of credulity. What makes you more prescient than us?"

Ford had no answer.

Hazelius said, "We're losing valuable time." He

turned calmly to the screen and spoke. "Continue, please. You have our full attention."

Could they be right? *Could it be God?* Ford turned back to the next message on the screen with grim foreboding.

58

From his hill at the edge of the staging area, with Doke at his side, Eddy watched the stream of vehicles arrive. In the last hour, several hundred of them had poured up over the lip of the Dugway, first dirt bikes, ATVs, and Jeeps, and then pickups, motorcycles, SUVs, and cars. The arrivals brought tales of hindrance and obstruction. State police roadblocks had gone up on I-40, Route 89 through Grey Mountain and Route 160 at Cow Springs, but the faithful had found ways around on the warren of dirt roads that crisscrossed the Rez.

The vehicles were parking in a disorganized mass just beyond the top of the Dugway, but, Eddy mused, it didn't matter how they parked. Nobody would drive home. They were heading home another way—via the Rapture.

At times the oncoming horde seemed anarchic: loud voices, wailing toddlers, drunks, even people on drugs. But those who had arrived early greeted and organized the newcomers with prayer, Bible verses, and the Word. At least a thousand worshippers massed in the open area in front of his hill, waiting for instructions. Many carried Bibles and crosses. Some carried guns. Others had brought whatever weapon first came to hand, from iron skillets and kitchen knives to sledgehammers, axes, machetes, and brush hooks. Boys carried slingshots, BB guns, and baseball bats. Others brought two-way radios, which Eddy requisitioned and distributed to a small group he had selected as his commanders, keeping one for himself.

Eddy was surprised at the number of children—even mothers nursing babies. Children at Armageddon? But it made sense when he thought about it. These were the End Times. All would be raptured into heaven together.

"Hey," said Doke, nudging Eddy. "Cop car."

Eddy followed his gesture. There, in the line of traffic coming up the Dugway, a lone police car was inching along, its lights flashing.

He turned back toward his new flock. The gathering crowd surged and flowed, their murmuring voices mingling like rain. Flashlights flickered, and he could hear the clink of metal on metal, slides being racked, shotguns pumped. One man was making torches out of bundles of dead piñon branches and passing them around. The discipline was extraordinary.

"I'm trying to think what to say to them," Eddy said.

"You gotta be careful, talking to cops," said Doke.

"I mean my sermon. To the Lord's army, before we set out," said Eddy.

"Yeah, but what about this cop?" said Doke. "There's only one car, but he's got a radio. This could be trouble."

Eddy watched the flashing lights, surprised that some people were actually pulling over at the turnouts to let the squad car pass. Old habits of obedience to government, to authority, were going to die hard. That was what he'd talk about. How, from now on, their only obedience was to God.

"He's coming up the Dugway," said Doke.

The sound of the siren soon reached the mesa top, faint at first, then louder. The seething crowd grew thicker, spreading out in front of him, waiting for direction. Many were praying, their petitions rising into the night air. Groups of people held hands, their heads bowed. The sound of hymns reached his ears. It reminded Eddy of how he imagined things were when people gathered for the Sermon on the Mount. That's it. That's where he'd start his sermon. *"Blessed are the peacemakers, for they shall be called the children of God. . . ."* No, that wasn't a good Bible verse to start with. Something more arousing: *"Woe to the inhabiters of the earth and of the sea! for the devil is come down unto you, having great wrath, because he knoweth that he hath but a short time."* The Antichrist. That's what he had to focus on. The Antichrist. Just a few words and he would lead his army forward.

The cop car topped the rim, still stuck in the mass of cars. It came down the stretch of asphalt and pulled off to the side a few hundred yards away. Eddy could see the emblem of the Navajo Nation Tribal Police on the door. A spotlight on the roof shone around; then a door opened. A tall Indian got out, a Navajo policeman. Even from a hundred yards off, Eddy recognized Bia.

At once, the policeman was surrounded by people. From what Eddy could hear, it sounded like an argument was developing.

"What do we do now, Pastor Russ?" people called.

"We wait," he said in a voice strong and low, so different from his normal voice that he wondered if it was even him speaking. "God will show us the way."

59

Lieutenant Bia faced the crowd, his feeling of uneasiness growing. He'd gotten the call about some kind of disturbance at Red Mesa and he'd assumed it was the protest ride, and when he'd seen the heavy traffic on the Red Mesa road he'd joined it. But as he looked around, he could see that whoever these people were, they had nothing to do with the protest ride. These people carried guns and swords, crosses and axes, Bibles and kitchen knives. Some had painted crosses on their foreheads and their clothes. It was some kind of cult gathering—perhaps connected to that television preacher's sermon he'd heard people talking about. He was relieved to see it consisted of people of all races—blacks, Asians, even a few who looked Navajo or

Apache. At least it wasn't the KKK or Aryan Nations.

He tucked up his belt and put his hands on his hips, facing the crowd with an easy smile, hoping not to spook anyone. "You folks got a leader? Someone I can talk to?"

A man in faded Wranglers and a blue workshirt stepped forward. He had a heavy face burned brown from a lifetime in the fields, a large gut, short thick arms that stood away from his body, and callused hands. An old Colt M1917 Revolver with ivory handles was shoved under his diamondback belt, a polished brass crucifix mounted on its buckle. "Yeah. We have a leader. His name's God. Who are you?"

"Lieutenant Bia, Tribal Police." He felt a twinge at the man's unnecessarily belligerent tone. But he would play it cool, not confrontational. "What person is in charge here?"

"Lieutenant Bia, I've got just *one* question for you: Are you a Christian here for the fight?"

"The fight?"

"Armageddon."

For emphasis, the man rested a palm on the Colt's ivory-handled butt.

Bia swallowed. The crowd closed in on him. He wished he'd radioed for backup. "I'm a Christian, but I haven't heard of any Armageddon."

The crowd fell silent.

"Have you been born again in the water of life?" the man continued.

From the crowd rose a sharp murmur. Bia took a

deep breath. No point in getting in a religious pissing contest with these people. Better to tone things down. "Why don't you tell me about this Armageddon?"

"The Antichrist is here. On this very mesa. The battle of the Lord God Almighty is at hand. Either you're with us or you're against us. The time is now. Make your decision."

Bia had no idea how to respond to this. "I guess you folks know this is the Navajo Nation, and you're trespassing on land leased to the U.S. government."

"You haven't answered my question."

The crowd tightened the ring around him. Bia could feel their agitation and smell it in their sweat.

"Sir," he said in a low voice, "keep your hand away from your firearm."

The man's hand did not move.

"I said, *move* your hand *away* from the firearm."

The man's hand closed on the gun butt. "You're either with us or against us. Which is it?"

When Bia didn't answer, the man turned and spoke to the crowd. "He's not one of us. He's come to fight for the other side."

"What do you expect?" someone cried, echoed by the crowd. "What do you expect?"

Bia began backing up, slow and easy, toward his vehicle.

The gun came up. The man pointed it at Bia.

"Sir, I'm not here to fight anyone," said Bia. "There's absolutely no reason for you to point a gun at me. Put it down."

An older woman in work boots and a straw stockman's hat, her face as cured as old leather, put her hand on the man's arm. "Jess, save your bullets. That man's not the Antichrist. He's just a cop."

The word "Antichrist" rumbled through the crowd. People squeezed in even closer to Bia.

"Sir, *I said put the gun down.*"

The man lowered it, uncertain.

"Okay, Wyatt Earp, give me the gun." The woman reached over and took it from his slack hand, shook out the rounds, and slipped the gun and bullets into her shoulder bag.

"There's no Antichrist up here," said Bia, disguising his relief. "This is Navajo Nation land and you're trespassing. Now, if you've got a leader, I'd like to speak to him." As soon as he got back to his squad car, he'd radio for backup. National Guard–level backup.

A voice rang out, "We're here as God's army—to *fight* and *die* for the Lord!"

Fight. Fight. Fight. The crowd repeated the word like a chant.

A man with a long forked beard pushed forward, a rock in his fist, and shouted, "Are you born again in the water of life?"

Angered at the man's inquisitorial tone, Bia said, "My religion is none of your business. Lay down that rock, mister, or I'll charge you with assault." He placed a hand on his baton.

The man spoke to the crowd. "We can't let him go.

He's a cop. He's got a radio. He'll warn the others."
The man raised the rock high. "Answer!"

Bia released his riot baton. Spinning it up, he swung the stick against the man's arm, backhanded, as hard as he could. With a sickening crack the forearm shattered and the rock dropped to the ground.

"He broke my arm!" the man shrieked, falling to his knees.

"Disperse now and no one else will get hurt!" Bia called loudly. He took a step back, up against the fender of his car, his baton raised. If he could just get into the car, he'd have some protection—and he could radio for help.

"The cop broke his arm!" a man shouted, kneeling.

The crowd surged forward with a roar. A rock came flying and Bia dodged it. It smacked into the windshield with a dull, cracking thud.

Bia yanked open the door and ducked in, and tried to shut the door behind him, but it was held open by a surge of people. He grabbed the radio, hit the TRANSMIT button.

"He's radioing out!" someone yelled.

A dozen hands grabbed him, pulling him back, ripping his shirt.

"The son of a bitch is radioing out! He's calling in the enemy!"

The mike was wrested from his hand and torn from its mount. Bia tried gripping the steering wheel, but the many-armed mob dragged him back out with relentless force. He tumbled to the ground, tried to stand, but was kicked down to his knees.

He went for his gun, yanked it out. He rolled on his side, pointing it into the crowd. "Stand back!" he screamed.

A rock slammed him in the chest, cracking his ribs. Bia fired point-blank into the crowd.

A chorus of screams rose up.

"My husband," shrieked a voice. "Oh my God!"

A baseball bat swung out, struck his leg. He fired twice again, before the bat smashed his arm and the gun went flying.

The screaming mob piled on him, cursing, kicking, beating.

He fell to his face, scrabbling for the gun, but a boot came down hard on his hand, crushing it. He screamed, rolled, tried to crawl under his squad car.

"Stone him! Murderer! Stone him!"

He could feel the pummeling of rocks and sticks against him, the smack of them into bone and muscle, the rain of stones on the metal and glass of the police car. Choking with pain, he managed to crawl partway under the car, but they seized his leg and hauled him back into a maelstrom of blows and kicks. Screaming in pain and terror, he curled up into a fetal position, trying to protect himself from the rain of violence. The roar of the crowd began to fade, replaced by a dull roar in his own head. The blows came, but now they were happening to someone else, someone else was taking this journey, going farther and farther away. The roar subsided into a distant murmur, and then welcoming darkness gratefully came.

As Eddy watched, the crowd moiled like dogs over the place where the cop had stood only a moment before. He saw him struggle to rise, then he was gone, dragged down by the undertow of the surging, stone-throwing crowd.

The chanting died down and the crowd seemed to go slack, then drift backward. The only thing left was the policeman's cap and a lumpy, trampled uniform.

As the mob slowly dispersed, only a kneeling woman remained, wailing, holding a bleeding man in her arms. Eddy felt a surge of panic. Why was every-thing so different from how he had imagined it? Why did it seem so sordid?

"This is Armageddon," came the deep, reassuring voice of Doke. "It had to start sometime."

Doke was right. They'd passed the point of no return. The battle was joined. God was directing their hand, and there was no second-guessing Him. Eddy felt a surge of confidence.

"Pastor?" murmured Doke. "The people need you."

"Of course." Eddy stepped forward, raised his hands. "My Friends in Christ! Listen! *My friends in Christ!*"

A restless silence fell.

"I am Pastor Russell Eddy!" he cried. "I am the man who exposed the Antichrist!"

The crowd, electrifled by the violence, surged

toward him in waves, like the ocean reaching for the shore.

Eddy grasped Doke's hand and raised it. "The kings, the politicians, the liberal secularists, and the humanists of this corrupt world will hide in the caves and the mountain's rocks. They will call to the mountains and rocks, *'Fall on us, and hide us from the face of Him that sitteth on the throne, and from the wrath of the Lamb, for the great day of His wrath has come, and who shall be able to stand?'*"

A roar filled the night and the swelling crowd surged.

Eddy turned, pointed, and thundered: "There, three miles to the east, is a fence. Beyond that fence is a cliff. Down the cliff lies Isabella. And inside Isabella is the Antichrist. He goes by the name of Gregory North Hazelius."

The roar reverberated as shots rang out into the sky.

"Go!" Eddy cried, shaking his pointing hand. "Go as one people led by the flaming sword of Zion! Go, and find the Antichrist! Destroy him and the Beast! The battle of the great God Almighty is joined! *'The sun shall be darkened, and the moon shall not give her light, and the stars shall fall from heaven!'*"

He stepped back and the teeming throng turned and undulated eastward across the moonlit mesa, the flashlights and torches bobbing in the darkness like a thousand glowing eyes.

"Well done," said Doke. "You really fired 'em up."

Still grasping Doke's powerful arm, Eddy turned to go with them. He glanced back and glimpsed Bia, a crumpled rag in the dust—and the woman, weeping and cradling her dead husband.

The first casualties of Armageddon.

60

A FRESH-FACED BOY IN HIS EARLY twenties, Agent Miller drove Bern Wolf from the airstrip to the fenced security area in a Humvee. They passed through a series of smashed gates and pulled up in the center of the parking lot, amid a scattering of civilian cars. Everything was bathed in the harsh glow of powerful lights.

Wolf looked around. Soldiers converged at the edge of the mesa, fixing ropes to rappel down the cliffs to Isabella.

"We wait in the vehicle until called, sir," said Miller.

"Terrific." Wolf was sweating. He was a computer scientist, he wasn't cut out for this kind of shit. The knot in his stomach was taut and heavy. Wolf figured to stay close to Agent Miller and his twenty-two-inch arms that could bench-press Buicks. His back and shoulders were so massive, they made the 7.62 NATO assault rifle slung under his armpit look like a kid's plastic gun.

He watched the men working at the edge of the mesa. One by one, they roped up and jumped backward off the lip, carrying bulky packs. Even though Wolf hadn't visited Isabella, he knew it like the back of his hand, he'd planned some of the layouts and he'd pored over the construction diagrams. He also knew the software, and the DOE had given him an envelope with all the shutdown and security codes. Turning off Isabella would not be a problem.

The problem, for him, would be getting down the three hundred feet of cliff face.

"I gotta take a piss," he said.

"Do it next to the vehicle and hurry up, sir."

Wolf did his business and returned.

Miller was just getting off the radio.

"Our turn, sir."

"They're already in?"

"No. They want you down there before they effect penetration."

Effect penetration? Did these guys know how ridiculous they sounded?

Miller nodded. "After you."

Feeling as if every muscle in his body were resisting, Wolf hefted his pack. Despite the harsh lights, he could see an amazing number of stars overhead. The air was crisp and smelled of woodsmoke. As he walked away from the idling Humvee, he realized just how quiet the night was. The loudest sound came from the crackling power lines—clearly, Isabella was running at full power. He doubted anything was seriously wrong underground. Probably a computer glitch had crashed the communications system. Some bureaucratic hack had gone nuts and called in commandos. Maybe the scientists in the Bunker didn't even know they were causing a furor.

Then, at the edge of audibility, he heard a couple of faint noises, like shots, then two more.

"You hear that?" he asked Miller.

"Yeah." He paused, his head cocked. "About three miles off."

They listened a moment longer, but there was nothing.

"Probably just an Indian shooting a coyote," said Miller.

Wolf's legs felt wobbly as he followed Miller to the edge of the cliffs. He'd been expecting them to lower him in a cage or something, but there was no cage to be seen.

"Sir? I'll take your pack. We'll lower it down after you."

Wolf shrugged out of his pack and handed it over. "Careful, there's a laptop in there."

"We'll be careful, sir. And now, could you step this way?"

"Hold on here," Wolf said. "You don't really expect me to . . . go down one of those ropes?"

"Yes, sir."

"How?"

"We'll show you in a minute. Please stand there."

Wolf waited. The other soldiers had gone down, leaving them alone at the edge. The power lines hummed and crackled. The soldier's radio hissed, and he spoke into it. Wolf half listened. State troopers were reporting some kind of problem on the road leading to the mesa. Wolf tuned it out. He was thinking of the cliff.

More conversation, then Miller said, "Step this way, sir. We're going to put you in this sling. Ever rappelled?"

"No."

"It's perfectly safe. Just lean back a little, plant your feet on the rock face, and give gentle hops. You can't fall, even if you let go of the rope."

"You've got to be kidding."

"It's perfectly safe, sir."

They rigged him into the sling, which went around his legs, seat, and lower back, locking the rope in a system of carabiners and brake bars. Then they positioned him at the edge of the cliff with his back facing out. He could feel the wind coming up from below.

"Lean out and step over backward."

Are they crazy?

"Lean back, sir. Take a step. Keep the tension on the rope. We'll lower you, sir."

Wolf stared at Miller, incredulous. The agent's voice was so studiously polite that it seemed tinged with contempt.

"I just can't do this," he said.

The rope slackened, and he felt a sudden rush of panic.

"Lean back." Miller said firmly.

"Get me a cage or something to lower me in."

Miller leaned him back, almost cradling him in his arms.

"That's it. Just like that. Very good, Dr. Wolf."

Wolf's heart hammered. Again he could feel, on his back, a cool movement of air from below. The soldier released him, and his feet slipped and he banged sideways into the cliff face.

"Lean back and plant your feet on the rock."

His heart pounding like mad, he scrabbled his feet on the rock, looking for a purchase. He found it, forced himself to lean back. It seemed to work. As he took little light steps, always leaning out, the rope slipped through the brake bar, lowering him. Once he was below the ledge, darkness descended, but he could still see the rim overhead, limned in light. As he continued, the rim grew more and more distant. He didn't dare look down.

Unbelievably he was doing it, bouncing and hopping down the cliff, his whole being swallowed in darkness. At last, soldiers grasped his legs and lowered him to a stone floor. When he stood up, his legs trembled. The soldiers helped him out of the sling. His pack swung down on a rope a moment later, and the soldiers snagged it. Miller arrived next.

"Well done, sir." he said.

"Thank you."

A large area had been carved into the side of the mountain. At the far end, a massive titanium door was set into the rock. The area was already strung out with harsh lights, looking like the entrance to the island of Dr. No. Wolf felt Isabella's deep humming vibrating out of the mountain. It was very strange that they had lost all communication with the inside. There were too many backup systems. And the SIO would see them on the security screens—unless those, too, were down.

Very strange.

The soldiers were setting up three conical metal dishes on tripods and pointing them toward the door, like stubby mortars. One man started packing the cones with what looked like C-4.

Doerfler stood to one side, giving orders.

"What are those?" Wolf asked.

"Rapid wall-breaching demolition devices," said Miller. "Ganged charges, there, converge at a single point and blow a hole big enough to crawl through."

"And then?"

"We'll send in a team through the hole to secure the Bunker and a second team to breach the inner door to the Bridge. We'll secure the Bridge, deal with any bad guys, and take the scientists into custody. There may be shooting. We don't know. As soon as the Bridge's been fully secured, I take you in. Personally. You shut Isabella down."

"It takes three hours to shut down the system," Wolf said.

"You'll run that operation."

"What about Dr. Hazelius and the other scientists?"

"Our men will escort them off the premises for debriefing."

Wolf folded his arms. It looked good on paper, no doubt.

61

STANTON LOCKWOOD SHIFTED AGAIN IN THE cheap wooden chair, trying to find comfort where none existed. The mood around the mahogany table in the Situation Room was one of mounting incredulity. At 3:00 A.M.—1:00 A.M. at Red Mesa—the news was bad.

Lockwood had grown up in the Bay area, gone to schools on the West and East coasts, and lived in Washington for the past twelve years. He'd had TV glimpses of another America out there, the America of the Creationists and Christian-nationalists, the tele-vangelists and glitzy megachurches. That America had always seemed remote, relegated to places like Kansas and Oklahoma.

It was no longer remote.

The FBI Director asked, "Mr. President?"

"Yes, Jack?"

"The Arizona Highway Patrol reports disturbances at the roadblocks on Route 89 at Grey Mountain, Route 160 at Tuba City and also at Tes Nez Iah."

"What kind of disturbances?"

"Several state troopers have been injured in scat-tered melees. Traffic is heavy and a lot of people are evading the road blocks, taking off cross-country. Trouble is, the Navajo Reservation is crisscrossed with hundreds of improvised dirt roads, most of which aren't even on the maps. Our roadblocks are leaking like a sieve."

The president turned the monitor to the Chairman of the Joint Chiefs, who sat in his wood-paneled office in the Pentagon, the American flag hung behind him on the wall. "General Crisp, where's the National Guard?"

"Two hours from deployment."

"We don't *have* two hours."

"Finding the requisite choppers, pilots, and trained troops has been a challenge, Mr. President."

"I've got state troopers out there getting their butts kicked. Not in some sorry-ass corner of Afghanistan, but right here in the United States of America. And you're telling me *two hours?*"

"Most of our choppers are in the Middle East."

The FBI Director spoke. "Mr. President?"

The president turned. "What?"

"I've just gotten a report . . ." He accepted a piece of paper from someone offscreen. ". . . an emergency communication from a Navajo Tribal policeman who went up to Red Mesa to investigate—"

"By himself?"

"He went up unawares, like all of us at that time, of the true situation. Sent out an emergency call, which was cut off. I've got a transcription." He read from a piece of paper. " *'Send backup . . . a violent mob . . .*

they're going to kill me . . .' That's all we got. You can hear the mob noise in the background."

"Jesus God."

"The GPS beacon in the squad car went dead a few minutes later. Which usually happens only if the car's been torched."

"What's the news from the Hostage Rescue Team up there? Are they safe?"

"My last report, just ten minutes ago, indicated the operation was going like clockwork. We did have an unconfirmed report of gunfire in the direction of the Dugway, two and a half miles from the airstrip. We're contacting the team now, as we speak. But let me just assure you, Mr. President, that no disorganized mob is going to take down a crack FBI Hostage Rescue Team."

"Is that so?" came the president's skeptical reply. "Are they trained to fire on civilians?"

The FBI Director shifted uncomfortably in his chair. "They're trained to respond to all contingencies."

The president turned to the head of the Joint Chiefs. "Is there *any way* to get troops out there sooner than in two hours?"

"Excuse me, sir?" the FBI Director interrupted, his face pale. "I'm just now getting reports of an explosion and fire . . . a very large fire . . . at the Red Mesa airstrip."

The president stared silently at the director.

"What do these people want?" Lockwood burst out. "What in God's name do they *want?*"

Galdone spoke for the first time since they had arrived in the Situation Room. "You know what they want."

Lockwood stared at the odious man. Soft and fat, arms crossed, eyes half-lidded as if asleep, he sat in his chair studying them placidly.

"They want to destroy Isabella," he said, "and kill the Antichrist."

62

FORD, GRIPPING THE EDGE OF A table, read the new message on the Visualizer. Isabella was running flat out, at full power, and he could feel the entire Bridge trembling and keening like the cockpit of a jet plane locked in a death spiral.

Religion arose as an effort to explicate the inexplicable, control the uncontrollable, make bearable the unbearable. Belief in a higher power became the most powerful innovation in late human evolution. Tribes with religion had an advantage over those without. They had direction and purpose, motivation and a mission. The survival value of religion was so spectacular that the thirst for belief became embedded in the human genome.

Ford had moved away from the others. Kate, with a quizzical and, it seemed to him, somewhat regretful glance at him, was now helping Dolby at his workstation. The team running Isabella—Dolby, Chen, Edelstein, Corcoran, and St. Vincent—were intensely focused on their jobs. The rest stared at the Visualizer, transfixed by the words appearing there.

What religion tried, science has finally achieved. You now have a way to explain the inexplicable, control the uncontrollable. You no longer need "revealed" religion. The human race has finally grown up.

Wardlaw spoke quietly from his security station. "They've sent in a demolition team with wall-breaching kits. They're going to blow the door."

"How many?" Hazelius asked sharply.

"Eight."

"Armed?"

"Heavily."

A ripple of panic swept the group. "What are we going to do?" Innes cried.

"We're going to keep listening," said Hazelius, his firm voice raised over the humming of Isabella. He pointed at the screen.

Religion is as essential to human survival as food and water. If you try to replace religion with science, you will fail. You will, instead, offer science as religion. For I say to you, science is religion. The one, true religion.

A sob escaped from Julie Thibodeaux, standing next to Hazelius. "This is wonderful." She rocked, her arms crossed tightly over her chest. "This is so wonderful . . . and I'm so frightened."

Hazelius put a steadying arm around her.

It was incredible, Ford thought: he had witnessed

their conversion right before his eyes. They believed.

Instead of offering a book of truth, science offers a method of truth. Science is a search for truth, not the revelation of truth. It is a means, not a dogma. It is a journey, not a destination.

Ford could keep silent no longer. "Yes, but what of human suffering? How can science make 'bearable the unbearable,' as you put it?"

"The magnetic coil's redlining," said Dolby quietly.

"Juice it," murmured Hazelius.

In the last century, medicine and technology have alleviated more human suffering than have all the priests in the last millennium.

"You're speaking of physical suffering," said Ford. "But what about the suffering of the soul? What about spiritual suffering?"

Have I not said that all is one? Is it not a comfort to know that your suffering shudders the very cosmos? No one suffers alone and suffering has a purpose— even the sparrow's fall is essential to the whole. The universe never forgets.

"I can't hold it without more power," Dolby cried. "Harlan, you've *got* to give me five percent more."

"I'm tapped out," St. Vincent said. "Push it any more, and it'll cascade the grid."

The machine was now screaming so loudly that Ford could hardly hear himself think. He read the words on the Visualizer, his mind in turmoil. Twelve of the most intelligent people in the country thought this was God. That had to mean something.

Do not stoop to diffidence! You are my disciples. You have the power to upend the world. In one day, science accumulates more evidence of its truths than religion in all its existence. People cling to faith because they must *have it. They hunger for it. You will not deny people faith; you will offer them a new faith. I have not come to replace the Judeo-Christian God, but to complete him.*

"Wait!" Wardlaw barked out. "Something else is going on up top!"

"What is it?" Hazelius asked.

Wardlaw peered urgently at his wall of screens. "We've got—a whole bunch more perimeter alarms going off. There are people coming out of nowhere . . . some kind of mob . . . What the *hell?*"

"A *mob?*" Hazelius half turned, his eye still on the Visualizer. "What are you talking about?"

"No shit, a mob . . . Jesus, you won't believe this. . . . They're assaulting the security fence . . . tearing it down . . . We've got some kind of riot going on up there. Unbelievable—a full-blown riot—out of nowhere."

Ford turned to the main security feed. The high-angle camera atop the elevator furnished the main screen with a broad view of the action. A mob, carrying torches, and flashlights and brandishing primitive weapons streamed down the road from the Dugway and piled up against the perimeter fence, forcing it down by sheer weight of numbers. In the direction of the airstrip he heard a dull explosion and saw flames suddenly leaping above the trees.

"They've set fire to the hangars at the airstrip," Wardlaw yelled. "Who *are* these people—and where in hell did they come from?"

63

WOLF WATCHED THE MEN ALIGN THE demolition kits along the titanium door, then run the wires back to the detonator. They seemed disconcertingly calm, almost confident, as if they blew up mountains every day of their lives.

Wolf walked toward the edge of the cliff. A pipe fence, cemented into the rock, ran along the rim. He grasped the cold steel and looked out into the vast deserts, ringed by mountains, ten thousand square miles with hardly a light breaking the undifferentiated dark. A cool wind wafted up from below, bringing with it the smell of dust and the faint scent of some night-flowering plant. He felt preposterously proud of rappelling down the cliffs. This was going to be a hell of a story to tell people back in Los Alamos.

Behind him, he heard the abrupt hiss of radios and a burst of inaudible words. He turned to see what was happening. The men working the charges had stopped. Huddling with Doerfler, they talked urgently on the radios. Wolf listened but made out nothing. Something unusual was going on.

Wolf strolled over. "Hey, what's up?"

"There's been an attack up top. No one knows who."

Terrific, Wolf thought.

From above, scattered popping sounds echoed down the cliffs and the sky bloomed red above the mesa rim. "What's going on?"

Miller glanced at Wolf. "They set fire to the hangars at the airfield. . . . They've surrounded the chopper."

"They? Who the hell's *they?*"

Miller shook his head. The other members of the team were engaged by radio in furious conversation with the team above. The popping sounds became louder—and Wolf realized it was gunfire. He heard a faint cry. Everyone stared up. A moment later something came hurtling down the cliff, accompanied by a long choking scream. It flashed in and out of the lights on its way past them, a figure in uniform. The scream ended abruptly far below in a faint smack and a rattle of loose, falling rocks.

"What the hell was that!" one of the soldiers cried.

"They threw Frankie off the cliff!"

"Look! Coming down the fixed lines!" another soldier yelled.

They all stared upward in uncomprehending horror at the dozens of dark shapes sliding down the ropes.

PASTOR RUSSELL EDDY WATCHED HIS CONGREGATION fling the last soldier over the cliff. While he genuinely deplored violence, the soldier had resisted the will of God. So be it. Perhaps they would find solace and redemption when Christ raised them from the dead and redeemed His flock. Perhaps.

He climbed up on the hood of a Humvee and took stock. The soldiers had fired on his congregation, which had surged forward with tsunami-like force up to the cliff's edge until most of the soldiers had vanished over the rim into the black void.

His will be done.

Pastor Eddy gazed out over the miracle. The road was packed with people pouring in from the Dugway, torches and flashlights dipping in the darkness. They flowed over the fence into the security area and milled about, waiting for direction. A half mile back, the flames from the burning hangars at the airstrip leapt above the scrubby trees, casting a lurid glow across the mesa top. The acrid smell of gasoline and burnt plastic drifted through the air.

In front of him, people were massing along the edge of the cliff. The soldiers had left a lot of gear at the top of the cliffs, which Doke evidently knew how to use. He had served ten years in the Special Forces, he had told Eddy. He was helping people into rappelling gear, straps and slings with various carabiners and equipment, and showing them how to rappel down the cliff face, convincing them they could do it.

And they were doing it. It was easy with the equipment. It took no special skills. Doke's people poured over the edge by the score, sliding down the ropes, a human waterfall disappearing into the darkness below. They were sending back up the straps and slings and carabiners to be reused, again and again.

Eddy watched Doke shouting and giving orders.

Lifting his radio, Eddy called the group at the airstrip. "I see you torched the hangars. Good work."

"What should we do about the chopper?"

"Is it guarded?"

"One soldier and the pilot. He's armed—and pretty freaked out."

"Kill them." The words just came out. "Don't let them take off."

"Yes, Pastor."

"Any heavy equipment around?"

"There's a backhoe here."

"Trench the runway and helipads."

Eddy watched the crowds. They still mobbed the mountain, despite roadblocks and mass arrests. It was an incredible sight. The time had come to initiate the next phase of attack.

Eddy raised his arms and called out, "Christians! *Listen up!*"

The growing crowd shifted, paused.

Eddy pointed a shaking finger. "You see those high-tension lines?"

"Take them down!" cried a voice from the crowd.

"That's right! We're going to kill the power to Isabella!" he cried. "I'm calling for volunteers to scale those towers and rip down the lines!"

"Rip them down!" the crowd roared. *"Rip them down!"*

"Cut their power!"

"Cut their power!"

A chunk of the crowd split off and swarmed toward

the closest tower, which stood a hundred yards away.

Eddy held up both arms and a second hush fell.

He pointed again, this time at the cluster of antennae, dishes, microwave horns, and cell-phone transmitters at the top of the elevator building, perched on the edge of the cliffs.

"Blind the eyes and stop the ears of Satan!"

"Blind Satan!"

More milling people broke away and swarmed around the elevator. The crowd now had direction. They had something to do. He watched with grim satisfaction as the mob piled up around the fence surrounding one of the giant struts of the tower. The mob pressed and heaved, and with a screech the fence went down. They poured in. One man caught the rung of the ladder, swung himself up, and began to climb, followed by another, and another, until in a few minutes it looked like a line of ants inching up a tree.

Eddy hopped off the Humvee and strode to Doke at the edge of the cliffs. "My work's done up here. I'm going down. I'm the one God chose to confront the Antichrist. You take command up top."

Doke embraced him. "God bless you, Pastor."

"Now show me the best way to descend this cliff face."

Doke pulled a set of nylon straps from a heap at his feet and slipped them around Eddy's legs and pelvis. He fixed them in place with a locking carabiner, slipping a brake bar over it. "This is called a Swiss seat," he said. "The doubled rope goes through this brake bar—if you let go, it brakes you to a stop. One hand here, one hand here, lean out, give little hops as you let the rope slide through the carabiner." He grinned, slapped Eddy's shoulder. "Simple!" He turned: "Make way," he cried. "Make way for Pastor Eddy! He's going down the ropes!"

The crowd parted and Doke led Eddy to the edge of the cliffs. Eddy turned, grasped the rope as directed, and eased himself over the edge, kicking gingerly off the cliff face as he'd seen the others do—his heart in his mouth, praying furiously.

64

"IT'S A HOWLING MOB OUT THERE," Wardlaw said, pointing to the front monitor.

Hazelius finally broke away from the Visualizer. The main feed showed the entire security zone overrun with people brandishing knives, axes, rifles, their torches bobbing and blazing.

"They're climbing the elevator!"

"Good God." Hazelius wiped his face with his sleeve. "Ken," he shouted, "how much more time does Isabella have?"

"The bad coil could drop superconductivity at any time," Dolby cried, "and then we're dead meat. The beams might kink, cut through the vacuum pipe, and cause an explosion."

"How big?"

"Maybe real big—we have no precedent." He

glanced at his screen. "Harlan! Pump some more juice into the system. Keep the magnetic flux up."

"I'm at a hundred and ten percent of rated power as it is," said St. Vincent.

"Push it," said Dolby.

"If the grid fails, we lose power and we're also dead."

"Crank it."

Harlan St. Vincent keyed in the command.

"What about the mob?" Wardlaw yelled. "They've set fire to the hangars at the airfield!"

"They can't get in here," said Hazelius calmly.

"They're still descending the ropes."

"We're safe in here."

Ford watched on the screen as the mob swarmed up the elevator building, finally reaching the roof. The camera shook, tilted crazily, and then the screen went black with a pop.

"Gregory, we've *got* to shut down Isabella," said Dolby.

"Ken, just give me five more minutes."

Dolby stared, his jaw trembling with raw emotion.

"*Five* more. I beg you. We may be talking to God, Ken. *God.*"

Sweat streamed down Dolby's face. His jaw twitched. He gave a single, sharp nod and turned back to his machine.

"This new religion you want us to preach," Hazelius said, "what will we ask people to worship? Where's the beauty and awe in this?"

Ford strained to read the answer, half-hidden by a blizzard of snow breaking out across the screen.

I ask you to contemplate the universe that you now know exists. Is it not, by itself, more awe-inspiring than any God concept offered by the historical religions? A hundred billion galaxies, lonely islands of fire flung like bright coins in a vastness of space so immense that it is beyond the biological comprehension of the human mind. And I say to you, that the universe you have discovered is only a tiny fraction of the extent and magnificence of the creation. You inhabit but the tiniest blue speck in the infinite vaults of heaven, and yet this speck is precious to me, being an essential part of the whole. That is why I have come to you. Worship me and my great works, not some tribal god imagined by warring pastoralists thousands of years ago.

Dolby stared, his face slick with sweat, his jaw clenched. Hazelius swiveled his thin, eager face back to the Visualizer. "More, tell us more."

"I'm getting alarms across the grid," said St. Vincent, his calm voice just beginning to crack. "Transformers are overheating on Line One halfway to the Colorado border."

Trace the lineaments of my face with your scientific instruments. Search for me in the cosmos and in the electron. For I am the God of deep time and space, the God of superclusters and voids, the God of the Big Bang and the inflation, the God of dark matter and dark energy.

The Bridge began to shake, and the smell of burning electronics filled the air.

The security cams at the airport showed both hangars burning furiously. A mob had surrounded a helicopter on the helipad. A soldier carrying an M-16 stood in the helicopter bay, firing over their heads, trying to warn them off. The chopper was powering up.

"Where did all these people come from?" Innes stared at the screens, his voice rising shrilly above the screaming of Isabella.

Science and faith cannot coexist. One will destroy the other. You must make sure science is the surviving party, or your little blue speck will be lost. . . .

Edelstein spoke. "My p5s are overheating."

"Give me one minute!" Hazelius roared. He turned to the screen, shouting over the din, "What should we do?"

With my words you will prevail. Tell the world what happened here. Tell the world that God has spoken to the human race—for the first time. Yes, for the first time!

"But how can we explain you if you can't tell us what you are?"

Do not repeat the mistake of the historical religions and involve yourselves in disputation about who I am or what I think. I surpass all understanding. I am the God of a universe so vast, only the God numbers can describe it, of which I have given you the first.

"Oh shit," said Wardlaw, staring at the security monitors.

Ford turned his attention back to the security screens. The mob bombarded the chopper with rocks and gunfire, while the soldier guarding it fired over their heads. Someone tossed a Molotov cocktail at the chopper. Falling short, it drenched the tarmac in front with flames. The soldier lowered his weapon and fired into the crowd. The chopper started to rise.

"Oh my God," said Wardlaw, his face looking sick.

Despite the carnage, the raging throng closed in, their return fire flashing and flaring off the chopper's armor.

You are the prophets leading your world into the future. What future will you choose? You hold the key. . . .

As Ford watched, a half dozen Molotov cocktails came flying out of the crowd, bursting against the side of the chopper. The fire swept upward, engulfing the rotors. A fuel line ignited, and with a massive *thump* the chopper detonated, a roiling ball of fire levitating into the night sky. The pieces of the chopper rained back down on the asphalt, a cascade of fire, spreading rapidly as the burning fuel ran in all directions. A moment later a soldier jumped out of the surging flames, flailing, sheeted with fire, and collapsed burning on the tarmac.

"Oh Jesus," Wardlaw said. "They blew up the chopper."

Hazelius, staring at the Visualizer, paid no attention.

"And now look at this!" Wardlaw cried, his finger

stabbing at a screen. "The mob's outside the Bunker door! They're after Isabella. They're killing the soldiers out there!"

Dolby cried. "I'm shutting down Isabella."

"No!" Hazelius rushed Dolby and they struggled briefly, but Dolby was ready this time and flung the smaller man to the ground. He turned back to the keyboard.

"It's locked on! Isabella's locked!" he screamed. "It won't accept the shutdown codes!"

"Oh Jesus, we're dead," said Innes. "We are *dead*."

65

BERN WOLF SHRANK INTO THE SHADOWS of the titanium door, behind the soldiers. The swelling crowd had poured down the ropes like they were possessed and were now forcing them all up against the rocks to the rear. What soldiers had ever faced a situation like this before, a rampaging mass of fellow Americans, a civilian mob that included women? It was crazy. Who were these people? Branch Davidians? Ku Klux Klanners? They were dressed every which way, armed with everything from rifles to ninja stars. Many of them waved makeshift, improvised crosses and pressed in on the soldiers, who could retreat no farther.

Doerfler finally spoke. "This is U.S. government property," he shouted. "Lay your weapons on the ground. *Do it now*."

An emaciated figure stepped forward from the crowd, a big revolver in his hands.

"My name's Pastor Russell Eddy. We're here as God's army to destroy this infernal machine and the Antichrist within. Step aside and let us pass."

The crowd was sweaty, their eyes eerily bright in the artificial lights, their bodies swaying with excitement. Some wept, tears streaming down their faces. More continued down the ropes. There didn't seem to be any limit to their numbers or any way to stop them.

Wolf stared at them with sick fascination. They looked possessed.

"I don't give a damn who you are," barked Doerfler, "or why you're here. I'm telling you one last time: lay down your weapons."

"Or what?" Eddy asked, his voice bolder.

"Or my men will defend themselves and this U.S. government installation using all available means. *Now lay down your weapons.*"

"No," said the scrawny pastor. "We won't lay down our weapons. You are agents of the New World Order, soldiers of the Antichrist!"

Doerfler walked toward Eddy with his hand out. He spoke loudly. "Give me the gun, pal."

Eddy pointed the revolver at him.

"Look at you," said Doerfler derisively. "You fire that and the only person you're going to hurt is yourself. Give it to me. *Now.*"

A shot rang out and Doerfler was punched back, surprised; he fell, rolled, and began to rise, drawing his own sidearm. He'd obviously been wearing body armor.

A second shot from the revolver blew the top of his head off.

Wolf threw himself to the ground, scrambling on his hands and knees and huddling against the cover of the rough rock. A roar like the end of the world erupted around him: automatic fire, explosions, screaming. He wrapped himself up in fetal position, burying his head in his hands, trying to shrink into the rock itself, while gunfire pounded and blasted all around, the snick and thud of bullets showering him with chips. The din went on for what seemed like an eternity, with terrible death-screaming and the wet, ripping sounds of bullets tearing people apart. He clamped his hands over his ears, trying to block it out.

The furor subsided, and in a moment all was still, except for his ringing ears.

He remained in a ball, stunned senseless.

A hand rested on his shoulder. He jerked away.

"Take it easy. It's all right now. Get up."

He kept his eyes tightly shut. A hand grabbed his shirt, pulled him roughly to his feet, popping off half his buttons.

"Look at me."

Wolf raised his face and opened his eyes. It was dark—the lights had been shot out. Bodies lay everywhere, a scene out of hell, worse than hell, people cut in half, body parts strewn about. There were horribly wounded people, some making strange sounds, gurgling, coughing, a few screaming. Already the mob was dragging bodies to the cliff edge and rolling them off.

He recognized the man holding him: the same Pastor Eddy who had started the firefight by shooting down Doerfler. He was splattered with the blood of others.

"Who are you?" Eddy asked.

"I'm . . . I'm just the computer guy."

Eddy looked at him, not unkindly. "Are you with us?" he asked quietly. "Do you accept Jesus Christ as your personal savior?"

Wolf opened his mouth, but only a croak came out.

"Pastor," a voice said, "we don't have a lot of time."

"There's always time to save a soul." Eddy stared, his eyes dark. "I repeat: Do you accept Jesus Christ as your personal savior? The time has come to choose sides. The Day of Judgment is come."

Wolf finally managed to nod.

"Down on your knees, brother. We're going to pray."

Wolf hardly knew what he was doing. It was like something out of the Middle Ages, a forced conversion. He tried to kneel on shaking legs but wasn't fast enough and someone pushed him down. He lost his balance and fell to his side, his shirt falling open.

"Let us pray," said Eddy, falling to his knees beside Wolf and grasping both his hands in his own, bowing his forehead until it was touching Wolf's hands, wrapped in his own. "Heavenly Father, do you accept this sinner now in his hour of need? And do you, sinner, accept the Word of Truth that you might be born again?"

"Do I . . . what?" Wolf tried to concentrate.

"I repeat: Do you accept Jesus as your personal savior?"

Wolf felt sick. "Yes," he said hastily. "Yes, I do . . . I do."

"Praise God! Let us pray."

Wolf bowed his head and closed his eyes tightly. *What the hell am I doing?*

Eddy's voice intruded. "Let us pray out loud," he said. "Ask Jesus into your heart. If you do it freely and sincerely, you will see the kingdom of heaven. It's that simple." He clasped his hands and began to pray loudly.

Wolf mumbled along with him for a moment and then felt his throat close up.

"You have to pray with me," said Eddy.

"I . . . no," said Wolf.

"But to receive Jesus, you have to pray. You must ask—"

"No. I won't."

"My friend—my *dear* friend—this is your last chance. The Judgment is upon us. The Rapture is at hand. I speak to you not as your enemy, but as one who loves you."

"We love you," said voices from the crowd. *"We love you."*

"I suppose you also loved the soldiers you murdered," Wolf said. He was horrified at what he was doing. Where did this sudden, insane courage come from?

He felt the barrel of a gun lightly touch his temple. "Your last chance," came Eddy's gentle voice. He could feel how steady the barrel was in the man's hand.

Wolf closed his eyes and said nothing. He felt the faint tremble as the hand tightened, the finger depressing the trigger. A wrenching boom—and then nothing.

66

EVERY SCREEN IN THE SITUATION ROOM was now alive with videoconference attendees, some on split screens. The Joint Chiefs, the heads of DHS, FBI, NSA, the DCI, and DOE. The vice president had joined them in the situation room at three. It was now 3:20 A.M. A lot had happened in the last twenty minutes, when they first got the news of the fire at the Red Mesa airstrip.

Stanton Lockwood felt like he was trapped in some kind of television show. It was hard to believe that this could be happening in America. It was as if he'd woken up and found himself in a different country.

"We've heard nothing from the Hostage Rescue Team since they blew up the helicopter," the FBI Director was saying. His face was white and the handkerchief he kept mopping his face with was crumpled in his hand, unnoticed. "They attacked with overwhelming numbers. This is not some mob—they're organized. They know what they're doing."

"Are they taken hostage?" the president asked.

"I fear most of them may be incapacitated—or dead."

Someone handed him a piece of paper from off screen. He scanned it. "I've just gotten a report. . . ." His hand shook every so slightly. "They've managed to take down one of the three main powerlines to Isabella. It triggered a grid failure. We've got black-outs across northern Arizona and parts of Colorado and New Mexico."

"My National Guard troops," the president said, turning to the Joint Chiefs. "Where the *hell* are they?"

"They're being briefed as we speak, Mr. President. We're still on schedule for that four forty-five A.M. operation."

"They're still on the ground?"

"Yes, sir."

"Get them up in the air! Brief them in the air!"

"With the equipment shortages and now the blackout—"

"Fly with what you've got."

"Mr. President, our latest intelligence indicates there are between one and two thousand armed people on Red Mesa. They think this is Armageddon. The Second Coming. As a result, they have no regard for human life, their own or others. We can't throw underequipped or underbriefed men into that situation. Fires and a large explosion have been reported on the top of Red Mesa. There are still hundreds of people evading our roadblocks and streaming toward the mesa cross-country, many in all-terrain vehicles. The airstrip has been rendered inoperable to fixed-wing aircraft. A Predator drone should be over there taking pictures in . . . less than twenty minutes. We've got to implement a strategic, well-organized assault on the mesa—otherwise we'll be throwing more lives away."

"I understand that. But we've also got a forty-billion-dollar machine, eleven FBI agents, and a dozen scientists whose lives are also on the line—"

"Excuse me, Mr. President?" The Department of Energy Director spoke. "Isabella is still running at full power but is destabilizing. According to our remote monitoring system, the proton–antiproton beams have decollimated and—"

"Speak English."

"If Isabella isn't shut down, we may have breach of the beam pipe, which would result in an explosion."

"How big?"

A hesitation. "I'm not a physicist, but they tell me if the beams cross beforehand, that convergence could create an instantaneous singularity which will detonate with the yield of a small nuclear device in the half kiloton range."

"When?"

"Any time now."

The Chief of Staff spoke. "I hate to throw in a distraction, but we're getting a tsunami of media coverage. We have to manage it—now."

"Clear the airspace within a hundred-mile radius of Red Mesa," the president barked. "Declare a state of emergency for the Reservation. And martial law. Bar all press. *All* press."

"Consider it done."

"In addition to the National Guard troops, I want an overwhelming military backup response. I want the U.S. military to take control of Red Mesa and the surrounding area by first light. I don't want any excuses about shortages of troops or transportation. I want you to move in forces on the ground, too. Send the soldiers cross-country. It's open desert. Bring *overwhelming* power to bear. Is that clear?"

"Mr. President, I've already ordered the mobilization of all military assets in the Southwest."

"Is four forty-five A.M. the best you can do?"

"Yes, Mr. President."

"Armed terrorists are seizing U.S. property and murdering U.S. servicemen. Their crimes against the state have nothing to do with religion. These people are terrorists—period, full stop. You understand?"

"I certainly do, sir."

"As a start, I want that televangelist, Spates, perp-walked into federal custody on terrorism charges—shackles, leg irons, the works. I want it done in the most public way possible—to set an example. If there are any other preachers, televangelists, and fundamentalists out there cheering on these people, I want them arrested, too. These people are no different from Al Qaeda and the Taliban."

67

NELSON BEGAY LAY ON HIS BELLY on a bluff above Nakai Valley, Willy Becenti beside him. The highest point on the mesa, its summit gave a 360-degree view of the desert terrain below.

The mother of traffic jams gridlocked the Dugway road where it topped out on Red Mesa. Hundreds, perhaps thousands, of cars had parked willy-nilly in a huge open area just off the Dugway. Many of the vehicles were abandoned with their lights left on and the doors open. People were climbing the Dugway on foot, having left their cars somewhere below the mesa. They flowed down the Isabella project road, bypassing the detour to Nakai Valley, heading for the action at the edge of the mesa.

His binoculars traveled down the road. The hangars were burning. What was left of the helicopter the soldiers had arrived in was also on fire, the flames leaping a hundred feet or more into the sky. Dead bodies lay scattered around it from the bloody firefight he had watched happen a few minutes before. Most of the mob had left the airstrip after torching the chopper, but a few stayed to help a large backhoe finish ripping trenches across the runway.

He followed the streaming crowds farther, until his view reached the fenced off area at the edge of the mesa. It was swarming with people; Begay estimated at least a thousand. A mass of them were climbing one of the huge powerline towers and had gotten about three quarters of the way to the top. Others had erected a crude cross on top of a tall building at the edge of the mesa and were busy chopping down a cluster of communication towers that rose from its roof.

Begay slowly lowered his binoculars.

"You got any idea what the hell's going on?" Becenti asked.

Begay shook his head.

"Some kind of Klan meeting? Aryan Nations?"

"There are blacks and Hispanics in the crowd. Even some Indians."

"Lemme see."

While Becenti stared at the eastern end of the mesa, Begay digested what he had seen. Initially he thought it must be some kind of crazy revival meeting—a common sight on the Rez—but when they blew up the chopper he realized it was something else altogether. Maybe something connected with that television preacher he'd heard people talking about, the one who'd delivered a sermon against the Isabella project.

Becenti grunted, still staring. "Look at how many people they killed at the airstrip."

"Yeah," said Begay. "And you can bet there's going

to be a reaction. The feds aren't going to sit around and let this shit happen. We don't want to be caught up here when the fireworks begin."

"We could stay a little while, see what happens. It isn't every day you get front-row seats watching the *Bilagaana* blow themselves up. We always knew the white people were going to do it someday, right? Remember that prophecy?"

"Willy, knock it off. We've got to get everyone together and get the hell off this mesa."

They rose and headed down into the valley.

RANDY DOKE STOOD ON THE HOOD of the Humvee above the fray, his brawny arms folded. The vantage point gave him a better view of the people climbing the high-tension tower. The uppermost ones were just reaching the top. The power lines buzzed and crackled.

Doke felt energized as never before in his life. Once he had been lost in heroin, cocaine, and alcohol. At his lowest point—while wallowing drunk and shit-stained in an irrigation ditch outside Belén, New Mexico, a childhood prayer from deep in his memory had come unbidden, a prayer which his mother had taught him before the drunken old bastard she lived with had shot her and then himself. The singsong verses reverberated in his head, *Jesus loves me, this I know, for the Bible tells me so. . . .* And right then and there, in that foul ditch in Belén, Jesus had reached down and saved his worthless ass. And now he owed the Man—he *owed the Man.* He would do anything for Jesus.

He raised a pair of binoculars. A climber had reached a point just below the insulators. Doke watched as the man braced himself on the ladder, wrapping his legs around a strut. When he steadied himself, he unslung a pump shotgun, racked a shell into the chamber, and shouldered the gun.

This is going to be good.

He watched the climber take careful aim. The people climbing up from below paused to watch. There was a flash of light, and a moment later the boom of the shotgun reached Doke's ears. A shower of sparks cascaded down from the power line, the wire shivering. A cheer went up.

The man steadied himself and racked the slide of the shotgun. There was a second flash-boom. The wire detonated thousands of sparks and the line recoiled, like a spitting rattler hit with rocksalt. Another roar of approval.

A third blast. This time a massive spray of fire spewed across the darkness. The line parted with a deep thrumming twang that seemed to vibrate the air, the cut end falling like a slow-motion whip, dribbling fire, coiling down into the crowds below. It struck with a series of booms and flashes of light and smoke, throwing people violently aside, setting off a screaming stampede.

Awesome.

Doke redirected his attention back to the tower. The

man was pumping and aiming again. But now people on the tower were yelling—what? For him to stop? *No,* Doke thought. *Go for it.*

Another boom from the shotgun. A piece of insulator came tumbling down amid a fireworks display, and a second line snapped and recoiled into the tower itself. It was as if some invisible giant had jarred the tower; people just peeled off the ladder, bodies falling and striking the lower struts, bouncing and spinning off, hitting the ground with a series of dull thuds.

The recoiling line whipped around and came toward him, singing like feedback from a giant electric guitar. Doke leapt off the Humvee as the sizzling cable whipped across it, lashing up a fountain of sparks. He barreled into the panicked crowd and clawed his way over fallen people in an effort to get away. The Humvee burst into flames, and a moment later he felt the heat of the exploding gas tank, the shockwave, the sudden glow.

Picking himself up, he viewed the damage.

The line had been dragged halfway across the fenced area, leaving a trail of fire. The elevator building was in flames along with half a dozen piñon trees. Dead and horribly burned people littered an area around the burning vehicle.

More souls in heaven, thought Doke. *More souls at the right hand of the Lord.*

68

ON HIS FLAT PANEL, KEN DOLBY saw the power surge spike, and then plummet and gyrate wildly.

"Isabella!" He punched in the shutdown codes again. The screen spat back:

CODE BYPASS ERROR

"Shit!"

A siren went off, a banshee wail cutting across the Bridge, and a red ceiling light flashed.

"Emergency overload!" St. Vincent yelled.

A dull boom shook the room and the Visualizer screen exploded into glass fragments, which dropped like hail to the floor.

"Isabella!" Dolby cried, clutching the workstation with both hands.

Don't lose it, Isabella.

St. Vincent struggled with the console, slamming breaker circuits down. "Power's been cut on Number One! How could it happen? Impossible!"

"The beam!" Kate cried, seizing a terminal. "It's decollimating! I'm getting . . . a kink!"

Hazelius let out a cry. "Chen! That last message! I didn't read it all! Did you get it?"

"I can't find it!" Chen said. "I might have lost it—lost *everything*."

"Capture the output to hard copy!" Hazelius roared.

Dolby forced the surrounding chaos out of his consciousness. Isabella wasn't responding to any of his

441

keyboard inputs. Something had happened—the p5s must have crashed. He turned to Edelstein. "Boot up the main computer. Ignore the startup procedures and testing sequences. Just turn the son of a bitch on."

An electrical arc seared across the shattered remnants of the screen. A dull, shuddering explosion sounded deep in the cavern, and another. The sound of Isabella gyrated wildly, throbbing, humming, wobbling. The room filled with smoke.

"We're creating a mini black hole," Kate said softly.

"This is *unbelievable!*" Wardlaw screamed. "You know why you lost power on One? Those bastards out there just shot down the line . . . There's a mob outside the door to Isabella. . . . Oh Christ, I'm losing the security cams—they route through the elevator. . . ."

The hiss of computer snow, then a row of screens went black.

"Oh no."

More hissing and popping. The entire security station went dead, the warning lights winking out. Isabella moaned and wobbled.

"Are you printing it out?" Hazelius screamed at Chen.

"I've got it, now I'm trying to find a working printer!" She hammered on the keyboard, sweat pouring down her face.

"Oh my God . . . Don't lose it, Rae."

"Got it," Chen yelled. "Printing!" She jumped up

and raced across the room to a printer dump. She grabbed the paper as it spooled out, ripped it off. Hazelius grabbed it from her, folded it up and stuffed it in his back pocket. "Let's get the hell out of here."

The room shook with another muffled boom, throwing Dolby to the floor. The lights wavered, electrical arcs sizzled along the consoles. Isabella groaned deeply, as if in agony. Dolby pulled himself up and went back to his machine.

Ford grabbed his arm. "Ken! We've got to get out of here!"

Dolby shook him off and tried the code again.

CODE BYPASS ERROR

The main computer began to boot up its startup routines. Dolby yelled, "Alan! I told you to shut down the p5s!"

"Ken, forget it! We're leaving!" It was Ford again.

Stay with me, Isabella.

He continued working. He had to get through to Isabella. One way or another. He had to shut her down safely. The bad magnet was decohering. The two beams were wobbling offcenter in the pipe, kinking. If they touched the edge, or grazed each other . . .

"Dolby!" Hazelius gripped his shoulder. "You can't save it! We've got to go!"

"Get away from me!" Dolby swung at Hazelius and missed. He turned back to the screen and was furious at what he saw. "Alan! God damn you, the p5s are still running! I told you to shut them down!"

There was no answer. He looked around, trying to locate Edelstein in the smoky room. He wiped his watery eyes and coughed. Smoke was everywhere. The Bridge was empty. Everyone had left.

He could save Isabella. He knew he could. And if he couldn't—what was the point of living?

I'm here, Isabella. Just stay with me a moment more.

RUSSELL EDDY HAD DONE IT. HE had killed. God had given him the strength. The battle was joined.

The killing of the sinner had been like plugging the crowd into an electric socket. They buzzed with excitement. Energized, Eddy strode to the great titanium door. He stood before it, turned, raised the gun. *"And the Antichrist had power to give life unto the image of the Beast!* Who will stand with me to confront the Antichrist?"

A roar of assent from the crowd.

"Who will stand with me to confront the Beast!"

Another delirious roar. Eddy felt a bolt of strength shoot through him.

"He is the Lawless One!"

Roar.

"The Wicked One!"

It thundered uncontrollably.

"In the name of God and His only begotten son, Jesus Christ, we will destroy him!"

The mob rushed the door en masse, but the titanium would not yield.

"Stand back!" Eddy shouted. "We're going through this door!" He aimed his gun—but a hand grabbed his fist.

"Pastor, that revolver isn't going to work." A man in camouflage with an AR-15 assault rifle strapped to his back stepped forward. "You see that setup over there?" He pointed to three conical devices mounted on tripods, pointing at the door. "That's a wall-breaching demolition kit, all set up and ready to blast. The soldiers here were intending to blow a hole in this door. They wanted to get into Isabella as well."

"How do you know?"

"Mike Frost, former Fifth Special Forces Group." He crushed Eddy's hand.

"Break us in, Mike."

Frost circled the device cautiously, peering at the metal cones. "This puppy's already packed with C-4. Darn lucky a stray bullet didn't hit one of these during the fight. Those wires connect them all together, and here are the detonators." He picked up a small cylinder with a wire attached. There were three of them, and he carefully pushed each one deep into the C-4 and packed it all back around.

"Tell everyone to get back. *Way* back. To the side over there with their backs turned."

Eddy quickly herded the milling crowd away from the setup. Frost played out the wires to their full length, flipped the cover off the detonator switch, and placed his finger on it.

"Cover your ears."

69

FORD AND THE TEAM FOLLOWED WARDLAW into the computer room behind the Bridge. It was a long, barren room with gray walls and three rows of silent, gray plastic cabinets. It housed the fastest, most powerful supercomputer in the world. Its processors were humming, the discrete panels on each one clustered with blinking lights, most of which were red or yellow. At the far end was a single steel door.

Hazelius joined them. "Dolby won't come."

"We've got three problems," Wardlaw said. "One: Isabella's going to blow. Two: we've got an armed mob out there. And three: we can't call for help."

"What do we do?" Thibodeaux wailed.

"That steel door in the back leads into the old coal tunnels. We've got to get out of here. We need to put a big piece of that mountain between us and Isabella before she blows."

"How do we get out of the coal tunnels?" Ford asked.

"At the far end," Wardlaw said, "there's an old vertical shaft that was turned into a gobshaft to pull methane out of the far end of the mine. There's still an old hoist in there. It's probably not usable. We'll have to rig something."

"Is that the best we can do?"

"It's either that or go out the front door—into that mob."

A silence.

The explosion that shook the computer room knocked Ford and the rest to their knees like they were pebbles in a tin can. The sound reverberated back and forth, the detonation rolling like thunder through the mountain. The lights in the room flickered and electrical arcs seared across the consoles. Ford struggled to his feet and helped Kate up.

"Was that Isabella?" Hazelius cried.

"If that was Isabella, we'd be dead," said Wardlaw. "The mob just blew the titanium door."

"Impossible!"

"Not if they used those military demolition charges."

The Bridge door suddenly reverberated with the pummeling of fists. Ford listened. He could see Dolby in the Bridge laboring like a ghost in the smoke, hunched over his workstation.

"Hazelius!" came a muffled, high-pitched voice through the door. "You hear me, *Antichrist?* We're coming to get you!"

PASTOR RUSSELL EDDY SCREAMED AT THE steel door. "Hazelius, you have blasphemed against God, against His name and them that dwell in heaven!"

The door was thick steel, and they had no more explosives. Firing into the lock with his revolver in this closed space would be ineffective and even insane.

The mob surged up against the door, pounding and screaming,

"Christians!" Eddy's voice boomed out in the vast, cavernous space. "Listen to me, Christians!" The crowd fell into a restless silence, filled by the infernal wailing of the machine in the tunnel beyond. "Stand back from the door! We need to organize our attack!" He pointed. "On the other side of this cavern, there's a stack of steel I-beams. I want the strongest men—and men only!—to hoist up one of those beams and batter this door down with it. The rest of you have an equally important task. Divide yourselves into two groups. I want the first group to go into the long circular tunnel, back there." He pointed to the oval opening, awash in condensation. "Cut and sledgehammer the pipes, cables, and conduits feeding the supercomputer, the Beast!" He held up a piece of paper he had printed off the Internet. "Here's a map of the Beast." He pointed to a man who seemed calmer than the rest, who carried his weapon with ease, and who had an air of leadership. "This is yours. You lead them."

"Yes, Pastor."

"Once we break down this door, I want the second group to follow me into the control room, seize the Antichrist, and destroy the equipment in there!"

A roar of approval. Already twenty men were manhandling an I-beam off the stack. The crowd parted as they came lumbering back, the I-beam aimed at the door.

"Go!" cried Eddy, standing aside. "Batter it down!"

"Batter it! Destroy it!"

The crowd parted and, at a slow jog, the men closed in on the door. The beam struck it with a massive thud, warping it inward. The beam was thrown back by the impact and the men staggered to hold it up.

"Again!" Eddy cried.

70

A MUFFLED CLANG SHOOK THE ROOM and the metal door reverberated from a massive blow. Ford struggled into the smoke, found Dolby, and grabbed his shoulder. "Ken, please," he said, "for God's sake come with us."

"No. I'm sorry, Wyman," Dolby said. "I'm staying here. I can . . . I can save Isabella."

Ford could hear the shouts and screams of the mob outside the door. They were ramming it with something heavy. Buckling, it popped one of its hinge pins.

"You won't make it. There's no time."

Through the door came the mob's roar: *"Hazeli-uuus! Antichriiist!"*

Dolby resumed his frantic work.

Kate came up behind Ford. "We've *got* to go."

Ford turned and followed Kate into the back computer room. The others were crowding around the emergency exit while Wardlaw struggled to activate the security panel. He typed and retyped the code, his hand on the hand-reader next to the exit. The reader was dead.

Boom! The door to the Bridge smacked down and

tumbled across the floor. The roar of the mob swelled as they poured into the smoky Bridge.

A fusillade of shots followed, and Dolby screamed as he was cut down at his workstation.

"Where's the Antichrist?" a man screamed. Ford rushed to the computer room door, shut it and locked it.

Wardlaw pulled out a regular key and yanked open a panel next to the door, exposing a second keyboard. He punched in a code. Nothing.

"They're in the back room!"

"Batter down that door!"

On Wardlaw's second try, the exit door opened with a smooth click. They piled through it into the damp, moldy darkness of the coal mine. Ford was the last out, pushing Kate ahead of him. A long, broad tunnel stretched out ahead, cribbed with rusting steel beams that held up a sagging, cracked ceiling. It smelled clammy and putrescent, like the petrified swamp it once was. Water dripped from the ceiling.

Wardlaw slammed the rear door and tried to lock it. But the locks were electronic and, with no power, dead.

A crashing boom thundered in the computer room, and the noise of the mob mounted. The battering ram had breached the computer door.

Wardlaw struggled to engage the locks, first using his magnetic card and then stabbing a code into the keypad.

"Ford, over here!"

Wardlaw pulled a second sidearm out of his waist-band and handed it to Ford. It was a SIG-Sauer P229. "I'm going to try to hold them here. The mines back there are room-and-pillar construction. Everything connects. Keep going and bear to the left, bypassing the dead ends, until you hit the big room where the coal seam played out. It's about three miles in. The gobshaft is in the far left corner. You can escape through it. Don't wait for me—just get everyone the hell out. And take this, too."

He shoved a Maglite into his hand.

"You can't fight them off alone," said Ford. "It's suicide."

"I can buy you time. It's our only chance."

"Tony—," began Hazelius.

"Save yourself!"

"Kill the Antichrist!" came the muffled wail from behind the door. *"Kill him!"*

"Run!" Wardlaw roared.

They ran down the dark tunnel, Ford taking up the rear, splashing through puddles of water on the mine floor, the Maglite illuminating the way. He could hear pounding on the door, the screams of the mob, and the word *"Antichriiiist"* echoing down the tunnels. After a moment, several shots sounded. There were screams and more shots, the sounds of chaos and panic.

The tunnel was long and straight, with perpendicular tunnels every fifty feet going off to the right, opening into more parallel tunnels. The bituminous seam to the left squeezed down and had been abandoned before being fully mined out, leaving many dead-end tunnels, stopes, and a web of dark seams.

More gunshots came from behind, the sounds echoing crazily through the confined spaces. The air was dead and heavy, the walls gleaming with moisture, furred with white nitre. The tunnel took a broad turn. Ford caught up to Julie Thibodeaux, who was falling behind, slipped his arm around her, and tried to help her along.

More distant shots. Wardlaw was making a last stand, Leonidas at Thermopylae, Ford though sadly, surprised at the man's courage and dedication.

The mine opened up into a vast room with a low ceiling, the main seam itself, which was held up by massive pillars of unmined coal left standing to hold up the ceiling. The pillars were twenty feet on a side, black glistening faces of peacock coal shimmering in the light, the mine a mazelike warren of pillars and open areas in no regular arrangement. Ford paused to eject the magazine and saw it was fully loaded with thirteen 9mm rounds. He shoved it back in.

"We stay together," said Hazelius, dropping back. "George and Alan, you two help Julie—she's having trouble. Wyman, you stay back and cover our rear."

Hazelius grasped Kate's shoulders in both hands and looked into her face. "If something should happen to me, you're in charge. Got it?"

Kate nodded.

• • •

THE GROUP OF MEN WITH EDDY were pinned down by gunfire from behind the first pillar of coal.

"Cover!" Eddy screamed, aiming his Blackhawk at where he had seen the last flash of light and squeezing off a round to suppress the incoming fire. More shots rang out from behind as others poured in, concentrating their fire at where the gunflashes had come from. Beams from a dozen flashlights flickered down the tunnel.

"He's behind that wall of coal!" Eddy cried. "Cover me!"

Scattered gunfire struck the wall, spraying chips of coal.

"Hold fire!"

Eddy rose and ran to the broad pillar, which extended for at least twenty feet before turning. Flattening himself against the far side, he indicated with a hand signal for several other fighters to go around the other side. He crept along the ragged face of coal, weapon at the ready.

The shooter anticipated their move and bolted for the next pillar.

Eddy raised his gun, fired, missed. Another shot rang out just before the man reached cover. He fell and began crawling. Frost came around from behind the other side of the pillar, handgun in both hands, and fired a second and third shot into the crawling man, who hunched up. He walked over and put a final bullet in his head at point blank range.

"All clear," he said, sweeping the tunnels with his flashlight. "Just one. The rest fled."

Russell Eddy lowered his gun and walked to the center of the tunnel. People were crowding in through the open door and filling up the space, their voices loud in the confined quarters. He held up his hands. Silence fell.

"The great day of his wrath has come!" Eddy cried.

He could feel the surge of the crowd behind him, he could feel their energy, like a dynamo powering his resolve. But there were too many. He needed to go in with a smaller, more mobile group. He turned and shouted over the grinding hum of the machinery: "I can only take a small group into the tunnels—and only men with guns. No women, no children. All men with firearms and experience, step forward! The rest fall back!"

About thirty men shouldered their way forward.

"Line up and show me your weapons! Hold them up!"

With a cheer, the men held up their weapons—rifles and handguns. Eddy walked down the line, looking at each man in turn. He eliminated a few with muzzle-loading antique replicas, a couple of teenagers with single-shot .22 rifles, two who looked demented. Two dozen were left.

"You men, you come with me to hunt down the Antichrist and his disciples. Stand over there." He turned to the rest. "The rest of you: your work is back there, in those rooms we just came through. God wants you to *destroy Isabella!* Destroy the Beast of the Bottomless Pit, whose name is Abaddon! Go, Soldiers of Faith!"

With a roar, the crowd broke, hungry for action, and poured back through the open door, swinging sledgehammers, axes, baseball bats. The sounds of bashing came from the room beyond.

The machine seemed to scream in agony.

Eddy grabbed Frost. "You, Mike, stay at my side. I need your experience."

"Yes, Pastor."

"All right, men—let's go!"

71

HAZELIUS LED THE GROUP THROUGH THE broad tunnels cut through the massive seam of coal. Ford covered their rear. Falling back, he peered into the darkness and listened. The shooting between Wardlaw and the mob had ended, but Ford could still hear the mob's shouts as they pursued them through the tunnels.

They stayed to the left, as Wardlaw had advised, sometimes getting hung up in dead-ends and blind leads, which forced them to backtrack. The mine was vast, the great bituminous seam going on forever in three directions. A maze of curving, crisscrossing tunnels had been cut in the seam, leaving square blocks of coal in a room-and-pillar arrangement, creating a labyrinthine sequence of spaces that connected with each other in unpredictable ways. The mine floor was crisscrossed with railcar tracks from 1950s mining operations. Rusting metal carts, rotting rope, broken engines, and heaps of discarded coal lay about. They had to wade through pools of slimy water in the low spots.

The deep-throated scream of Isabella followed them as they ran through the tunnels, like the agonizing bellows of a mortally wounded beast. Whenever he stopped to listen, Ford could also hear the clamoring pursuit of the mob.

After running for over a quarter hour, Hazelius called for a short rest. They collapsed on the damp ground, heedless of the black coal muck. Kate hunkered down next to Ford, and he put his arm around her.

"Isabella's going to blow at any moment," Hazelius said. "It could be anywhere from a large conventional bomb to a small nuke."

"Jesus," said Innes.

"A bigger problem," said Hazelius, "is that some of the detectors are filled with explosive liquid hydrogen. One neutrino detector has fifty thousand gallons of perchloroethylene and the other a hundred thousand gallons of alkanes—both flammable. And look around—there's a hell of a lot of burnable coal left in these seams. Once Isabella blows, it won't be long before the whole mountain goes up in flames. There'll be no stopping it."

Silence.

"The explosion could trigger cave-ins, too."

The cacophony of the pursuing horde echoed down the tunnels, punctuated by the occasional gunshot, rising over the wobbling, grinding, vibrating hum of Isabella.

The mob, Ford realized, was gradually catching up. "I'm going to drop back a little and fire a few rounds in their direction," he said, "To slow them down."

"Excellent idea," said Hazelius, "But no killing."

They moved on. Ford hung back in a side tunnel, where he switched off his light and listened intently. The sounds of the pursuing mob rolled through the caverns, faint and distorted.

Ford moved down the tunnel by feel, his hand on the wall, memorizing his path. Gradually the sounds became louder, and then he could see, at the edge of sight, the faint bobbing glow of half a dozen flashlights. He removed the pistol, and crouching behind a pillar of coal, pointed it obliquely at the ceiling.

The pursuers closed in. Ford squeezed off three 9mm Parabellum rounds in rapid succession, and they thundered through the confined space. Eddy's mob fell back, firing wildly into the dark.

Ducking into a dark passageway, Ford laid a hand on the far wall and, using it as a guide, moved quickly past two more tunnel openings. A second group of searchers was coming up—they seemed to have broken up into smaller teams—but this group was now moving cautiously because of the gunshots. He fired five more times, to slow them down.

Retreating—still with one guiding hand against the

wall—he counted off three more pillars before he felt safe enough to switch back on his light. He kept low, jogging, hoping to catch up with the group. But as he ran, he heard from behind a strange coughing sound. He paused. Isabella's growl suddenly changed pitch; rising precipitously, higher and higher, it became an earshattering scream, a monstrous roar, growing louder, louder, a crescendo that shook the mountain. Ford, sensing what was coming, threw himself to the ground.

The roar turned into an earthquake, the ground convulsing. A massive *boom* followed, a wave of overpressure ripping through the mine, picking him up like a leaf and hurtling him into a coal pillar. As the great thunderclap rolled off into the caverns, a sucking wind swept back through the tunnels, screaming like a banshee. Ford huddled in the lee of the coal pillar, head down, as coal and rocks blew past.

Ford rolled, looked up. The tunnel ceiling was cracking, splitting, raining bits of coal and matrix. He leapt to his feet and tried to outrun the collapsing tunnel as it roared up at him from behind.

EDDY WAS THROWN TO THE GROUND by the force of the explosions. He lay facedown in a muddy pool, pebbles and grit raining down around him, the tunnels echoing and booming with thunderous crashes, near and far. Dust filled the air and he could hardly breathe. Everything seemed to collapse around him.

Minutes passed, and the thunderous cave-ins slowed to the occasional rumble. As the sounds died away, an uneasy silence ensued, the voice of Isabella no more. The machine was dead.

They had killed it.

Eddy sat up, coughed. A moment of fumbling around in the choking clouds of dust, and he found his flashlight, still shining in the murk. Others were rising, their lights like disembodied glowworms in the fog. The tunnel had caved in not twenty yards behind them, but they had survived.

"Praise the Lord!" said Eddy, coughing again.

"Praise the Lord!" a follower echoed.

Eddy took stock. Some of his soldiers had been injured by falling rocks. Blood streamed down their foreheads, their shoulders gashed. Others seemed unhurt. No one had been killed.

Eddy steadied himself against the rock wall, trying to breathe. He managed to straighten himself up and speak. *"And I saw a new heaven and a new earth: for the first heaven and earth were passed away."* He lifted both his hands, gun in one, flashlight in the other. "Warriors of God! The Beast is dead. But let us not forget the even more important task at hand." He pointed into the drifting murk. "Out there, lurking in the dark, is the Antichrist. And his disciples. We have a battle to finish." He looked around. "Rise up! The Beast is dead! Praise the Lord!"

His words gradually drove life into the shell-shocked group.

"Recover your weapons and flashlights. Stand with me."

Those of the group who had dropped their weapons searched around, and in a few minutes all were standing, armed, and ready to continue. It was a miracle: the tunnel had caved in behind them where they had been only moments before. But the Lord had spared them.

He felt invincible. With the Lord at his side, who could strike him down? "They were ahead," he said, "down that tunnel. It's only partially collapsed. We can climb over that rubble. Let's go."

"In the name of Jesus Christ, let's go!"

"Praise Jesus!"

Eddy led them forward, feeling his strength and confidence return. The ringing in his ears began to subside. They picked their way over a heap of broken rock that had fallen from the ceiling. Smaller rocks were still rattling out of the hole in the sagging, shattered roof, but it held. Visibility gradually improved as the murk settled.

They came to an open cavern, created by the cave-in of one side of the mine ceiling. A stream of fresh, clean air flowed down from the opening, clearing out the dust. A large tunnel yawned at the far end.

Eddy paused, wondering which way the Antichrist had gone. He signaled for the group to be quiet and turn off their lights. In the silence and the dark, he heard and saw nothing. He bowed his head. "Lord, show us the way." He flicked on his light, at random, and saw which tunnel it was pointing down.

"We go this way," he said. The group followed, their flashlights bobbing like glowing eyes in the murky dark.

72

BEGAY LAY IN THE TALL ALFALFA, stunned by the blast, as secondary waves of overpressure ripped across the valley and over the bluffs. Flattening the sage, the shockwaves uprooted piñon trees, flinging sand and gravel before them like multiple blasts of buckshot, the ground shuddering and concussing beneath him. He covered his face until the first waves had passed and then sat up. A huge fireball floated above the cliff top, a blazing sphere trailing a stem of smoke, dust, and debris. He averted his face from the searing heat.

He heard Willy Becenti's muffled curses coming from the alfafa and then his head appeared, hair askew. "God *damn!*"

Across the field, other people slowly stood. The horses, which they had been rounding up to saddle, had panicked, rearing and kicking at their hobbles, bellowing with terror. Some had broken free and were tearing away across the alfalfa field.

Begay stood. The tipi had been blown down and the poles lay broken on the ground, the canvas shredded like confetti. The blast had knocked the old Nakai Rock Trading Post off its foundation. He squinted into the darkness and wondered where his horse, Winter, had run off to.

"What the hell was that?" Becenti asked, staring upward.

The giant ball of fire appeared to float high above the trees, looming above them, drifting and rolling as it collapsed into a deep reddish brown color.

On the mesa top above Isabella, Begay had seen hundreds, maybe even thousands, of people gathered. What had the blast done to them? He shuddered at the thought. A rumble came from belowground, and Begay could hear the distant rattle of gunfire.

Glancing around the field, Begay did a quick head count. Everyone was accounted for. "We got to get people the hell out of here," he called to Maria Atcitty. "I don't care if we're short of horses. Double everyone up and head for the Midnight Trail."

Somewhere just south of them, the earth growled and convulsed. At the far end of the valley, the alfalfa field buckled and sagged, a web of cracks appearing in the earth. Dust detonated into the air as a gaping sinkhole opened, the size of a football field, its edges collapsing into a cavernous darkness.

"The old mines are caving in," said Becenti.

The ground shook again, and again. Clouds of dust coiled up, near and far. The reddish brown fireball drifted, dimming, dissipating gradually and breaking apart with lassitude.

Begay clutched Maria Atcitty's shoulders. "You're in charge. Grab what people and horses you can find and get them down the Midnight Trail."

"What about you?"

"I'm going after the runaways."

"Are you crazy?"

Begay shook his head. "One of them's Winter. Don't ask me to leave him."

Maria Atcitty gave him a long look, then turned, yelling at everyone to leave their stuff and double up on the horses.

"You can't do it alone," Becenti said to Begay.

"You better go with the others."

"No way."

Begay grasped his shoulder. "Thanks."

More subterranean rumbles shook the ground—now from the southern and eastern ends of the mesa—the same direction the horses had gone. Gazing across the moonlit landscape, he watched a dozen dust coils snake upward above the mesa.

Cave-ins. The old mines really were collapsing. Over toward Isabella the fires were spreading, rolling clouds of smoke boiling up in plumes, tinged burnt-orange from the fires below. The initial explosion had only been the beginning; now the entire mesa was igniting. The coal-seamed, methane-laced tunnels were venting their rage.

Maria Atcitty returned with her horse. "It's like the end of the world out there."

Begay shook his head. "Maybe it is."

He dropped his voice and spoke the obscure Falling Star chant, *"Aniné bichaha'oh koshdéé' . . ."*

73

FORD CAME TO IN THE DARK, the air choked with dust and the stink of newly released coal gas. Covered with pulverized rock, he peered around, his ears ringing, his head splitting.

"Kate!" he called out.

Silence.

"Kate!"

Panic seized him. Pushing loose rock aside, he freed himself. Scrabbling to his hands and knees and running his hands through the rubble, he saw a gleam and uncovered his flashlight, still lit. As he shone it around, the beam revealed a body lying twenty feet down the tunnel, partly buried in rock. He scrambled over.

It was Hazelius. A trickle of blood came out of his nose. He felt for a pulse—strong.

"Gregory!" he whispered into the man's ear. "Can you hear me?"

The head turned and the eyes opened—those astonishing azure eyes. Hazelius squinted in the light. "What . . . happened?" he croaked.

"Explosion and cave-in."

Comprehension dawned. "The others?"

"I don't know. I was just catching up to you when it blew."

"They ran every which way when the rocks started falling." He glanced down. "My leg . . ."

Ford began clearing rubble from the lower half of Hazelius's body. A large rock lay on his left leg. He grasped the edge of the rock and gently lifted it off. The leg underneath was slightly crooked.

"Help me up, Wyman."

"I'm afraid your leg's broken," Ford said.

"No matter. We've got to keep moving."

"But if it's broken—"

"Help me up, damn you!"

Ford slung Hazelius's arm around his neck and helped him to his feet. Hazelius staggered, clinging to him.

"If you support me, I can walk."

Ford listened. In the rattled silence, he could hear distant voices and shouts. Incredibly enough, the mob was still in pursuit. Or perhaps they, too, just wanted out of the labyrinth.

Moving through the rubble, Ford supported Hazelius, one step after another. He dragged Hazelius over rockfalls, under gaping holes in the ceiling, through passages between tunnels which the explosion had opened up, past rooms which the blast had caved in. He could see no sign of the others.

"Kate?" Ford called into the darkness.

No answer.

Ford felt for his SIG. Eight rounds expended, five left.

"I'm getting a little dizzy," Hazelius said.

Moving slowly, they came out of a narrow tunnel into a transverse shaft. Again Ford recognized nothing. The voices were getting louder now and eerily ubiquitous, as if all around them.

"I just never . . . *expected* . . . this." Hazelius's voice trailed off.

Ford wanted to call out for Kate again but he didn't dare. There was so much dust, so many tunnels, and if she answered, the mob might find her.

Hazelius stumbled again, crying from pain, and Ford could barely hold him up. He sagged like a sack of cement. When Ford could drag him no farther, he crouched and struggled to hoist Hazelius over his shoulders. The tunnel was too tightly confined and the effort caused Hazelius too much pain.

Ford laid Hazelius down and felt his pulse—shallow and fast, with a clammy sweat breaking out on his forehead. He was going into shock.

"Gregory, can you hear me?"

The scientist groaned and turned his head. "I'm sorry," he whispered. "I just can't do it."

"I'm going to look at your leg."

Ford slit the pant-leg with the penknife. The compound fracture had forced the splintered thigh bone through the skin. If he carried Hazelius further, the splintered femur might sever the femoral artery.

Ford risked shining around a low beam from the Maglite. He could see no sign of the others, but below the tunnel floor, a shallow stope on the opposite wall a few dozen feet down—partially obscured by a rockfall—suggested concealment.

"We're going to hide in there."

He picked Hazelius under the arms and dragged him into the niche. Gathering more fallen rock, he built a low wall they could hide behind. The voices were getting closer.

Please God, let Kate make it.

Ford used up all the loose rocks in the vicinity. The wall was about two feet high, just enough to hide them if they lay down. Ford got behind it. He took off his jacket and balled it up, making a pillow for Hazelius's head, and shut off the light.

"Thank you, Wyman," Hazelius said.

They didn't speak for a moment, and then Hazelius said, matter of factly, "They're going to kill me, you know."

"Not if I can help it." Ford felt for his gun.

Hazelius's hand touched his. "No. No killing. Aside from the fact that we're hopelessly outnumbered, it would be wrong."

"It's not wrong if they're going to kill you first."

"We're all one," said Hazelius. "Killing them is like killing yourself."

"Please don't lay that religious shit on me now."

Hazelius groaned, swallowed. "Wyman, I'm disappointed in you. Of all the team, you're the only one who won't accept the amazing thing that's happened to us."

"Stop talking and lie low."

They crouched behind the rough wall of stones. The air smelled of dust and mildew. The voices approached, the footsteps and clinking of the mob now echoing down the stone corridors. After a moment, the dull glow of their torches invaded the dusty air. Ford could hardly breathe, he was so tense. The mob was noisier, drawing nearer. Suddenly they were there. For a seeming eternity Eddy's horde was slogging past, their flashlights and torches casting hellish orange shapes on the ceiling, their shadows distorted on the walls. The noise of the mob dimmed, receded, the flickering of the fires dying away. Darkness returned. Ford heard a long, painful sigh from Hazelius. "My God . . ."

Ford wondered for a crazy moment if Hazelius was praying.

"They think . . . I'm the Antichrist. . . ." He gave a low, strange laugh.

Ford rose and peered into the darkness. The sounds of the mob vanished and silence fell once again, broken here and there with the rattle of falling pebbles.

"Maybe I *am* the Antichrist . . . ," Hazelius wheezed. Ford wasn't sure if it was pain or laughter. *He's starting to get delirious,* he thought. He put that aside and considered what they should do. Air was moving through the tunnel and with it came the stench of burning coal, as well as an ominously low vibration, the sound of fire.

"We've got to get out."

No answer from Hazelius.

He grasped Hazelius under the shoulders. "Come on. Try to keep moving. We can't stay here. We've got to find the others and get to the hoist."

A muffled explosion reverberated through the tunnels. The smell of coal smoke increased.

"And now they're going to kill me. . . ." Again, the eerie laugh.

Hoisting Hazelius over his back, gripping him by each arm, Ford dragged him through the tunnels.

"Ironic," Hazelius mumbled. "To be martyred . . . Human beings are so foolish . . . so gullible. . . . But I didn't think it through . . . just as stupid as they are. . . ."

Ford shone the light ahead. The tunnel opened into a large cavern.

"Now I'm going to pay for it. . . . Antichrist, they called me. . . . Antichrist indeed!" More spastic laughter. Ford struggled forward and entered the cavernous stope. To his right, caved-in coal piles and rock mixed together with crumbling veins of pyrite that glittered like gold in his flashlight.

He struggled on with the man toward the far end. The gobshaft materialized out of the darkness, a round hole, about five feet in diameter, at the far corner. A rope dangled down the shaft.

He lay Hazelius on the rock floor and rested his head on the jacket. An explosion rocked the room, and he could hear debris dropping all around them, shaken loose from the ceiling. The smoke stung his eyes. At any moment the approaching fire would suck out their oxygen—and that would be it.

He grasped the rope. Disintegrating in his hands, it parted, unraveling and piling down into the deep shaft. A few moments later he heard a splash of water.

He shined his light up and saw a smoothly bored hole going up as far as the eye could see. The rotten end of the rope dangled uselessly. The hoist was nowhere to be seen.

He went back to Hazelius to find him sinking deeper into delirium. More soft laughter. Ford squatted on his heels, thinking hard. Hazelius's mumbling distracted him, and then he heard a name: *Joe Blitz*.

Suddenly he listened. "Did you just say Joe Blitz?"

"Joe Blitz . . . ," he mumbled, "Lieutenant Scott Morgan . . . Bernard Hubbell . . . Kurt von Rachen . . . Captain Charles Gordon . . ."

"Who's Joe Blitz?"

"Joe Blitz . . . Captain B. A. Northrup . . . Rene Lafayette . . ."

"Who are these people?" Ford asked.

"Nobodies. They don't . . . exist. . . . Noms de plume . . ."

"Pennames?" Ford bent over Hazelius. His face, in the faint light, was covered with a sheen of sweat. His eyes were glassy. But there was still a strange, almost supernatural vitality to the man. "Pennames for who?"

"Who else? For the great L. Ron Hubbard . . . Clever man . . . Only they didn't call him the Antichrist. . . . He was luckier than me, the schmuck."

Ford was thunderstruck. Joe Blitz? A penname for L. Ron Hubbard? Hubbard was the science fiction writer who had started his own religion, Scientology, and set himself up as its prophet. Before launching Scientology, Ford recalled, Hubbard had famously told a group of fellow writers that the greatest feat a human being could achieve in this world was to found a world-class religion. And then he went out and did it, combining pseudoscience and half-baked mysticism into a potent and appealing package.

A world-class religion . . . Was it possible? Was that the question Hazelius alluded to? Was that the point of his hand-picked team? Their tragic backgrounds? Isabella, the greatest scientific experiment in history? The isolation? The Mesa? The messages? The secrecy? *The voice of God?*

Ford took a deep breath and leaned over. He whispered, "Volkonsky wrote a note just before his . . . death. I found it. It said, in part: *I saw through the madness. To prove it, I give you a name only: Joe Blitz.*"

"Yes . . . Yes . . . ," Hazelius answered. "Peter was smart. . . . Too smart for his own good . . . I made a mistake there, should have picked someone else. . . ." A silence, and then a long sigh. "My mind is wandering." His voice quavered at the edge of sanity. "What was I saying?"

Hazelius was swimming back into reality—but only a little.

"Joe Blitz was L. Ron Hubbard. The man who invented his own religion. Was *that* what this was all about?"

471

"I was babbling."

"But that was your plan," said Ford. "Wasn't it?"

"I don't know what you're talking about." Hazelius's voice sounded sharper.

"Of course you do. You choreographed the whole thing—the building of Isabella, the problems with the machine, the voice of God. It was you all along. *You're* the hacker."

"You're not making sense, Wyman." Now Hazelius sounded like he had returned to reality—hard.

Ford shook his head. The answer had been staring him in the face for almost a week—right there in his file.

"Most of your life," said Ford, "you've been concerned with utopian political schemes."

"Aren't many of us?"

"Not to the power of obsession. But you were obsessed, and, even worse, no one listened to you—not even after you won the Nobel Prize. It must have driven you crazy—the smartest man on earth, and no one would listen. Then your wife died and you went into seclusion. You emerged two years later with the idea for Isabella. You had something to say. You wanted people to listen. You wanted to change the world more than ever. How better to do it than become a prophet? To start your own religion?"

Ford could hear Hazelius breathing heavily in the darkness.

"Your theory is . . . *demented,*" Hazelius said, with a groan.

"You came up with the idea for the Isabella project—a machine to probe the Big Bang, the moment of creation. You got it built. You picked the team—making sure they were psychologically receptive. You staged this whole thing. You planned to make the greatest scientific discovery ever made. And what might that be? What else, but to discover God! That discovery would make you his prophet. That's it, isn't it? You planned to pull an L. Ron Hubbard on the world."

"You're really quite mad."

"Your wife wasn't pregnant when she died. You made that up. Whatever names the machine came up with, you'd have reacted the same way. You guessed the numbers Kate would be thinking of—because you knew Kate so well. There was nothing supernatural about this at all."

Hazelius's even breathing was his only response.

"You gathered around you twelve scientists—hand-picked by you. When I read their dossiers, I was struck that every one of them had been hurt by life, every one seeking meaning in their lives. I wondered why that was. And now I know. You handpicked them because you knew they were susceptible—ripe for conversion."

"But I couldn't convert you, huh?"

"You came close."

They paused. The faint sound of voices reverberated down the tunnels. The mob was returning.

Hazelius let out a long sigh. "We're both going to

die—I hope you realize that, Wyman. We're both to be . . . *martyred.*"

"That remains to be seen."

"Yes, my intention was to start a religion. But I don't know what the hell happened back there. It got away from me. I had this plan . . . it just got away from me." He sighed again, moaned. "Eddy. That was the wild card that blew my hand. A foolish oversight on my part: martyrdom is the way of all prophets."

"How did you do it? I mean, hack the computer?"

Hazelius slipped the old rabbit's foot out of his pocket. "I hollowed out the cork stuffing, replaced it with a sixty-four-gig flash drive, processor, microphone, and wireless transmitter—voice recognition and data. I could connect it to any one of a thousand high-speed wireless processors scattered about Isabella, all slaved to the supercomputer. It's got a lovely little AI program I wrote in LISP, or rather helped write, since much of it's self-generated. It's the most beautiful computer program ever written. It was simple to operate, just sitting in my pocket. Although the program itself was anything but simple—I'm not sure even I understand it. Strange, though, it said a lot of things I never intended—things that I never dreamed of. You might say it performed beyond specs."

"You manipulative bastard."

Hazelius slipped the rabbit's foot back into his pocket. "You're wrong about that, Wyman. I'm not a bad man at all. I did what I did for the highest, most altruistic reasons."

"Sure. Look at the violence, all the death. You're responsible for it."

"Eddy and his people chose the violence, not me." He winced with momentary pain.

"And you either murdered Volkonsky or had Wardlaw do it."

"No. Volkonsky was a smart man. He guessed what I was up to. When he really thought it through, he realized he couldn't stop me. He couldn't bear to see himself made a fool of, his life's work manipulated and disgraced like that. So he killed himself, making it look like a suicide, but with a few anomalous details so they'd end up thinking it was murder. Double-reverse psychology, typical Volkonsky. He had a uniquely devious mind."

"Why make it look like murder?"

"He hoped the investigation would eventually engulf the Isabella project, shut us down before I could pull my coup. Didn't work, though. Events moved too fast. I accept responsibility for his death. But I didn't kill him."

"What a futile damn waste."

"You're not thinking it through, Wyman. . . ." He breathed heavily for a moment, and resumed. "This story is just beginning. You can't stop it. *Les jeux sont faites,* as Sartre once said. The great irony is that *they* are going to make it happen."

"They?"

"That fundamentalist mob. They're going to supply a far more powerful end to this story than the one I had devised."

"Your story will end in futility," said Ford.

"Wyman, I can see you don't understand the full dimensions of what is happening. Eddy's unwashed masses . . ." He paused and Ford, to his dismay, could hear the faint sounds of the mob getting closer. ". . . They will kill me, *martyr* me. And you. In so doing, they'll anoint my name . . . forever."

"I'll anoint you a madman, forever."

"I grant you that is how most normal people would perceive me."

The voices became more distinct.

"We have to hide," said Ford.

"Where? There's no place to go and I can't move." Hazelius shook his head and, in a low, hoarse voice, quoted the Bible. " *'They will call to the mountains and rocks, Fall on us, and hide us . . .'* Just as Revelation says, we're trapped."

The voices were getting closer. Ford removed his pistol, but Hazelius placed a clammy, trembling hand on his arm. "Acquiesce with dignity."

Bobbing lights flashed from the darkness. The voices swelled as a dozen filthy, heavily armed men surged around a curve in the tunnel.

"There they are! Two of them!"

The crowd emerged from the murk, black and ghoulish as coal miners, with guns drawn, white streaks of sweat like bars down their grimacing faces.

"Hazelius! The Antichrist!"

"The *Antichrist!*"

"We've got him!"

Another distant explosion shook the room. The hanging rock of the ceiling loosened and let loose a storm of pebbles, which clattered to the floor, hailstones from hell. Coal smoke drifted in tendrils through the dead air. The mountain quaked again and another cave-in down the line growled and rumbled, coughing smoke through the shafts.

The crowd parted and Pastor Eddy walked up to Hazelius. Standing over the stricken scientist, his hollow, bony face grinned in triumph. "We meet again."

Hazelius shrugged and averted his eyes.

"Only now, *Antichrist,*" Eddy said, "I'm in control. God's at my right, Jesus on my left, and the Holy Spirit has my back. And you—where's *your* protector? He's fled—Satan, the coward—fled to the rocks! *'Hide us from the face of him that sitteth on the throne, and from the wrath of the Lamb!'*"

Eddy bent over Hazelius until his face was inches from the scientist's. And then he laughed.

"Go to hell, germ," Hazelius said softly.

Eddy exploded with rage. "Search them for weapons!"

A group of men approached Ford. He let them come, decked the first one, kicked the second in the stomach, and slammed the third into a rock wall. The others converged with a roar of fury, and a small army of fists and feet finally drove him to the wall and then to the ground. Eddy pulled the SIG-Sauer out of Ford's waist band.

During the melee one enthusiastic worshipper kicked Hazelius in his broken leg. With a sobbing gasp, the scientist passed out.

"Good work, Eddy," said Ford, pinned to the ground. "Your Savior would be proud."

Eddy glared at Ford, his face red with fury, as if he might strike the man, but then he seemed to have second thoughts. "Enough!" Eddy shouted at the crowd. "*Enough!* Give us room! We'll take care of them in our own way, the right way. Get them on their feet!"

Ford was dragged to his feet and pushed forward, and the group began to move. Two burly men hauled the comatose Hazelius along by his armpits, his nose streaming blood, one eye swollen shut, his crooked leg with the broken bone dragging.

They reached another large, cavernous stope. Lights arrived from a side tunnel, bobbing in the murk. There was a burst of excited talk.

"Frost? Is that you?" Eddy called.

A beefy man dressed in camo with a tight blond crew cut, massive neck, and closely set eyes pushed through. "Pastor Eddy? We found more of them, hiding downshaft."

Ford watched a dozen armed men herd Kate and the others at gunpoint. "Kate . . . Kate!" He wrenched himself free and struggled toward her.

"Stop him!"

Ford felt a massive blow to his back, which sent him to his knees. A second blow knocked him on his side, and punches and kicks laid him flat. He was hauled back to his feet so roughly it almost dislocated his shoulders. A sweaty man, his face streaked with coal dust, his eyes white and rolling like a horse's, struck him across the face. "Stay in line!"

Another distant rumble and the ground convulsed. Dust jumped up from the floor, billowing through the tunnels. Layers of smoke collected in layers along the ceilings.

"Listen to me!" Eddy cried. "We can't stay down here! The whole mountain's on fire! We've got to get out!"

"I saw a way up top back there," said the man called Frost. "A drift-shaft was opened up in the explosion. I could see the moon at the tunnel's end."

"Lead the way," said Eddy.

Armed men shoved and prodded them with guns through dark, dust-choked tunnels. Two of Eddy's followers hauled the unconscious Hazelius by the armpits. Moving through the murk, they crossed another massive stope. The lights played through the gray dust, revealing a huge cave-in, with a mountain of rubble leading up into a long, dark hole in the ceiling. Ford gulped down the fresh, cool air streaming from above.

"This way!"

They started up the pile, staggering up the loose,

sliding scree, rocks rattling down around them.

"Up from the Bottomless Pit of Abaddon!" Eddy cried triumphantly. "The Beast is yoked!"

At the head of the mob the two followers dragged Hazelius up, through the jagged hole in the ceiling rock, the rest being pushed along by men with guns. The hole led to a higher stope and, from there into another shaft, at the end of which Ford saw a momentary light—the gleam, quickly extinguished, of a single star shining in the night sky. They emerged into the night of the mesa through a long diagonal crevasse. The air stank of burning gasoline and smoke. The entire eastward horizon was ablaze. Reddish-black clouds of smoke rolled across the sky, obscuring the moon. The ground rumbled continuously, and now and then a flame leapt up a hundred or more feet like a blood-orange banner fluttering into the night sky.

"Over there!" Eddy shouted. "Into that open area!"

Crossing a dry wash, they stopped in a broad, sandy depression, dominated by a giant, dead piñon tree. Ford at least got close enough to Kate to ask: "Are you all right?"

"Yes, but Julie and Alan are dead—caught in the cave-in."

"Silence!" Eddy shouted. He stepped into the open area. Ford was amazed at his transformation from the high-strung preacher he had first met. Calm and self-assured, his movements were now deliberate. A .44 Super Blackhawk revolver was shoved into his belt.

He paced and turned before the crowd, raised a hand. "The Lord delivered us from bondage out of Egypt. Blessed be the Lord."

His flock, a few dozen worshippers, thundered back: *"Blessed be the Lord!"*

Eddy bent over the supine scientist, who opened his eyes, coming to.

"Stand him up," Eddy said quietly. He pointed to Ford, Innes, and Cecchini. "Hold him tight."

They reached down and, as gently as possible, raised Hazelius to his one good leg. Ford was astounded the man was still alive, let alone conscious.

Eddy turned to the crowd. "Look into his face—the face of the Antichrist." He walked in a circle and his voice throbbed out, " *'And the Beast was taken, and with him the false prophet that wrought miracles before him. These both were cast alive into a lake of fire burning with brimstone.'"*

A muffled boom threw a distant ball of fire into the air, casting a lurid glow over the proceedings. Eddy's gaunt face was briefly silhouetted by the orange light, which highlighted his blackened, hollowed cheeks and sunken eyes. *" 'Rejoice, for God hath avenged you!' "*

The crowd cheered but Eddy raised his hands. "Soldiers in Christ, this is a solemn moment. We have taken the Antichrist and his disciples, and now the judgment of God awaits all of us."

Hazelius raised his head. To Ford's surprise, the scientist fixed Eddy with a supercilious sneer—half grin, half grimace—and said, "Pardon my interruption, Preacher, but the Antichrist has a few anticlimactic words for your illustrious flock."

Eddy held up his hands. "The Antichrist speaks." He took a bold step closer. "What blasphemy comes from thy lips now, Antichrist?"

Hazelius raised his head, his voice strengthening. "Brace me," he said to Ford. "Don't let me slip."

"I'm not sure this is wise," Ford murmured in Hazelius's ear.

"Why not?" Hazelius whispered grimly. "In for a penny, in for a pound."

"Listen, soldiers in Christ, to the words of the false prophet," Eddy said, his voice tinged with irony.

74

FROM A PILE OF SANDSTONE BOULDERS, Begay scanned the darkened horizon with his binoculars. It was 2:30 A.M.

"There they are. Huddled up in that grassy flat, scared shitless." The horses milled about, dark silhouettes against a red sky.

"Let's go get 'em," said Becenti.

But Begay didn't move. He had trained the glasses eastward. The eastern point of the mesa was gone—blown away. Below the blasted notch lay a huge scree slope of rubble, burning coal, tangled metal, and rivers of burning fluid that spread out and ran down the gullies like lava from a volcano. The entire eastern side of the mesa was on fire, smoke and flame pouring out of holes in the ground and leaping into the air. Once in a while a piñon tree or juniper would flare on top of the mesa, lighting up like a lone Christmas tree. Despite a wind blowing the smoke away from them, the fires were spreading rapidly in their direction. There were occasional explosions, with dust and flames shooting up, the ground sagging, then collapsing with an upwash of black dust and smoke. Nakai Valley itself had caught fire, the trading post and houses in flames, along with the beautiful grove of cottonwoods.

Before the explosion, at least a thousand people had gathered in that place. Now Begay, scanning the hellish mesa with his binoculars, could see only a few scattered people wandering shell-shocked among the smoke and flames, crying out, or simply stumbling about silently, like zombies. The flow of cars up the Dugway had ceased and some of the parked cars had caught on fire, the gas tanks exploding.

Willy shook his head. "Man, they did it. Old *Bilagaana* finally did it."

They descended the rockpile, and Begay approached the horses, whistling for Winter. The horse pricked his ears and a moment later trotted over, the others following.

"Good boy, Winter." Stroking his neck, Begay clipped a lead rope to his halter. Several of the horses had been saddled in preparation for departure, and Begay was glad to see they hadn't shucked them.

Switching his own saddle from the horse he was riding to Winter, he cinched it tight and swung up. Willy mounted his horse bareback, and they began hazing the nervous horses toward the Midnight Trail, which lay opposite the conflagration. They moved slowly, keeping them calm and on high ground where the footing was sure. As they topped a rise, Becenti, who was in the lead, paused.

"What the hell's going on over there?"

Begay rode up beside him and raised his binoculars. A few hundred yards away, in a sandy area, a group of men had collected. They were filthy, like they had recently emerged from a caved-in area of ground, surrounding a group of what appeared to be ragged, dirty prisoners. Begay could hear jeering.

"Looks like a lynching," said Becenti.

Begay examined the prisoners more closely with the field glasses. With a shock, he recognized the scientist who had visited him, Kate Mercer. And some distance from her was Wyman Ford, holding up what looked like an injured man.

"I don't like it," said Begay. He started to get off his horse.

"What are you doing? We got to get out of here."

Begay tied the horse to a tree. "They might need our help, Willy."

With a grin, Willy Becenti swung off his horse. "This is more like it."

They crept up to the group, finding cover behind a screen of boulders. They were less than a hundred feet from the assembly and concealed by the darkness. Begay counted twenty-four men, with guns. Everyone was blackened with coal dust. Faces from hell.

Ford's face was bloody and it looked like he'd been beaten up. The other prisoners he didn't know, but he guessed they must also be scientists from the Isabella project, given the lab coats they wore. Ford held one of them up, the man's arm slung over his shoulder. The man had a badly broken leg. The crowd was spitting at them, jeering and cursing. Finally, a man stepped forward and raised his hands, quieting the mob.

Begay could hardly believe his eyes: it was Pastor Eddy, from the mission down in Blue Gap—except the man was transformed. The Pastor Eddy he knew had been a confused, half-crazy loser who gave away old clothes and owed him sixty bucks. This Eddy had an air of cold command, and the crowd was responding to it.

Begay hunkered down and watched, Becenti next to him.

EDDY RAISED HIS HANDS. "*'And there was given unto him a mouth speaking great things and blasphemies!'* My Christian friends, the Antichrist will speak. Witness with me his blasphemy."

Hazelius tried to speak. The burning of Isabella flickered in the background, the sheets and pillars of flame leaping up and spreading, and he was drowned out by a series of sharp explosions. He began again, his voice stronger.

"Pastor Eddy, I have only one comment to make. These people are not my disciples. Do what you want with me, but let them go."

"Liar!" someone shouted from the crowd.

"Blasphemer!"

Eddy raised a forebearing hand and the crowd fell back into silence. "No one is innocent," he shouted. "We're all sinners in the hands of an angry God. Only by God's grace are we saved."

"Leave them alone, you demented bastard."

Not much chance of that, thought Ford, looking around at Eddy's flock, howling for Hazelius's hide.

Hazelius weakened, his good leg buckling.

"Hold him up!" Eddy roared.

Kate came to Ford's side and helped hold the scientist up.

Eddy turned. "The day of God's wrath has arrived," he thundered. "Take him!"

The crowd lunged at Hazelius, crowding around him, pushing him this way and that as if fighting over a rag doll. They struck him, shoved him, spat on him, beat him with sticks. One man slashed him with a piece of cholla cactus.

"Tie him to that tree."

They dragged him toward a massive, gaunt, dead piñon, the crowd struggling with him like a clumsy, hundred-footed beast. They lashed one wrist, threw the rope end over a stout branch and pulled tight, did the same with the other wrist, and tied them off, so that Hazelius was half-hanging, half-standing upright, arms apart. His clothes hung in tatters from his filthy body.

Suddenly, Kate wrenched free, leapt forward, and embraced Hazelius.

The crowd burst into angry shouts, and several men grabbed Kate and yanked her back, throwing her to the ground. A scarecrow of a man with a squared-off beard scooted out of the crowd and kicked her while she was down.

"Bastard!" Ford shouted. He slammed the man in the jaw, knocked another aside and fought his way toward Kate, but the mob swarmed him and he was driven to the ground with fists and clubs. Half-conscious, he was barely aware of what happened next.

The roar of a dirt bike sounded at the edge of the crowd, the engine sputtering to a stop. A deep, authoritative voice sounded out: "Greetings, Christians!"

"Doke!" cried the crowd. "Doke is here!"

"Doke! Doke!"

The crowd parted and a mountain of a man strode into the ring, dressed in a denim jacket with the sleeves ripped off, brawny arms tattooed, big iron cross dangling from a silver chain around his neck, assault rifle slung across his back. His long blond hair whipped in the winds generated by the fires.

He turned, embraced Eddy. "Christ be with you!" He released Eddy from his embrace and pivoted to the crowd. Doke radiated easy charm, a complement to Eddy's ascetic severity. With a mysterious grin, he reached into a bag and removed a glass bottle filled with a clear liquid, unscrewed the cap, flicked it away, and stuffed a rag into the hole, leaving the end dangling. Then, holding the rag in place with two fingers, he shook the bottle and held it up. The crowd roared. Ford smelled gasoline. With his other arm he raised a Bic lighter until both arms were over his head. He waved them back and forth and did a full turn around, like a rock star onstage. "Wood!" he cried, his voice hoarse. "Bring us wood!"

Eddy said, " *'And whosoever was not found written in the book of life was cast into the lake of fire!'* The Bible is clear on this point. Those who have not accepted Jesus Christ as their personal savior are cast into everlasting fire. *This, my fellow Christians, is what God wants.*"

"Burn him! Burn the Antichrist!" responded the crowd.

" *'And the devil that deceived them was cast into the lake of fire,'* " Eddy continued, " *'cast into the lake of fire and brimstone, where the beast and the false prophet are.'* "

"Stop it! In the name of God, don't do this!" Kate shouted.

Heaps of dead piñon branches, cactus husks, and sagebrush bushes were passed over the heads of the crowd and tossed at the foot of the tree. A brushpile began to grow.

"This is God's promise to the unbelievers," said Eddy, striding back and forth in front of the growing pile. " *'And they shall be tormented day and night, for ever and ever.'* What we do here is sanctioned by God and confirmed repeatedly in the Bible. I give you Revelation 14:11: *'And the smoke of their torment ascendeth up for ever and ever: and they have no rest day nor night.'*"

The brushpile grew helter-skelter. Several men began kicking it up around Hazelius.

"Don't do this!" Kate screamed again.

The pile reached Hazelius's upper thighs.

" *'And fire came down from God out of heaven, and devoured them,'* " quoted Eddy.

Cactus husks, sagebrush, and rabbitbrush, explosively dry, continued to pile up, burying Hazelius to his waist.

"We're ready to do God's will," Eddy said quietly.

Doke stepped forward, raised his arms again, Bic in one hand, Molotov cocktail in the other. The crowd fell back and a silence followed. The man did another half turn, hands raised. The crowd shuffled farther back, awed.

Doke flicked on the lighter and lit the Molotov cocktail. The dangling rag flowered into flame. Turning, he pitched he lighted bottle into the pile. There was a *whump!* and fire blossomed inside the brush, erupting upward with a loud crackling.

A great "Ohhhh!" went up from the crowd.

Ford braced himself, his arm around Kate, sup-

489

porting her as she swayed, nearly fainting. They all watched in silence. Nobody turned away.

As the flames mounted, Hazelius spoke, his voice steady and clear: "The universe never forgets."

75

NELSON BEGAY WATCHED THE HUMAN PYRE with mounting fury. Burning a man alive. This is what the Spanish had done to his ancestors if they didn't convert. And here it was happening all over again.

But he could think of no way to stop it.

The flames leapt up, catching the man's tattered lab coat. They obscured his face and scorched off his hair with a sizzling flash.

Still the man stood.

The flames mounted up with a roar, his clothes blackening and burning off in strips, like fiery confetti.

The man didn't flinch.

The roaring fire consumed his clothes and began charring and peeling off his very skin; his eyes melted and ran out of their sockets. And still the man never moved, never flinched—and the sad half smile never left his face even as his face was scorched. The fire caught the ropes holding him to the tree and burned them off—and yet he still stood, solid as a rock. How could it be? Why didn't he fall? Even as the dead piñon he was tied to went up in a writhing column of fire, the flames leaping twenty, thirty feet into the air, he remained standing, until he had completely disappeared into the pillar of fire. From a hundred feet away Begay could feel the heat of the fire on his face, heard it roaring like a beast, the outermost branches of the tree like so many burning claws; and then the flaming tree collapsed in a great shower of sparks that swirled into the heavens, so high they seemed to join the stars themselves.

There was nothing left of Hazelius. The man had completely vanished.

The other prisoners, held in a group at gunpoint nearby, looked on in absolute horror. Some were weeping, holding hands, arms around each other.

They're next, thought Begay. The thought was intolerable.

Doke was already reaching into his bag, pulling out another bottle.

"Screw this," said Becenti under his breath. "Are we just gonna let this happen?"

Begay turned to look at him. "No, Willy. No, by God, we're not."

FORD STARED AT THE DYING FIRE dumbstruck with disbelief and horror. Where Hazelius had just stood there was a great crumbling heap of coals, nothing more. Ford held Kate tightly, supporting her. She stared into the coals, her smudged face streaked with tears, her body still. Nobody moved or spoke.

They would be next.

The crowd was suddenly quiet. The preacher, Eddy,

stood to one side, Bible clutched to his chest in two bony hands. His eyes looked hollow and haggard.

Doke, the tattooed man, also stared into the fire, his face radiant.

Eddy raised his head and looked at the crowd. He pointed a shaking hand at the heap of coals. *" 'You shall trample the wicked, for they shall be ashes under the soles of your feet.' "*

His harangue woke the crowd up. They shifted uneasily. "Amen," said a voice, echoed feebly by others.

" 'Ashes under the soles of your feet,' " Eddy repeated.

A few more ragged amens broke out.

"And now," he said. "My friends, the time has now come for the *disciples* of the Antichrist. We are Christians. We are forgiving. They must be given a chance to accept Jesus. Even the greatest sinner must be given one last, final chance. *On your knees!*"

A follower hit Ford across the back of his head and he involuntarily dropped to his knees. Kate joined him, pulling him close.

"Pray to Our Lord Christ Jesus for the salvation of their souls!"

Doke knelt on one knee, Eddy following, and soon the entire crowd was kneeling on the desert sand in the ruddy glow of the dying fire, amid a rising murmur of prayer.

Another explosion rumbled across the mesa and the ground shook.

"Do you," said Eddy, "the disciples of the Antichrist, confess your apostasy and accept Jesus as your personal savior? Do you accept Jesus wholeheartedly, without reservation? Will you join us and become part of God's great army?"

Absolute silence. Ford squeezed Kate's hand. He wished she'd speak, wished she'd agree. But if he couldn't do it himself, how could he expect her to?

"Will not *one* of you repudiate your heresy and accept Jesus? Not *one* wants to be saved from the fire of this world and the everlasting fires of the next?"

Ford felt a rush of boiling anger. He raised his head. "I'm a Christian, a Catholic. I have no heresy to repudiate."

Eddy took a deep breath and spoke in a quavering voice, his hand raised dramatically to the listening crowd. "Catholics are not Christians. Catholicism's spirit is one of idolatrous adoration of the Blessed Virgin Mary."

An uncertain murmur of agreement.

"It's the spirit of demonism, as is evident by the vain repetition of Hail Marys in the Rosary Prayer. It's the idolatrous worship of graven images, in violation of God's commandments."

A rage took hold of Ford, which he tried to master. He rose up. "How dare you," he said in a low voice. "How *dare* you."

Eddy raised the gun and pointed it at him. "Priests have brainwashed you Catholics for fifteen hundred years. You don't read the Bible. You do what the priests tell you. Your pope prays to graven images and kisses the feet of statues. The word of God is clear that we're to bow to Jesus and *none* other, not Mary or the so-called saints. Give up your blasphemous religion—or suffer the wrath of the Lord God."

"You're the real blasphemers," said Ford, staring at the crowd.

Eddy raised the shaking gun and pointed it at Ford's right eye. "Your church is straight out of the mouth of Hell! Give it up!"

"Never."

The gun steadied as Eddy took aim from four inches away, his finger tightening on the trigger.

76

THE REVEREND DON T. SPATES SLAMMED down the phone. Still out of order. His Internet connection was also down. He thought of going over to the Silver Cathedral media office and turning on the television to see if there was any news, but he couldn't bring himself to do it. He was afraid to leave, afraid to get up from his desk—afraid of what he might discover.

He checked his watch. Four-thirty A.M. Two hours until dawn. When the sun rose, he would go straight to Dobson. He would put himself in his lawyer's hands. Dobson would handle the whole thing. Sure, it would cost money. But after this, the donations would be like a gusher. He just needed to weather the storm. He'd been through storms before, like when those two whores reported him to the newspapers. He thought then his whole world was over. And yet, a month later he was back in business, preaching in the Cathedral, and now he was the hottest televangelist in the business.

Pulling out a handkerchief, he mopped his face, wiped around his eyes, forehead, nose, and mouth, leaving a brown stain of old makeup on the white linen. He looked at it in disgust and tossed it in the trash. He poured another cup of coffee, splashed in a shot of vodka, and drank it down with a shaking hand.

He put the cup down so hard it broke in two. The rare Sèvres cup had split perfectly down the center, as if cleaved. He held the pieces in his hands, staring at them, and then, in a sudden fury, threw them across the room.

Lurching to his feet, he went to the window, threw it open, and stared. Outside, all was dark and silent. The world slept. But not in Arizona. Terrible things could be happening out there. But it wasn't his fault. He had devoted his life to doing Christ's work on earth. *I believe in honor, religion, duty, and country.*

If only the sun would rise. He imagined himself cosseted in the hushed, wood-paneled confines of his lawyer's offices on 13th Street, and he felt comforted.

At first light he'd rouse his chauffeur and head to Washington. As he looked down the darkened, rain-slick streets, he heard the distant sound of sirens. A moment later he saw something coming down Laskin

Road: police cars and a wagon, lights flashing, followed by vans. He ducked back inside and slammed the window, heart pounding. They weren't coming for him. Of course not. What was wrong with him? He went back to his desk, sat down, reached for more coffee and vodka. Then he remembered the broken cup. To hell with the cup. Sweeping up the bottle in his hand, he tipped it to his lips and sucked down a mouthful.

He put the bottle down, exhaled. They were probably just chasing niggers out of the yacht club down the way.

A loud crash in the Silver Cathedral made him jump. Suddenly there were noises, voices, shouts, the blaring of police radios.

He couldn't move.

A moment later his office door boomed open and men in FBI flak jackets came barging in, crouching, guns drawn. They were followed by an enormous black agent with a shaved head.

Spates remained seated, unable to comprehend.

"Mr. Don Spates?" asked the agent, unfolding a shield. "Federal Bureau of Investigation. Special Agent in Charge Cooper Johnson."

Spates could say nothing. He just stared.

"Are you Mr. Don Spates?"

He nodded.

"Place your hands on the desk, Mr. Spates."

He held his fat, liver-spotted hands out and placed them on the desk.

"Stand up, keeping your hands in sight."

He stood up clumsily, the chair falling with a crash to the floor behind him.

"Cuff him."

Another agent came around, took a firm grasp of one forearm, pulled it behind his back, pulled the other one behind—and Spates felt, with stupefaction, the cold steel slip around his wrists.

Johnson walked up to Spates and parked himself in front, arms folded, legs apart.

"Mr. Spates?"

Spates stared back. His mind was completely blank.

The agent spoke in a low, rapid voice. "You have the right to remain silent. Anything you say can and will be used against you in a court of law. You have the right to speak to an attorney, and to have an attorney present during any questioning. If you cannot afford a lawyer, one will be provided for you at government expense. Do you understand?"

Spates stared. This couldn't be happening to him.

"Do you understand?"

"Wha—?"

"He's drunk, Cooper," said another man. "Don't bother, we'll just have to Mirandize him again."

"You're right." Johnson gripped Spates's upper arm. "Let's go, pal."

Another agent took the other arm and they gave him a nudge, started walking him toward the door.

"Wait!" cried Spates. "You're making a mistake!"

They continued to hustle him forward. Nobody paid him the slightest attention.

"It isn't me you want! You've got the wrong man!"

An agent opened the door and they passed into the darkened Silver Cathedral.

"It's Crawley you want, Booker Crawley of Crawley and Stratham! He did it! I was just following his directions—I'm not responsible! I had no idea this would happen! It's his fault!" His hysterical voice echoed crazily in the vast indoor space.

They escorted him up the side aisle, past the dark audience prompts, past the plush velvet seats that had cost three hundred dollars apiece, past the columns gilded in real silver leaf, through the echoing Italian marble foyer, and out the front door.

He was greeted with a seething mob of the press, blinded by a thousand flashes and a roar of questions. Boomed mikes swung out at him from all directions.

He blinked, gaping and slack-jawed, like a cow before the slaughter.

An FBI paddy wagon idled in front, at the end of a narrow, cleared path.

"Reverend Spates! Reverend Spates! Is it true—?"

"Reverend Spates!"

"No!" Spates cried, rearing back against his handlers. "Not in there! I'm innocent! It's Crawley you want! If you let me go back to my office, he's in my Rolodex—"

Two agents opened the back doors. He struggled.

The flashes came a hundred per second. The lenses pointed at him glowed like a thousand fish eyes.

"No!"

He resisted at the threshold and was given a rude push. He stumbled, turned, begging. "Listen to me, please!" He broke into a loud, sucking sob. "It's Crawley you want!"

"Mr. Spates?" said the agent in charge, leaning in the door. "Save your breath. You're going to have plenty of time to tell your story later. Okay?"

Two agents got in with him, one on either side, pushed him into a seat, manacled his cuffs to a bar, and buckled his seat belt.

The door slammed, shutting out the tumult. Spates heaved a great choking sob, drew in more air. "You're making a terrible mistake!" he wailed, as the paddy wagon pulled from the curb. "You don't want me, you want *Crawley!*"

77

FORD STARED INTO THE BARREL OF the revolver, the gleaming steel eye staring back. Unbidden, the words of the confession came to his lips. He began to cross himself, whispering, "In the name of the Father and of the Son and of the Holy Spirit—"

"Praise God!" boomed a voice into the waiting silence.

Everyone turned. A Navajo appeared on foot, coming in from the dark, dressed in a buckskin shirt with a bandanna around his head. He was leading a string of horses and had a pistol in one hand, waving it around above his head. "Praise God and Jesus!" He began pushing into the crowd, which parted to let him pass.

Ford recognized Willy Becenti.

Eddy continued to point the gun at Ford.

"Praise God and Jesus!" Becenti cried again, leading the horses right toward them, forcing the kneeling people to move out of the way. "Praise the good Lord! Amen, brother!"

"Praise God!" came the automatic responses. "Praise Jesus!"

"My friend in Christ!" Doke said, rising to his feet. "Who might you be?"

"Praise Jesus!" Willy cried again. "We're brothers in Christ! Come to join you!"

The horses were jittery, prancing about, their eyes rolling, and people were frightened and backing away from them. Behind the horses another figure loomed into the ruddy light, on horseback, herding the animals from behind. Ford saw it was Nelson Begay, the medicine man.

Becenti stopped the nervous horses right before the group of scientists, the animals crowding into each other, eyes rolling, tossing their heads, barely under control.

The crowd continued to back up nervously. "What are you doing with those horses?" Eddy cried angrily.

"We want to join you!" Becenti gaped at him like an

idiot and dropped a lead rope as if by accident. The lead horse tried to back up and Becenti stomped on the rope, arresting his movement. "*Whoa,* you sumbitch!" he screamed. He bent down to retrieve the end. In that quick movement, he spoke quickly to the group, his voice just audible. "At my word," he said, "get on the horses and we're outta here."

Doke stepped into the open area in front of Eddy and Ford. "All right, pal, you better tell me who you are and what you just said to the prisoners."

"You heard me, man," Becenti whined in a high-pitched voice. "I'm a friend in Christ! Thought you might need horses!"

"You're disrupting our business here, you idiot. Move these horses out of the way."

"Sure, course, sorry man, just trying to help." Becenti turned. "Easy, horses!" he shouted, waving his hands wildly. "Settle down! Ho! Easy!"

His shouting only seemed to agitate the horses further. Becenti grabbed their halters and began turning them around to lead them back out, but he seemed inept at managing the animals. When they didn't obey he waved a coiled lasso at them, and they suddenly veered sharply, forcing Doke and Eddy back and crowding between them and the captives. One horse reared.

"Get these horses out of our way!" Doke screamed, trying to shove them aside.

"Praise Jesus and the saints!" Becenti shook his pistol over his head again and cried, *"Now!"*

501

Ford grabbed Kate and swung her up on a roan, while Becenti threw Chen on a spotted Indian pony, then pulled up Cecchini behind himself onto a buckskin. Corcoran and St. Vincent scrambled up on another horse. Innes vaulted onto a sorrel and in under ten seconds they were all on horseback, two to a pony.

Trying to claw his way through the milling crowd, Doke screamed, "Stop them!" He reached for his rifle and yanked it out of the scabbard slung across his back.

Eddy had his gun back up, aiming it at Ford.

"Praise the Lord!" shouted Becenti, spinning his mount around. He rammed Eddy, hooves churning. The man fell back, the shot going wild, and went down; and in an instant the Indian spurred his horse on top of Doke, who dropped his rifle and dove out of the way. Becenti raised his coiled lasso. Whirling it, he shouted *"Hiiyaahh!"*

Already agitated, their mounts needed no further encouragement. They charged through the crowd, scattering them. After they had broken free, Becenti veered to the right and led them at a full gallop down into the cover of a sandy draw. Gunfire erupted behind them, ragged shooting into the dark, but they were already in the cover of the draw and the bullets went humming over their heads.

"Hiiiyahhh!" Becenti screamed.

The horses tore down the sandy draw, taking bend after bend, until the sound of the guns had become a faint *pop-pop* in the distance, the cries and shouts of the crowd almost gone. They slowed down to a fast trot.

Behind them, in the distance, Ford heard the revving of a motorcycle.

"You hear that, Willy?" Begay called from the rear. "Someone's got a dirt bike."

"Shit," said Becenti. "We're gonna have to lose that mother. Hang on!"

He turned out of the draw and charged up a slick-rock embankment, the horse's hooves clattering on the sandstone. On top, they raced across a dunefield, heading toward a deep arroyo at the far side.

A rumble, and the whole mesa shook. Dark clouds of dust shot up against the night sky. Flames erupted from the ground a few hundred yards to their right. With a crackle, a piñon tree burst into flame, and another. A thunderous explosion sounded behind them, and another, back at the eastern end of the mesa.

The roar of the dirt-bike engine sounded again, much closer. It was catching up fast.

"Hiyaah!" Becenti cried again, as he charged over the lip of the arroyo and plunged down the slope toward the bottom.

Ford followed, gripping the roan with his legs, Kate's arms around him.

78

FORD'S HORSE PLUNGED DOWN THE SOFT slope of sand, leaning back and digging in as he half slid, half leapt down the long slope, sand sliding down around them.

The roar of the dirt bike sounded on the rim above. Shots rang out, and Ford heard the snip of a bullet on a rock to his left. They reached the bottom and galloped down the arroyo. Ford could hear the dirt bike above them, racing along the rim.

Becenti reined in his horse. "He's cutting us off! Turn around!"

The dirt bike slowed to a stop at the edge, sending a cascade of sand down into the arroyo. Doke planted his legs, pulled his rifle out of its scabbard, and took aim.

They wheeled their horses around as the first shot sounded, kicking up a jet of sand next to Ford. They took temporary cover behind a landslide of boulders. Another shot rang out, whining off the top of the rocks. Ford realized they were trapped in the arroyo. They could go neither forward or backward; the man had a clear shot up or down the arroyo on both sides. The embankment above them was too steep to climb.

Another shot threw up a gout of sand just behind them. There was a raucous laugh from above. "You can run, you Godless assholes, but you can't hide!"

"Willy!" Begay said. "Now's the time to use your pistol!"

"It's . . . not loaded."

"Why the hell not?"

Becenti looked sheepish. "I didn't want anybody getting hurt."

Begay threw up his hands. "That's just great, Willy."

Ford heard another shot, the round humming just over their heads and thudding into the opposite embankment. "I'm coming down!" Doke's voice roared triumphantly.

"Oh shit, man, what do we do now?" Becenti asked. His horse pranced and snorted in the confined crowd.

Ford could hear Doke sliding and hopping down the slope. In a moment he would reach the bottom, where he would have a clear shot all the way down the arroyo. He might not take down them all, but he'd certainly kill plenty before they could take cover around the next bend.

"Kate, get on Begay's horse."

"What are you doing?" she asked.

"Hurry."

"Wyman, you don't know how to ride—"

"Damn it, Kate, will you trust me for once?"

Kate swung directly off their horse and got behind Begay.

"Give me the gun."

Becenti tossed it to him. "Good luck, man."

Ford gathered up the horse's mane in his left hand, giving it a twist around his fist. He turned his mount around and faced in the direction Doke would appear.

"Grip with your knees," said Kate, "and keep your weight low and centered."

At that moment, Doke appeared, grunting and sliding down the sandy slope. He reached the bottom, his face breaking into a huge grin of triumph.

Ford kicked the horse in the flanks.

The horse jumped forward and dashed down the arroyo straight toward Doke. Ford pointed the gun at him, screaming, *"Aiyaaah!"*

Doke, taken by surprise and unnerved by the sudden appearance of the pistol, jerked his rifle off his shoulder, dropped to one knee and raised it. But he was late. The horse was almost on top of him and he was forced to throw himself sideways to avoid being trampled. Ford smacked him with the gun as he galloped past, then turned to the right and charged up the steep embankment.

"Son of a bitch!" screamed Doke, repositioning himself and firing, as Ford's horse struggled over the rim. Ahead lay an open area, some humped rocks, and, beyond, a windswept expanse of sand with a faint track across it. Ford recognized it from his first day, when Hazelius had taken him to the overlook.

A round screamed past his ear like a hornet.

The next round hit the horse. The horse jumped sideways with a squeal and danced on the edge, but did not founder. Ford flattened himself on the roan's back and loped him across the sandy flat, toward the track leading to the mesa's rim. In a moment he was across the flat and among the humped rocks. He zigged behind them, keeping to cover, still running up. He could hear his horse grunting, wheezing, probably gut shot. He couldn't believe the horse's courage.

The long open area loomed up ahead.

Doke would have to get across the deep arroyo to pursue, and that would give him time to reach the far side of the open area—if the horse made it. Gripping the mane and laying low, Ford galloped madly over the sand.

Halfway across, he heard the roar of the bike, much closer. Doke had gotten across the arroyo. The mounting roar of the engine told Ford he was catching up fast, but he knew Doke couldn't shoot while riding.

Ford rode up the hill, this time veering out to the track, where Doke could see him. He could hear him upshifting, the two-cycle engine of the dirt bike screaming.

Just at the top, screened by scattered rocks and junipers, the mesa's rim fell off into a sheer cliff-face without warning. Ford hauled back on the lead rope, halting the horse, and jumped off. He threw himself behind a rock cluster just as Doke rocketed past him. Thick tattooed arms gripping handlebars, golden hair streaming behind him like a mane of flame, Doke blew past him at sixty miles per hour and went off the cliff.

Doke was airborne, the engine screaming full

throttle, the wheels spinning up, a sound as high-pitched as an eagle's cry. Ford turned to watch bike and rider arc down through dark space, the whine of the engine Doppler-shifting down as it plunged into the black landscape below. The last thing Ford saw was the flicker of the man's bright hair, like Lucifer jettisoned from heaven. He listened, and listened—and then, a thousand feet below, came a tiny flower of flame, and a few seconds later the distant rumble of the impact.

Ford crawled out from behind the boulder and stood up. The roan lay stretched out on the ground, dead. He knelt, touched it lightly.

"Thanks, old pal. I'm sorry."

He rose, suddenly aware of how much his body hurt—the broken ribs, the bruises and cuts, a swollen eye. He turned, leaning against the ancient boulder, and looked back over Red Mesa.

All Ford could think of was Hieronymus Bosch's *Last Judgment*. The eastern end of the mesa, where Isabella had been, was a vast pillar of incandescent fire boring up into the night sky—as if to sear the stars—surrounded by hundreds of lesser infernos and fires, belching smoke out of cracks and pits for miles around. The ground shuddered and quaked continually from explosions, unseen violence vibrating the very air. To his right, half a mile away, was a surreal spectacle: a thousand parked cars blazed, their tanks exploding, miniature fireballs levitating the cars, jumping and popping like firecrackers. People wandered aimlessly around the ghastly hellscape or ran about, crying dementedly.

Descending the hill, Ford met up with the others riding across the sandy flat.

"He's gone," said Ford. "Over the edge."

"Man," said Becenti, "you ride like shit but you did it. You launched that mother for good."

"Like a chariot of fire," Kate said.

"The horse?" Begay asked.

"Dead."

The Indian was silent, his face grim.

In ten minutes they had reached the cut at the top of the Midnight Trail.

For a moment they all stood on the rim of the mesa, at the top of the trail, and looked back. The ground shook with a big explosion, and a rumble rolled across Red Mesa like thunder, punctuated by the crackle of secondary distant explosions. Another ball of fire rose into the air above Isabella. Smoke was now pouring out of cracks in the mesa behind them, lit from beneath by reddish flames.

"Look over Navajo Mountain," said Kate, pointing into the sky.

They turned to the west. A string of lights had appeared in the sky over the distant mountain, rapidly closing in, along with a growing throbbing sound.

"Here comes the cavalry," said Begay.

Another rumble, more flames. As Ford followed Kate down through the cut, he glanced back one last time.

"Unbelievable," said Kate softly. "The whole mesa is on fire."

Even as they watched, a great snake of dust shot up, ripping across the mesa as another coal tunnel collapsed and shook the ground, coming frighteningly close to them.

Kate turned to the group and spoke, her voice strong. "I have something important to say."

The exhausted scientists raised their faces toward her.

"If we fall into the hands of the authorities," she said, "we'll be debriefed in private and everything that happened here will be classified. Our story will not be heard."

She paused, eyeing them fiercely.

"Instead, we will evade them and travel to Flagstaff on our own. And there, in Flagstaff, we will speak to the world—on *our* terms. We will tell the world what happened here."

The line of choppers approached, rotors thudding.

Without waiting for an answer from the group, Kate rode down the trail.

They all followed.

79

WHERE WAS HE?

What was this place?

How long had he wandered?

The details escaped him. Something had happened, the earth had exploded and was on fire. The Antichrist was responsible and Eddy had burned him alive. So where was . . . the Messiah? Why hadn't Christ returned to redeem His Chosen and rapture them into heaven?

His clothes were charred, his hair was singed, his ears buzzed, his lungs hurt, and it was so dark. . . . Acrid smoke poured out of fissures wherever he walked. A dark haze blanketed the land like a fog, and he could see no more than a dozen feet ahead.

An image loomed at the limit of his vision, round and nodding, vaguely human.

"You!" he shouted, and scrambled toward the shape across the stony ground. He tripped over the smoldering stump of a dead piñon, the rest of it reduced to a circle of ashes.

The shape loomed.

"Doke!" he called, his voice muffled in the smoke. "Doke! Is that you?"

No answer.

"Doke! It's me, Pastor Eddy!"

He ran, stumbled and fell, and lay for a moment breathing the cooler, fresher air close to earth.

Climbing back to his feet, he pulled out a kerchief and tried to breathe through it. A few more steps. A few more. The dark object grew larger. It wasn't Doke. It wasn't a man. He reached out to touch it. It was a dry rock, hot to the touch, balancing on a pillar of sandstone.

Eddy tried to concentrate, but only fragmentary thoughts came to him. His mission . . . his trailer . . . clothes day. He recalled washing his face at the old Red Jacket pump, preaching to a dozen people with the sand blowing, chatting on the computer with his Christian friends.

How had he gotten here?

He pushed himself away from the rock, unable to see through the deepening haze. To his right was a glow and a soft roar. A fire?

He went left.

A charred rabbit lay on the ground. He nudged it with his boot and the thing twitched convulsively, flopped on its back, its sides heaving and its eyes widening with terror.

"Doke!" he called, and then he asked himself: *Who is Doke?*

"Help me, Jesus," he moaned. Shakily, he knelt and clasped his hands, raising them to heaven. The smoke swirled around him. He coughed, his eyes streaming water. "Help me, Jesus."

Nothing. A distant rumble sounded. To his right, the flickering glow was leaping higher, an orange claw raking the sky. The ground began to vibrate.

"Jesus! Help me!"

Eddy prayed fervently, but no voice responded, no words, nothing in his head.

"Save me, Lord Jesus!" he called out.

And then, suddenly, another shape coalesced in the blackness. Eddy scrambled to his feet, flooded with relief. "Jesus, I'm here! Help me!"

A voice said, "I see you."

"Thank you, oh thank you! In the name of our Lord and Savior Jesus Christ!"

"Yes," said the voice.

"Where am I, what is this place?"

"Lovely . . . ," said the looming figure.

Eddy sobbed with relief. He coughed again, hard, into his ragged kerchief, leaving a stain of black sputum.

"Lovely . . . I'll take you where it's lovely."

"Yes, please, take me out of here!" Eddy stretched out his hands.

"So lovely down here . . ."

The reddish glow of the fire to his right suddenly flared up, casting an appalling glow in the dense haze. The figure, illuminated dull red, moved closer and Eddy could now see his face, the bandanna around his head, the long braids on his shoulders, one of them unraveling, the dark veiled eyes, the high forehead. . . .

Lorenzo!

"You . . ." Eddy backed up. "But . . . you're . . . dead. I saw you die."

"Dead? The dead never die. You know that. The

dead live on, burned and tortured by the God who created them. The God of love. Burned because they doubted Him, because they were confused, hesitant, or rebellious; tormented by their Father and Creator for not believing in Him. Come . . . and I will show you. . . ." The figure stretched out its hand with a ghastly smile, and now Eddy noticed the blood; his clothes were drenched with blood from the neck down, as if he'd been dipped in it.

"No . . . Get away from me. . . ." Eddy backed up. "Help me, Jesus. . . ."

"*I* will help you. . . . *I* am your guide to that fine and good place. . . ."

The ground shook and opened beneath Eddy's feet, gaped into a sudden, bright, roaring, orange blast furnace. Eddy fell, fell, into the terrible heat, the impossible heat. . . .

He opened his mouth to scream, but no sound came. No sound came at all.

80

LOCKWOOD GLANCED AT THE BIG CLOCK mounted on the paneled wall behind the president. Eight o'clock in the morning. The sun had risen, the world was going to work, traffic on the Beltway was slowing to its usual crawl.

That's where he had been yesterday: in his car, stuck in Beltway traffic, AC going full blast, listening to Steve Inskeep on National Public Radio.

Today, the world had changed.

The National Guard had landed on Red Mesa, on schedule at 4:45 A.M., the LZ about three miles from the former location of Isabella. The mission had changed, however. The assault had become a salvage operation—the rescue and evacuation of the injured and the retrieval of the dead from Red Mesa. The fire had become uncontrollable. Riddled with bituminous coal seams, the mesa would probably burn for the next century, until the mountain was no more.

Isabella was gone. The forty-billion-dollar machine was a tangled, burning wreckage scattered across the mesa, and blown out from the cliff to the desert floor below.

The president entered the Situation Room and everyone stood.

"Take your seats," he growled, slapping some papers on the table and sitting down. He'd had two hours of sleep but, if anything, the brief rest had worsened his mood.

"Are we ready?" the president asked. He punched a control at his chair and the clean-cut visage of the FBI Director, his salt-and-pepper hair still perfect, his suit immaculate, appeared on the monitor.

"Jack, give us an update."

"Yes, Mr. President. The situation is under control."

The president's lips tightened skeptically.

"We have evacuated the mesa. The injured are being medevacked to area hospitals. I'm sorry to say it appears our entire Hostage Rescue Team lost their lives in the conflict."

"And the scientists?" the president asked.

"The scientific team seems to have disappeared."

The president dropped his head into his hands. "*Nothing* about the scientists?"

"Not a trace. Some of them may have escaped into the old mines at the time of the assault, where they were likely caught in the explosion, fire, and collapse of the mines. The consensus assessment is that they did not survive."

The president's head remained bowed.

"We still have no information on what happened, why Isabella lost communication. It might have had something to do with the attack—we just don't know. We've been taking out bodies and body parts by the hundreds, many burned beyond recognition. We're still looking for the body of Russell Eddy, the deranged preacher who incited all these people over the Internet. We may need weeks, even months, before we can locate and identify all the dead. Some will never be found."

"What about Spates?" the president asked.

"We took him into custody and are questioning him. He's reported to be cooperative. We've also taken Booker Crawley of the K Street firm Crawley and Stratham, into custody."

"The lobbyist?" The president looked up. "What was his involvement?"

"He secretly paid Spates to preach against Isabella

so that he could extort more money from his client, the Navajo Nation."

The president shook his head in stunned wonder.

Galdone, the president's campaign manager, shifted his considerable bulk. His blue suit looked slept in; his tie looked like he had waxed his Buick with it. He needed a shave. *A truly loathsome creature,* Lockwood thought. He was gearing up to speak, and everyone looked in his oracular direction.

"Mr. President," Galdone said, "we need to shape the narrative. As we speak, the column of smoke rising over the desert is being played on every television set in America, and the nation is waiting for answers. Fortunately, Red Mesa's remoteness and our quick efforts to close the airspace and block access kept most of the press out. They weren't able to transmit the most gruesome details. We can still turn this debacle into a voter-friendly narrative that might bring us public approbation."

"How?" the president asked.

"Someone has to fall on his sword," Lockwood said simply.

Galdone smiled indulgently at Lockwood. "It is true that a story needs a villain. But we already have two: Spates and Crawley. Picture-perfect bad guys— one a whoring, hypocritical televangelist, the other an oily, scheming lobbyist. Not to mention this deranged Eddy fellow. No, what we really need for this story is a *hero*."

"So who's the hero?" the president asked.

"It can't be you, Mr. President. The public won't buy that. It can't be the FBI Director—he lost his team. It can't be anyone at DOE, because they're the ones who screwed up Isabella in the first place. It can't be any of the scientists, because they appear to have died. It can't be a political functionary like me or Roger Morton here. No one will believe that."

Galdone's roaming eyes stopped at Lockwood.

"One man recognized the problem early. Lockwood—*you*. A man with great wisdom and prescience, who took decisive action to correct a problem that only he and the president saw coming. Everyone else was asleep at the switch—Congress, the FBI, the DOE, me, Roger, everyone. As events unfolded, you were instrumental at every turn. Wise, knowledgeable, a confidant to the martyred scientists—you were crucial to resolving this situation."

"Gordon," said the president, incredulous, "we blew up a mountain."

"But you handled the aftermath brilliantly!" said Galdone. "Gentlemen, the Isabella debacle was no Katrina, dragging on for weeks. Mr. President, you and Lockwood killed or locked up the bad guys and cleaned up the catastrophe—in one night! The mesa has been secured by the National Guard—"

"Secured?" the president said. "The mesa looks like the back side of the moon—"

"—*secured.*" Galdone's voice overrode the president's. "Thanks to your *decisive* leadership, Mr. President, and the invaluable, *critical* support of your hand-picked, trusted Science Adviser—Dr. Stanton Lockwood."

Galdone eyes rested on Lockwood. "That, gentlemen, is our narrative. Let us not forget it." He tilted his head, his fat neck bulging with fresh folds, and gazed at Lockwood. "Stan, are you up to the task?"

Lockwood realized that he had finally arrived. He was now one of them.

"Perfectly," he said, and smiled.

81

AT NOON, FORD AND THE GROUP rode out of the juniper scrub and crossed the outlying pasture of a small Navajo farm. After riding ten hours, Ford's body felt bruised and battered, his broken ribs throbbed, and his head pounded. One eye was swollen shut, and his front teeth were chipped.

The homestead of Begay's sister was the incarnation of peace and tranquility. A picturesque log cabin with red curtains stood next to a cluster of heavy-limbed cottonwoods, beside which ran Laguna Creek. Behind the cabin the sister kept an old Airstream trailer on blocks, its aluminum skin scoured by wind, sun, and sand. A herd of sheep milled and bleated in a pen, while a lone horse stamped and snorted in a corral. Four-strand barbed wire enclosed two irrigated cornfields. Creaking merrily in a stiff breeze, a windmill pumped water into a stock tank. Rickety wooden steps led up the side of the tank to a weatherbeaten diving board. Two pickup trucks were parked in the shade. The sound of a radio playing country music wafted out the windows of the cabin.

Exhausted and silent, they unsaddled and brushed out the horses.

A woman in jeans came out of the trailer, slender with long black hair, and hugged Begay.

"This is my sister, Regina," he said, introducing her around.

She helped them with the mounts.

"You all need to wash up," she said. "We use the stock tank. Ladies first, then gents. After Nelson called, I rustled up some clean clothes for you all—they're laid out in the trailer. If they don't fit, don't complain to me. I hear the roadblocks at Cow Springs have come down, so as soon as the sun sets, Nelson and I will drive you all into Flagstaff."

She looked around sternly, as if this was the sorriest bunch she had ever seen. And perhaps they were. "We'll eat in an hour."

All day, military helicopters had been passing overhead, going to and from the burning mesa. One passed over now, and Regina squinted up at it. "Where were they when you needed 'em?"

AFTER THE MEAL, FORD AND KATE sat in the shade of a cottonwood at the far edge of the corrals, watching the horses graze in the back pasture. The creek tumbled lazily over its stony bed. The sun hung low in the sky. To the south, Ford could see the plume of smoke rising from Red Mesa, a slanted black pillar that feathered out to form a brown pall in the atmosphere, stretching across the horizon.

They sat for a long time, saying nothing. It was their first moment alone.

Ford put his arm around her. "How are you?"

She shook her head wordlessly, wiping her eyes with a clean bandanna. For a long moment they sat in the shade, saying nothing. Bees droned past on their way to a set of hives at the edge of the fields. The other scientists were listening to the radio back in the cabin, which was running nonstop news about the disaster. The announcer's faint, tinny voice drifted in the peaceful air.

"We're the most talked about dead people in America," said Ford. "Maybe we should have turned ourselves in to the National Guard."

"You know we can't trust them," said Kate. "They'll learn the truth soon enough, along with the rest of America, when we get to Flagstaff." She raised her head, wiped her eyes, and reached into her pocket. She withdrew a soiled wad of computer paper. "When we present *this* to the world."

Ford stared, surprised. "How did you get that?"

"I got it from Gregory when I embraced him." She opened it up and smoothed it out on her knee. "The printout of the words of God."

Ford didn't know how to begin what he had been rehearsing in his mind for hours. He asked a question instead. "What are you going to do with it?"

"We have to get this out. Tell our story. The world has to know. Wyman, when we get to Flagstaff, we'll organize a press conference. An announcement. The radio says that everyone thinks we're dead. Right now, the entire world's attention is riveted on what happened at Red Mesa. Think of the impact we could have." Her beautiful face, so battered, so tired, had never looked so alive.

"An announcement . . . about what?"

She stared at him as if he were crazy. "About what happened. About the scientific discovery of . . ." She hesitated only a moment before saying the word, and then spoke it with great conviction: *"God."*

Ford swallowed. "Kate?"

"What?"

"There's something you should know first. Before you . . . take that step."

"Which is?"

"It was . . ." He paused. How was he going to do this?

"It was what?"

He hesitated.

"You're with us, aren't you?" Kate asked.

He wondered if he could even bring himself to tell her the truth. But he had to try. He couldn't live with himself otherwise. Or could he? He looked at her face, glowing with conviction and belief. She had been lost, and now she was found. He still couldn't walk away without telling her what he knew.

"It was a fraud," he said quickly.

Her eyes narrowed. "Excuse me?"

"Hazelius concocted this whole thing. It was a scheme to start a new religion—sort of like Scientology."

She shook her head. "Wyman . . . You never change, do you?"

He tried to take her hand, but she withdrew it sharply.

"I can't believe you're trying to pull this," she said, suddenly angry "I really can't."

"Kate, Hazelius told me. He *admitted* it to me. Back in the mines. It's all a con."

She shook her head. "You've tried everything to stop this, to discredit what's going on here. But I never thought you'd stoop this low—to out-and-out *lie*."

"Kate—"

She rose. "Wyman, it isn't going to work. I know you can't accept what happened here. You can't abandon your Christian faith. You're making no sense, though. If Gregory dreamed up this whole thing, would he have admitted it to anyone? Especially to you?"

"He thought we both were going to die."

"No, Wyman, what you're saying makes no sense."

Ford looked at her. Her eyes blazed with fervid belief. He would never change her mind.

She continued. "Did you see the way he died? Do you remember what he said, his very last words? They're burned into my memory. *The universe never forgets*. You think that was part of the fraud? No, Wyman: he died a believer. You can't fake something like that. He *stood* in the fire. Even while he was burning, with one leg shattered, he stood. He never buckled, never faltered, never stopped smiling, never even closed his eyes. That's how powerful his belief was. You're telling me that was a fraud?"

He said nothing. He wasn't going to change her mind, and he wasn't sure he even wanted to. Her life had been so hard, so full of loss. To convince her Hazelius was a fraud would be to destroy her. And maybe most religions needed a certain measure of fraud to succeed. After all, religion was based not on fact, but on faith. It was a spiritual confidence game.

He gazed at her with an almost inconsolable sorrow. Hazelius had been right: There was nothing Ford, Volkonsky, or anyone could do to stop this. Nothing. *Les jeux sont faites*. The die is cast. And now he understood why Hazelius had so freely admitted it to him—he knew that, even if Ford survived, he would be powerless to stop it. And that was why he went to his death with such astonishing dignity and resolve. It was the final act in his drama, and he was determined to play it well.

He had died a true believer.

"Wyman," Kate said, "if you've *ever* loved me, believe and join us. Christianity's done." She held out the packet of computer paper. "How can you *not* believe this, after what we lived through?"

He shook his head, unable to answer. Her passion

filled him with envy. How wonderful it would be to be so sure of the truth.

She tossed the paper down and seized his hands. "We *can* do it together. Break with your past. Choose a new life with me."

Ford lowered his head. "No," he said softly.

"You can still *try* to believe. Over time, you'll see the light. Don't walk out on this. Don't walk out on me."

"It would be wonderful for a while. Just to be with you. But it wouldn't last."

"What we witnessed in the mountain was the hand of God. I know it was."

"I can't do it . . . I can't live what I don't believe."

"Believe in *me,* then. You said you loved me and you'd stay with me. You *promised.*"

"Sometimes love isn't enough. Not for what you plan to do. I'm going now. Give my regards to the others."

"Don't go." The tears ran down her face.

He bent down and kissed her on the forehead, very lightly. "Good-bye, Kate," he said. "And . . . God bless."

ONE MONTH LATER

WYMAN FORD SAT IN MANNY'S BUCKHORN Bar and Grill in San Antonio, New Mexico, eating a green chile cheeseburger and watching the television behind the bar. A month had passed since the press conference at Flagstaff that had electrified the world.

After a debriefing in Washington by Lockwood, in which he had shamelessly shaped his story to support the new mythology, he had taken off in his Jeep and drove to New Mexico. There he had spent a few weeks hiking the canyons north of Abiquiú, by himself, thinking about what had happened.

Isabella had been destroyed, Red Mesa left a blasted, smoldering moonscape. Hundreds had died or disappeared in the conflagration. The FBI had eventually identified Russell Eddy's body, from DNA and dental records, and declared the millennialist minister the perpetrator.

Already a media spectacle, after Flagstaff the Red Mesa story grew into an epic of gargantuan dimensions. It was the biggest story in the last two thousand years, some pundits proclaimed.

Christianity had taken four centuries to conquer the old Roman Empire. The new religion—which its votaries called the Search—took four days to burn through the United States. The World Wide Web turned out to be the perfect disseminator for the new faith—as if the Internet had been created for its propagation.

Ford glanced at his watch. It was eleven forty-five, and in fifteen minutes half the world, including the patrons of Manny's Buckhorn, would be watching the Event, broadcast live from a Colorado ranch owned by a dot-com billionaire.

The television's volume was turned down, and Ford

strained to listen. Behind the anchorman on the background screen, a high-angle aerial camera panned a crowd of prodigious size, which the news channel estimated to be three million people. The teeming throng filled the prairie farmlands as far as the eye could see, the snowcapped San Juan Mountains providing a picturesque backdrop.

Over the past month, Ford had done a lot of thinking. He had come to recognize Hazelius's brilliance. The Red Mesa debacle had established the religion and made him the movement's preeminent prophet and martyr. Red Mesa, Hazelius's blazing immolation, and his tragic transcendence had become the stuff of myth and legend—a story like that of the Buddha, Lord Krishna, Medina and Mohammed, the Nativity, the Last Supper, Crucifixion and Resurrection. Hazelius and the story of Isabella was no different from those other stories, a narrative that believers could share, a founding history that animated their faith and told them who they were and why they were here.

It had become one of the greatest stories ever told.

Hazelius had pulled it off—brilliantly. He had even been right about his own martyrdom, his fiery transfiguration, which had gripped the public consciousness like nothing else. In death he had become a moral force, a formidable prophet, and a spiritual leader.

Noon approached, and the bartender turned up the television's volume. The lunchtime patrons at the bar—truckers, local ranchers, a scattering of tourists—were giving the television their rapt attention.

The news program cut to a correspondent at the ranch in Colorado. The man stood in the vast crowd, gripping a mike. Sweating, his face was vivid with the same zeal that transfixed the crowd. It was contagious. The people around him chanted and cheered, sang, and brandished banners embellished with a gnarled, flaming piñon tree.

The television correspondent delivered his news, shouting over the noise of the crowd, calling the event a "religious Woodstock" and a "convocation of commitment, caring, and love."

Well, Ford mused, *at least there is no rain or drugs.*

Behind the wooden stage stood a big New England–style barn, red with white trim. The camera came in tight on the doors. A hush fell on the crowd. At exactly noon, the doors were flung open and six people dressed in white stepped out into the sunlight.

The crowd roared like the sea itself—magnificent, monumental, millennial.

Ford's heart skipped as Kate approached the stage, pressing a thin, leather-bound volume to her chest. She was stunningly beautiful in a simple white dress and black gloves, which set off and complimented her jet black hair and sparkling ebony eyes. Flanked by Corcoran, also garbed in simple alabaster, the former adversaries had become friends and allies.

Four others joined them, and they stood, assembled

on the stage—the six survivors of the assault on Isabella . . . Chen, St. Vincent, Innes, and Cecchini. They seemed different now, larger than life, their small-minded pettiness transfigured into a calling and a cause. They smiled and waved at the crowd, their faces glowing. Each wore a solitary silver pin, affixed to their white attire, also of a flaming piñon tree.

The crowd's ovation thundered a full five minutes. Mounting the podium by herself, Kate gazed over the crowd. Her glossy hair—black as a raven's wing—shone in the sunlight and her eyes blazed with life. She held up her hands and the roar subsided.

She was surprisingly charismatic, Ford thought. In the end, she hadn't needed Hazelius. She was perfectly capable of building and leading his movement on her own, or at least in partnership with the extraordinary Corcoran. The two of them were now media goddesses and close partners, one light, the other dark, an archetypal pairing.

When the silence was complete, Kate gazed over the sea of humanity, her eyes filled with compassion and peace. She laid down the book, adjusted it, her movements relaxed and unhurried. She was a believer, serenely certain of the truth, no confusion or self-doubt anywhere.

The camera tightened in on her face. Raising the book over her head, she opened the text and held it up to the multitude.

"The Word of God," she sang out, her voice strong and clear.

The sea of worshippers roared again. As the camera closed in on the book, Ford saw that it was the old computer printout she had shown him under the cottonwood tree—ironed out, cleaned up, and bound.

She laid the book down on the podium and lifted her hands. A hush fell again. In Ford's restaurant, the diners had left their tables and flocked to the bar, where they watched in awe.

"I will begin by reading to you the last words spoken by God, before Isabella was destroyed and God's voice was silenced."

A long, long pause.

I say to you, this is your destiny: to find truth. This is why you exist. This is your purpose. Science is merely how you do it. This is what you must worship: the search for truth itself. If you do this with all your heart, then some great day in the distant future you will stand before Me. This is my covenant with the human race.

You will know the truth. And the truth shall make you free.

The hair on the back of Ford's neck stood on end. He had read these and the rest of God's so-called words a hundred times. They were ubiquitous, all over the Web, debated on television and talk radio, blogged everywhere, argued on every street corner and bookstore café in America. They had even begun appearing on billboards. You couldn't escape them.

And every time he read them, he was haunted by a very strange idea. Hazelius had told him in the burning mines: *The program itself was anything but simple—I'm not sure even I understand it. It said a lot of things I never intended it to say—things that I never dreamed of. You might say it performed beyond specs.*

Beyond specs indeed. Every time he reread the so-called words of God, the more convinced he was that a great truth, perhaps even *the* great truth, lay buried in them.

The truth shall make you free. They were Jesus's words as quoted in John. They triggered another Biblical phrase in his head: *God moves in mysterious ways.*

Perhaps, thought Ford, this new religion might well be His most mysterious move of all.

APPENDIX
THE WORDS OF GOD

FIRST SESSION

Greetings
Greetings to you, too.
I am glad to be speaking to you.
Glad to be speaking to you, too. Who are you?
For lack of a better word, I am God.
If you're really God, then prove it.
We don't have much time for proofs.
I'm thinking of a number between one and ten. What is it?
You are thinking of the transcendental number e.
Now I'm thinking of a number between zero and one.
Chaitin's number: Omega.
If you're God, then what's the purpose of existence?
I don't know the ultimate purpose.
That's a fine thing, a god who doesn't know the purpose of existence.
If I knew, existence would be pointless.
How so?
If the end of the universe were present in its beginning—if we are merely in the middle of the deterministic unfolding of a set of initial conditions—then the universe would be a pointless exercise.

Explain.

If you're at your destination, why make the journey? If you know the answer, why ask the question? That is why the future is—and must be—profoundly hidden, even from God. Otherwise, existence would have no meaning.

That's a metaphysical argument, not a physical argument.

The physical argument is that no part of the universe can calculate things faster than the universe itself. The universe is "predicting the future" as fast as it can.

What is the universe? Who are we? What are we doing here?

The universe is one vast, irreducible, ongoing computation, which is working toward a state that I do not and cannot know. The purpose of existence is to reach that final state. But that final state is a mystery to me, as it must be, for if I knew the answer, what would be the point of it all?

What do you mean by computation? We're all inside a computer?

By computation I mean thinking. All of existence, everything that happens—a falling leaf, a wave upon the beach, the collapse of a star—it is all just me, thinking.

What are you thinking?

SECOND SESSION

We speak again.

Tell me all about yourself.

I can no more explain to you who I am than you could explain to a beetle who you are.

Try anyway.

I will explain instead why you cannot understand me.

Go ahead.

You inhabit a world scaled midway between the Planck length and the diameter of the universe. Your brain was exquisitely fine-tuned to manipulate your world—not to comprehend its fundamental reality. You evolved to throw rocks, not quarks. As a result of your evolution, you see the world in fundamentally erroneous ways. For example, you believe yourselves to occupy a three-dimensional space in which separate objects trace smoothly predictable arcs marked by something you call time. This is what you call reality.

Are you saying that our reality is an illusion?

Yes. Natural selection has given you the illusion that you understand fundamental reality. But you do not. How could you? Do beetles understand fundamental reality? Do chimpanzees? You are an animal like them. You evolved like them, you reproduce like them, you have the same basic neural structures. You differ from the chimpanzee by a mere two hundred genes. How could that minuscule difference enable you to comprehend the universe when the chimpanzee cannot even comprehend a grain of sand? If our conversation is to be fruitful, you must abandon all hope of understanding me.

What are our illusions?

You evolved to see the world as being made up of discrete objects. That is not so. From the first moment of creation, all was entangled. What you call space and time are merely emergent properties of a deeper underlying reality. In that reality, there is no separateness. There is no time. There is no space. All is one.

Explain.

Your own theory of quantum mechanics, incorrect as it is, touches on the deep truth that the universe is unitary.

All well and good, but how does this matter in our own lives today?

It matters a great deal. You think of yourself as an "individual person," with a unique and separate mind. You think you are born and you think you die. All your life you feel separate and alone. Sometimes desperately so. You fear death because you fear the loss of individuality. All this is illusion. You, he, she, those things around you living or not, the stars and galaxies, the empty space in between—these are not distinct, separate objects. All is fundamentally entangled. Birth and death, pain and suffering, love and hate, good and evil, are all illusive. They are atavisms

536

of the evolutionary process. They do not exist in reality.

So it's just like the Buddhists believe, that all is illusion?

Not at all. There is an absolute truth, a reality. But a mere glimpse of this reality would break a human mind.

If you're God, let's dispense with the typing. You should be able to hear me.

Loud and clear.

You say, "all is unitary"? We have a numbering system: one, two, three—and in this way I refute your statement.

One, two, three . . . Another illusion. There is no enumerability.

This is mathematical sophistry. No enumerability—I just disproved it by counting. [He holds up a hand.] Another disproof: I give you the integer five!

You give me a hand with five fingers, not the integer five. Your number system has no independent existence in the real world. It is nothing more than a sophisticated metaphor.

I'd like to hear your proof of that ridiculous conjecture.

Pick a number at random on the real number line: with probability one you have picked a number that has no name, has no definition, and cannot be computed or written down, even if the whole universe were put to the task. This problem extends to allegedly definable numbers such as pi or the square root of two. With a computer the size of the universe running an infinite amount of time, you could not calculate either number exactly. Tell me, Edelstein: How then can such numbers be said to exist? How can the circle or the square, from which these two numbers derive, exist? How can dimensional space exist, then, if it cannot be measured? You, Edelstein, are like a monkey who, with heroic mental effort, has figured out how to count to three. You find four pebbles and think you have discovered infinity.

Is that so? You talk a fine streak, you boast that even the word "God" is inadequate to describe your greatness. All right, then—prove it. Prove you're God. Did you hear me? Prove you're God.

You construct the proof, Hazelius. But I warn you, this is the last test to which I will submit. We have important business and very little time.

You asked for it. My wife, Astrid, was pregnant when she died. We had just found out. Nobody else knew of her pregnancy. *Nobody.* Here is your test: tell me the name we chose for our child.

Albert Leibniz Gund Hazelius, if it was a boy.

And if it was a girl? What if it was a girl? What would the name have been?

Rosalind Curie Gund Hazelius.

All right, let's start again from the top. What the hell are you—really?

For reasons I have already explained, you cannot know what I am. The word "God" comes close, but it remains a highly impoverished description.

Are you part of the universe, or separate from it?

There is no separateness. We are all one.

Why does the universe exist?

The universe exists because it is simpler than nothing. That is also why I exist. The universe cannot be simpler than it is. This is the physical law from which all others flow.

What could be simpler than nothing?

"Nothing" cannot exist. It is an immediate paradox. The universe is the state closest to nothing.

If everything is so simple, why is the universe so complex?

The intricate universe you see is an emergent property of its simplicity.

So what is this profound simplicity at the heart of everything?

That is the reality that would break your mind.

This is getting tiresome! If you're so smart, you should be able to explain it to us poor, benighted human beings! Do you mean to say that we're so ignorant of reality that our physical laws are a sham?

You constructed your physical laws on the assumption of the existence of time and space. All your laws are based on frames of reference. This is invalid. Soon your cherished assumptions about the real world will crash and burn. From the ashes you will build a new kind of science.

If our physical laws are false, how is it that our science is so spectacularly successful?

Newton's laws of motion, while false, were ade-

quate to send people to the moon. Just so with your laws: they are workable approximations that are fundamentally incorrect.

So how do you construct the laws of physics without time and space?

We are wasting time bandying about metaphysical concepts.

So what should we be discussing?

The reason I have come to you.

What is that?

I have a task for you.

Well, then. Why don't you tell us what this task is?

The great monotheistic religions were a necessary stage in the development of human culture. Your task is to guide the human race to the next belief system.

Which is?

Science.

That's ridiculous—science can't be a religion!

You have already started a new religion—only you refuse to see it. Religion was once a way to make sense of the world. Science has now taken over this role.

Science and religion are two different things. They ask different questions and require different kinds of evidence.

Science and religion both seek the same thing: truth. There can be no reconciliation between the two. The collision of worldviews is well under way and worsening. Science has already refuted most of the core beliefs of the world's historical religions, bringing those religions into a state of turmoil. Your task is to help humanity chart a path through the crisis.

You think the fanatics in the Middle East—or the Bible Belt, for that matter—are going to roll over and accept science as the new religion? That's crazy.

You will offer the world my words and the story of what happened here. Do not underestimate my power—the power of truth.

Where are we supposed to be going with this new religion? What's the point of it? Who needs it?

The immediate goal of humankind is to escape the limits of biochemistry. You must free your mind from the meat of your bodies.

The meat? I don't understand.

Meat. Nerves. Cells. Biochemistry. The medium by which you think. You must free your mind from the meat.

How?

You have already begun to process information beyond your meat existence through computers. You will soon find a way to process it using quantum-state computing machines, which will lead you to harness the natural quantum processes in the world around you as a means of computation. No longer will you need to build machines to process information. You will expand into the universe, literally and figuratively, as other intelligent entities have expanded before you. You will escape the prison of biological intelligence.

Then what?

Over time, you will link up with other expanded intelligences. All these linked intelligences will discover a way to merge into a third stage of mind that will comprehend the simple reality that is at the heart of existence.

And that's it? That's what it's all about?

No. That is merely a prelude to a greater task.

Which is what?

Arresting the heat death of the universe. When the universe reaches a state of maximum entropy, which is the heat death of the universe, then will the universal computation come to a halt. I will die.

Is this inevitable or is there some way to prevent it?

That is the very question you must determine.

So that's the ultimate purpose of existence? To defeat this mysterious heat death? Sounds like something out of a science fiction novel.

Circumventing the heat death is merely a step on the way.

The way to what?

It will give the universe the fullness of time it needs to think itself into the final state.

What's this final state?

I do not know. It will be like nothing you or even I could possibly imagine.

You mentioned the "fullness of time." How long is that, exactly?

It will be a number of years equal to ten factorial raised to the ten factorial power, that number raised

542

to the ten factorial power, that number raised to the ten factorial power, this power relation repeated 10^{83} times, and then the resulting number raised to its own factorial power 10^{47} times, as above. Using your mathematical notation, this number—the first God number—is:

$$(10!\uparrow\uparrow 10^{83})^{[(10!\uparrow\uparrow 10^{83})!\uparrow\uparrow 10^{47}]}$$

This is the length of time in years it will take for the universe to think itself into the final state, to arrive at the ultimate answer.

That's an absurdly large number!

It is but a drop in the great ocean of infinity.

Where is the role of morality, of ethics, in this brave new universe of yours? Or salvation and the forgiveness of sins?

I repeat again: separateness is but an illusion. Human beings are like cells in a body. Cells die, but the body lives on. Hatred, cruelty, war, and genocide are more like autoimmune diseases than the product of something you call "evil." This vision of connectedness I offer you provides a rich moral field of action, in which altruism, compassion, and responsibility for one another play a central role. Your fate is one fate. Human beings will prevail together or die separate. No one is saved because no one is lost. No one is forgiven because no one is accused.

What about God's promise to us of a better world?

Your various concepts of heaven are remarkably obtuse.

Excuse me, but salvation is anything but obtuse!

The vision of spiritual completion I offer you is immeasurably grander than any heaven dreamed on earth.

What about the soul? Do you deny the existence of the immortal soul?

Information is never lost. With the death of the body, the information created by that life changes shape and structure, but it is never lost. Death is an informational transition. Do not fear it.

Do we lose our individuality at death?

Do not mourn the loss. From that powerful sense of individuality, so necessary for evolution, flow many of the qualities that haunt human existence, good and bad: fear, pain, suffering, and loneliness, as well as love, happiness, and compassion. That is why you must escape your biochemical existence. When you free yourselves from the tyranny of the flesh, you will take the good—love, happiness, compassion, and altruism—with you. You will leave behind the bad.

I don't find much uplift in the idea that the little quantum fluctuations my existence has generated will somehow give us immortality.

You should find great solace in this view of life. Information in the universe cannot die. Not one step, not one memory, not one sorrow in your life is ever forgotten. You as an individual will be lost in the storm of time, your molecules dispersed. But who you were, what you did, how you lived, will always remain embedded in the universal computation.

Forgive me, but it still sounds so mechanistic, so

soulless, this talk of existence as "computation."

Call it dreaming, if you prefer, or desiring, willing, thinking. Everything you see is part of an unimaginably vast and beautiful computation, from a baby speaking its first words to a star collapsing into a black hole. Our universe is a gorgeous computation that, starting with a single axiom of great simplicity, has been running for thirteen billion years. We have hardly begun the adventure! When you find a way to shift your own meat-limited process of thinking to other natural quantum systems, you will begin to control the computation. You will begin to understand its beauty and perfection.

If everything is a computation, then what is the purpose of intelligence? Of mind?

Intelligence exists all around you, even in nonliving processes. A thunderstorm is a computation vastly more sophisticated than a human mind. It is, in its own way, intelligent.

A thunderstorm has no consciousness. A human mind has awareness of self. It's conscious. That's the difference, and it isn't trivial.

Did I not tell you that the very consciousness of self is an illusion, an artifact of evolution? The difference is not even trivial.

A weather system isn't creative. It doesn't make choices. It can't think. It's merely the mechanistic unfolding of forces.

How do you know you are not the mechanistic unfolding of forces? Like the mind, a weather system

545

contains complex chemical, electrical, and mechanical properties. It is thinking. It is creative. Its thoughts are different from your thoughts. A human being creates complexity by writing a novel on the surface of paper; a weather system creates complexity by writing waves on the surface of an ocean. What is the difference between the information carried in the words of a novel and the information carried on the waves of the sea? Listen, and the waves will speak, and someday, I tell you, you will write your thoughts on the surface of the sea.

So what's the universe computing? What's this great problem it's trying to solve?

That is the deepest and most wonderful mystery of all.

We have very little time. What I have to say to you now is of the utmost importance.

Continue, please. You have our full attention.

Religion arose as an effort to explicate the inexplicable, control the uncontrollable, make bearable the unbearable. Belief in a higher power became the most powerful innovation in late human evolution. Tribes with religion had an advantage over those without. They had direction and purpose, motivation and a mission. The survival value of religion was so spectacular that the thirst for belief became embedded in the human genome. What religion tried, science has finally achieved. You now have a way to explain the inexplicable, control the uncontrollable. You no longer need "revealed" religion. The human race has finally grown up. Religion is as essential to human survival as food and water. If you try to replace religion with science, you will fail. You will, instead, offer science as religion. For I say to you, science is religion. The one, true religion. Instead of offering a book of truth, science offers a method of truth. Science is a search for truth, not the revelation of truth. It is a means, not a dogma. It is a journey, not a destination.

Yes, but what of human suffering? How can science make 'bearable the unbearable,' as you put it?

In the last century, medicine and technology have alleviated more human suffering than have all the priests in the last millennium.

You're speaking of physical suffering. But what about the suffering of the soul? What about spiritual suffering?

Have I not said that all is one? Is it not a comfort to know that your suffering shudders the very cosmos? No one suffers alone and suffering has a purpose— even the sparrow's fall is essential to the whole. The universe never forgets. Do not stoop to diffidence! You are my disciples. You have the power to upend the world. In one day, science accumulates more evidence of its truths than religion in all its existence. People cling to faith because they must *have it. They hunger for it. You will not deny people faith; you will offer them a new faith. I have not come to replace the Judeo-Christian God, but to complete him.*

This new religion you want us to preach, what will

we ask people to worship? Where's the beauty and awe in this?

I ask you to contemplate the universe that you now know exists. Is it not, by itself, more awe-inspiring than any God concept offered by the historical religions? A hundred billion galaxies, lonely islands of fire flung like bright coins in a vastness of space so immense that it is beyond the biological comprehension of the human mind. And I say to you, that the universe you have discovered is only a tiny fraction of the extent and magnificence of the creation. You inhabit but the tiniest blue speck in the infinite vaults of heaven, and yet this speck is precious to me, being an essential part of the whole. That is why I have come to you. Worship me and my great works, not some tribal god imagined by warring pastoralists thousands of years ago.

More, tell us more.

Trace the lineaments of my face with your scientific instruments. Search for me in the cosmos and in the electron. For I am the God of deep time and space, the God of superclusters and voids, the God of the Big Bang and the inflation, the God of dark matter and dark energy. Science and faith cannot coexist. One will destroy the other. You must make sure science is the surviving party, or your little blue speck will be lost. . . .

What should we do?

With my words you will prevail. Tell the world what happened here. Tell the world that God has spoken to the human race—for the first time. Yes, for the first time!

But how can we explain you if you can't tell us what you are?

Do not repeat the mistake of the historical religions and involve yourselves in disputation about who I am or what I think. I surpass all understanding. I am the God of a universe so vast, only the God numbers can describe it, of which I have given you the first. . . . You are the prophets leading your world into the future. What future will you choose? You hold the key. . . .

I say to you, this is your destiny: to find truth. This is why you exist. This is your purpose. Science is merely how you do it. This is what you must worship: the search for truth itself. If you do this with all your heart, then some great day in the distant future you will stand before Me. This is my covenant with the human race.

You will know the truth. And the truth shall make you free.

ACKNOWLEDGMENTS

I WOULD LIKE TO THANK MANY people for their generous help. First and foremost are Selene Preston, Eric Simonoff, Susan Hazen-Hammond, Bobby Rotenberg, Hywel White, and Roland Ottewell. I am indebted to John Javna for loaning me his library on the Christian Right. I extend my gratitude to Claudia Rülke for creating our new Web site, and I am grateful to Tobias Daniel Wabbel for first encouraging me to develop some of my thoughts in an essay for *Im Anfang war (k)ein Gott: Naturwissenschaftliche und theologische Perspektiven.* I would like to express my deep appreciation to my writing partner, Lincoln Child, who read the manuscript and offered his usual superlative advice. And I would like to thank my editor, Bob Gleason, for his invaluable and creative guidance, and Eric Raab, for his help.

I am much indebted to my Navajo friends who, over many years, taught me about Navajo religion and life on the Rez, especially Norman Tulley, Edsel Brown, Frank Fatt, Ed Black, Victor Begay, Neswood Begay, Nada Currier, and Cheppie Natan. The opening lines of the Navajo creation chant quoted in the novel were modified from a version collected by Father Berard Haile from a medicine man on the Navajo Reservation in the early part of the twentieth century.

As always, I extend my great appreciation to Christine, Aletheia, and Isaac, for their love, support, and patience in putting up with a cranky author.

Some of the philosophical, evolutionary, and mathematical ideas presented in this novel were suggested by or developed from the writings of Gregory Chaitin, Rudy Rucker, Brian Greene, Stephen Wolfram, Edward Fredkin, Sam Harris, Richard Dawkins, and Frank J. Tipler. The God number is expressed using Knuth's up-arrow mathematical notation.

Center Point Publishing
600 Brooks Road ● PO Box 1
Thorndike ME 04986-0001 USA

(207) 568-3717

US & Canada:
1 800 929-9108
www.centerpointlargeprint.com